# The Reform Plan

Bill Blanchet

Order this book online at www.trafford.com
or email orders@trafford.com

Most Trafford titles are also available at major online book retailers.



Printed in the United States of America.

ISBN: 978-1-4269-3637-1 (sc)
ISBN: 978-1-4269-3638-8 (hc)
ISBN: 978-1-4269-3639-5 (e)

Library of Congress Control Number: 2010931619

*Our mission is to efficiently provide the world's finest, most comprehensive book publishing service, enabling every author to experience success. To find out how to publish your book, your way, and have it available worldwide, visit us online at www.trafford.com*

*Trafford rev. 10/26/2010*

Trafford PUBLISHING www.trafford.com

**North America & international**
toll-free: 1 888 232 4444 (USA & Canada)
phone: 250 383 6864 • fax: 812 355 4082

# Dedication

David L. Dowd

Teacher and Professor of History

***"EDUCATION IS THE ENGINE THAT MAKES AMERICAN DEMOCRACY WORK"***

*DREW GILMORE FAUST, PRESIDENT: HARVARD UNIVERSITY*

# *CHAPTER I*

## *A Meeting*

"Excuse me." She was exasperated. Her words were slow, distinct ... patronizing. Manicured nails of long, slender fingers tapped the edge of the rostrum. The demanded silence, however, was not forthcoming. Chin pinched with left middle finger and thumb, pinky extended, the marquise diamond on the fourth finger flashed dutifully. "If our agenda is not resolved this afternoon. . .", she waited imperiously, ". . . then, ladies and gentlemen," . . . pause, eyes rounded, . . . "then, it will simply *have* to be resolved: subsequently. At a later meeting!"

That notwithstanding: continuing, blatant, non-compliance! The faded blue eyes narrowed combatively. Thin lips pursed, jaw set, the third entreaty was strident. Piqued, she enunciated distinctly, voice rising several semi-tones, warbling at the edges, "Ex-cu-use me: pl-e-a-es-e? May-we-have-your-attention!"

No result. If anything, the private conversations became even more earnestly self-centered. The scurrying between seats progressed to an erratic kind of darting, accompanied by dramatically intense stage commands: theatrical mouthing of incomprehensible words, pantomime pointing, and semaphore gesticulations with pencils, roll books, purses, textbooks, a large plastic right-angle triangle, disorganized wads of semi-corrected papers. The communication efforts were augmented by facial contortions registering incredulity, exasperation, confusion, and exaggerated agreement. The apparently random movements were underscored, moreover, by haphazard efforts to stifle loud giggles and grating laughter as a number of individuals, in their eagerness to find their seats, backing or climbing, stumbled and clutched, for steadying support, the most proximate shoulder, arm, or what evoked the loudest guffaws and squeals ... leg.

Now overtly bellicose, Dr. Allsbury gripped the microphone as if it were the throat of a particularly vexing member of her audience. "Ladies and gentlemen!" The appeal was shrill. Lips compressed to a thin line, eyes dilated, she personified indignation: the stymied teacher—outrage ineffectively masking impotence. "It is now-ow [she separated the syllables] af-ter th-ree-e [she rolled the "r"'s ] ... and if we cannot get started by th-ree-e ... we will simply have to continue after fo-o-o-r!"

"Wanna bet," came from a baritone voice in a confused area towards the back. The irascibility of the comment was obvious because, immediately, occurred one of those momentary, open silences, which often punctuate interpersonal resentment. No longer thoughtlessly immature, the scenario was now combative. The cacophony recommenced with renewed vigor.

Allsbury's expensive, high-heeled, mauve cocktail sandal was turned compulsively on its side, a gesture at odds with the immaculate presentation of silk violets, whispering among multiple tiers of organdy and chiffon, which floated above thin and superbly shaped legs. *Décolletage* revealed the alabaster complexion. Lavender ribbons fluttered from auburn hair, twisted precisely into a chignon.

She looked over her shoulder. The tiers rising behind were designed for the Gospel Choir. Now, the administrative group were congregated at the top around a scarred upright piano.

The unpleasantness of the audience subsiding somewhat, she seized the opportunity, and plunged into the parañá-infested waters. The voice quavered. The elegant ankle bone was glued to the floor. "The first topic on our agenda—if you pl-e-e-a-se, ladies and gentlemen—will be a presentation that will elucidate the anticipated legislation and differentiate the critical role substantiated by our school in a proposed Reform Plan: how it will ameliorate the education of youngsters in our community . . . our students at Fillmore High. Now, I-am-sur-ure," she paused for emphasis, "that *all* of us realize how *very* important this topic will be to each and every one of us!"

She nodded solemnly having convinced at least one person of the gravity of the situation. "Moreover, I am *absolutely* confident we will *all* give our *complete,"* significant pause, "and *total* attention? In that way we can be totally apprised of its connotations." There were smirks in the audience.

"Also . . . may I add," she was condescending, "that it is *not* frequent that a leading citizen from the *business community* is willing to depart from an already demanding schedule to visit with us and inform on issues. And I am *sure* we all appreciate that."

She rotated inquisitively toward the command post, mouth turned down at the corners, jaw lifted, head tilted back. The plucked eyebrows, arched in expectation, however, fell immediately, and the thin lips constricted into a skeletal line. Impossible! The anticipated guest was not there!

Indifferent to the sycophant grins of his colleagues, one of the administrative group stirred his bloated appearance: large hips and expanding waist evidencing lack of exercise and acquiescence to the junk food culture. The flopping, well-worn camel hair jacket did little to conceal the burgeoning pear shape.

"Hi everybody. I was just telling the Superintendent earlier? How you guys are just the greatest? Bunch of teachers? Absolutely! Numero Uno! And I know you're zonked from just a super hard day! Slugging it out in the trenches! Wow!"

Exhaling noisily, the Principal moved his head wearily to underscore the veracity of his observation. And his empathy. "Now, as most of you already probably have heard, Mr. Pritchard is in a delay mode. But when he gets here he's gonna fill us in about possible new kind of reform plan? Reshuffles that will impact us here at Fillmore. And our Cathedral Heights community? Stuff that's going to help us to continue your just super dedication to helping Fillmore kids. So, obviously, his words will impact on each and every one of us. Big time! And I believe," he was coy, "that he might even have some information about a salary increase?" The Cheshire smile was Number Seven on his List of Facial Responses.

"Hey! Right on!" Female twittering reinforced the remark.

"And hey! After School Board's been using the salary increase plan for their seat cushions now for how many umpteen months! Go for it."

"How about a new school? Got any new skinny on that consideration, Joe? As of yet?"

Speaking quietly and slowly, a device intended to mask insecurity as well as barrio accent, the speaker, grasping at the perceived approbation, allowed his smile to persist, motioning with a thrust of his jaw. "All good questions. Let's let our guest to resolute them." He nodded crisply to Allsbury. "They'll be waiting to continue with you until Mr. Pritchard gets here."

Allsbury overlooked the rudeness. "While we're *waiting*," she stressed the verb; "we have some updates about CAHSEE. Word has come down that State might revise it."

A few derisive cheers broke the hostility. "Yeah! Say it!"

"It'd be a cold day in hell when they revise something that's not working anyway. Marginalized on the dark side as per usual. That's us!"

"Of course none of us wants more tests that's unfair to minorities."

Deaf to the comments, Allsbury looked to the command post for support; and receiving none, continued, "I know we all agree on fairness." She smiled emptily. "However, it does seem that we *will* administer the test again this year. I know that's a big concern for all of us: testing possibly six to seven hundred youngsters, with CAHSEE alone?" Allsbury's next statement—clipped, spoken through her teeth—seemed ironic. "But I think we all know how important Assessment is!"

"Even though tests don't measure what kids could know?"

"What's the point? Our kids can't do the questions anyhow."

"Waste of everybody's time!"

"What you talkin' about? Cay-see?"

"The *point*," she stressed the word, "ladies and gentlemen, is, that it *appears* that we're going to have to test again this year for CAHSEE: as well as the other mandated tests. Both NRT's and CRT's. CAHSEE is mandatory. I know it entails additional work and is stressful for us but if State wants it, well, we have to be in compliance. Not a site-level decision."

"Is there a testing schedule yet? I mean for all the tests we'll have to be doing this year?"

"At this early date? I imagine we'll follow last year's path? EXIT probably in October, February, and April. GATE in March; Golden State in May; AP's in Calculus, Spanish, U.S. History, Social Studies, Biology, Chemistry, Foreign Languages, I believe in May; ASVAB probably in April. Of course CELDT and language placement tests will continue in the usual way on an 'as needed' basis, and there will be the regular PSAT and SAT's as well as the special scholarship tests from SAT. SDC and RSP placement testing will continue in the usual norm."

"Is that all? And when kids supposed to learn for testes in the subject matter? I mean teacher-made testes? For stuff we're teaching? Stuff they're supposed to be learning? Day after day? In the classroom?"

"What about re-testing?"

"Will the Christmas break be the same as last year? I heard it might be longer? Teacher in Santa Obesso told me might could be? There?"

"One point? If I might, Dr. Allsbury? We lose three days a month on federal and state mandated tests. Already. We never know what's going to be on most of them. Neither teachers nor students get the results. I wonder about the purpose? Of losing fifteen percent of instructional time? Demoralizing to teachers and kids."

"Assessment is a challenge: assuredly. For everyone. Then, again, we've been through all this before."

"Business as per usual! Muddle through!"

"What about . . .?"

She interrupted her interlocutors. "GATE testing as well as language placement will be handled in the regular way as will Reading and Math for proper in-grade adjustments: on an 'As Needed' basis. Also, for your information, as we progress in Standards Based Instructional strategies—and we do need more improvement in that area?" She paused, tongue caressing the inner part of her upper lip, looking askance at blank faces. "We will have norm referenced assessment in curriculum content as well. And be apprised that OCR will be including their requirements, plus Title I and Title IX compliance issues."

Ever prescient, she tossed her head indignantly, ribbons bobbing, a gesture intended to communicate social and intellectual hauteur. She stood in the conductor's place, the vertex of a three-dimensional parabola, with the choir—teachers—arranged in tiers in front and the orchestra—administrators—arranged at the top of the tiers behind. The entire ensemble was struggling, competing really, to establish individual tempi, heedless either of the score—the Agenda—or the conductor—Maistra Allsbury.

A paw-like fist at the end of a massive, hairy, sweaty forearm shot up. Immediately, murmuring recommenced. It was accompanied by shuffling of chairs and somewhat muffled epithets suggesting that finally, the choir's discordant interpretation of the composition would prevail over the struggle of the conductor. "Union contract says Agenda issues has to be told to us. So? Why wasn't Agenda put out *before* meeting? Contract says it's gotta be in our boxes! At *least* twenty-four hours *before* faculty meeting. Max! So! What gives? For today?"

The speaker was Bruce Warfles, Teachers' Union representative. With back to Dr. Allsbury, his glance, upward and to the periphery, swept a one hundred and fifty degree angle: triumphant indignation mingled with inherent belligerence. "And, all this other kinds of testing makes it pretty darn hard for classroom teachers to be teaching the stuff kids is supposed to be tested on. No wonder they do so bad on testes. And on CAHSEE! And don't let somebody say it's teacher fault! For sure! Not! Everybody knows our kids are miles behind already, when we get 'em and we got to spend all our time playing 'catch up' for the next four years. Administration shoots an overload on us with testes. We should spend more time teaching the kids what they should know then in finding out what they don't know." The audience broke into an irascible *fortissimo* of solidarity.

Allsbury turned to the Principal, who, moving with unexpected agility, again descended and took the microphone without acknowledgment. "Thanks, just a whole lot Bruce? For that 'head's up'. Input has it that Agenda was attended to, but Marvella tells us the copier's been down? Service people said we're maxed out on our usage. But, we should have a copy for you in your mailboxes by tomorrow, hopefully, morning? 'Way of the Hill', folks. Always."

A hollow groan was the resentful response:

"Come on Joe. Give us a break!"

"Who does he think he's kidding? Anyhow?"

"No matter, they'd follow their own Agenda anyway."

Basking in this approbation, Bruce seized his advantage. "Yeah. And there's something other. I don't see why the union rep is always left to last? On the Agenda? Never enough time left over at the end and we get cut off. Have to go into our own time? How about it Joe? How about giving us our turn up to bat? I mean before the tenth inning?"

Intermittent laughter accompanied chairs re-dragged into position, changing seats, inquiries for the 'place' in their hymnals.

The principal stood his ground. Smiling vacantly like one of his orchestral cronies at the piano group, he parried the attack skillfully, exuding Response Number Three—Bemused Indifference—that also failed to inspire confidence. "We'll take care of that too. Next time, Bruce, g'buddy." He gave a thumbs-up sign, chuckling, "You'll be Numero Uno on the Agenda."

A sardonic, "Sure, you will!" came from one side of the room and "When hell freezes over," from another.

Joe Baques—he eschewed the traditional José—was the Principal of Fillmore High, one of the largest in the state: over 5000 students. 'Joe' connoted the 'pal' image he craved but was denied. Also, there was lingering confusion regarding pronunciation of his name. And Mr. 'B' was too intimate.

Without looking at Allsbury, he returned to the command post: the managerial inner sanctum: Assistant Principals; Marvella, the school secretary, still absorbed in ticking off absent teachers from her three-page roster; four Resource Teachers; three Mentor Teachers and five Counselors. None of these dignitaries deigned to take seats among regular teachers. They authenticated separateness by their posture, females aping males, lounging together, in comradely fashion around the piano, and by the intensity of private exchanges—whispering, rolled eyes, palms cuffed over mouths, shrugged shoulders—about confidential issues, erudite, transcending teacher blather.

With a toss of her head, setting off another lavender flurry, Allsbury again confronted her opponents. "We need to skip then to Item Number Four on the Agenda and hear from our Assistant Principal, Mr. Brampton Falange." She looked up myopically. "Sir! If you would?" She nodded effusively to the agitated individual already at her side.

"Bomb threats! Mucho serioso, folks! Now! Here's the deal! Last call that happened answered by one of our counselors, Mrs. Brauphman? So, let's us have her to tell us all about it. And folks, this *is* serious. So, let's give it *all* our attention!" His nodding did not indicate confidence in their collaboration. "OK?"

Falange turned, looked up to the administrative group and motioned to the lady waddling down the steps. Hair frizzed, an over dyed blonde, she projected subterfuge coyness. A 'large' woman who had capitulated in the struggle to maintain a figure, she had a tiny, rounded nose with miniscule, shining eyes. Her words, a whining rendition of baby talk, aped a 'southern' accent.

"Now, how's ever-thang? Now that my daughter [she pronounced it daater] has her AP class early—these GATE kids are so darn *smart*, now—I come right from her school to here, so I guess I'm usually the, well, first one here? In the morning? To arrive?" Giggling to reassure herself, she smacked her lips. "Anyhow, as I'm sayin', this here call comes in? I try to keep this jerk on the phone so as to better trace him? Then what happens? Ms. Donner? Blonnel? Now, she comes waltzing in, pretty as a picture, not thanking anythang's wrong, just all ready to start her. . . whatever? Typing? As per usual? So, quick like a bunny, I signals her to get into the other phone! Call police?" Her voice was excitedly conspiratorial and, mouth hanging, she made the telephone sign with thumb and little finger, head cocked to the side, eyes rolling.

"Anyhoo, you know how these bombers are real sickos. Big time! Really! What happens? Nut Bar ups and hangs up! So police left standing there, holding a empty bucket. But that's what we're told: keep 'em on the phone! As long as possible so to trace the call? Then, by that time the first bell rings and the kids starts going in to class—at least some of them?" She looked furtively at Falange. "Then Mr. Baques, he gets here and tells us to fetch all the kids *outside* the classrooms because no one knows where the bomb is." She tugged at the folds of her enormous Cleveland Browns shirt, possibly to allay suspicion of concealed bombs on her own person. "Now, like I'm sayin', these guys are gettin' scary—*real* scary! I sure wouldn't want to meet up with one. Like in a dark alley somewheres. Preverts!"

Falange, smiling over clenched teeth, shook her hand solemnly, indicating, with a nod, she should return to her place. "*Mucho gusto*, Rayella. So very much! For your life-force. You know it's quick thinking like yours that saves the day! Every time! You'll be a significant asset to school reform." He pursed his lips. "OK. Now, back to the drill, folks. Here's game plan! So, listen up! Let me have all your ears! Now, when we get a bomb threat—and as Rayella just said, they *are* getting more frequent, and all the time, we had three last month alone—this *would* be the game plan! What we do is: we're going to mobilize all the male teachers to go into the classrooms and make a total search? We can't expose everybody. Ms. I believe you have your hand up?"

"Doesn't the school district carry insurance on classroom items? Is there anything there that's irreplaceable? That's worth risking someone's life for? Globes, maps, textbooks? Potted plants? Or lesson plans? As I understand it, these bombs could be in any kind of container, fastened beneath furniture or what have you. I just don't get the logic of your 'game plan'. I'm sorry! But I really don't." Sandra Weatherby, Biology, was indignant.

"Well, as I just said, these are *contingency* measures so's you can stick to your Biology classes. I enunciated how we *will* be formatting permanent policies at a future date. But right now, in the meantime, this is *our* school and we're *all* here to protect kids! That's all of us's responsibility!"

"Why can't the police do it? Don't they have trained bomb squads?"

"Right! So, let's get some skinny on this. You might not think so, but we're in close touch both with FBI, State Highway Patrol, SWAT, School District police, sheriffs, local police, county law enforcement: the whole spiel! And their policy is to send over somebody to check things out. OK? But, folks—have to lay it on the line here—there's just too *darn many* calls to come check out each and every one of these weirdoes! Nut bars!"

"Exactly how many weirdoes *can* they check out?"

"Yeah! Ten? Twenty-three? One? There's a limit? Isn't that what police get paid for? Dangerous jobs? And presumably they're trained to know how to look for bombs? At least they might know the packaging? It seems to me that this is one area where the amateur looking for a bomb, however well intentioned *he* is, might not only kill *himself* but other people as well. And incidentally: why are males more competent *amateur* bomb detectors than females? Women get paid as much as men, don't they? Male lives are worth less? Or just expendable?"

"Mr. Pemberton? Your point escapes me!"

"Then I'll explain. The *logic* of your plan, to say nothing of the lack of regard for teachers lives, is astounding. It's OK to kill a male teacher? But not a female teacher? Not a certified bomb squad technician?"

"Mr. Pemberton, once again, I *said* this was a *contingency* measure."

Lyndon Pemberton, Heath/Driver Education, continued peevishly. "What's worse, you assume—why I don't know—that the bomber has technical expertise! Brauphman implied these bombers—perverts—are insane. I agree. That compounds the danger of 'amateurs' doing the searches. So, your plan is to expose the lives of *male* teachers, totally untrained, in a normally highly specialized and dangerous activity, on the assumption that the 'pervert', the 'nut bar', has what? Technical proficiency? You assume, that in no way are his technical skills—assuming he has them, and that's a big if—affected by his obvious psychopathic and criminal dementia? If he says the bomb will explode in one hour, you accept that as accurate? What if the bomb explodes in fifteen minutes, not sixty? What if it explodes in three hours, *after* students and teachers, including female teachers, have returned to the classroom?"

"As I said Lyndon—Mr. Pemberton—and let me restate: this is a *contingency* plan. We'll modify it: as-we-uncover-the-glitches!" Again, Falange searched the ceiling for inspiration. Finding none, he sighed pontifically, muttered, "OK" and left the podium.

Allsbury resumed her place with refurbished rigidity. "We're getting behind and have to move on. Claudia Obesso from District Bicultural/ Bilingual Education is here to assist."

Whether Allsbury was directing the contempt in her smile to the audience or the new speaker was unclear. In any case, without warning, there was a jarring interruption from the Command Post: inordinately hearty introductions and forced laughter. Startled, Allsbury pivoted, brows furrowed, elongated skeletal hand draping itself across her chest. Audience truculence shifted to curiosity. Baques, oblivious to them, having waved Obesso back to her place, was introducing a new arrival to the administrative group. Only after these protracted greetings had spent themselves, did he turn to the teachers.

"Right now, folks! To listen up? I'm going to have to interrupt." He looked around proudly brandishing his broadest grin. "You can see the guest of honor *has* arrived!" He raised his voice excitedly. With a comradely arm over the new arrival's shoulder, Baques escorted him down the steps to the rostrum. Without acknowledging Allsbury, he basked in the glory of his trophy. "Folks. I always say, whatever happens: happens. He finally got here! This is a superlative honor for us here today. And we sure do appreciate it." He spoke with ponderous sincerity. "If this idea for our school reform goes through, and I can assure you, Mr. Pritchard, we are all behind it: one hundred percent. Change is the name of the game. Always."

Obviously buoyed by the new arrival, Baques' front teeth glistened. "We know that the Reform Plan will quite considerably benefit our school. And our kids." He became reverential. "So, folks, if there *is* any kind of concerns, in your minds, then Reform Plan will change them." He turned to his guest with adulation. "Now, folks, I don't have to introduce you: to Mr. Peter Pritchard! But for those of you who might be new, he is only the CEO of the biggest investment company in the state: EduCom". He sniggered. "He's a mortgage banker and industrialist. A hard-charger, go-getter type! And over the years has demonstrated in a multiplicity of ways that he's a straight-shooter! Mega old school!"

Baques restrained himself from bowing. "So, let's cut to the quick! And! His whole family are Fillmorians! Warriors!" Triumphantly, he searched the audience for approbation but found affirmative head shaking only from the 'Sucks': staff who robotically agreed with Administration on everything. "His grandfather and father were also proud Fillmore graduates. Folks: this man and his family are proof that Fillmore *does* and *can* produce: leaders! In spite of how some might try to bad-mouth inner city schools. And minorities. We already heard some of that here today. And let me tell you, I can get pretty darn P-O'd, when I hear our own teachers bad mouthing: trying to put on that we're not doing all we can for kids? Wow! Now, I won't lie to you! Hassles me! Sure does! And we *will* be conferencing with those individuals!"

Bobbing his head, his affability returned. "Mr. Pritchard'll be going to explain all about new Reform Plan to us. How it'll help us to help kids. He has the totality of support of our Superintendent, Dr. Jones-Laporte and School Board members." With an adoring expression, he inclined his head and asked, "Your father and his father: both members of our School Board, if I'm not mistaken? So, and without further ado . . . " Leaving completion of his paean to the imagination, Baques cautiously touched Pritchard's arm, and bobbed himself off the rostrum.

Peter Pritchard masked his reaction to the introduction with a dignified smile directed to his audience. "Good afternoon, ladies and gentlemen. Thank you for inviting me. For permitting me to speak with you. I know you are busy. I will be brief."

The speaker's confidence, dignity and appearance commanded attention: the substitute teacher evaluated by the class. The embodiment of leadership, Pritchard projected power and authority. His intensity, his immediacy, flattered them.

"It has been said that you, classroom teachers, are important in maintaining our great democracy?" His tone was a challenge. "That as instructors of future generations, you are inextricably bound up with the continuation, the expansion, even the survival, of this, the greatest democracy in the history of humankind."

Looking into the back rows, his dark eyes widened. He rode the wave of uneasy tension, which he permitted to roll over the room. The light spray of applause invigorated him.

Leaning forward, he lowered his voice to a theatrical whisper. The room fell into total silence. For the first time.

"My own belief, however, may surprise you." He waited as their anticipation crescendoed. "I have to tell you something: different." They were stunned. "Ladies and gentlemen, I *disagree* with that view." There was a rippling of uneasy laughter, twitters from the female contingent: an embarrassed hush.

"Here is what I believe." His voice regained its original resonance. "I believe that you, *you*, comprise the *most* important, the *essential* component of our great nation—this greatest possible democracy. You: are the crucible of our democracy. You: hold in your hands. . .its survival. . . its flowering. You: molding young minds, enable it to repulse attacks from subversives of all kinds: terrorists, gangsters, free-thinkers, Communists, Socialists, flag-burners, atheists, drug dealers: the compendium of unpatriotic naysayers who are conspiring to pull our great nation down from the principles on which it was founded: from its achievements! Inside and outside our borders! Over the past two centuries."

"Sadly, the media are complicit in anti-school attacks: assaults against what they call incompetent, immoral, self-serving teachers." The pall of audience caution was lifting. "My friends, when people attack teachers, what are they really doing?" He waited. "When they attack our educators, teachers, they are attacking a fundamental pillar of our God-given democracy: education itself. Attacks, therefore, against our teachers, our schools, are attacks against this sacred shrine of democracy. That nurtures us. That protects us."

His voice regained its original stentorian vibrato, as acceptance submerged their initial doubt. He extended his palms, interrupting the burgeoning applause. "No! Ladies and gentlemen, because of the pivotal place of education in our democracy, I believe yours is the *most* honorable profession to which a person can aspire." He waited. "You, as sculptors of our next generation, form the *essential* component of our God-given democracy." A moment of silence; then the anticipated applause filled the room. "You are its hallmark! And I salute you for your dedication."

He spread his arms. "Each of you, therefore, holds in her or his hands, the essence of our democracy: its survival against those who envy us. Who seek to destroy us. It is *you* who have the power to shape the future of our God-given democratic heritage. Preserve it. Strengthen it. Expand it."

Unable to contain themselves, the room, now amazed, exploded into cheers: shouts of approval. Catapulted into action, several stood, nodding vigorously, motioning with pounding hands to their colleagues.

Shifting his stance, Pritchard continued. "My friends, it is not so long ago that I myself walked these halls as a young person on the threshold of his own destiny." He paused just long enough to initiate the next demonstration of approval which he immediately silenced. "Well, perhaps somewhat longer than I would like to say." He smiled at the self-conscious chortling from the older teachers. "It was you who shaped that destiny. You shaped my philosophy. My beliefs." Arms extended, he permitted them to savor the hallowed content of his message.

"It was in those Art courses with Mr. Sternberg and English with Mrs. Staples?" He looked back to the Command Post. "Are they here?" The faces there were expressionless, unsure of the direction of his discourse. "Possibly they have retired? And God bless them! So now: their mantle falls to you: to shape other future leaders. God bless them. And you."

He took a long sip from the glass at his side, requiring the audience to hang suspended. "Ladies and gentlemen, I prefer *not* to call teaching a profession, as we have heard today. Rather, I will call it, as we did formerly at Fillmore: a *vocation.*" He was intimate. "Allow me to speak frankly! When I was younger, I lacked your courage. I lacked your fortitude: to go down into the trenches day after day and assist our young people. May I add, with due respect to Mr. Baques and his excellent staff, your struggle is sometimes without the reinforcement you deserve! Support that administration want to give you, yes! But from which they, too, are hampered by budgetary constraints. In many ways, under the present system, they are as frustrated as you in their efforts to bring our school to the highest level of academic excellence. Occasionally, we need to remind ourselves that we are all on the same team! Let no one say differently."

"Ladies and gentlemen, I only wish teaching had been my spiritual calling—as it is yours. To be responsible for molding young minds and young personalities. To be entrusted with a sacred and God-given responsibility: the guidance of young adults to their so richly deserved destiny: a destiny nurtured in this crucible of democracy. My friends, I was not *called,* as were you. And may God love you for it!"

The cheers escalated. He waited benignly allowing the applause to undulate to the edges of the room, eddy, and spray back on itself. "Yes. It is for that reason that I acknowledge the honor you do me by permitting me to share my thoughts on this vital topic—school reform—with you today."

The speaker knew his art and did not press for additional accolades. Poise and confidence—concomitants of power and money— fascinated them. The slight gesture of his hand re-engaged them, calming the waters, soothing possibly breaking waves into smoothly undulating swells and troughs. Potentially dangerous, yes. But a master was at the helm. The room was wafted into a silent sheen.

"Ladies and gentlemen! Student advocates! It is quite appropriate that you want to know about Reform: how it will work to benefit your students. And you. Before you accept it. Accordingly, without taking more of your professional time, I would like to discuss the essence of our Plan. Its overall thrust. What sets it apart from other school reform plans. I hope you will see my suggestions as viable: that you will consider them. The decision, of course, remains yours."

He stepped in front of the podium, hands at his sides. Attractively trim, he was in his early sixties but could have passed for mid forties. The *Canali* suit enhanced the svelte silhouette. Speaking without notes, his voice was strong and his enunciation precise.

"How will Reform help you? Teachers are pragmatic: they deal in facts. Not superfluities. Very well, then, permit me to explain. The facts." Their attention was complete.

"My friends, *our* Reform Plan comprises two phases. They set it apart from other reform efforts: make it unique. Its bi-furcated strategy, it's double-pronged assault, is the key to its success. It is why our Reform is indeed 'new'. Why it will succeed where plans elsewhere have failed."

He accepted a bottle of water from a lady in the front row, brushing aside the requisite tissue. "Phase One: reform from inside our school. Phase One itself is two-pronged. In Part A we take back our school. The key word here is 'We'. We, not outsiders, know what our problems are. The small cracks in the dam. We will repair them."

"And Phase One, Part B? We will retain what is working for us now. We, allow me to emphasize 'we', will not make changes for the sake of change. Change? Yes. Selective change."

"You said it, guy! Tell the gooks in State to just tend to their own business."

"Thank you, sir. A critical issue? Teacher evaluations? Our Reform is based on teacher *effort* in the classroom, our progress with the reality of the students we have: not with what students 'should be' as defined by politicized test makers, hundreds, even thousands of miles away. A fantasy. A politicized fantasy designed not to help students. But to further the careers of politicians!"

He quieted the applause. "No, ladies and gentlemen. Our Reform is predicated on reality. The reality that some of our students are deficient in reading, Mathematics, English, Science when they arrive on our doorstep. Teacher evaluations based on student progress? Of course! But! From the reality of *our starting* point. Not from the whimsy of the Traditionalist *achievement* point."

"Another teacher concern: Assessment. Testing. To evaluate teachers? Fine. So long as tests are based on what is taught. Not on subject matter the student cannot learn. Not designed by paid government test makers, by politicians, the content of which, somehow, magically, students are supposed to imbibe, in a process of mental osmosis, without considering the reality, as pointed out, that our minority youngsters, are deficient when they arrive here. Do politicians in the state capital, in Washington, know that? Do they care? When they impose *their* strictures on us?"

"Right on, guy! And them wanting to deny us money because we're helping kids to know what they can. Not testing them to find out what they don't know. And can't learn."

"Let us *help* them. Not test them to death."

Pritchard was reassuring. "Federal politicians either do not know. Or do not care. And their ignorance is making *us* their pawns—their political pawns. And in the process, hindering our children. Not helping them. Destroying, not *helping*, public education."

"Tell it again, guy: the politicians' song and dance: 'we're the shepherds, you're the sheep: bah!"

"You said it, Peter! If kids already were at the level to be tested, what would be the point of having us? I mean, ho-o-ly!

"And tests? Those guys want our kids only to study for tests! Big deal. They get to parrot stuff they don't like and don't understand? That's education? I don't think so. Not what I went into teaching for! No way, José!"

Peter absorbed their comments. "Our Reform means fairness and common sense: *our* teachers—make *our* tests—for *our* students! Yes, perhaps, down the road, in the future, we *can* have government made tests. But not now. Later."

"Right! And a ten percent increase by our kids tests could be the same as a fifty percent increase by other kids in Traditionalist schools tests."

"And everybody knows Traditionalists cheat to get their great big fat wonderful 'increases'."

"We don't need to put our kids in a leaky boat and expect them to row across the lake. I mean, come off of it!"

"Teachers like coaches! But nobody expects the Track coach to have her kids run a marathon in less than a hour. Can't be done."

"In the interests of time, ladies and gentlemen. Phase Two? May I outline that in general terms?"

The enthusiasm for Peter was cresting. "Go for it!" "This guy's one smart, cookie. Knows his beans!"

"Phase Two, ladies and gentlemen: the second prong of our bifurcated Reform Plan, will focus *outside* the school. Phase Two will restructure our community. You ask why? And how?"

"Why? Why is community reform essential? To the success of school reform? Because many, most, of the problems you deal with in your classrooms, especially discipline and academic disinterest, emanate, not from the school but from the community. How often are you, the classroom professionals, expected to deal with, solve, problems, extraneous to academics, which impede student learning?"

He allowed their interest to swell. "Broken homes? Out of work parents? No parents? Drive-by shootings? Gangs? Drugs? Unwanted pregnancies? Alcohol? Eviction? Lack of transportation? Imprisoned parents? Lack of academic preparation? Foster Home children? To mention a few." Peter was commiserate. "My friends, until we devise a strategy to solve *community* problems, our *school* problems cannot be solved. Indeed, they will escalate. School reform at best will be a band-aide."

"This guy's hit his hammer on the nail. For sure."

"How? How will Phase Two of our Reform transform our community of Cathedral Heights into a place where youngsters are nurtured, emotionally, and made safe: given the security they deserve—made confident instead of fearful—so they are psychologically, socially, economically *prepared:* to absorb your instruction?" He held up his hands to silence the approval. "Of course they cannot learn now: in the present environment. They come from a disruptive place. And we, our Reform, must change what happens *to* them. *Out there!* If we want to change what happens *for* them. *In here!*"

"How? How to save our youngsters? The solution, the bedrock of our reform plan is: partnership! Join schools and community in a partnership. Let schools and community act in concert rather than in opposition: mutual isolation."

The applause was vigorous: foot stomping and slapping of backs and shoulders. Falynn Smedley, General Mathematics, leapt from his chair and bawled the Rebel Yell.

Peter was conversational. "My wife is my bulwark. My inspiration. She is a ballet aficionado. In our discussions she likens school and community to dance partners, moving together as one: complimenting one another to produce a beautiful totality. A unified whole! Not martial arts opponents; battling each other; one survives at the expense of the other. No, our Reform does away with school versus community: isolated segments unaware of each other. Combating each other. Our Reform *fuses* school and community by reform *both* in the school *and* in the community. Separate but entwined: a union, perfect synchronization. Achieving the common goal."

"Why shouldn't we do the Reform ourselves, then? Why you? An outsider?"

"Thank you, Mr. Mugwabe. Point well taken. First, *our* Reform is *entirely* in *your* hands. Already. *You* design it. *You* implement it. I merely present the seed. If you like it, you plant it. Nurture it. Watch it flower. Reform? It *is* yours. Now. Not mine."

"Second, why me? An outsider? Given, we agree that our schools must be an integral part of *our* community. Phase Two will accomplish that partnership in a way that is unique. Permit me to say, that my business associations may allow me to offer experience in community activities for which, perhaps, some of you, may not have the time. I provide the frame. You paint picture. *Your* picture."

"Hey, guy! How about number one? Salaries?"

"Critical point. Reform will increase salaries. How? Our community will become financially resourceful. Let me explain the partnership of schools and community." He held them baited. "We will bring in new businesses. New businesses will create the kind of community that nurtures youngsters—prepares them for your instruction—a community that is economically prosperous, safe, politically innovative."

"Tell us."

"We offer tax and other incentives to entice business entities, corporations. And they will come. Eagerly. Because they will be the purveyors to our school district and to our municipality: equipment, plumbing, construction, electrical, catering, police, health. The myriad of things schools need. These businesses will recreate our community. And? They will be minority owned. Gender leveled."

Shrill, tongue-twirling Bedouin screeches cascaded over the assemblage.

"Salaries? Increased tax revenues will give us—us—*discretionary* income—ours—to spend where? Where *we* see fit. *Including teacher salaries!* On *our* citizens. Results? There are many."

"Many new jobs for our graduates. Management jobs. Not fast-food jobs. And speaking of jobs. We are working on a plan whereby teachers may participate in this economic boon."

"He's gotta be kidding!"

"Mr. Baques and his staff will be speaking with some of you to show how you may, while teaching, gain stipends to assist these businesses with Reform needs: supplies, equipment. Result? Increased revenue for you. And? In the highly unlikely event that the state does mandate salary increases? That will be icing on the cake. For you. Our salary increases will no longer be the pro forma minimal State subsistence increases. We will be able to offer *professional level* increases. You! *You* decide *your* salaries!"

"Wow! If that's not reform then I'm not a . . ."

"Teacher burnout? Understandable. Our Plan envisions class size reduction and sabbatical leave. No other Reform plan acknowledges teachers in these ways."

"And speaking of the nurturing environment essential to preparing students to receive your instruction? Cathedral Heights, our own community, with economic revitalization, will become the haven for persons hitherto either excluded or marginalized from economic and political advancement elsewhere. Persons who epitomize the causes which are the backbone of this great democracy: single parents, feminists, ecologists, animal rights advocates, victims of child abuse, mothers against drunk drivers, victims of domestic violence, advocates of ethnic diversity, opponents of capital punishment, multi-culturalists, victims of gender abuse, of domestic violence, and, if you wish, advocates of Free Choice."

He permitted the applause to subside. "Now, right now, how many of you own your own homes?" They exchanged puzzled looks.

He was patient. "I count seven hands. Next question: how many expect to own their own homes?" Pritchard scrutinized them. "I counted what? Three hands? The point is that right now, most teachers do not own their own homes. And do not, cannot, expect to do so. In the future."

He smiled. "That also will change! Phase Two will provide low interest and eventually, as we expand financially, reimbursed Interest for home loans. So teachers, our teachers, may have gracious, dignified, residences. Appropriate to their professional status. Not, what is the term. . .?"

"Fixers! Fixer-uppers?"

"None of that. Result? Gracious housing for professionals. The best teachers will want to come here from other districts: we will provide the academic atmosphere, the security to manage their own classrooms. And financial security, with a professional living standard. In a safe, diversified, self-governing community."

"Another point. About Phase Two. Community based schools? What politicians say they want? But do not provide? Fine! We *shall* provide! Charter Schools? Name is unimportant. *Our* schools—intertwined culturally and financially with *our* community—to benefit *our* students, *our* teachers, *our* welfare. That is what is important. That is *our* reform."

"I neglected to mention one advantage. Our Plan: community based schools, community integrated schools, may lead you to separate our community of Cathedral Heights from Los Altos: set up our own self-governing city that will allow, will ensure, that here—in our own city, that we control, financially and politically—we will have teachers holding political office."

"Get this you guys! He's off his rocker! How?"

Another lady offered bottled water. "What if State and Federal government don't like what we're doing? Try to stop us?"

"Excellent point. They might! Try to stop us! So? To prevent that, it may be that when you approve Reform next June you may want to attach a codicil that we take the step, the daring step, of separating Cathedral Heights from Los Altos and establishing ourselves as an independent city. That we control."

"Incredible."

"Back to teachers holding political office." His eyes, which never lost their intensity, pinpointed several in his audience, and shining, stopped at Arnida Hollyfield. "It may be that this young lady, will be willing to sacrifice her Science class to become our next mayor! Our next Superintendent of Schools? Imagine: a *teacher* giving the orders! Managing that one hundred sixty million—plus—dollar budget! Appointing teachers. Administrators! Incredible things are possible ladies and gentlemen. Our Reform is more than change. It is a revolution. In contemporary public education. In contemporary local government." He quieted the ovation. "Yes, revolution. Federal and state politicians want community based schools? Our Reform Plan will show them community based schools: in a way they never imagined! We take the Reform bit in our teeth. My friends, we are going to run with it! And? We are going to win the race. Thank you."

The approbation was thundering. Mike Moran, Consumer Math was ebullient: "This guy is definitely a class act!"

Allsbury returned from the sidelines, cautiously taking her position at the podium and speaking carefully. "Isn't that wonderful! To have such public-spirited leaders? So, ladies and gentlemen? Moving on? We are just a wee bit behind and we have Ms. Rikki Bacon-Gaither and Dr. Cyndye Hernandez here with us today from the District to help us with the topic of upcoming accreditation?"

"Thank you, Dr!" Baques was motioning from the command post. "We need to reach finality. It's past the hour! Wow! So ladies we're just going to have to put you on a back burner until next opportunity. Ho-ly! Teachers! You guys need to get to your homes!"

"Hey! What about Union?"

"Sorry, Bruce. You'll be first next time. Trust me!"

"Sucks, man! Teachers get it again. Need a special meeting to say how District trampled on the salary increase proposal we made. How they won't protect our cars from vandalisms: but got insurance to cover administration cars. How cost of dependent health care will be costing us more! Mega old school, man!"

Baques was patronizing. "Right on Bruce! But, if, quickly? It seems notices didn't get out to our parent advisor so she's not here today. And, I believe you have a few introductions, Dr? And then you might take us to closure?" He bobbed his short neck towards Allsbury.

"I believe we have some new teachers with us today? New arrivals? Helping out in Foreign Languages will be, ah, Huguette Cortère? Mme. Huguette Cortère: our resident French expert?" Allsbury looked up blankly and myopically. "Will you please stand and be recognized, Mme. Cortère?" Pointed chin raised, she swung her gaze imperiously around the semicircle of the audience, plucked eyebrows arched, thin smile stretched to breaking point.

No response. Several offered gratuitous explanations: "Must have quit already!" "One smart girl!" "Didn't take her long to get the skinny." The anti-Allsbury faction shot baleful expressions at the administrator.

"That must be her?" Large frame, square jawed, dark complexion, with a mass of jet hair arranged in a 60's bouffant, a lady stood beside her chair.

"I guess you mean me. I'm *Ms.* Cort-high-err," giving the Canadian pronunciation. Speaking from the side of her mouth, she corrected Allsbury's Parisian pronunciation. There was muted applause intermixed with overt sniggering at the rebuke.

"Well, I know you come from Canada."

"Prrro-vauce-day-Kay-bec!", was the second reprimand.

"And thank you so *very* much. We are delighted. To join your expertise to our professional staff."

"Now, something else ladies and gentlemen. A recognition. The Civitans have selected one of our teachers as their Teacher of the Year. And now would *you* please stand, Mr. Besserian? And I know I got that one right." There was some giggling.

A large smile did not conceal a hint of shyness. Assuming his full height of five feet ten inches, the leg of his folding chair slipped and he would have fallen had not two ladies in the row behind scrambled to support his one hundred and seventy pounds. Grasping Blaise Martyn-West's shoulder, he righted himself with an athlete's agility. There was an aroma of musk, and the sweat on his face defined the outline of beard. His voice was clear.

"I'm pleased to receive this award. And I know it's well intentioned. But it should go to students. They did the work. The role of the teacher is off stage. In the background. Helping kids: they're the ones who should get the awards." His smile was infectious but his recessed eyes did not invite intimacy. Reaching through his legs, he grasped the chair and sat down.

"Mr. Baques, did you wish to add anything before we move forward to closure?" Allsbury's right slipper was pressed against the floor. The Principal gave his traditional "thumbs up" gesture without taking his attention from the papers which Marvella was handing him to sign. "Bruce? Don't forget! Next time g'buddy?"

Bruce Warfles was Allsbury's antithesis. Already having maneuvered himself to the front, his pungent aroma obliterated her scented, *Tigress,* chiffon. Nostrils compressed, Allsbury smiling vacantly, yielded the podium. Short, disheveled, with a pronounced paunch, both Bruce and his clothes were adverse to washing. His '70's Hawaiian shirt, faded from unskilled use of bleach, was soaked at the armpits. A person who relished confrontation, there was belligerency in his walk—an aggressive waddle. With short, wide feet, his tire-tread, ergonomic sandals were cracked from rain and sun. He wore no socks. There were conflicting stains on his rumpled, cotton trousers.

He called over the emptying room, "Meeting next week! Give you guys the scoop on salaries. And vandalisms to our cars." He smirked at Baques. "Gottcha man. You owe me! " He called to the retreating Baques who returned a thumbs-up sign without looking back.

There was considerable scraping of chairs as the remaining teachers filed out calling parting encouragement to Brian and each other: "Get 'em tiger." "Hang in there, big guy." "Happy days are here again", the lyrics intoned in a mocking, high-pitched tone.

A few teachers collected personal items scattered on the floor or chairs. "They don't know and they don't care." "Who appoints these administrators, anyhow? Joseph E. Newman?" "Happy Hour at *Tamarino's*, anyone?" "Another wasted hour and a half." "Numero uno consideration? Protect what we've got! Otherwise could be worse for us!"

Scented skin lotions and sweat mingled with school smells: books, paper, varnished desks, negligent air conditioning, floor wax, disinfectant.

Besserian sat with his briefcase on his knees, thumbs gripping the front latches and nurturing a predilection to introspection. The meeting triggered futility and isolation. Resignation to the ineffective carping and faultfinding didn't make the feelings more pleasant.

He frowned and the combination of fading light, heavy shadow of beard and deeply recessed eyes, combined to shroud his face. Tilting his chair, he looked up at the ceiling partially discolored by water seepage.

The Reform Plan bothered him. "An innovative idea: involve the community. Maybe?"

"Hey! Mr. B! Good award there, buddy! Administration likes teachers to get into the community. Not go too far, of course!" Brian McCauley, Football coach, teasing, retrieved a misplaced issue of *Football Digest*. The exchange snapped Besserian back to his usual outward demeanor: uninvolved and distant. He smiled mechanically. "Right! Not too far." He slapped the case affectionately, his eye following Brian through the door.

In fact, however, he was not alone in the silence. Sandra Weatherby, Biology text at her side, was rummaging in an oversized tapestry purse. He spoke carefully. "I liked what you said today."

She looked up, her initial irritation eddying into a meticulous observation. Chin lifted, she scraped a fingernail against a lower front tooth. "OK. I'll accept that. And congratulations to you! Your award!"

"Maybe. Say: one thing you might help me with. Some advice! About several kids in my first period. I'm not reaching them. Actually, some in period five, too."

"A few must be getting something. Or you wouldn't have the award. So? What's wrong with the 'some'? Better than none. But, I guess survival is the answer, here. For most people."

As much to relieve the tension as anything else, Besserian ignored the inference. "So? What did you think of our little speech today?"

"That? Pritchard? Not sure."

"Sounded like it might be pretty good."

"Sounds that way."

"You're not overly, what? Optimistic? Enthusiastic?"

"Skeptical, perhaps. Yes, skeptical is a good word."

"Higher salaries. Smaller classes. Skeptical? About that?"

"Skeptical about Reform from the outside?"

"What's the expression? Any port in a storm?"

"Precisely. But who chooses the port? And why?"

"You heard him. He's got business management and community connections. School reform? Tied to community reform? Could be a winner? Seems to be OK?"

"Listen, my friend. . ." She hesitated. Then, cutting off the thought, "I have to go", she swept up purse and books hurriedly. Petulantly.

He watched her uneasily, gathering up her paraphernalia. "Kids?"

"Sure. I'll let you know. Later."

"Hold on! Hey! Something the matter? Did I say something."

He had caught the tip of her sleeve. She turned, glaring at him. Then at his slowly retreating fingers. "No, you didn't say anything." She fumbled with her purse. "And you didn't do anything."

He relaxed, still slightly confused. "OK? So, what . . .?"

"And you didn't *think* anything. Look! We're not kids. I have to go." Her heels echoed through the open door, as she picked her way along the passage between the buildings.

# CHAPTER II

## *An Incident*

*Esta es una facilidad escolar cerrada.*
*Las personas que entren a esta facilidad escolar deben*
*de reportarse a la oficina del director.* [1]

The sign at the bottom of the hill asserted no admittance, a warning reinforced both by the eighteen-member Security force, and the physical site itself. Because it was impossible to check five thousand ID cards—frequently mutilated and often shared—twice a day, in addition to verifying numerous early and special dismissal slips, Security was reinforced by metal detectors and guard dogs. Guards were authorized to search students once they had navigated the pot-holed macadam to the top of the hill: the administration building.

Then there was the hill itself: daunting, a steep slope up to the massive, crenellated main portico. As for the rest of the campus, high embankments isolated athletic fields, stadium, auditorium, classrooms, cafeteria, support buildings and administrative offices from the surrounding neighborhood.

Most of the original Oak, Sycamore, Cedar, and Palms were gone, as were the sculpted flower beds. At one time the largest of these had framed, in brilliant color, two bronze plaques: WWII Memorial to fallen students

1 Campus is locked. Anyone wishing to enter must report to the Principal.

and the school motto: '*Quaecumque Vera Docete Nos*'.[2] Now, both were almost obliterated by clumps of weed overgrowth.

Besserian was struck by the mood of abandonment that permeated the campus after three o'clock: and particularly now, after five, following the faculty meeting. Gates were supposed to be chained, padlocked, and doors bolted by five-thirty, however, aggressive security officers often locked them earlier. Teachers, privileged to have classroom keys only, ran the risk of being incarcerated if they delayed their departures. Then there was the 'AP Johansson Directive No. 14-G', warning faculty to quit the campus "in the interests of personal safety, by four-fifteen: max!".

Few of the daily, after-school 'Student Enrichment' programs, funded for two hours, therefore, ran to completion. Nor was this curtailment, in spite of the monetary waste, deemed serious. Contrary both to District publications and school PR releases regarding these government-funded Intervention programs, dismissal did not open floodgates of intellectual inquiry.

Contravening administrators sermons to the few parents who attended infrequent 'Parent Night' or 'Back to School So Glad to See You' Get-Togethers, the school, after dismissal, did not blossom into a center of intellectual vigor where dedicated teachers, surrounded by inquiring, receptive, and brilliant young minds, sitting wide-eyed at their feet, expanded the fine points of ideas and skills presented earlier in the day. Nor was such a metamorphosis expected: by anyone.

In point of fact, administration eschewed supervision of 'Enrichment'. These classes were paid 'perks'. The monthly stipends, one thousand dollars plus, expanded the eligibility pool: Baques 'team players'. Funded for ten hours a week, Intervention classes met for perhaps five or six. Students received academic credit based on attendance as recorded by the instructor, not its reality, and not by demonstrated knowledge of the sporadic assignments.

Classes were generic only. The teacher created the curriculum: English, Mathematics, Reading, Science: not Algebra I, Geometry, US History, Government—substantive courses under the state curriculum. Two or more subjects might be taught by one teacher; different grade and proficiency levels notwithstanding. Pre and post assessments were unknown. Instruction, far from being remediation determined by student need, was at the convenience of the teacher. Intervention faculty were not

2 Teach us Whatever is True.

accountable. Many were not credentialed in the subject they, purportedly, were teaching.

The reality was that once the throng of five thousand had surged out. . . pushing. . . .running. . . shouting. . . Intervention students, isolated throughout the complex of buildings, passed the time perusing magazines, often provided by the instructor, socializing, and occasionally completing regular class assignments or homework. Legitimacy of an Intervention class was determined by attendance only, and it was easy to adjust the numbers accordingly. Food, drinks, and make-work assignments were further inducements, especially since they often pre-empted instruction. In excess of one hundred twenty thousand dollars annually were allocated from the school budget: faculty 'Enrichment' stipends.

The depressing atmosphere pushed the recollection, lingering and unpleasant, of Weatherby's cryptic remarks into the recesses of Besserian's mind. Looking across the expanse of campus, Besserian could hear several adolescents scrambling and slapping one another, petulantly, with feigned resentments. Across the track and field area, he could make out several couples, lying on the grass enjoying mutual caresses. Occasionally they surveyed their surroundings but always indifferently, zombie-like. They were apathetic to the distant squeals of infantile play: a single parent from the neighborhood with her offspring, able to navigate the one precarious path snaking up from the 'flats' below.

As he altered his direction to the parking lot, intending to stop first at his own classroom, he saw a secluded quartet imitating a game of handball. Two, with their shirts off, glistened in the late afternoon sun; skirt-like, silken shorts, clinging precariously to their hips, dangling below their knees.

They swatted at the ball, sometimes powerfully and aggressively, but mostly with indifference. Their partners, one in low-rise short-shorts and the other in a bikini, the bottom, bearing stenciled lettering: *Men's Athletics*, wore tank tops: one proclaiming *I'm Having a Maalox Movement* and the other *Work Sucks But I Need the Bucks*, compensated for their own disjointed efforts, by jeering at the exertions of their respective partners, interfering in the play and giggling petulantly or gleefully that they had either 'junked' or 'ragged' the males. All four were seized with paroxysms of hilarity.

The *Maalox* player, alleging injury, ran to the side, flinging matted tresses violently. Screaming obscenities, she rummaged furiously in a *Hello Kitty* backpack, flinging out the contents: lotions, lubricants, bra, a 'Personal Gratification' DVD, pony tail Ties, self-rolled cigarettes, an issue of *Persona*.

"It's cool! I got it." Brandishing a gargantuan plastic bottle, she gurgled a protracted drink, wiped her mouth with a forearm, and then, rolling on the ground deliriously, legs fanning the air, was consumed with self delight.

From another area the cheerleaders were rehearsing, chanting in disjointed effort at rhythm:

"Oh! Get 'em good! Get 'em hard!
Get 'em where it hurts!
Give it to 'em! Give it to 'em!
Go Warr'eeers! Go! Warr'yr Power! All the way!
Show 'em what you got, guys!"

The *Adorables*, were leaping, legs wide. They attempted back-flips, hugged each other, and collapsed, sprawling on the ground. At the behest of their leader, extricating themselves from bouts of compulsive hilarity, it was only with difficulty that the young ladies formed themselves into a serrated chorus line. And the leader, delineated by her sequined crimson and brown Shako—a Jekyll and Hyde personality who alternated between bouts of uncontrolled laughter and vitriolic commands worthy of an enraged Baron von Stüben—prodded her minions with a gold-flaked baton urging them into their next 'routine':

"We the Best: We the Rest: You don't need to
Pass no Test! Go Warr'yeers!
Girl Power! All the Way!"

Their leaps, restricted by skill and coordination, were unfortunate, and they fell on each other haphazardly; flailing their arms, amid yelps of resentment—"You get your snooker out my face, girl!"—echoing in the receding light.

Near the football field was an ROTC detachment. Using their rifles as batons, they twirled them awkwardly, warily; then, crouching, heaved the weapons into the air. Lurching to retrieve them—if dropped, there were explosions of unabashed laughter—the cadets snatched the rifles desperately and scurried to contort themselves into a choreographed stance which, to Besserian, seemed eccentric: heads inclined sharply downward, one leg bent exaggeratedly, leaning on the stock, barrel buried in the sand: a caricature of a $19^{th}$ century pose of mourning. He recalled a multi-figured monument, "Warriors for the Confederacy" in a Georgia cemetery.

The crash of a ponderous pushcart resounded from a nearby building, as a custodian, alternately whistling, crooning and cursing, tugged the contentious conveyance, precariously loaded with buckets, brooms, mops, spray bottles, and oil-soaked rags over a cement threshold. Manipulating it with resounding thumps, punctuated with gratuitous curses—*¡los cuicos! Este lugar se encabrone me*[3]—down a flight of concrete stairs, she heaved a steel-belted door, and oblivious to the din, the nasty little wheels of the obdurate vehicle spinning stupidly in absurd defiance, yanked the cart through, allowing the door to hurtle closed with a reverberating crash, leaving an unpleasant emptiness in her wake.

Perhaps it was the silence? The enveloping darkness? The strain of the meeting? In any case Weatherby's innuendo that he, personally, was 'out of sync' with genuine reform kept recurring. It bothered him. No: irritated him. What did she know? Talk about the pot calling the kettle black! How was she better? Although a pillar of the Biology Department, her outspoken complaints about inadequate response to student need, had relegated her to the Fillmore hinterlands. An idealistic and competent teacher, Besserian's impression was that she undermined the validity of her criticisms by her contempt. He, on the other hand, was regarded as a mainstay of any faculty claim to intellectuality. Also, the Civitans Award was more than anyone else had received!

As he ruminated, it was her 'out of sync' inference that especially rankled him. It was used by teachers to castigate students who wouldn't or couldn't 'learn': who ignored assignments and, physically and verbally, made life miserable for teachers and students alike. "It's their culture", was the explanation. "They don't value academics".

So, he, Besserian was 'out of sync'? With what? Reform? He wasn't involved in reform! Her innuendo was a good example of why many found her irritating: why her Administrative Credential would remain a useless appendage.

"Me? 'Out of sync'! What nerve!" In his mind the epithet was a cover-up: code, used to shift blame for student failure, Drop-outs and Opt-outs, away from staff onto students: victims of the crime held responsible for it.

3 This place ticks me off! People are a bunch of pigs!

The Drop-out rate was over fifty percent! Drop-outs were students who disappeared from the system. No one bothered to trace them. Opt-outs were a shifting percentage of those who remained: but did not work: usually gang members and drug 'pushers'. They were the chronic discipline problems: perpetrators of physical and verbal violence against students, teachers and security guards. Often caught with concealed weapons, they were the chronic offenders who defied the veneer of administrative authority, contemptuous of calls to parents and suspensions.

No. It was her simplistic analysis, naiveté really, that bothered him. Where was reform supposed to start? What could staff do? Expulsion, mandated for possession of weapons, was seldom enforced. In the eyes of the dominant campus liberals, expulsion violated the mantra of Due Process: it was not politically correct to 'deny' a student their 'right' to public education. For any reason. Ever. To Besserian who considered himself a quasi liberal, liberals had painted themselves into a corner. What about the rights of hard-working students? What about school responsibility to parents of conscientious youngsters to protect *them*? Intellectually as well as physically? So far, he had kept his opinions to himself.

It occurred to him that he had adopted the same stance at Fillmore that governed his marriage: don't rock the boat. But that left the unpleasant question of what precisely were his duties? On ship or ashore?

A construction barricade interrupted his reverie. He shook his head to clear it of the pointless daydream. He knew a short-cut: the passageway between the back walls of the antiquated Science Building—it still bore the bronze plaque acknowledging the first Pritchard as its donor—and the auditorium. The adjacent buildings concealed a narrow walkway between.

Dusk was approaching: the passage was dim. High above, however, still gleaming in the sunset, the soaring scenery vault of the auditorium towered over the campus, and shimmered in color: green, red, gold, blue and black. It was a blazing Aztec calendar, geometric radiations filled with symbols and pictograms. Surmounting it, a heroic male figure, proud and arrogant, carrying in his bronzed, herculean arms, a swooning female, every detail of his sexuality emphasized, exaggerated even, by the abbreviated and bulging loin cloth, distended thigh, calf, abdominal and shoulder muscles. The stance was heroically defiant: dark eyes flashing, brilliant feathered headdress undulating. Above them, a soaring eagle, beak opened defiantly, flaunted its own writhing captive.

Entering, Besserian stepped cautiously. More narrow and longer than anticipated, the passage was, perhaps, eight feet by sixty. He was unprepared for the darkness. Groping, he could not see the end, and the walls were changing to a deep purple. He moved cautiously, immersing himself in the shadows and gloom.

Inching his way, he detected an unusual sound. Whistling, perhaps? If so, it was strange: more of a hissing? Wheezing? It altered into a muted.... squealing? He stopped—inquisitive and irresolute. And the sound stopped. He could not identify it precisely. It elicited disturbing reactions. Guilt? Fear?

"Go back?" He was irresolute. The sound again. His own apprehension? The stress of the day? The intimidating environment? The purple shades were dissolving into black. Although he detected movement in the gloom, he could see nothing. Whatever it was, however, couldn't be far away. His feelings were imploding, convulsing: excitement, danger.

Besserian stepped sideways, instinctively positioning his back against the rough, clammy, stone wall. He sensed he was beside an open space to his left and it was from there the sound came: intermittent but desperate. He held his body immobile. . . rigid.

As his eyes adjusted he realized that the recessed space was a stair well. His hand was slipping on the smooth steel of the pipe railing.

He could make out that the steps below—a quirk of the shadows enabled him to decipher the bottommost—descended in his direction. Arching his neck, he saw a line of light under the door at the foot of the steps. It permitted him, increasingly, to make out shapes. Now he was sure. The shrouded pulsations were clear.

The sound increased: powerful, intense. He became taut and sweat matted the hair on his chest and thighs. Heedless of its own volume, the sound, surged in intensity and Besserian was transfixed and rigid in his immobility. His eyes glistened: wide. His body must broadcast his presence: the pungent, murky aroma of damp hair comingled with moist wool.

Finally . . . now. . . hyperventilation. Then . . . silence. But it was the screaming silence of his own fear: the danger surrounding him. His mouth locked. Increasingly, he could make out details.

"Go back? No! Impossible". The reality held him: mute and motionless: desperate to know. To see. To find out.

Buttocks were thrust up to him; wringing the final ecstasy from the encounter. A leg was raised. A compulsive movement of the pair changed their positions, enabling Besserian to decipher the struggling figure on the bottom. Wrists still grasped by his partner, the broad shoulders were braced on a step, supporting both. The figure on top, still contorted in the final moments of consummation, threw back long hair, tossing it wildly from side to side. Finally, head drooping back in delirium, almost to the shoulder blades, she brought her eyes balefully upward . . . and they gleamed, mounds of fire, upon the interloper. She gasped. Heaved. And there was silence.

Besserian ground his back into the wall. He waited for the scream. The shout. But . . .neither. Possibly he hadn't been seen? His imagination? Body taut, his eyes bore into the impenetrable wall opposite; trying to blot out the reality. The silence, the blackness of the alley, imprisoned him, saturating him with its menace.

His reactions spun him into physical immobility. Trapped! Fear? Yes. But of what? He had done something wrong? He should not have seen it? He was an intruder? No! He hadn't sought this. A violator? No! Yes! Because their reality was unendurable.

His mind raced. Action? Solution? If they were students he had legal and professional obligations. Panic. He was involved! Mechanically, he felt for his briefcase. The wool stuck to his thighs and his shirt clung to rigid abdominals. The stubble on his face formed a sculpted mask. The back of his shirt was saturated. His aroma, intoxicating, could not conceal his presence.

In the enveloping darkness, a paralyzing hysteria overcame him. What had he witnessed? Rape? Murder? He was transfixed with indecision. He was certain she had seen him. She must have! He had breached, no matter how inadvertently, an alien world.

Three landings above, a ponderous metal door heaved open and the ubiquitous cleaning person began the ritual crashing: banging her wheeled trash cart down the metal steps. *"¡Carajo! ¿Una escuela? Es una mierda! ¡éste no es un lugar apropiado para tener un perro!*[4] The sounds reverberated through the alley then stopped as she allowed another metal door to crash behind her.

Forcing himself, he moved cautiously, carefully groping the remaining distance of the cave. Emerging, he stumbled his way toward the parking lot. "Now, how the hell to break out of this Gulag?"

Escape. He had only his classroom key. The campus was completely enclosed by a twelve foot steel-link fence, and at the periphery of the

4 Damm! Call this a school? Shit! I wouldn't teach a dog in this place!

eighteen acres, at the top of the embankments, even behind the ROTC building, and the stadium, the wall was topped with barbed wire. By now each building within the locked compound would be bolted: the heavy fire/burglar doors on the main buildings secured. Interior areas of the compound—main courtyard, library, gym, classrooms—were doubly guarded by metal gates sheeted in perforated steel.

Only the front fence was not decorated with razor wire. Male students were notorious for their agility in vaulting it. So it must be possible. Perhaps he could too, even without the seventeen-year old male psyche. Muscular, but not well coordinated, he discarded the idea! And the absurdity in any other profession, of an executive, being required to scale a series of walls and barbed wired fences to get out of his place of employment! In spite of his predicament he grinned at the thought of Allsbury's skeletal figure shinning up the fence in high heeled sandals and billowing lavender organdy. He recalled stories of a secret path carved out of the back slopes of the campus? But he'd never find it, especially in the dark. In any case to avoid incrimination, it was imperative that he get his car.

The previous day, the construction crew, needing a bulldozer entrance, had knocked down two interior barriers and replaced them with temporary fences. Now, eyes gleaming, he picked his way through and reached the parking lot under the "D" building. The smells saturated his clothes: oil, grease, exhaust, gasoline, dampness. Then! A fluke? The pedestrian gate was unlocked. He could get in! Now, how to get his car out!

The automobile gates, sheeted with steel grating, were held together by trailing padlocked chains. Swinging on enormous hinges, and because the entrance sloped steeply down into the structure from the street, the gates had no secure central footing. Swinging loosely at the center, they should have been held rigid by iron turn rods but the holes drilled into the filthy, oil-stained concrete were misaligned, and they swung loosely even when locked; menacing and confrontational. On the verge of panic, he saw his nemesis!

The steel padlock! Bolt cutters might have severed it: if they had six-foot handles! Indeed, five weeks earlier, vandals had done just that: penetrated three locked barriers, entered the administration building, and sprayed it with graffiti, wrecking equipment and furniture. Baques' office particularly had suffered: files burned, partitions smashed. The vandals' parting gesture had been to race their cars in circles on the lawn, destroying the remaining grass and plantings, leaving ugly welts of criss-crossed tire tracks.

His mind was speeding. Back there! In the alley! Maybe he really hadn't seen anything! Self-delusion! The kids were always teasing him about his age...he was forty, although he looked younger. They hoped to see him bristle at barbs about loss of memory, growing bald spot... teasing, implicit suggestions of diminished sexuality: "That's OK. Don't feel too bad! You got your memories, Mr. B."

He should make a report? To whom? There were security officers somewhere but how to call them? After hours they vanished. The main Security Office was at District Headquarters, four miles away. His cell phone was in the car.

And the repercussions? He could imagine Falange or Baques: 'Mr. Besserian, we know it's stressful teaching here at Fillmore. Are you sure you saw this: what? 'Copulation'? We have to be careful that *we* don't *pry!* Into student private lives, even with the best of intentions. And the Board is pledged to support Due Process. And, at the risk of being prolix, let me state there *have* been cases, other cases mind you, of teachers who said they had seen, well, what they *imagined* or, quite frankly, *wanted* to see! Vicariously?'

"However, consider also, that the law is very precise in such cases. It requires you as a state employee to stop *each and every* occurrence of violence, certainly of sexual activity, between students. Now, by your own admission you failed to do that! How do you explain your turpitude to intervene on behalf of student safety?" He could almost hear the fatuous sermonizing. "Let me remind you of your imposed duty, abandoned it seems, to protect? Each student? And that *could*—mind you I'm not saying does, at this time—might construe dereliction of duty? Recall Ed Code §44421; §44424; also Title 5, State Code of Regulations, Section 5530; and 36 A.L.R. 3d 330,340; and please recall, if you would, *Blasnost v. Salvador Union SD* in 1947? A truly landmark case! Also it appears *you could*—and note my use of the gerundive voice—be charged with negligent reporting under the Child Abuse Law'[5]!

Falange's litany of intonations, unctuously kneading his smidgen of power, would meander on with their nasty malapropisms. Besserian should jeopardize his security? Reveal himself as another sexually frustrated Mr. Phillips?[6] Deny the jeopardy of getting involved? So far, he had avoided those potholes. He was to start now?

5 Mandates penalty for not reporting possible as well as actual child abuse

6 See Chapter 7

Right now, the present, was the pivotal problem. He was infuriated at being trapped. Stymied. "You dumb shit! What the hell are you doing with your life? Hiding? Putting up with crap like this? This place is a *job*?" He kicked the gate, struck his shin, and yelled in pain and frustration. "Damm this place! There must be some kind of Security in this hole. You could be killed and nobody would know. Raped?"

Then he saw it. The gates were lurching under his assault. Unbelievable! The ponderous links rattling through the grating! Whoever had left the pedestrian gate unsecured also must have left the car gates 'dummy locked'. Talk about inefficiency! And luck! He tore furiously at the lock until it gave way. It required some fidgeting until he could extricate the bulky shaft from the links but he tugged frantically until the entire assemblage clattered resentfully through the metal keeper, heaped itself on the concrete floor, and the gates, misaligned and overlapping, liberated, careened open, dangerously and uselessly. He ran against the grated panels, shoving one against the inside wall and the other alongside the pedestrian railing opposite. The hooks were flimsy. It was a matter of minutes before the ponderous barriers would teeter, and once again hurtle mindlessly toward each other. He raced to his car.

Whoever they were on the stairs, by now, must have heard the noise: would have recognized his car parked near the entrance? Digging the key into the ignition, the car exploded into gear, and, tires squealing in pain, he shot through the zigzagging breech, leaving behind the misaligned barricades as they accelerated past each other under the force of their own weight. He left them dangling absurdly. Looking at each other stupidly. Impotent.

# *CHAPTER III*

## *An End, End Run*

"Who's the jackass who took it off my desk? Shit! God Damm! And just when I need it." He rapped the side of his head with his knuckles. "Need to crack this report. Now! Find out what the hell's going on with those guys. Get my ass in gear."

"Here it is. You put it in the EduCom folder. And I'm the jackass."

He scowled, frustrated, and rubbed the back of his neck inside the collar. "What? Right! Guess I did. Thanks." His russet hair was closely cropped to lessen the evidence of beginning bald spot. And by eleven-thirty, the distinct shadow was outlined on his face. He scowled petulantly, gulped a huge amount of air and loosened his paisley Massimo Bizzocchi tie. "Right. OK. This is it. And ... I didn't mean you. Sorry." His grin lit the room. With a large open palm he touched her shoulder heavily, absently, the full force of his absorption directed to the file.

Penny arranged the contents of the second part of the folder sequentially, at the end of the Louis XIV mahogany and ormolu table that served as his desk. "Here, you forgot your milk. All you have to do is sit down. Decelerate. Analyze the situation. And I need your revisions to this outline. For the TV program. Two-thirty. Max. There's a deadline. Producer wants Notes three months before air time."

He nodded aggressively, took off his jacket and handed it to her without looking up from the file. The Isaia suit was a chestnut windowpane: not so loosely cut as to conceal the trim waist. The tailored, blue oxford cloth shirt, damp at the armpits, emphasized shoulders and chest.

Buck scanned each page quickly with formidable intensity, frowning in disagreement, nodding approval, his head moving methodically, biting his lower lip, occasionally moving an index finger inside his collar across the auburn shadow on the back of his neck. He whispered small sounds, hyperventilating, exhaling strongly, as he settled into the report. She assumed her accustomed place, chair to the side of the desk, enabling easy movement; to lean over, comment on a particular point, occasionally place a manicured, uncolored nail, on a strategic phrase. Buck's eyes, recessed cobalt lasers, bored through the paper.

Her dress was silk; a muted emerald foulard. Her only jewelry a plain gold Baume et Mercier.

"This is good. Good job. Damm good! But something else bothering me."

"Pritchard?"

"Yes. His Reform Plan. Can't put my finger on it. Somehow, Mr. Hot Pants Peter plans to make himself a bundle."

She brushed his ear with her pen as she leaned over to emphasize the figures."Of course. You know he is. So? Two things. We find out his plan. And? We do it instead of him."

He swiveled to the left and looked past the wall of glass, scanning the tops of adjacent buildings. "Do it? Us? Instead of him?"

"We could . . ."

He was thinking. Furiously. "Maybe. Just maybe! Yes. And I'm ready."

"But we need more information. To move into it."

"Inside information!"

"Exactly. Details. Specifics. As they happen. What he's really up to. And how. So we can counter with your own plan."

Not taking his eyes from the paper, he shook his head and grimaced. Absently, he ran thumb and middle finger over his face, savoring the rasping sound.

She motioned with a raised finger for the receptionist to finish the arrangement of Birds of Paradise on the glass conference table. And leave. Impulsively, she moved her chair closer, placing her forearms on the table. "Yes, you *are* ready. And you *can* get the details."

His eyes, now indigo, were slits under the dark projection of his forehead. He inhaled powerfully, lips tightly rounded. "OK. Tell me."

"Inside information. Details. So you can make your move. Fine tune your own strategy. To eliminate him." She fidgeted with the top of her gold Cross pen. "But you have to have inside data. Whatever he's up to, this Reform Plan, might just be the ticket to you easing him out: TriDelta replacing EduCom. Buck Henderson replace Peter Pritchard. It's the chance you've been waiting for. It's perfect: for you!"

She had one hundred percent of his attention. "I have a good feeling about this. But we need to act now. Fast. There are only, what, seven months, until the teachers' vote."

"So? Tell me."

"Inside information. A contact."

"I've got somebody."

"That token female VP? Jackie Stevens? Had lunch with her last week. Pritchard hasn't told her anything. Yet. She needs coaching. To get the information you need."

He scowled. She continued. "We need details: specifics, dates, amounts, about the Plan as it happens: who, what, when, where, how. So you can block. And counterattack." She relaxed. "As I said, I have a good feeling about this."

"A good *feeling*?"

"You know how women are! It's a skill we have. Intuition?"

Buck marked his place on the columns of numbers. "Maybe." He surveyed her warily. "Don't know about that. Could be." Elbows resting on the desk, palms pressed together, he tapped the tips of his fingers against his front teeth, scraping the bottom of his chin with his thumbs. "Basically then, it's a counter assault? Like we did last year with ACROM?"

A whiff of musk, barely covering the perspiration, hit her. "Similar." She looked at the wall covered in russet suede, the mounted water buffalo head, commendations, awards, trophies. The morning light, reflected from the top floors of the surrounding had not yet created its glare on the glass wall. The display of trophies, plaques, citations—silver, gilt, crystal—on the wall opposite glimmered softly in response. Beneath the display, hating its glass case, easily twelve feet in length, mouth opened menacingly, tail poised viciously, was a stuffed crocodile.

She toyed with her watch. "At the same time we could shelter our reserves and . . ."

"Cut the old queen off at the pass. I like it. I like it. You realize that if we try something like this and fail? It will be the end? Of TriDelta. Of me? That deal involving Lakeside Financial two years ago? Inside story is that Lakeside screwed him. Their two top executives ended up in a car accident. Incinerated. Pritchard controlled the DA's report, the investigation. That was no accident. Believe me. Pritchard doesn't like to be double-crossed. He's one dangerous SOB."

"We're on the same track. I hear you. So, we have to be sure of every step we take. Therefore? Back to my original point. We need details. Inside details. Someone who's competent. In the middle of things. And won't double cross us."

"I'm listening."

She permitted her strategy to filter through the labyrinth of his logic and smiled imperceptibly. She had set the wheels in motion. He was making the initial calculations. The wheels were spinning: rechecking his mental calculations. He took the silver pen from his jacket pocket, corroborating his reckoning on the paper she slid under his hand. Numbers were punctuated with heavy straight lines tipped with needle-like arrowheads and placed within fiercely drawn rectangles, sketched box-like, one inside the other. The hair on the backs of his hands, was moist. His intensity was absolute. He was transfixed: the starting line. The chase.

"OK." He swiveled the chestnut tufted leather chair, eyes burning with intensity. "This 'insider'? You have somebody in mind. Don't you?"

"I have a suggestion."

"OK. Who?"

"Has to be somebody they've already decided they want. Trust. And respect. Not jockeyed in at the last minute. Not a radical; either on the left or the right. Perceived to be apolitical. Someone they wouldn't suspect: especially if this person himself wasn't aware he was our, well, 'Go-between'?"

"You obviously have somebody in mind. Who?"

"Besserian. My husband."

Buck looked at her sharply, pushing back his chair, genuinely surprised. "What? Him? You mean that? He's a *teacher* isn't he?" He mouthed the word carefully. "Does he know about administration? Any kind of management? You think he could operate in something as slippery and dangerous as this?"

"No."

"No? then why the hell . . ."

"You guide him. Help him over the managerial hurdles. The political pitfalls. In the process? He gives you the information—that you need."

"Me? Teach him? When he doesn't know anything? And this is dangerous. He could foul us up. Get hurt himself."

"What are the first two lessons you taught me? About management?"

He stared at her.

"Number One: Take risks. Number Two: turn the situation to your own advantage. Risk with him is minimal because he'll need you. He knows the Administration credential is zero preparation. Vaguely aware of his own idealism: enough to realize he could be a duck out of water in administration. But he genuinely does want reform. True reform. So? He'll need advice. About management. From you. And you'll need his information. It's a win-win situation. For you both."

Buck swiveled, got up slowly, walked the seven steps to the wall of glass behind him, staring down at the tops of the neighboring buildings. He stood, reflecting, then came back to the desk and depressed a button on a lighted control panel. The sheer drapes moved silently from behind their mahogany panels, turning the now uncomfortable glare into a soft, muted haze. "You're a hell of a manager yourself. Glad you're on my team. So? We need to talk. Like we always do. You're up to something. So, tell me. What you're really after. Let's sit over here." He selected a burgundy leather couch and she took the one opposite, adjusting the gold suede pillows. "You sure you want to do this? With Besserian?"

"When I came here, I changed. I found a new world. A new life." She reflected, smiling. "Rewarding. Exciting. A new part of myself. That I hadn't seen before. That I always wanted. But hadn't admitted to myself. And I feel what? Complete. In a way I never have before." There was a muted, faraway sound, maybe from the street far below. "You gave me that."

He relaxed. "You took it. You liberated yourself. The way it should be. I didn't *give* you anything."

"This way? Me? Help Tri-Delta? And? Help him too." She waited. "Successful reform will . . ."

"It may not be as successful as he wants. Perfect."

"That's where he learns from you. Pragmatism. Some reform. Better than none. With your backing he replaces Baques. Then Jones LaPorte. Then State Superintendent of Education. Who knows? Washington? School reform is a hot issue. Anyway . . ."

"Anyway what?"

"If B and I don't change together, we'll drift apart. Already . . ."

"Hold on! Don't tell me. We have a good relationship. A business relationship. It works because we know what the boundaries are. We need to keep it that way. I got your point."

"Excuse me, sir. Sorry to break in. You said it was top priority, Ms. Besserian? And sir? Mr. Henderson? It's that call from Costa Rica. The one you said was so important.""

"Good man, Jeffrey. Thanks." Buck nodded approvingly. "And as for you, young lady! You put a different perspective on loyalty. On management. Relationships. Glad you're on my side. Enough talk. Let's get out of here. I'm hungry. So we learn what's going on. Have a strategy. For dislodging Mr. Big Shot Peter. Good idea. Glad I thought of it."

# CHAPTER IV

## *At Home*

Although the reality—the failure—by now should not have been denied; it was. There were a number of reasons why the situation was still encrypted. It was not what they should have undertaken: the problems more difficult and the solutions, for all practical purposes, impossible. They had made their decision, impulsively, naively, the first time they saw it, without looking further. The solution—the perfect setting for the successful professional couple—now was the problem. The idyllic joint venture, the consummate project, had deteriorated into an obligation. Then an albatross.

A 1928 Spanish revival, it sprawled up the property. There were several magnificent vistas from the terraces and the living room, but what had especially appealed to them was the view from the master bedroom. With its tiled fireplace and carved beamed ceiling—the colors were discernable although faded—it overlooked a park, that, immediately, seemed to be their own. Center city buildings were visible, and due to the prevalent haze, often wrapped in an ethereal, vaporous gauze—late Turner or Monet—far away, unattainable. A distant world. That too had captivated them. Now, construction across the street, was proposed. If not prevented, it would cut off their vista: their would-be escape. Their outside illusion jeopardized, they continued it inside.

The doors of the living room, dining room and library—ponderous Honduran mahogany with original art deco stained glass panels—opened to a sweeping tiled loggia decorated with a profusion of the plants they both said they loved: potted Snow White gardenias; massive ceramic pots for the orange trees and jasmine; gleaming green Ficus, thick, tall; and overhanging the mélange, dripping sensuous vermillion; luxuriant Fuchsia. The plants, however, needed a great deal of care and, increasingly, that became difficult. Perhaps they hadn't recovered from last year's draught. Whatever the reason, the accumulation was diminishing and the once vibrant color was fading. In the event of rezoning, they would have only this truncated perspective.

The original plan had been to improve both house and grounds by working on a series of joint projects. Each would alternate, architect and laborer, between landscaping and structural maintenance. It would be fun. And they could use their combined talents to hide the frustrations of his job and her domestication.

Their mutual naiveté was revealed unpleasantly, however, as they uncovered a series of problems. What were envisioned as fun—manual labor enterprises, that 'anyone could do if they set their minds to it': cleaver successes, things to laugh about and relate wittily to friends, while sipping Blue Goose martinis—had evolved exponentially, into minor and then major fiascos. No longer the blissfully innocent Bobsey Twins 'At Home', 'At the Seashore', 'At Happiness Lake', or anywhere else; increasingly they were the stymied couple in 'Goin' South'.

In fact, the mutual projects were not 'charming', as a housewarming guest had parroted, beaming delightedly. Unanticipated complications had burgeoned, ensnaring them in financial and structural obstacles.

For example, there was the landscaping. The property was extensive, almost two acres. High embankments, however, made much of it inaccessible. The slopes were rocky, barren really, and much steeper than initially had been apparent. The sprinkler system, ineffectual except along the driveway, necessitated hand watering—time consuming, difficult because of the hill, and, increasingly, avoided. After constant, irritating, efforts at repair, a landscape gardener had recommended a system of terraces. The cost was prohibitive. So, instead of nourishing the soil, much of the water ran uselessly over the increasingly barren ground into the street. Plants and foliage remained listless and flaccid. In many places rocks projected through scrub and weeds. Much of the property was compacted clay that resented their efforts, increasingly sporadic, to establish Italian cypress, fruit trees, and ground cover. Vegetation, sparse and unattractive clung to fissures in the rock. The ivy was receding and the property was taking on an unkempt appearance: weed-like growth and meager, listless brown sprouts.

His efforts to trim the scrub oak—'alluring' friends had informed them, and 'just so *marvelously* indigenous and needing to be preserved'—had resulted in painful bouts with poison oak: the one type of vegetation that flourished: unassisted.

Nor was moving an option. The housing market had declined, and now with two jobs, the complexities of looking for another house were impossible. In any case, they weren't sure what they wanted.

The interior was no more reassuring. Structural problems persisted. Plumbing and heating needed replacement. There was also the expense of air conditioning which originally, both had maintained they did not need, since, in the 1930's, people—and guests had corroborated this—had 'survived quite well without it'. The original tile roof which seemed so 'culturally relevant' proved to be inordinately costly to replace. They considered asphalt shingles until indignant neighbors screeched 'cultural rape'. To add insult to injury, the glass-enclosed second living room roof was developing seepage. While not yet critical, it made what they had envisioned as a private retreat, uncomfortably damp, fireplace notwithstanding.

More distressing, the antiquated heating system was unable to produce or circulate adequately. They had not thought to inquire about insulation, of which there was none. On clammy winter days, it was colder inside than out. Heating experts advised them to scrap the original. Cost was exorbitant and would require replacing some of the original walnut flooring and 'irreplaceable' 1920's Spanish tile. Here again, decision remained in limbo.

Yet, from the street the property presented a neat, orderly and well-tended façade. The driveway, its macadam only slightly cracked, was bordered by thick ivy, and, for a portion of the year, a profusion of lavender bougainvillea, flowering jasmine, orange blossom and roses. All these created an inviting appearance as the asphalt wound itself upward toward the house. There, it made an interesting turn, and disappeared into the garage.

And there, the attraction stopped. The cavernous space, designed for three cars, was another liability discovered too late. Burrowed into the hill under the house, it was sunless: cold in winter and during the summer, an inhospitable refuge, unpleasantly dank.

Intended as the hub of household repairs and projects, the workshop at the end of the garage was used infrequently. The work bench was a repository for items to be discarded.

Of more interest was the sequestered apartment behind the workshop. Originally servants quarters, Besserian had converted the single large room—combined living room, bedroom and kitchen—into his private gym. The refracted light from the west—three rows of glass block—created an aquatic atmosphere; caused reflections, contingent on the hour and season, to undulate across ceiling and walls. An unusual arrangement, the bathroom entrance was through the closet, making it a secret room. There, the original art-deco tile, left over from the master suite bathroom, still gleamed in geometric patterns: black, green and mauve. Unlike the master bathroom, there were no cracks and the showerhead still produced a gushing cascade totally at variance with conservation. Besserian loved it.

The gym had a self-spotting weight system: bench press with three hundred pounds and overhead pull-down bars. Recently he had added, at the other end of the room, a heavy bag and speed bag. Narrow doors opened onto a private enclosure where he could jump rope. Facing west, in the afternoon it was flooded with sun and became his secluded sun deck. A place for various kinds of meditation.

A unique spiral staircase wound up from the garage to the vaulted octagonal entrance hall. Spacious and attractive with its muted gold, plastered walls, the previous occupants—the Bolivian Consul, or so the real estate agent maintained—had used it, when entertaining, as an overflow from the dining or living rooms. The original sconces, yellow-brown corrugated glass, hanging from the tips of wrought-iron lances, remained. An electrician had detected dangerously outdated wiring: another expense. The floor tile was distinctive: squares of hardened leather: deeply lustrous Cordovan, impossible to replicate. Fortunately, it seemed in good condition.

Unfortunately, seepage had crept into the foundation of the house, causing the iron-studded oak front door to shift; misaligning the frame and making it embarrassingly difficult to use. In fact, it negated the function of the flagstone path leading from the street. By default, therefore, the entrance was through the garage and the spiral staircase. The reactions of their sporadic guests were, "enthralling", "enchanting", "outré". In reality, it was another excuse for infrequent entertaining.

The entrance to the library was cleverly hidden by one of the octagon panels. This was his favorite room and not only because of its seclusion. Its paneling, Columbian linenfold mahogany; handsome Regency couches: tufted auburn leather and tapestry; a ponderous black oak Spanish refectory table as a desk; a wall of bookcases. On the far wall, in matching walnut and steel frames he had designed himself, were two Piranesi: *Carceri d'Invenzione.*[7] He still had the framed 'Very Likely to Succeed' from Brébeuf High School. And there were the certificates of his varsity letter in lacrosse, his two Master's Degrees and the Achievement Award, Second Class, from the summer institute at the Toronto Royal Conservatory of Music: 'Piano Accompaniment'.

The mindless beep of the answering machine greeted him.

"Been a day from hell". Penny's voice was excited: a chirping staccato that irritated him. "Got to run, now. Tonight? Don't know how late. Dinner. Business talk. Reform Plan information. Lining up our ducks . . . the usual you-kno-what. Don't wait up. I'll be exhausted." He could hear background noise, obviously distracting her, and it sounded like the phone fell from her shoulder, probably gesticulating frantically with hands and head as she gave orders to staff members.

There was more. "Almost forgot! Be sure and tape the *Denise Show.* Replay at nine. Buck is arranging for me to be on in a couple of months to make sure Denise Something or Other—you won't like her or the program—handles this Reform thing the right way. Set it up without telling me. Last minute. Ciao".

He went into the living room, settling into the large, high-backed couch.

The achievement of the room was its fourteen-foot ceiling: "cathedral" in the parlance of the real estate woman. Although now faded, the intricate fern and acanthus leaf design carved into the walnut beams originally had been decorated in green, yellow, red and blue. His sole inheritance from his parents, a silk and wool Tabriz, almost too large for the room, with its brilliant pinks, blues and reds set off by an unusual black background, provided the distinctive color.

Another remnant of their original naiveté—'this is so really *different*?'—was the unusual style of the furniture. Early in their marriage they had enjoyed poking around antique stores for '20's pieces to go with the house: heavy, dark, straight legged, tapestry and horsehair upholstery: 'Neo Jacobean' was the trade designation although a guest, not invited again, had made an unfunny joke: 'Neo-Uncomfortable': an unfair jibe

7 Piranesi, Giovanni. 18th century Roman engraver: "Prisons of the Mind".

because chairs and couches were, after all, relieved by exotic 'middle eastern' cushions.

There were the appropriate wrought-iron accoutrements. The ponderous seven-foot candelabra, for example, had brackets arranged on tiers of concentric circles. The illumination was always mysterious, always soft, even when all eighteen were burning. The massive candles, coated with hardened drippings, surprisingly, always seemed to have more life. The undulating flames softened the black metal with flickering amber and could be hypnotic. But then again, in recent years, they seldom shared the room. At least not in that way.

Here he could luxuriate in the richness of the reverberating sound. Penny, uncharacteristically had, in a moment of pique, called it 'typical male overkill'. Maybe, but that's what he relished: the power of the stereo system, its ability to delineate the nuance of individual words and instruments: vibrato of the piccolo, shattering trombones and the reverberating resonance of double bases. He loved to feel the majestic chords of a concert grand accompanying one of his favorite singers. And Besserian loved to sing. But only when alone.

Penny had no interest in music and, therefore, his interest isolated them further. Music often made her discover an unfinished task elsewhere.

Now, in his present seclusion, he was transported from disillusionment and frustration into the sensual, '20's exoticism, sheltered by the warmth of color and fabric as well as resonating acoustics. On private evenings, like this, following the aggravations of the day, the security of the three divans, the carpets and wall hangings were especially welcome.

Here, he could be transported to his own reverie which, somehow seemed to lead, ultimately, along the same tortured path. It still bothered him after all these weeks: 'My fault. Shouldn't have been there. In the alley? Somebody could still say something. Even now. Does Trouble just find me? Or do I seek it out? Am I immature? Maybe we both are? Probably everyone has their regrets. I wonder how deep hers are.'

The music began to sooth him: draw him into its opulence. In vocal music he loved the intricacies and complexities of the accompaniments: change of key, modulations of rhythms, shifts in harmony. He was a passionate disciple of Schubert for the lyrical depiction of sexual intimacy; Wagner for the powerful dynamics reaffirming the quest of spiritual rejuvenation; and Verdi: the *ensemble* pieces describing agonies of frustrated relationships, dangerous coincidences, and conflicting obligations. He slid back in the cushions, half speaking, half singing, accompanying with his dark baritone, allowing the words of the female voice and her music to embrace him:

| | |
|---|---|
| *Che mai feci!* | *What have I become!* |
| *Qual fantasima ovunque* | *What phantom* |
| *Il mio delitto* | *Appears to me?* |
| *M'appar? Mi lacera il rimorso!* | *I am torn by remorse* |
| *Temo che ognun mi legga* | *I fear that everyone* |
| *A lettere di fuoco* | *can read the letters* |
| *Scolpita in fronte la parola:* | *of fire on my forehead:* |
| *Colpa!* | *Guilty!* |
| *Ciel, que feci mai!* | *Heaven! What have I done?* |
| *Mi lacera il rimorso!* | *I am torn by remorse!* |
| *Ohimè, che feci mai?* | *Fate! What have I done?* |
| *Salvami, Salvami tu, grand Dio;* | *Dear God. Spare me.* |
| | *Save me.* |
| *Tu che mi leggi in core* | *You, who can see the* |
| | *Innermost depths* |
| | *of my soul!* |
| *E sai l'angoscia e* | *And knows the extent* |
| *Il pentimento mio!* | *Of my anguish and torment!*[8] |

The mood allowed him to savor his own sexuality. The frustrated longing, so poignantly reiterated, compensated for the emptiness of what he seemed to have become. He luxuriated in the heroine's grief, her isolation, her frustrated passion. That the language was not his own heightened the eroticism: the mystery, the secret. He knew the words perfectly and relished her passionate self-recrimination: aria and cabaletta. He was saturated with the remorse of the self-incriminated lover. . . dishonor. . . betrayal of obligation. In these moments of reverie they became his reality. . . his escape. He felt the warmth and sting of her tears in his own eyes. His was the dilemma of conflicting frustrations, the male beset by fate, stymied, unsure of which way to turn. In these secluded moments, music again tried to break the cipher of his innermost fears and yearnings.

He savored the beat: the strong, bold rhythms and the rolling collisions of the brasses. It was his favorite recording of the work: the excitement of a live recording. He counted: one-two-three-four, rapping repeatedly on the cushion, signaling with a frown to members of the orchestra, to the singers

8 Verdi, G. *Aroldo*: Act I, Scene 1.

with a clenched fist or encompassing movement of his arm. Now came the lilting melodies of the cellos and violas, he chided '*andante sostenuto*' and scowled at the lethargy of the reeds.

But this was self-indulgence. He lowered the sound and went to the piano, his cherished *Bechstein*. They both had questioned its nine foot length: 'over-kill' perhaps? But he loved the resonance of the treble and the power of the bass. Badly mistreated, he had salvaged it from a school sale. Recognizing that the frame and soundboard were intact, he found a gifted restorer and, with great expense, this time willingly made, its magnificent tone, splendid burled walnut case, somber ivory keys were revealed in their original grandeur. Amfortas' Act I soliloquy was on the music rack.[9]

But enough retreat into reclusive self indulgence. He sorted through yesterday's mail: her unopened magazines: *Fortune, Wall Street Journal;* bills from Barney's; catalogue from PRO Boxing; the *American Teacher*; bills; catalogues: clothes, tools, health products. He ignored them.

With the music, still enveloping him, enhancing the bronze detail of the staircase railing, he went up to a guest bedroom: still accompanying the tragic self-recrimination of Mina's opening aria, his baritone, whispering to strain for the higher notes. Without losing a beat, he began to change. Reveling in the rhythm, Besserian overlooked the disharmony of the clutter in the Master suite, arranging his clothes meticulously, opening the small window at the end of the closet, wiping, polishing really, the gleaming cherry of the ponderous dresser with his undershirt before tossing it in the hamper. Again, reveling in the harmonics of their agony, the soaring melodies, he admired a still-attractive physique in the triptych of the dressing room mirror. The words were memorized:

<table>
<tr><td>Il pianto non vale:<br>Nessuno sospetti l'evento<br>  fatale.<br>Sia come in spulcro<br><br>  Celato l'errore,<br>Lo esige, lo impera<br><br>  Del sangue l'onore.</td><td>Tears are useless:<br>No one will discover<br>the malignant crime.<br>I shall keep it<br>  hidden<br>as if in a tomb,<br>The honor of our<br>  family<br>Both commands and<br>  demands it.[10]</td></tr>
</table>

9 Wagner, R. *Parsifal.* Act I.

10 Verdi, G. *Aroldo*: Act I, Scene 1.

Here the quintessence of obligation. But: enough dreaming. Pulling on jeans, no underwear, he took the back stairs, his 'secret passage', to the kitchen. Opening the cans for 'their' dinners, *Ms* purred heavily, scratching him unintentionally as he placed her bowl on the 'kitty' floor mat. *Klingsor* was more patient, favoring him with thank you nudges, savoring the caressing of his thick bluish coat, and licking the strong wrist appreciatively, prior to burying his nose in the bowl.

The kitchen had brought them only a modicum of success. They had never been able to find time to refine their sketches—cabinets, hardware or tile. Initially Penny had demonstrated creativity in her effort to restore the 1920's style. But gradually they had been distracted. '50's 'Knotty Pine' cabinets and walls, red and white rubber tile, and café curtains remained. A constant irritation to him. *Il pianto non valle.* He grunted. He recalled Allisandro Piñeda, in his Period Four: "Guy's gotta roll with crap, Mr. B."

But the problems were not only stylistic. Misled, duped really, by the contractor's estimate, the actual cost of remodeling this 'Fifties Fiasco', an expression sure to provoke an unpleasant silence between them, had been, in student parlance 'out of sight': clogged pipes, mildewed floor boards, layers of paint, and an arcane electrical system fluctuating between dangerous and hopeless, all had to be added to the original estimate.

Extricating himself from pointless reverie, he could take advantage of the evening by enjoying the second of his diversions.

He retraced his steps down to the garage, to the gym. The evenings were slightly cooler now and he turned on the electric heater. Penny had laughed, 'needs airing out' and then 'makes me want to hold my breath' the two times she had contemplated accepting his invitation. But he hated the omnipresent 'Health Clubs' or 'Spas': crowds, parking, mindless chatter about hair and diets, wailing masquerading as singing: vapid adolescent vows—to Besserian they were threats: 'I'll sta-a-a-nd by yo-u-u, alw-ay-ay-s-s'. Here, in his own inner sanctum, he could lose himself in strenuous physical release. His private meditation. When he was lucky enough to get home by four, he could finish before Penny came in, normally by seven or eight. With the speed bag and heavy bag he could push himself to exhaustion. It was exhilarating. He could feel the tension leaving him. And the resurgence of energy. Afterwards, at relative ease, he had two hours to correct papers and plan the next day's work. They had dinner together infrequently.

He appraised himself in the full length adjustable mirror. Lycra shorts and cotton tank top complimented him. And in hot weather, regular gym gear seemed superfluous. The routine he had set for himself included crunches and push-ups. Then the weights. Then the two bags. It was more than the appreciation of his physique and health. This was his time to reflect on the events of the day. Things which he had pushed aside. Occasionally, he reconsidered former ideals: teaching, personal.

Again, the situation in the Alley intruded itself. "Who were they—it had been what? Two months, now? Had they seen him? Why did they choose that place? Why them? Why me? Probably they were students. From another school? Staff? Administration? Outsiders?"

Students knew the physical plant of the school better than teachers and administrators. They had their hideaways and he may have stumbled on one. Hadn't Ms. Qu-Yahni Lewis, Geometry, aroused by the sickeningly sweet aroma from under her 'bungalow', found a club house retreat, comfortably constructed from cardboard and plywood, furnished with auditorium seat cushions, and gym mats? Even a kerosene heater? And it was common belief that students were active sexually: more than adults.

He strained to complete the set. Student pregnancies were now a matter of course. He arched, inching up the bar. Why would they choose the stair well: damp and uncomfortable? Certainly dangerous? Maybe danger was the attraction? What if he had been someone else? Some kind of pervert? Who had seen them? Their compulsion? They couldn't wait for a safer, more comfortable place?

He luxuriated in the sensuality of the resistance of the weights. The exertion. The burning of his muscles. The heat enveloped him and he savored his glistening body. The stairs incident receded from his attention. Maybe he had an obligation to pursue it. He didn't know. For now, alone in his retreat, he blotted out the future as well as the past—and devolved into the delirium of the present: exotic fantasy.

---

# *CHAPTER V*

## *Discussion*

Bruce Warfles adjusted his bulk on the couch, drew his knees to the fetal position, muffling half-heartedly a belch and opened one eye. “It'll be cool. For teachers who want to play ball. Anyway, it's about time *somebody* stood up for *teachers*. Let Pritchard do his thing.” Burying his face in the soiled cushion he gave a final insight, “Couldn't be worser than the other reform boon-doggles.”

The overstuffed piece of furniture was canted, and not only by his weight: one bulbous foot had a missing wheel, so that the cushion, around which his massive, sweaty forearms were clenched, his life-preserver, was careening off the couch, inches from the floor, throwing into focus the yellowish strands sticking to the sweaty scalp. He snorted, settling into a new position, inhaling the moist aroma of the discolored brown, red and orange tapestry, toes twitching through holes in mismatched socks.

Obviously discarded from someone's Family Room, Bruce's ‘crib’, as it was affectionately known, set the tone of the room. There were two similar pieces of furniture, equally dirty, also refugees from better days. One was dark brown vinyl, a long tear across the back revealing grimy, matted, stuffing. It retained a single cushion. The other boasted a gold mohair fabric—Cynthia Rowland, Government-Economics, thought it might be the original 1950's covering, “... get a load of those stains! Eeek!

I sure wouldn't want to park *my* butt there. Not with AIDS and e-bucoli, STD's, warts, Terrorists! Whatever! No, m'am. No way."

Its three, probably original, pillows, brownish-green-orange velveteen, retained vestiges of silver tasseled fringe, now clinging tenaciously, in matted clumps. An obvious relic, the 'di-ván' as Myron Lancaster, Social Studies, called it, seemed determined, despite its present embarrassment, to maintain a semblance of its erstwhile glory: the showpiece of an Islington parlor. There were an assortment of overstuffed chairs, also stained and discolored, competing for discomfort with wood, folding metal and blue molded plastic seats.

Three, frayed, imitation oriental carpets—Mr. Bathersea, Geography, had opined that one "might possibly be a Tabriz or even a Turkish Kashan"—bore the marks of both solid and liquid droppings. Their success in hiding the chipped black and green asphalt floor tiles was moderate.

Sections of the *TIMES:* comics, sports, Calendar, were strewn across the floor. Partial issues of *Arizona Highways; Today's Teacher; Tools for the Farm; The Idiot's Guide to History,* littered two varnished 40's tables. Sections of textbooks, competed with mutilated issues of *Football Digest.* A copy of *Retirement: Your Choice,* was partially visible from under the refrigerator: the door ajar due to lack of defrosting. Scattered on and under chairs were brochures: *Disneyland; Magic Mountain; Raging Waters; pamphlets: "Finding Your Second Career in Real Estate and Insurance";* a travel guide: *"Your Slice of the Good Life—Singles Get-Aways: the Solomons, Tonga, Bora-Bora".*

Three tables, pushed together unevenly due to their different heights—and the perversity of cracked floor tiles—were in the center of the room. At one end a card game was in progress, the players attired in matching polyester sun visors emblazoned: *Life: Take the Bait!* At the far end, several individuals munched sandwiches, celery sticks, popcorn, Trail Mix, or Gummy Bears. A table against the wall designated "Send-Out/Pick Up", held culinary treats, all competing for the dominant aroma: chow mien, pepperoni, teriyaki, sauce-drenched ribs, salsa-covered chicken burritos. There was a half-consumed jug of *Dr. Pepper.*

"Everybody went ape over that corporate guy?"

"Pritchard?"

"Whatever. Reform? I didn't hear him say how he was to reform administrators. Probably'll still fill quotas. Not selected for competence."

"Reform to evaluate administrators? That's a joke!"

"Or school boards? Made up of wanna be politicians. Don't give a you-know-what-about education."

"Or care. Or know."

"And all the problems having disturbed kids in our classes? Special Ed? Least Restrictive Environment? Hell, it's more restrictive when they're in a normal class where they can't do the work. And drive the teacher, and other kids, crazy."

"Right. Regular teacher doing the job people with Special Ed credentials get paid extra for not doing? Give me a break! How about reforming that?"

"Pritchard not say anything about that stuff."

The door burst open and she screamed the greeting. "How ya'll doin'? Hey gir-r-r-l-l-l! Hel-l-l-l-o-o Arnida Hollyfield!" Lydia Hastings-Bruce, Art and Ceramics, raced over to Arnida embracing her deliriously. "O-o-o-o-o-h! Scrump-tious! Day-lic-i-óus! Love ya' girl-friend!" The greeting was punctuated with hugs, kisses and resonating squeals, cemented by mutual clasping of little fingers, "Pinky Swear?".

"Just one more time!" Lydia Arlekian, Reading IV, was livid. "One! Just One! And lemme tell you! If that G-D Alfonso Martinez mouths off to me: One-More-Time! Just One! And just who in hell's name does he think he's talking to? One of his *cholas*? And I told him keep his perverted paws off my girls! I had his older brothers! All out of the same cookie cutter! Girls complain: one-more-time! Just-One-Time! Lemme tell ya'! I'll run his tight little ass through the wringer! And that sexist dude'll be *outa* here! Like gangbusters! Here's *one* female he'll wish he hadn'ta tangled asses with. Learn his butt!"

"Wait till parents night!" Arnida Hollyfield, Science, laughed. "Once you meet daddy? The old saying . . stuff never falls far from the tree?"

Cindye Jacobson, Special Education, adjusted large, gold-rimmed glasses under a light blue *Houghton Mifflin* cap. "Don't blame them. It's their culture. Women are trash. Objects! Only there to serve them. And, you know? Their women put up with it! Machismo."

She scraped her chair. "But Alfonso's grown up a lot since last year. Know something? Some girls told me he was actually a *model* in some magazine? They're bringin' it in to show me? But just you wait 'till that guy hits his twenties! Gets some experience under his belt! Holy Mother Theresa! And let me tell you girl, don't you just *know* he's *already* got what it takes! Gol-ll-y! Eat your heart out, girl! That equipment! You catch him in his 501's yesterday! And if they hadda been *any* tighter ..."

"Who's going to 'Reform'—Narda Teklebrahan, Spanish II, waggled fingers in quotation marks—parents without steady income and working two or three jobs? Of course kids have family problems! And single parents with live-in boy friends. No wonder education isn't a 'today thing' in their culture."

"Reform? Start with ending social promotions in elementary and junior high. So we don't have to re-teach most of them."

"You guys carrying on like banshees! At that meeting? I ask you? Where's-the-money-going-to—come—from—for—these—new—reforms? For teacher salaries?"

"Hear that special deal to increase salaries." Cyril Jacobs, affectionately known as 'Milton', Junior English, moved around the room with irritable energy and hopped up on the counter. "You people can just go ahead yakkety-yakking all you want. I am just *determined* to get rid of this *dirt*: get some *clean* in here. If it *kills* me. This is dis-*grace*-ful!" He jumped aggressively—a futile effort—to reach the smudged windows above the chipped tile counter on which he was standing. Faded chintz curtains hung limply from the few remaining rods.

'Deh vieni alla finestra, O mio tesoro;
Deh, vieni a consolar, il pianto mio.' [11]

Cyril spread his arms imploringly. An amateur opera singer, his voice was a small tenor. "And this place does *not* have to look like *this*! A pig-sty! Staff *could* clean it out. If, and let me emphasize the word *If*,"—he pronounced it 'aahff'—glaring icily into the chattering room, "they *wanted* to."

"Professional means to reform younselves."

"*Professionals*? When's the last time anybody ever called us that?"

"Show me where you work and I'll tell you who you are?"

"Some truth in that, Narda. There's a world hiding outside of these mucky windows. This place reminds me of Dracula's basement. A cave."

Cyril persisted. "Maybe this school isn't dead! Just sleeping? Hibernating? In the meantime we got it pretty good. We want to rock our boat?"

Arvetis Jamgotchian, Grade 12 Algebra I, grinned cynically. "Why not find out whether we like it or not, first? His Reform Plan? Toss it

11 Mozart, W.A. *Don Giovanni*: Act II, Scene 3. "Come to the window my Treasure! Come! Console my throbbing heart…take away my sorrow!"

around some in the bowl, then see if it makes salad? Sure don't want teaching to tests. Us responsible!"

"Especially when tests are culturally biased and our kids can't learn the material!", Arnida observed, knitting needles flashing. "Nonlevel playing field all over again, if you ask me. Our kids can't do it. Not prepared. Any way you slice it, teachers get the short end of the stick. And from the brie tasting, chardonnay sipping, 'caffescienti' in Palos Hermosa: the ones who write in to newspapers complaining about teachers and schools. And know diddley. Not care about kids!"

"Arnida, they're making a fuss about things they don't care about?" Sandra Weatherby, isolated at a center table, observed without interrupting her own knitting. "Must be some legitimate concerns if the papers are full of education problems. Every day. Fact is our kids aren't where they should be in reading, writing, math, science. And what about 50% plus dropouts? Somebody must be responsible. If it's not schools: who? I'm hearing conflicting things here: excuses—no responsibility or accountability—but more money. If we're not going to do anything about Education problems, or can't, then maybe we're the ones who need some help. To be reformed! Question is are we going to put in Reform? Solve the real problems? You guys just mentioned some. Somebody just said: that means risking what's pretty comfortable and safe for a lot of us. Now."

"You know, Miss, if you're not happy here, why stay? You could go somewheres else. But again, maybe you can't."

"Let's not cut to the personal. Keep it clean, folks!"

"You guys should wonder why there's a number of teachers who never come here. To the lounge?"

"They think they're superior, that's why."

"Not team players. Isolationists."

"If it makes you happy to think that." Bartholomew Huerta, Physics, spoke resignedly. "There are some teachers in this school, who think there's more to education than protecting ourselves. But they're called Fascist, terrorist, subversive? And we're supposed to be educated people? Ourselves?"

Marquis Mugwabe, Algebra II, moved restlessly in his chair. "Why not fault parents? Administrators? District pogues with their six figure salaries? Superintendent? Board of Education? State legislature? The overall culture? Why always us?"

"Why you think I got so many kids to deal with? Cherry Hamilton was the Parole Office permanently assigned to Fillmore. "Now, we getting more drug babies. And hyper actives. Ritalin side-effects! Kids on drugs! And alcohol. Lots of our kids not have a permanent place to live: few weeks here, few weeks there. Not do homework? Got no home to do it in. No family. No structure. Unless we give it. No way teachers can do that. How's Reform Plan gonna solve that?"

Narda looked up at Milton on the countertop. If 'Reform' is anything like programs they already paid for? *Little Country Schoolhouse*? *Best of America*? Millions of dollars down the drain. To outside consultants. And then never used them?"

"I hear kickbacks on those went to Superintendent. And Board members."

"Whatever! Point is nothing ever happened. Millions of dollars and time wasted. Wonder if tax payers know that?"

"I say give even part of that money to us. We know the problems. Can do the changes."

"Reform is always their agenda. Not ours."

Sandra Weatherby, turned down the heat under the bubbling coffee. "First of all we have to agree on what the problems are. Change isn't necessarily reform. The questions need to be: 'What kind of reform? Reform for whom? Will it do what's best for students? And who decides what's best for students? What's best for us to assist students? What is the real motivation of the School Board in their support of Pritchard?"

"You know what really gets me?" The 'College for Every Student' non-idea. Why? With college courses like *Ghetto Affiliations* or *Realizing Your Sexual Persona?* Most college kids never take a course in Shakespeare . . ."

"Can't. Not in the curriculum."

". . . or Wordsworth? Or Chemistry? Or Math? Or Statistics? And wonder why graduates can't get jobs? Maybe Reform needs to ask: why us? We're the ones supposed to push our kids into Algebra and Biology and History when most of the college courses they actually take have nothing to do with academics?"

"But it's us that get dumped on. A lose-lose situation."

Bruce rolled over, adjusting his bulk to a more comfortable position, blinking tiny eyes. "Reform'll get the team players some good bucks. Baques'll be talking to some of you. Don't sweat it."

The Teachers Lounge, located inconveniently at the far end of the campus, an antediluvian structure which had evolved from boiler room to storage facility prior to inadequately serving the needs of its present tenants, had been their temporary housing for the past seven years. Ducts criss-crossed the ceiling, too much even for Milton's efforts.

Adjacent, the former auto shop, now remodeled as the Women's Self-Awareness Center, blocked the lounge skylight.

But lighting wasn't the only problem. Competition for the copy machines aggravated tensions. Invariably, one—there were two—was inoperative. Competition ensued chiefly from teachers who, on a daily basis, copied dozens of pages; often from unauthorized materials. Disagreements and name-calling were not uncommon. AP Marion Johansson had sent home Blaise Jackson, Computer Graphics, after Laura Yi reported he had thrown her papers—she was copying ten pages, forty copies, of *Today's Bride: A Wedding Made in Heaven* for her PE class—on the floor and called her the 'B' word. And Mr. Falange had 'written up' Falynn Smedley, General Math, after Reshma Smythe-Goode, Authentic Choir, had slapped his face for muttering that she was 'hogging' the machines. Smythe-Goode claimed Smedley "had issues": was insensitive, a sexist, and had called her a pig.

The peculiarities of lighting, obscured somewhat the wall decorations. Over the microwave table was a dusty lithograph of the battleship *Maine,* stacks billowing. Entitled *Dastardly Assault,* the ship was slicing angrily through spraying waters: arrogantly contemptuous—or blissfully unaware—of the torpedo burrowing furiously toward it. And on another wall, close-ups of terrified faces, panic-stricken women clutching screaming infants, running before a towering wall of angry water: *The Broken Dam. Johnstown, Pennsylvania: 1889.*

"We might could look at this from a different angle."

"What's that, sweetie?"

"New Reform? Turn it any direction you want and what do you think?"

"*Di me.*"[12]

"You'll see. More of the same. Political. Too many incompetents put in jobs for political reasons. Instead of being able to do the work. Been going on since the '70's." As soon as she spoke Narda Teklebrahan realized she had gone too far.

"What? You some sort of Fascist? Racist?"

"Traditionalists had all the privileges, up to now! How about giving some to somebody else? Do turnabout! For a change?"

"You're like sayin' if the shoe don't fit, you expect the person to cut off their leg! Get real. For once, lady!"

---

12 Tell me.

Narda rummaged in her bag to recheck the instructions for the argyle sweater.

Cyril, snapping his dust rag, watched the aggressive nature of Warfles' sleep: rasping snoring punctuated by erratic twists of his porcine body. He plopped himself into one of the overstuffed chairs, another discard from someone's garage. Several springs uncoiled with a resounding zing, causing him to leap aside to defend himself. Cyril repositioned himself gingerly. "Maybe we should give this Reform Plan a chance, then we'll find out what it can do."

He reflected:

> '. . . .what can be worse
> Then to dwell here, driv'n out from bliss, condemn'd
> In this abhorred deep to utter woe?' [13]

Brian McCauley ignored him and shook his head in reminiscence. "This is like when it's Fourth Down and twenty to go? We need to find ourselves a wide receiver. Like way back when that ole ass kicker, Tommy Czynowoski pulled the Broncs out of the trash heap in '74? Moved them into the pennant race? He sure didn't take it laying down. No sir! For sure not 'ole Tommy! And did he make those guys haul ass! And you wanna know something? I met him? Yup! In the flesh? At some bar one night? He said why he had to ran them ragged? Guys had been missing training, doin' drugs, drinking, sex—and not all with gals, let me tell you!" He arched his eyebrows and, after protracted deliberation, tossed out a card theatrically. "Pushed into their own end zone. But he was fragged from the git-go. Why? Owners didn't want 'em to win. Their own team. Some kind of tax benefits or signals 'under the table'? Out of Vegas, probably. A nuc'lr option and he didn't even know it. But dammit to hell if he didn't get them to the pennant race anyhow. And not even supposed to! So what happens? They dump him. So, he snags the ball then gets tackled by his own team! Just goes to show. Never can say who's going to nail you. Just because they're wearin' the same uniform? Not mean diddly. If they got a different game plan. Sucks!"

There were nods of agreement from a 'Ladders and Slides' game by the rear door.

---

13 Milton, John. *Paradise Lost*: Book II: Oration of Moloc.

> "Live to ourselves, . . . free, and to none accountable, preferring hard liberty before the easy yoke of servile pomp'." [14]

Milton had resumed his dusting.

A founding member of the card group, Millicent Pimmentade, Music Appreciation and Choral Director, interjected laconically, "At least we know what we have now. And in lots of ways we got it pretty darn good. So why change? Better to not rock the ship. Do we want even more supervisory pogues coming in here and telling us how to do our own work? Setting accountability goals? That group from EduCyber last year was the pits."

"And what about those 'consultants' the District hired from State College, UC wherever, last December? I hear it cost at least a couple hundred thou. Hey, Brian'll remember." Roger Mulhausen, Computers, called to him. "Hey, goo' buddy: remember that lady who said we should teach Math by having the kids to write poems! "Learn their multiply tables that way. . . which they never learned in Grade Four? C'est quel gar-báge! Excuse my French, ladies."

"You don't seem to understand. Those 'consultants'", Millicent fluttered her fingers as quotation marks, "are the pride of the Education Department at State! I don't think any one of those gals ever took a real Math course: even Algebra, to say nothing about Geometry, so ..."

"Calculus, Analytic Geometry, Statistics ..." Marquis Mugwabe completed the catalogue.

"So, what's wrong with teaching Math by having the kids to write poetry?" Qu-Yahni Lewis was struggling with the broken ice machine. "I've been teaching Geometry for seven years. They can't do theorems and postulates. They're sure not learning now. Who knows? If it works! Right now, I'd try anything with my Period Four. What a bunch of losers! Help!"

"Forget about Shakespeare, Milton, Wordsworth. Or advanced Math or Science: when we went to school, the culture valued academics. Now, there's nothing but 'Self-Awareness, Personality Explorations, Sexual Identification, Sensitivity Awareness, rap, hip-hop, bloggers and bling. Same in colleges. So why knock on us? At least we take a stab at academics."

"Wake up guys and get with it. That's what it is nowadays. That *is* the culture. Education supposed to fit into it. Not fight it. Culture makes

14 Milton, John. *Paradise Lost*: Book II. Oration of Mammmon.

education. Not the other way around. Reform that not know that: gonna fail!"

"Education? Whole system's rotten: kindergarten to college. Wouldn't make a difference even if we did change. So, why not get what we can for ourselves. Like corporate gurus do. Can't lick 'em? Join 'em."

"Fewer bibles in the school and more condoms! With due respect, Ms. Hamilton! Sor-r-r-y! But that's what I think." Millicent Pimmentade shrugged resignedly, mouth contorted.

"The Union needs to represent kids not teachers. Union not care about kids."

Bruce Warfles picked up his ears, adjusted his pillow and rolled over heavily, the three tiny wheels under the terrified legs screeching complaints. "Right on. Whatever." He wiped a sweaty forearm over his forehead before burying his head in the pillow. "When kids start paying union dues, then Union'll represent them. Simple."

The five by four lithograph hanging over the couch legitimized Bruce's occupancy. It depicted an enormous pig, ensconced in a hammock drooping precariously, inches from the ground, wearing a Dodgers cap, visor turned to the side, pink eyes rolled back expressionlessly, tongue hanging out, and pudgy forelegs and hoofs languidly placed on a bulging stomach. It wore short red pants with blue suspenders and a 'Go Dodgers Blue' T-shirt. Beside it, littering the ground were empty cans of Miller, Bud, Dr. Pepper; a *Mighty Ducks* pennant; slices of unfinished pizza; and partially consumed gargantuan bags of chips and pretzels.

Milton walked to the bookshelf and rearranged the paperbacks.

> 'Shall we accept this dark opprobrious Den of Shame:
> The prison of His tyranny, who Reigns by our delay?
> No!
> Better to reign in hell than serve in Heaven.'[15]

"Too bad you can't teach the kids that. Might get them somewhere. Like into some useless college program?"

"Interesting point, Pete." Arnida Hollyfield spoke from across the room to Mr. Czerney. "Since teachers have to be college graduates! Are you saying a college degree isn't good preparation for being a teacher? A degree in Chicana studies? It *does* qualify you to teach."

---

15 Milton, John. *Paradise Lost*: Book II: Oration of Moloch and Book I: Oration of Satan.

"You got a problem with that?" Brian McCauley was incensed. "And folks, there's some who's saying we should reform by not paying non academic teachers the same as those who got a Math credential and can teach Calculus and Analytic Geometry and Physics, Biology, and Literature! And History. And Algebra. Because they take the most IQ. Some teachers worth more than others? More than PE? They need to reopen Auschwitz for fascists who think like that."

"Still some bigotry!"

"And sexism." The comments came both from the Poker game and the 'Slides and Ladders' competition. "People like that need to get back into the Arc."

> "Far off from there a slow and silent stream,
> Lethe, the river of Oblivion rolls
> Her watery labyrinth. . ."[16]

"Lay off, Milton. You can already see it here. These cutesy programs that only pay more money in salaries and do diddly for kids: *Kick Start*! *Jump Start*! *Early Start*! *Head Start*! *First Start*! *Re-Start*! *Switch On to School*! *Fired Up to Learning*! *Hooked on Phonics*! And where did they get us?"

"False Start, if you ask me."

"How about 'Why Start'?"

"Anyway, more telling us how to do what we're supposed to know already. And we're supposed to be professionals? I don't think so."

"*Hecho lo ganas.*[17] That's what I tell my kids." Seraphina Meldonian, Biology, snickered as she wiped some spilled coffee from a faded polyester shirt and adjusted a yellowed wool ski cap. "Reform rolls off our backs like off a duck's you-know-what. It's talk. Never has happened. Never will happen. Why get ourselves in a tailspin? Not happen, folks. I clue you."

"You got me guys. Settle up later." Bartholomew Huerta, Physics, picked up the cards and shuffled them carelessly. "I lost my luck, today". His daily Poker game with Brember Bathersea and Brian McCauley was a Lounge institution. "Already, now? In addition, to our subject credential, we've got to have all kinds of other credentials and courses. For example: Diversity, Cross Cultural Learning, Minority Literature, Cultural Awareness, Ethnic Consciousness, Bi-cultural Assessment, Safety? Coping

16 Milton, John. *Paradise Lost*: Book II: Reflection of the 'Infernal Peers'

17 'Go for it!'

with Grieving? Terrorism: how to avoid it? Reform's going to do more of that uselessness? Actually now, that kind of BS is more important than subject matter credentials! So we still have to take extra classes at night. My take is Reform'll mean more add-on credentials, more 'intervention strategies' by Miss Uppty Allsbury, more un-paid 'in-services' training. Kids sense our frustrations. That's why they pull away from us. Now."

"Was that the bell?"

Bruce Warfles, stirred, rolled over and rubbed his eyes. "Better get goin' folks. Keep the zoo keepers happy."

# *CHAPTER VI*

## *A Luncheon*

"Hi, folks? And I'm Kelyee? And I *will* be your server here to-die?" She tossed crimped hair, nodding vehemently and emitting a wide and vacuous smile. "Oka-a-a?" She flourished an order pad from the back of bulging black trousers. "You folks care to hear our Spec-i-al-it-ies? To-die?"

"I know what I want." Buck grimaced and rubbed the inside of his collar. "Hamburger. Rare. Fruit. No potatoes. Bud."

"Same for me. Medium. Iced tea, please."

"Thank you m'am. And si-i-i-r!" Kelyee's patience was stretched thin. "We don't do them rare?"

"Well, how do you *do* them?"

She swiveled her neck over her shoulder, emitting a protracted sigh. She caressed the words. "Si-r-r! It's our *pol-i-cy*? We-don't-do-them-*rare*!" She extended her lower jaw. "Government's regulations. Customer protection?"

"Interesting place. At least they warn you about the food. OK—medium rare. If that's not against your policy."

Kelyee chronicled carefully and intently, brows furrowed. "And the other gentleman?"

"Hamburger. Medium. Iced tea."

Buck looked across the table. "Hear you got yourselves a 30's Spanish revival?"

"I told Buck about the house. Some of the projects."

"It's coming along. '20's." Besserian made an effort at a joke. "I guess you could say, it's what: 'challenged'? Got some problems." No one laughed.

"Penny tells me you set yourself up a workout room."

"Does the job."

"Guess so." He nodded appraisingly. "Look OK. What've you got?"

"What have I got? Weights! I don't follow you."

"How much weight? Bench press? Lat machine. I mean what? What the hell does anybody have in a gym? Shit, man!"

"About three hundred. Speed bag. Heavy bag."

"OK. That's all I meant. Nothing serious. Gimme a break!"

Penny shifted gears. "B, Buck is interested in Fillmore. And the Reform Plan? If it goes through TriDelt may be more involved with the school district. He was thinking that you might give him an inside perspective. Teacher's? Administrator's? As the Plan develops? Especially if you're AP?"

"You think you'll get it?"

"Get what? AP job? Not sure I want it. Interview sometime in January."

"Why not? Want it?"

"What do you mean?"

"Mean? Education's in a mess. Seems to me that some hard-charging guy would want to grab it. Good for reform. Good for himself."

"A 'mess'?"

"You think everything's fine? Nobody else does. I mean maybe I got the wrong information. Glad to hear they're no problems in public education. Guess I've been reading the wrong newspapers."

"Go to any party. Tell people you're a teacher and first thing you hear? How bad schools are. How bad teachers are. Why don't *they* solve the problems? If they know so much?" Besserian was already exasperated.

"Why not you?"

"Me?"

"Sure. Get the AP job. Then you make sure Reform Plan works. Makes changes that help kids. That's what you want, isn't it?"

"Easier said than done. They're a lot of variables."

"Shit! Variables. In business we . . ."

"Schools aren't businesses."

Buck shook his head. "Maybe they should be. Their 'non-business' management sure isn't working now. Give me a better solution, buddy."

"B, that's Buck's way. He's only saying . . "

"Forget it! The wonders of corporate America. Does nothing but strew blessings and goodness all over the world! Theft from investors! War profiteering! Unconscionable salaries! Schools follow that? To reform themselves? You give *me* a break: *Buddy*!"

"Pal, don't get ants up your . . ."

Besserian leaned closer into the table. "Schools aren't a business. Grubbing after money. And don't call me 'pal'."

"Not a business." Buck's laugh was exasperation. "OK. So, they don't have to be accountable? For their failure? Great! If people are dumb enough to pay taxes for it! Kids can't read and write? Damm! You living in Noah's Arc, guy? I mean, shit!"

"Capitalism: the panacea! Wonderful! Genocide? War? Bombing innocent people? While you guys prance around in your alligator shores, in one of your twenty-eight million dollar houses! Open your eyes!"

"Here's your orders? Sir, would you move your plate? Pull-eese? Now, these plates are just *super* hot! We have to tell that so that everyone don't pick them up and get theirselves burned."

"Makes sense. Might set the restaurant on fire. Or start a forest fire? You never know. I know you've got your policy!"

"Our policy, sir," Kelyee groused, "is to *protect* people! And would that be a problem for you?"

Penny smiled. B fidgeted. Buck seethed. And Kelyee finished distributing the plates. "Now, would there be anything *else* I could serve for you? At this time?"

"Nothing, thank you Kelyee. We'll let you know, sweetie." Penny touched the server's hand soothingly.

They ate in silence.

The painting over their booth was not inconspicuous. In too thick oil, it depicted patches of flowers—reds, blues, and yellows—clamoring to escape the profuse foliage of drooping willows and pink and white flowering hedges. The winding brook personified 'meandering', that is, until it eddied into the lower foreground. There, the surfeit of peculiarly aggressive bubbles caused the observer to consider the possibility of dangerous subaqueous activity. The eye of the viewer was then drawn upstream to the pseudo

Gothic stone bridge, its buttressed arches illuminated by flickering torches throwing an orange-yellow glow on the water. The bridge led, of course, to a thatched roof cottage displaying a prominent 'Welcome' mat. The interior, exuding a surfeit of coziness, was illuminated by the orange gold glow of a candle in the disproportionately large leaded, window. From the chimney, spiraled a haze encircling a full moon.

The frame was gilt baroque. From its swirls, a fixture leaned out precariously, its miniscule bulb casting a russet glow. A plaque at the bottom announced: *The Cottage in the Dell. Laura van Diemen-Peldt. Suggested: $3,600.*

Intrigued by the picture, Buck twisted his head back to his companions. "She'd cream at fifty bucks. So! What made you get into teaching? The money?"

Besserian gulped some air, as if to say something, then reconsidered, stroking the napkin beside his plate. A shadow masked his eyes: a combination of the projection of his brow and the subdued light of the room. "Basically, I like it. That's why." He glanced at his watch. "Why does anyone do what they do? What made you get mixed up in investments? Money?"

Buck rolled his shoulders as if the jacket was a nuisance. The booth was confining and the seat uncomfortably worn. He bit his lower lip. "Mixed up?" His face was also masked: a one o'clock five o'clock shadow. "Anyway!" He gulped the beer. "You get this AP job? Management is management anyway you look at it. OK! You got some kind of point. Sure the style is different. At the school. But you got to produce to make it in management. Even in a school. It's just hard to see what it is you're supposed to produce. There. Hard to keep your ass out of a bear trap."

"I'll try and remember. Thanks for the advice."

"No need to get bent out of shape. Only making conversation."

They resumed their silence.

# CHAPTER VII

## *Temporary but Permanent*

He was always early, never later than six thirty: avoid the fatuous mailbox camaraderie. Despite the 'mandated' six week cutoff—it was now late November—more student drops and adds; student over-due library books; a term insurance brochure; notice that a former teacher had 'passed'; attendance rosters. No Allsbury bombshells. He made his way to his classroom: one of the Portables.

For Besserian, portables were the salient characteristic of Fillmore. Bungalows? Pre-fabricated structures? Modular buildings? The name masked the issue. They were not portable. Temporary was code for permanent. Portables were a microcosm of the difficulty, the futility, of school reform: muddling through, apparent solutions: 'the best as we can come up with right now, given the . . financial, social, racial, legislature . . .' you name it, 'situation'.

Installed the year of Besserian's arrival eight years prior, removal was not a priority. Repairs, therefore, were a continuing exasperation. To everyone. Broken locks; inoperative doors and windows; electrical short circuits with defective lighting; damaged steps, holes in walls, defaced white boards, graffiti, malfunctioning fire alarms. Ms. Jamgotchian, overheard to say the potholes and protrusions in the asphalt surrounding Portables reminded her of 'black acne' elicited a Letter of Reprimand regarding use of 'racist epithets' from AP Falange.

The overriding complaint, however, concerned defective air conditioning and heating. The previous winter, Mrs. Park Chuoy, General Science, unable to turn off the cold air during two weeks of temperature in the forties, was required to use thirty days of Workmen's Comp to recover from 'double' pneumonia. Her complaint stated that she could get warm only by standing outside: 'flaring' her rheumatism. Also, when Johansson "wrote me up" for leaving the class unattended—she had gone several times to her car for additional sweaters, caps, gloves, and blankets—"he inflicted psychological damage, possibly permanent". In ensuing months, the discomfort remained; not only for Mrs. Chuoy. After April, 'squirrelliness' intensified when Portable temperatures reached the nineties.

Besserian recalled his first year when the Portables arrived three days prior to the opening of school. The last minute project had overlooked heating, cooling, electricity, white boards, teacher's desk, supply cabinets—or lighting. It took the administration six weeks to begin to resolve the deficiencies. In the interim, he and several others in the same predicament had spent their own money—some claimed over two hundred dollars—on supplies and equipment. Besserian bought an overhead projector and an industrial quality extension cord that he connected through the back window of Mr. Melvin's—Grade 12, Government/Economics—room, across a walkway, a distance of about thirty feet. The solution was sporadic. Passing students, intrigued by the iridescent orange color, tugged at the cord, disconnecting both his means of instruction and source of light. In any case, it became a moot point when Melvin, arbitrarily, rescinded permission: "It's my room, my space, my electricity, my plug, my window! Mi casa: mis reglas! And No! I don't have to! So, you can just to get your own!" Fortunately, Sandra Weatherby's room was adjacent.

To add insult to injury, there was, as usual, a sexual denominator to the problem of Portables. The three-feet space separating them provided convenient places in addition to the recessed doorways of classroom buildings for exchanges of student intimacy.

Underscoring the seriousness of this, Mr. Wilfrid Phillips, Grade 12 Health: Individual Living Strategies and Parenting, recounted at a faculty meeting, that he "was almost one million percent sure" he had seen "a male student with his underpants—red chili peppers on a canary background—down, around his thighs, mind you, and pushing up against a young lady student and not leastways," and he was "totally sure on this point—the boy had one hand up and inside her Scanties and the other inside her tank top! And this at six forty-three! And in the A.M! I kid you not!"

Although he affirmed that students should, "Of course, define their own beliefs and follow their individual persona," and that he, himself, was "in no way a prude, and certainly not judgmental", he did have "concerns about health issues. I mean, look at AIDS!"

In corroboration, several PE instructors and Counselors stated that female students were complaining, increasingly, of "date rape". Other female faculty reported an increase, on campus, of overtly sexual conduct of "different kinds—and not all of them bein'opposite sex members, neither!"

Possibly in response to these observations, Mr. Baques, at a special faculty 'dog and pony show', as teachers dubbed it, had reaffirmed that student activity was "always personal and teachers were not to get involved. It's all of our duties to protect students and their privacy. Always."

AP Falange, in a Greek chorus pronunciamento, cited numerous provisions of the Education Code prohibiting teacher "connections" of any kind with students, direct or indirect, on campus or off: "No person, no place, no time, no reason, no excuses, no mix-ups, no Involves. No Way! No 'ifs', 'ands', 'buts', or 'maybes'! So, let's keep it simple, folks: do a reality check! Involvement? A total No-No! This place is like a kaleidoscope. Changes constantly! When you look into it too close."

There were three additional reasons why bungalow replacement still had not occurred: budget constraints, the slow progress of construction of the proposed solution—the 'F' building—and administrative mishaps.

Inexplicably, District financial officers, maintained they had smaller budgets each year, even though funding was based on an increasing enrollment.

'F' building construction had progressed at a snail's pace. Appropriated funds were lodged in accounts that were now, mysteriously, empty. With the delays, 'temporary' fences, boarded over holes, machinery, mounds of earth, bulldozers, all remained, cluttering the area.

Still visible on the cracked asphalt, were the partial markings of displaced hopscotch squares; leap-frog and jump-rope areas, remote controlled model car racing sites. The reduced recreational space not only curtailed legitimate games. It aggravated physical and verbal conflicts.

Construction was a festering sore. Against the advice of the contractors, District administrators and the School Board had decided to save money by using plans for a structure designed sixteen years prior.

The results were unfortunate. And predictable. In the intervening years the increase in enrollment made the number of classrooms designated in the original $40 million structure—now $120 million—inadequate even at the time of groundbreaking. Exacerbating the problem, classroom space was reduced further by new services mandated in the intervening years but not provided in the original plans: resident Parole Officer suite, Parent Room, expanded Health service room, Women's Resources Rooms, Nursery, Reflection room.

The recently mandated Security Suite requiring space for Holding/ Interrogation Rooms, K-9 corps, personnel armor, crowd control equipment, weapons and offices, also had to be carved out of space originally designated for classrooms and teacher work rooms.

During the sixteen-year hiatus, technology had advanced. Original plans did not provide for computer wiring, ducts, equipment rooms, all of which had to be created from student activity space. OSHA requirements had burgeoned and on-the-spot construction adjustments were made to comply with the proliferation of new regulations: fire, earthquake, asbestos, flood, toxic waste storage and removal, drainage, graffiti removal; electrical, water and sewage requirements.

In adopting the old plans, the School Board discounted the architects warnings, emphasizing instead, cost savings to taxpayers. In fact, protracted rental of Portables, costs of redesign, constant structural modifications, implementation of new building and equipment codes, had obliterated the 'savings'. By using the old plans, overall costs had increased over one hundred percent and instructional classroom space was decreased in excess of twenty percent: during the same period that enrollment had increased by thirty percent. And still rising!

Moreover, there were non-monetary costs of the prolonged disruption: proliferation of trenches, temporary walkways and barriers, blockage by equipment and machinery, noise, congestion, dust and extreme inconvenience.

There was another snafu, not disclosed to the public. Through an administrative oversight, the site of the "F" Building–now affectionately termed 'Faulty Towers' by the more erudite—was the former varsity baseball field. Site for the new playing field proved a $600,000 oversight.

But to cap the construction malaise, a fiasco really, the contractors had sued the School District for pressuring them to utilize School Board relatives and friends as sub-contractors. For the same reasons contractors refused to accept responsibility for the findings by state inspectors of substandard quality of work and the failure to meet safety and environmental codes. Lacking the requisite government certifications, the project was mired in limbo. Legal costs, unbudgeted, would exceed several hundred thousand dollars. The entire 'F' building 'solution', far from a panacea, was a festering sore: managerial, logistical, legal, financial and ultimately, continuing.

Anyway, today he was in a bad mood. Perhaps the insolence of that brat at the restaurant. The possibility of repercussions from the Alley incident. Weatherby's not very veiled criticism after the faculty meeting still bothered him. Maybe she was right? He wasn't doing enough. For kids.

He brushed the thought aside and winced, thinking of that arrogant bastard in the restaurant. Probably couldn't use the pencil sharpener without that Jeffrey character. Never should have let Penny talk him into the lunch. But TriDelta was important to her.

Forget all this! Maybe it really was temporary: the place, the kids, him? The motto of this place is Indecision. Self Protection. CYA. Always. Why fight it? No one else seemed to. Sandra Weatherby? Well, maybe she and Huerta, Mugwabe, Pemberton, Leavering, and some others.

Right now he appreciated the quiet. He still had the room to himself. "What do they need? What do they want?" He reviewed the assignment papers, entering the remaining scores in the roll book. Retrieving a paper from the floor he noticed that the first page indicated a modicum of effort. The assignment, in the required format, was legible. The back of the page was quite different. He looked at it, amazement mounting. The script was a cacophony of styles, scrawls really, and the writing was both horizontal and vertical so that it was necessary to keep turning the page.

"I won. I won. Yeah! I won. You have that right-Very! Yuck! Fright. Night. How grose! Bad example-dope We we know it's practially always the ugly addict. Sad too. Why-oh why-are half the ones stuipd people [Mistake=thee-hee] Negro oh why. Artist or piano player-Now going for Cream-Just It's up yours. It's up mine. It's howdy doody time. Kidding-I only want his body-just it will make sense later. I promise kiddidng-Wait a minute No I'm not. All I know is he needs a haircut and 'badely' [mistake hee-hee] Nose slash. Sorry. How pretty. I like the long t's. And l's especially.

So God-I love myself. Should I or no. Draw more often girl. You can't do it next year. I got to get goin. Don't let somebody block me".

He replaced it in the pile.

Besserian had slept fitfully and, in the morning, when he kicked off the sheets, sweating and frustrated, there was a note on the bedroom door: "Big deal pending today. Late home." He had crumpled the paper in his fist: "Shit"!

And yesterday, as if the persisting Alley recollection plus the restaurant fiasco hadn't been enough, Dolores Lomerdosi, Grade 10 Counselor, passing him in the hall, emitting a vapid smile, tossing her waist-length hair pertly, observed, "How's your day, fella? You look wasted. Kids getting you down?" Moreover, when Baques had told him to call a parent whose child was being bullied, allegedly by one of his students, the principal had intoned the 'teacher responsibility' mantra, fending off discussion of Besserian's application for Assistant Principal.

His first period was restless; indifferent to History. Maybe the answer was simple: students were not "academically inclined" and study wasn't "a part of their culture". His irritation increased. He wrote the lesson plan on the board, arranged the assignment papers to be returned, and prepared himself for the blitzkrieg.

As it approached, they began to mill around outside. There were the usual contingents of couples absorbed in petting, slapping and teasing one another. The girls' attention to eye shadow, makeup and loudly whispered confidences, did not prevent them from hurling volatile accusations at the inattentive boys. The conversations were aggressive and belligerent. Several, conspiratorially, were transferring items of clothing, food, shoes, copies of 'Brides' magazines, *Hustler*, lotions, spray bottles, and gym attire from one back pack to another.

The door banged open, "How ya' doin' today, Mr. B?"

"Everything OK? Hey man! You look warped!"

"Hey, you know about Pruno? Make you feel good, man. Cool. You should try some."

"He's been workin' kinda hard."

"Guess years begin to show in a person."

"Get in touch with your pain, man."

"We gonna' have a sub today? I mean so's we could learn? I thought we were." They laughed loudly, exchanging mock punches, delighted with their own humor.

Besserian came outside: it helped him sense their mood and diffuse, somewhat, their exuberance. Some were leaning indolently against the metal paneling of the outer wall, undecided whether the class was worth their time. Opportunities to 'ditch'—avoid class—abounded: late teachers, or the office had neglected to get substitutes. Teacher absenteeism averaged about fifteen percent and on Mondays and Fridays was higher. Overburdened security, would ignore 'roaming' students, unless a fight broke out. A student could continue, period by period, moving from one group of displaced students to another, avoiding class entirely.

Several were pushing against each other in mock eagerness to enter. Those directly in front of the door shuffled aside with exaggerated deference. "Hey, step aside, dude. Let the man in." They shoved roughly, knocking one another off balance. "Hey, move youself, boy! You want to throw down after school?"

Besserian standing on the small porch, waited in front of the door. His mood lightened. "OK. Bell rang! And anyone who comes in after me will be tardy."

They seized the challenge. Scrambling aggressively, wrenching open the door, pushing him aside, they squashed several of the most vociferous between it and the outside wall.

"Comin' home!"

"Me first! Shag ass, girl!"

"Oncomin!"

From a pocket of females, there were squeals of mock consternation followed by shrieks of laughter: "Help! Pul-e-ee-ase!"

Allisandro elbowed Hector roughly. "Step aside, boy. Let a man to come on in first."

He called over his shoulder to Besserian, pointing behind him. "She be late, Mr. B! Monica! She be comin' in after me! Hey, boy, what you doing that for?" He shoved José roughly. "Got no respect?" They hooted, jostling each other, bobbing, weaving, ducking exaggeratedly, sparring, avoiding each other's punches. Shouts, squeals reverberated around the room.

Hector picked up the dialogue as he easily vaulted a desk. "Yeah. Hey, Mr. B! She barely got here! Griselda! Jesterday too. Same thing. That girl don't wanna' learn!" He swaggered magnanimously dispensing strokes of affection to several girls who had scrambled in during the melee.

Griselda scurried across the room, arms flying, a clattering of bracelets. Sliding, as if on ice, into her seat with the coordination of a gymnast, she slammed a pile of books on the desk, shrieking, "I was not! And Mr.

B: You-jest-better-make-him-stop-baggin'-on-me!" She wailed her denial in histrionic rage, slapping the male offender petulantly and turning for support to her female companions who looked away indifferently, rolling their eyes, giggling, hunching shoulders and covering their mouths as if to muffle their tittering. Among them, Destiny laDestina, voluptuous and curvaceous—a caricature of a Rubens painting, or a Playboy cartoon—doubled over in joviality, struggled to unwrap a stick of gum, contorting her bulbous torso with gusto—inflated, low-rise jeans, and bulging tank top notwithstanding—tore off the wrapping, threw it on the floor and inserted the morsel with a theatrical gesture onto her extended tongue which she rested on a flaming lower lip; long, gleaming eyelashes fluttering.

Besserian, keeping out of the way of additional arrivals who kept the door banging against the wall, went to his desk. "Destiny, pick up that paper please."

"Sure! Why not!"

José reached over Monica Alvarez' shoulder, grabbed the top of the door in his large fist, holding it open. "I'm in. Mark the teacher tardy."

The remainder of the class swarmed in.

"Hey boy. Get out of my seat. Mr. B, Jorge be in my seat. Hey, buddy, move it!"

Loud guffaws punctuated self-confident laughter.

At the desk, unshaved and swarthy, Aldo nudged Besserian conspiratorially, drawing attention to a massive bicep that he flexed to emphasize the tattooed Greek Key design. "Check that out, man. Cool, eh?" His body was rigid, leaning across the desk. Face inches from the other man, and nodding with a fierce intensity, he whispered, "Hey! Mr. B! You want me to pass out errands for you?"

"Just the books. Thanks."

"You got it! Give me the keys! To the cabinet. And your car!" He guffawed with laughter. "Hey, you like my chain?" He moved his face still closer, elevating the gleaming pendant hanging from the chain, opening his shirt wider.

"Very nice. What's that medallion? Looks like gold."

Aldo beamed, holding out the glistening emblem of the marijuana leaf from the hair in which it had been buried, forcing his chest close for Besserian's inspection, intensifying his pungent scent. "One hundred percent gold. It's the national flower of Mexico, Mr. B." He laughed exuberantly. "You wanna wear it? You can if you want to."

"Thanks anyway. Another time. Here you go, Aldo. The keys. Appreciate your help."

"No sweat. You tell me to spank the monkey—I spank the monkey."

Besserian raised his voice. "Table captains should begin collecting homework and report to Aldo to get your books. Let's go, everyone. We're losing time. Be in your correct seats. Sandra will be taking attendance. Who's Homework Collector this week?"

"Yo-oh!" Allisandro was raucous. "Right here! You got it!" Yeah! Hurry it up, people! Step on yourselves! Sir, she don't want to give me her homework. Guadeloupe don't."

"Be quiet, dumb ass! Still lookin' for it."

"That girl be lookin' a long time. A real long time. She not do it jesterday neither. Teacher says she don't do neat work like she supposed. Like me."

"Hey! I seen her at the Mall last night." Angel called from the front.

"Yeah. *El Emperador*!"

"Shut up, big mouth. What you doing there? Didn't see you with Nobody. You was stood! I seen you trashed, boy!" Guadeloupe rolled eyes, heavy with mascara, anger escalating. "Your Piece find something else?"

"You mind your dirty business, girl!" Allisandro bristled, his humor shifting instantly to dark indignation.

Monica Portillo, Guadeloupe's companion the previous evening came to her defense. "She did so do it and it was neat for your smart ass information! You mind your own business, anyhow, wet-back." Her tight, pink T-shirt advertised in balloon letters, "Powder Puff League. Girls Rule. Everyday. All the Way."

"I said that you mind your own business, girl. Screw off." Allisandro lunged at the paper but 'Lupe yanked it away.

"You stay out of my f-ing business!" She spat out the words.

"Give that to me, Guadeloupe". Besserian walked to her desk.

"I barely got here. Give it to you tomorrow."

"It's due now. Assignments are due at the beginning of class."

"Here it is." She smiled insolently, lower jaw extended, eyes dilated, and jerked it toward him. "OK?"

"That's not polite, Guadeloupe."

"Forget you, man!"

Ignoring the insult, Besserian pointed to the white board showing the date, assignment, Standard, pages and homework assignment. "I'll return your papers later. Let's get on with today's work. Thanks Allisandro. And Rigo."

"It's kick-back time."

"What's the date?"

"You can see the board, can't you?"

"What's the matter with you, boy? You a retard?" José upbraided Antonio. "Mr. B? It's like when his mother got him? But forgot to give him a brain?" José doubled over with laughter at his own joke. "Mr. B, he be goalie for the Dart team."

Antonio glared at his paper with malevolence and muttered under his breath, "You shut your big mouth, a-hole."

"Mr. Besserian, Antonio said a bad wo-o-o-rd." Griselda using a lilting, childish tone of mock sweetness fanned the continual combativeness between Jose and Antonio. The battles were frequent and last week had exploded into a classroom fistfight.

"Is that page twenty-two? Or ninety-two? Can't see it." Someone squinted with exaggerated concern at the White Board.

Besserian raised his voice. "It's a 'nine'. Perfectly clear." He signaled for attention. "There's the bell. Need to get settled. And you're going to find this topic very interesting—and important."

"What's it about?"

"Will it be on the test?" Omar ground his right fist into his left palm and gritted his teeth.

"Testing isn't what we're interested in now, Omar."

"Interested in? I guess! I'm a guy! Me, I'm always interested in it! Everyday, man." He shook his head delighted at his witticism, looking around to enjoy the effect of his insight.

"You wish, little boy." Marvella nudged a friend. Nonetheless, effusive snickering corroborated his philosophy.

Besserian took his place in front of the board. "Agenda? New Topic. Political Revolutions. 18$^{th}$ Century. France and America. State Standard 12-a. And is that your own seat, Angel?"

"Sure thing, Coach. Gettin' there."

"When did they happen?"

"It's good for us to learn this? Won't jingle-jangle our brains?"

Besserian continued. "In any subject as complex as this...are you paying attention, Lupe?"

"I think so."

"We're going to examine the main points of these two events, in order to get some ideas: their causes and general characteristics. Our purpose here is not to emphasize the details, you'll do that in your college

History courses, if you take History, but to look at the causes, the stated benefits and the actual accomplishments. Who really organized them? Who really benefited? Were the actual accomplishments the same as the stated, original, ideals?"

"Is this relevant? For inner city kids?"

"Relevant? You'll see that as we go on, Destiny."

"This could be real important. I seen this picture one time? Might of been a revolution, Mr. B?"

"Where, Marco? Which one?"

"Guess my mind's sort of clouded about that." He chortled conspiratorially. "It was some lady holding a big flag, real ragged and tore—sorta like the American flag, same colors—with lots of guys following her, and they all had rifles and s-words and stuff. Lots of bombs and smoke and crap. They was all shoutin' and runnin'."

"Sounds interesting."

"Real interesting." He looked around nodding, almost leering. "I guess: Revolutions? Don't freak out but I guess they don't wear: too many clothes? Or they get shot off? This lady was like real mad about somethin'? 'Cause she had lots of her clothes ripped and, well.... I mean they were, I mean she was, well, they were, like—huge!" Laughing, he illustrated by gesturing with his hands over his chest.

"Typical." Kasidy and Monica shook their heads in unison, contemptuously. "Male reaction. Immature."

"If you want to make stuff relevant, why don't we study about things that's happening now? Not thousands of years ago? It's like school is only about learning old stuff that happened in the age of the dinosaurs ands not happening anyhow, now."

"OK Allisandro. But hang on." Besserian noticed, smelled really, someone squeezing a large tube. Using the tips of her fingers, elaborately, she applied a scented cream—to him a nauseating, sickening aroma—into one concave palm, then, languidly, in an intricate, caressing motion, proceeded to kneed her legs and thighs with the thickness.

"Shaunisha. I asked you before. Several times. This is not the place for personal grooming. It may be allowed in other classes but not here. This is a classroom not a ..."

"Whorehouse?"

"Aldo. There are ladies present."

"Where?" The young man looked around with an exaggerated, searching expression. "I don't see none."

"Aldo! That's enough! Shaunisha, school rules prohibit personal grooming. So, put it away. And, also, are you chewing gum?"

She uncrossed her legs languidly, exhaled petulantly, and looked around the room, balefully rolling her eyes, heavy with mascara. Slowly, she squeezed more of the pink lotion on the back of one hand and caressed forearms, elbows and upper arms, sniffing to savor the pungent aroma now permeating the room.

Blinking her eyes she seemed to be emerging from a trance. "I really don't see that it's bothering somebody. I mean why should it?" She looked around for approbation. "Unless, of course, they're interested?" Lifting her torso on the seat, she took great pains to smooth the underside of a tiny skirt, caressing her thighs with the residue of the ointment as she repositioned herself; rolling her tongue over her teeth, sucking them, the corners of her cerise wet-look lips turned down. "So, who's interested?" With a contemptuous sigh she tightened the top of the tube and placed it in a zippered plastic bag. "Anyway, people only have to do what they want to do for themselves. Teachers can't make them. They ain't parents. And parents can't, neither."

"Can we get back to the work, Mr. B?"

"Of course, Monica, but Allisandro raised an important point. We're studying events of two hundred years ago precisely because we can follow them from beginning to end. They're complete. Also we have a great deal of information about them. As we do that—Shambra, would you look up here please—we can apply information about them to contemporary political, even social events."

"Mr. B? I don't see why we're learning all this stuff 'cause stuff change all the time anyhow. Why not learn something that's happen' right now. That's not changed yet?"

"Not sayin' anything personal, I mean you got to inflict the State Standards and all, but stuff is all in bygone years. About old people. Stuff that's not happenin' anymore."

"Good points. Ideally, we study history to get a frame of reference for what *is* happening now. Not to hide from the present."

"Mr. B? You sayin' History is the same sh. .  stuff happenin' over and over?"

"Perspicacious observation, Robert. No, I'm not teaching that. I'm presenting for your consideration: if certain conditions, situations, that occurred in the past seem to be happening now, the educated person should consider the possibility the educated person should consider the possibility of their relevance: to the present. They might serve as a guide to the present. To avoid the pitfalls of the past. The goal of the educated person being to control his environment, not let it control him. Or her."

"Go for it! How?"

"18th century France refused to tax the individuals and institutions that had the money: instead taxed those who could least afford it: lower classes. Second, it refused to stop waging wars that bankrupted the country. The government was run by the rich: for the rich. For their immediate financial profit. They ignored the long-term disastrous results: political, social, economic."

"Seems weird."

"It was done to benefit the military and the purveyors, the suppliers, to the military. And to cover up the political, social, economic problems at home. The result was the collapse of the richest country in the world. Why? The *real* war was waged by the government against its own people."

"But seems like school covers up stuff and all. Not this class, maybe. But my other classes? Don't learn stuff that's usable. We're here for four years and then move on. Stuff we learn's not permanent, either."

"Can I say something, Mr. B?"

He nodded to a girl in the back. "Please do, Amarantha."

"Why all this 'looking' and 'analyzing' about stuff nobody cares about? What's the point? Of school? Just makes lots of confusion and jumbled up thinking. I mean why not just enjoy our youth? Only young once. I know that's hard for older people to deal with."

"She just don't want to advance herself, Mr. B. Don't pay her no mind."

"Order and rules and Standards might be OK. But where to get us? Maybe we need to sort of jump overboard and see if we can swim. Or get eaten up by sharks?"

"You mean define our own education?"

"Could be. Make it work for us. I don't think it's working for most kids now. Like it should? What do you think, Mr. B?"

"Mr. B? Revolutions is about peasants? Taking over? Is that what we are? Peasants? Like we don't count? Just to do what we supposed?"

"The bell? So soon?"

"Short day. Pep rally, sir."

"Read these pages. We'll work on it together. Tomorrow."

# CHAPTER VIII

## *It's About Kids Helping Kids*

"And could we just make sure that you could grab that door, just real tight, would you sweetie? So we can activate?" Rayella Brauphman chortled, nodding vehemently at Mimi Zou. "Thanks, just a bundle? Can't have the whole world in here. Leastways not at this present moment in time."

Her colleague, Raven Lopez-Workman, also a counselor, began the class. "Young ladies, we got a big laundry list today. So ..."

"Ms. Weatherby, my Biology teacher? She says I couldn't take this? Not get credit for it? Peer Counseling not unapproved?" Paul Samir was hesitant. Confused.

Lopez and Brauphman stumbled over each other trying to reply at the same time. "OK. Right? Just you had better go ahead, Rave."

"Thanks, sugar. Good. Paul! This course is *totally* in an approve mode? You're on the receiving end of their bad-mouthing? Their gender bias and discrimination not ever going to stop? That group, and believe you me, we know who they are! Raised a ruckus about when we called our group *Ladies*! You guys recall that? So when we transitioned into *Peer Counseling*: Kids Helping Kids? Now they don't like that neither! What more do fascists like her want? Wow! Just to gimme a break!"

"And let me just to piggy back on that for a quick moment if I could, Rave?" Brauphman shook her curls vigorously. "And don't let them to forget: it's counselors: not teachers, not parents, not administration, not students, not anybody; who's the ones that decides what courses students take. And the credit they get! It's hands off to anybody else. And, Paul, sweetie," Rayella was commiserate, "Peer Counseling is most definitely in an approve mode. Your elective! So, you *will* get academic credit for it. So don't you worry that curly head of yours about teachers that's most definitely obstructionist anyhow. Against students. Anybody says something?" She looked knowingly at her associate. "And I know the teacher you are in reference to! Wow! Out of the Dark Ages. But not to worry. Let her or any other Neo Socialists tough it out with me! Personally! If they don't like it! Paddle their little—or should I say big—behinds, if they do! No! We're here for you! Counselors control student schedules. Period! Others? No way, José!"

She continued. "Right, and as Ms. Lopez was saying, Peer Counseling is students helping other students in ways that adults can't. Or, won't." Brauphman clucked her tongue and walked to the side of the room. "What's more, this room's been made permanent for us: in like Flynt! And sure, there's a shortfall of classroom space! So what else is new? This is more important than regular classroom stuff."

She looked knowingly at her associate. "Now, what that certain teacher ...

"You talking about Ms. Weatherby, Miss?"

"...that you're in reference to Paul, sweetie, couda intended, was, that all applicants to Peer Counseling, not being accepted. Humungous difference! True: all applicants don't surface on our acceptance list. What those fascists don't know is that this course not designed for everyone! We have to let some go by the wayside. Peer Counseling is training for our betterment. To tell ourselves that no: They can never hurt us. Not ever again! We learn that it's us who's in control. Now. To get what *we* want. For us. We got Them under our thumbs. By the you-know-whats! And that's where They're gonna stay!"

"And I was thinking?"

"Yes, Jackie?"

"Well, could I tell my boyfriend about what we say? In here? I mean he says he wants to know everything about me? What I think? To protect me? Be the mother of his children?"

Ms. Lopez interrupted the giggling. "Let's restate the Number One rule about Peer Counseling: 'What's Said In Here; Stays In Here'. Always! Your boyfriend? *His* children! We'll be cutting into just those kinds of Front situations, Jackie, a few classes from now. The point always is to be strong. It's for us to do the protectin'. And frankly, your boyfriend? Gonna be a problem for you, girl. With him. We'll be helping you to fend that."

The teacher nodded gravely. "Sure, there's some that says kids should tell parents about school. Who said what? But, think about it? Why do teachers have teaching credentials and parents don't?" Impressed by her own logic she summarized. "Destroy kid's right to privacy. To their self-hood. No, sweetie, this is a special class. And that's why regular rules can't obstruct here."

"Ms? I mean how about if we was to let some of Them, you know, guys? Come and tell us what *They* think? Maybe They don't know how we feel? That we think we should be, well, managing stuff? Maybe that way They wouldn't be so, well, so immature? And self-centered? I mean They might not even know?"

"Good point here, Melineh. Two concepts: first we don't need to beg anybody. To understand us. Those days are long gone. Long gone! In the ago! They can know or not know how we want to open up our windows. It's totally up to Them. They had their turn at bat. Now, it's ours. They got to find that out. For Theirselves. Gender Equality! It's Hard Ball time! And sure, it's a tough road. For Them. To hoe! But it's something They're gonna have to learn to live with."

"And let me just to add that for zillions of years, They never understood what we are and what we want, so how could They now? Even if They did want to dialogue? Anyway, the signage is that we're on a roller coaster ride, now! So? Ride it! No, we're not going to ask Them to ride with us! How can They? They're not going to the same place as us. A zero-sum game. But mindshare on that later."

Her eyes narrowed. "Now, back to the present. We're certain about self-empowerment. That's a given. Uncork our power. And we're never, never, ever, ever going back. To the before! It's about how They're gonna' have to live with that. So, here, we need to move into the affirmative! Counseling of others mode; who's still living in Jurassic Park. Review those students, kids, who are on each one of your Support Lists: that you're going to assist." She smiled gushingly. "So? Ms. Workman? Did you want to piggy back? On what I said? I mean we're totally about students, here? Right?"

"That would be a affirmative! Let me popcorn on your points, Ray. We're tight there. So, after we review each of your caseloads, we'll talk about some other goals we'll have for this year. Awesome goals! As you'll agree. Sandra?" She beamed approval. "Sweetie?"

"It's more than what Mimi just said. They'res teachers that say nobody should take this course. Credit or not credit."

"As we just said, sweetie, and I hate to repeat it, there's teachers that's fascists. Terrorists. Reactionaries. Negatize anything that's helping kids? Want to dump them out the window. But Sandra, that's why we have the 'what's said in here, stays in here' rule. This is your Safe House."

The day prior, Raven and Rayella had started decorating the room. There were framed mottos: "Tell Me the Glass Ceiling is the Name of a Fairy Tale"; Tell Me My Most Important Feature is My Self-Confidence"; "Tell You the Only Person I Need to Impress is Myself"; "Tell Me the World is Ready for a Girl Like Me": "Tell Me to Throw Every Inch of My Four-Foot Ten-Inch Frame into Everything I Do".

Sandra fidgeted in her seat, tossing streaked blond hair, lips stretched over upper front teeth. "Ms. Workman, there's talk like how's there's no boys in this class? And that's sorta discrimination? And that when kids get involved with other kids, they, well, find out too much about their personal problems. Personal stuff?" She looked at the others quizzically. "No. I mean it. Really. And kids not professionals. So, then professional standards might not apply to them? I mean to keep quiet. That they supposed to keep stuff to theirselves? And it's not really keepin' it to theirselves if they talk about it in here? Is it?"

"A biggie! Good point! Glad you brought that out to Group, here today, sweetie. We need to hear the alligators! I mean if there's dirt, well, you can't clean it up if you don't see it. If you only smell it! There's always a few smears every year. There's always somebody who's gonna poop on the carpet. Anything else? Anybody?"

"Ms. Brauphman, let's hopscotch for a minute here with this? Back up and do a survey? And then to move directly into the Rewards program that Peer Counseling students will be allowed to benefit from this year?" Lopez beamed what she hoped was an infectious smile. "So we need to roundtable? So, could we circle just a small bit tighter?" Workman nodded vigorously as, remaining seated, she led the others, by adroit manipulation of the heels of her cowgirl boots, in moving her own chair, to the center, smiling reassurance that intimacy and privacy would be safeguarded. "Great! So's we get to keep up our solidarity?"

She crossed her legs, hitching up her black jersey culottes, revealing the boots' carved design, inlaid with snakeskin. "Peer Counseling is for future leaders. That makes us different. Superior. So sure! That bothers some people. Change always does. Who don't want to change! Anyway, lots of kids can't relate to adults. Teachers or parents!"

Re-crossing her legs, Workman was intense. "People: a teacher, who don't understand kids: their special needs? At this very important time in their lives? School is much more than about what's in books. The nitty is that would it make sense for kids to be talking to other kids about personal problems lacking confidentiality? When the person supposed to be helping them might go and blab it all over the world? To their parents? To teachers? Administrators? Yakety-yakety?"

She shrugged. "Of course not. Parents don't need to know. Not their viewpoint. Ditto for other teachers. And for sure not those kinds of teachers, like we already heard about one such already today, that's not running in formation with our goals. Can't appreciate our Hurt! Our need to grieve. And if anybody should try to get you to talk, well, forget that! You just don't! Not if you want to stay here in Peer! You come to myself or Ms. Brauphman on any stuff! We'll tase 'em but good! No! Absolutely none of anybody else's business. What we say! Rayella?"

"Ms. Workman's sayn' it like it is." She snickered and heaved her bulk on the molded plastic chair. "And that other point. I just wanted to add that, sure, there's more young ladies in the group. But I think everyone here can see Paul. He's not a boy?"

"Maybe that teacher meant that, well, there's like one boy and about fifteen plus girls? And the topics here are, well, sort of based on, well, girl issues?"

"OK. Lots of personal things, problems here at the school, are personal to young ladies. In fact most of them. It's them that has the hardest time adjusting to high school. And it's different from Them. From the other gender. Why? Because this culture has always been rigged against us. From the git-go. We need to assert ourselves. So? . . ."

"So now we have to change the rules?" Stella Kincaid chortled in satisfaction.

Lopez' lips curled largely: a coy smile. "What we're saying now, sweetie, is, that women, our sisters, have much more personal problems. Than They do. And yes! Frankly. Our situation is how to phase in a new position for opposite sex members. So, OK, I think it's pretty clear that young ladies, can help others of their own gender better on those matters. I mean that's what their problems is about. I mean I sure don't know any young lady who would want to talk to a *boy* about stuff! Personal stuff? When all They can think about is Theirselves. Their own pleasure. So? It's good for Them to come to a understanding about how we need special heads up. It's for Them to develop sensitivity. Them to accept how it's *us* that's pushing the buttons now. How we're laundry listing our own needs."

"Miss, but if we don't know Their opinions?" Krystal interrupted.

"Good point." Brauphman was gushing. "There's two famous statements, sweetie, that answers your concern: First: 'It is, because it was'. And second: 'What goes around, comes around'. We can't be concerned with every other possible viewpoint in the whole world! It's about us. You do what you gotta do."

"And just let me jump in here right now, if I might Ray, to addition that we, in counseling courses, have found out that male gender members are not comprehending; are generally insensitive, to our gender needs. Basically, as I'm sure you've noticed, They are only inner-directed. Me! Me! Me! Everybody look at Me! But women, on the opposite side of the fence, are the natural care-givers. Outer directed."

"And, before I forget! Your other point! We do have a young gentleman in our group, with the idea, that if another boy should have a problem, well, they could maybe, receive some help from Paul? Boys aren't natural caregivers so they don't have the emotions girls do. Don't need much peer help. But, Paul's here. For them. What's not fair about that?"

"Miss? How's that not discrimination? Revenge?"

"Discrimination? Nada. No. Discrimination's when things gets worse. This is betterment, Twyla." She nodded agreement with herself. "So, Rave? Ms Lopez? Would you to get us started, please?"

"Fine, and with that as our modeling clay, let me slip into the Number One issue of today's class. Here's where you can see the special benefits of this course. Not available to outsiders. Scholarships? College scholarships?"

There were smiles around the circle and Lopez-Workman continued. "For right now, this is top secret. Shu-u-u-sh!" She depressed her lips with an index finger. "But, just let me pass on to you that with my connections at the Evergreen Foundation, I've found out that they'll be offering a scholarship to one of our seniors, *preferable from this group!* Scholarship will cover tuition, books, travel, room and board, and most living expenses at a major university of student choice. That is, so long as it's in sync with Evergreen goals! Sounds great? I can see by your reactions! And what's not to like?"

"To anywhere we want, Ms. Workman?"

"Just about. But, good. Actually, I'm glad you asked that question, Paul. Let me back pedal for a minute on this. Because, well, there's some—I wouldn't say 'restrictions'—but more like *qualifiers*? For the scholarship?"

"What Miss? Tell us?"

"Of course, you're interested, Stella. Who wouldn't be? 'Cause, basically, there's a new world out there. One we're helping to make. Evergreen is a woman's fraternity started about ten to fifteen or so years back by women executives who had cracked through the glass ceiling. So they got lots of money behind them. It's dedicated to others to continue smashing it. And the problems, well, they're still there. So, the young lady—don't get your hopes up too high, there, Paul—will have to demonstrate that she has been accepted in a school that is gender acceptable to Evergreen, and, quite frankly, except for some livestock technology schools—that nobody cares about anyhow—that's by now, ninety-nine percent of all the colleges. And she'll have to be a Business or Accounting or Pre-Law major. Or Pre-Med. But, and absolutely *no* give-way on this, there does have to be a double major to include 'Women in Management', 'Women's Studies', 'History of Gender Bias'. That sort of thing. Of course she has to have a Four Point GPA here at Fillmore."

"So she has to be a senior?"

"That's a true statement, Shambra. Now let me add a few other qualifiers. Evergreen's philosophy is that the Gender Equality movement won't be complete until women are in the predominate place. And that includes in the corporation world. Evergreen metaphysics is that women are naturally more logical, persuasive, and mature than Others, so, of course, they should! Be in control. Evergreen realizes that at the college time of life for many young ladies, they're pursued for personal commitments, even marriage, by Others. Evergreen feels that could break into the life dedication, of the scholarship receiver. So, she would have to agree not to be bound by any ties, legal or 'understood', while being in a scholarship mode. Now, I gotta tell you that Evergreen has been leading in the fight for single sex marriages. So, maybe they might could go for that. If it's passed. So, same sex marriage could be a pausibility! Whatever! But that's down the road: still up in the air. Alls we know as of right now, is that it's just super important for Evergreen to select a young lady who has the potential to go on to after-college college work: the Master's or even Doctor's. And share the metaphysics about gender absolutes. Of Evergreen! And funding can be continued so long as the candidate doesn't get side-tracked into well, say, marriage or children, or not be in a leadership mode for Gender Equality issues and all."

"Marriage after college, Ms. Workman? OK?"

"Sorry, Mimi. From my vantage point, right now, that would be a negativity. If the scholarship person chooses to continue on with her education? After the bachelor's."

"I mean, well, Evergreen wouldn't have to know, would they? I mean, gol-ly?"

"Not so fast! This is hard-ball, girl! There are personal interviews, family interviews, let's say some pretty detailed insights made. By pro-fayshionals. Background checks that keep going on! They found out two in past years: whose buckets couldn't hold the water. Let me clue you. The girls didn't get more money; plus, they had to do a pay back: on what they had received! Had broke their contract. And Evergreen won in the courts. So, it's serious! In one case, it was in the papers, the girl was found out her first year in After College school. That she had been married when she was a Junior? I think, if I'm not mistaken, Evergreen said she owed them, well, something like, let's see, was it, over forty or fifty thou? Plus? Room, board, books, clothes, travel? No, you wouldn't want to risk it."

"Couldn't she'dov sued?"

"They sued her! Contract was binding. She'd bitten into the conditions. Evergreen's politically correct certified. They got the best lawyers. So, she'll be paying back for umpteen years. In so much debt couldn't even transfer. A bummer. Trying to make it now as a waiter, last I heard."

"And if I could do a pop-up here? You bet she has regrets: the life that was waiting for her and she flubbed: penthouse, big office, BMW, designer jeans, vacations, travel? Wow! She had her chance to make Them dependant on her! And she self-destructed! You bet your you-know-what she's in the pits!"

"So, really, the point of all this; what Ms. Workman's saying, is that Peer Counseling has a lot going for it. We can help other students. And help ourselves along at the same time." Brauphman chuckled, walked over to the desk and sat behind it. "Wow! It's been a long one! Got some real losers in my counseling program! And my daater, the one in GATE at Manchester Academy? Now, that would be a private school, and believe you me, it's costing just a bundle! Anyhoo! Ms. Lopez has given us some mind candy to suck on." She giggled. "Some of it's licorice but, well, still candy!"

"Is this a non-academic course, Ms. Brauphman? I mean there's teachers sayin' non-academic is non-speak? Is non-sense?"

"We're goin' to have to have a special session on certain Obstructionist teachers. Straighten them out. For right now, we had better be moving toward closure. I know there's several here who's already begun working on the Spring Carnival preparations: Cinco de Maio? Rave? "

"You betcha. Just let me say that Peer Counseling is helping other kids in ways that parents can't. Or shouldn't. And there's several here who I just know for sure can qualify for Evergreen. And, another thing that makes it so good? It seems—now, don't any of you breathe this to a single soul—but it seems that Pritchard guy is hooked up to Evergreen! So, a word to the wise! We go all out for his Reform Plan. Make it a done deal! We do for him? He does for us: 'What goes around, comes around'!"

My point? Others? Them? Can be useful. So? Use 'em! Just now, everybody's throwing their hat in the ring to see how they can get the best deal for theirselves. From Reform Plan. So that's what we might just as well do here, too. Kasidy? You look confused?"

"We use Them? I mean what if Reform Plan's no good?"

"We need to cozy up to Pritchard: his Reform Plan. However direction it actually flows. Make it work for us."

Lopez flicked the ball to Rayella. "You need to look at who butters your bread. You have a question, Kasidy?"

"I know you hear a lot about Gender Superiority and such, but isn't that like, sort of, well, doing the same thing, but in reverse? Is that right? Do it to Them, too? Do stuff back to Them? I mean why would it be OK for us to do? I mean if it wasn't OK for Them? Isn't stuff wrong for, well, everybody? All the time?"

"As we go on together? Travel our road? You'll find out, sweetie, that things needs to be done? To level the playing field? You got to tilt it over more, so that it bounces back. And if the see-saw bounces back higher, then where They are? Well? There's the breaks. Right now it needs to be higher. To make up for when it was lower. And choices you make? There's no rule book. Play it by ear."

"Miss? Us superior? Like she jest said? That's revenge?"

"Hold that thought, would you Shambra? It's what some famous writer of long ago said: 'Survival of the Jungle'? I mean we are the strongest! So?" She reflected for several seconds. "So? That's why we have a democracy in this country. To let survival happen. Eat up whatever's in your way!"

"And that's what we learn to do here. In Peer Counseling. I see girls all the time, doing better in class than Them and going places and doing things they coudn've done before. And doin' them better. And they get special help for that. And others, Them, don't."

"On target there, Kenyon. We're ending the present. The oppression. Right now, it's all about Us. So we can grab hold of the power."

The bell rang. "Gender power. Leveling. All the way." They gathered the back packs and satchels scattered behind them.

"Don't forget! Young ladies? We'll be reviewing your interviews with other students next time! Remember! Who's got the power? Now? Always?"

# *CHAPTER IX*

## *A Wild Card*

"You didn't tell me! Guy's locked into himself."

Penny said nothing.

"And why? Beats the you–know-what out of me! Can't see beyond himself. Trust me. I know the type. A typical yuppie Liberal: carp from the sidelines. You say he's different? OK. But it didn't look that way. At the restaurant."

"You're taking the rational approach."

"Of course."

"He could do it. Would. Given expert help."

"The Assistant Principal thing?"

"Management. Yes."

"He has the what: the management, administration, credential?"

"A piece of paper. Certificate of attendance"

"Isn't school administration management?"

"Supposedly. Administration courses dumbed down to ensure political correctness and retain the politically correct minority mix: Principal wanna-be's. Come to class? You get the credential. B will tell you."

"You made your point. OK, he's got the license: credential. What's his other strong point?"

"He wants genuine reform. Academics. Wants to create alternative programs so all kids can succeed. End drop-outs and opt-outs. Keep kids from marking time in a nursery school. Prepare themselves for college—academic courses—or learning a marketable skill." She shrugged. "And."

"And what?"

"And Baques wants him—needs him—to get the support of the 'academic' or 'intellectual' factions. Of the faculty. The community. To support Pritchard's plan."

"Go on."

"Right now, you don't have the details of the Plan. You need them. Pritchard tells Baques. Baques tells B. B tells you."

"And then I make my move!"

"Exactly."

"He'll do that? Tell me?"

"*If* you're his mentor: his teacher: management teacher. Keep him from shooting himself in the foot. With his idealism. Ignoring the reality that he'll be crucified if he pushes Reform that demands accountability: consequences—teacher or administrator—too far. Anyway, staff always want any new AP to fail."

"So?"

"So, you make sure he's successful. In management."

"You've got this all worked out."

"A win-win situation. You need the details of Pritchard's plan. To push him out. B needs your help to implement Reform. To stay in."

"And I grab the benefits of the Reform Plan. For me."

"Right. You'll let—put it this way—you'll *help* B to implement reform. With some discrete modifications, of course."

He walked to the wall of glass and pressed a button. Noiselessly, the translucent drapes moved toward the center, infusing the room with a soft light. "Plan makes sense. One word comes to mind, however."

"What?"

"What I said before: loyalty."

It was her turn to move to the wall of light. "Mine? It's to both of you. You'll gain: whatever Pritchard was going to get. And B will gain. Administration where he can implement at least some genuine reform. As we said, he can move up. Principal. Superintendent? State Secretary of Education? He'll never get that now. Without your help, the politics of Reform will crush him. And he's not the correct race or gender. As I said: you as mentor? A win-win situation."

"Ms. Besserian? Mr. Besserian is in the conference room." The secretary cracked the door cautiously.

"Early dinner. Don't do it often." She motioned to Jeffrey. "Tell him I'll be right there."

Buck studied her carefully. "A win-win-win situation?"

**************************************************

"Great room. I come in here when I want to escape. And think." She indicated one of the leather couches. "My favorite. We don't leave at three o'clock here. And pretty soon, you won't be able to either, Mr. AP."

She squeezed his arm and laughed. "Welcome to the world where you can't walk out when the bell rings. Have to meet deadlines. Money doesn't come rolling in here from taxpayers." She brushed some imaginary lint of his shoulders. "Tri-Delt's about competition. Has to be to support the salaries. Buck makes more money than most people in this state. It's a different world. Who knows? You might get some ideas."

"I'm not like him! If that's what . . ."

"Never! You're totally different. OK. What? An hour? Don't go away."

The atmosphere was luxurious: deep piled, off-white carpet, a chiseled burgundy Greek-key border and concentric Greek Deltas in the center; the floor: white and green marble, gleaming, both from the concealed spotlights and the walls of glass. He made rough calculations of the heights of neighboring buildings; drank in the uninterrupted view of the mountains beyond; the unusually low snow line.

Burgundy leather upholstery, burnished gold tapestry pillows exuded comfort and sheer drapes muted the glass and chrome. He selected the supple cushions of the other couch. The aroma was pronounced; the comfort seductive. His eye moved to the side wall. Three large plates of glass, without frames, displayed architectural drawings—18$^{th}$ century bridges—two in Rome: *Pons Clemente XIV; and Pons Quirinale;* and another in St. Petersburg, *Pons Caterina Imperator.*

Refinement. Security. Self-confidence. Sanity. A different world of luxury—and power. Unknown at Fillmore. This bastion was undisturbed by jarring noises and frenzied altercations: hysterical laughing; whining teachers, frantic students, bellicose parents and security guards: bells; loudspeakers; buzzers; hallway disputes; shouting, running, perpetual indignation, fighting: "He took my pencil!", "She hit me!", "She be messin' with me!", "He be baggin' on my mom", "Her boy touched my little girl in her privates and what you gonna' do about it?", "I won't and you can't make me!", "She said the F-word: in Hispanic!" Constant interruptions: mindless trivia counterbalanced by genuine grievances: ricocheting non-stop from adults, to staff, to students, to teachers.

Chairs, upholstered bronze suede, one with a higher back and arms, framed a sweeping glass conference table. A series of luxuriant Ficus provided seclusion. Covering an entire wall but in perfect view from three sides of the table, highlighted by hidden spotlights, was an exhibit of trophies and commendations.

"Of course." Besserian put down the magazine and walked over to it.

Everything was in place: federal and state licenses; university degrees; varsity letters: football, baseball, boxing; photos with political, entertainment and sports celebrities. Certificates from Financial Planning Institutes legitimized his investment and managerial skills. Numerous pictures showed the inauguration of the TriDelta Corporation, groundbreaking for office buildings, malls and apartment complexes. In one, Peter Pritchard had his arm looped over the younger man's shoulder. In another Besserian could make out the name *Klingsor,* Pritchard's celebrated yacht: a gleaming, futuristic example of Italian shipbuilding. "Atomic powered and completely computerized": Besserian remembered an issue of *Architectural Environments* featuring the interior design of 'this floating Taj Mahal'.

There were the usual commendations from civic groups: the requisite County Commendations posturing as illuminated manuscripts. There were autographed pictures: governors and senators; Latin American presidents; and two prelates, effusive in scarlet or purple watered silk and jeweled pectoral crosses. Buck's name, reiterated throughout the testimonials, could have served as a descriptor of computer fonts. Accepting the accolades of the elite, his handsome face, sometimes smiling, always wore a mask: self-confidence, control.

Dwarfed by the gleaming metal and wood frames of the other tributes, was one with a smaller, plain frame: Blenheim Preparatory School: Talent Show; Music; 2$^{nd}$ Place.

"Mr. Besserian, I thought you might like some coffee. Cream? Sugar?" The receptionist smiled engagingly as she placed a silver tray, monogrammed with the three Deltas, on a glass table. There were Scottish tea biscuits and newspapers.

Surprised, he murmured thanks. One article extolled the advantages of the proposed Reform plan and possible new city. "A Boon to the Business and Education Communities: a mutual partnership: corporate world partnered with education." Another writer was relieved that "... maybe now education would 'wise up' and accept corporate management techniques—run our schools like a business and save taxpayer money." There was a large photo of Peter, and other executives, the ubiquitous Superintendent, Dr. Elayne Jones-Laporte and giggling School Board Members, waving their crimped manes.

"School reform: a timely, spontaneous partnership to make Cathedral Heights a truly democratic community; re-enhances the traditional American concept of fair play for all, in a democratic pluralistic society. At long last: education for those victimized by Traditional value systems."

Besserian skimmed through other comments: "Unique shared experience. . . All citizens winners. . . especially kids. . . alternative life styles live in dignity. . . influx of minority owned businesses... schools: foundation of our democracy. . . school-business partnerships: actually lower school taxes."

Another writer explained how an "academic revolution was needed to solve the debacle of education and the abandonment of our children". The back page featured an article lauding *Dr.* José Baques whose Fillmore High School would be achieving the "required—although unfair to minorities—API and AYP academic mandates of NCLB" [18]. The writer reflected that Baques' leadership would propel students into "top" universities and Fillmore "into [sic] the highest rung of the statewide academic arena". "Clearly Baques and his dedicated staff of professionals will be on the educational cutting edge, leading Fillmore into the vanguard, of educational excellence. In our state. In the nation."

The eloquence continued: "end once and for all . . . the dominant Traditionalist race concept and culture . . . together with the regrettable pall, of ingrained gender bias . . . so long overhanging education, indeed our entire culture."

The banner proclaimed: "School Reform: War For Kids."

******************************

"Hey, champ! What's this? Round Two!" He laughed confidently, clenching Besserian's hand, punching his shoulder. "No, seriously. Glad

18 NCLB: *No Child Left Behind.* Federal Law requiring academic progress of students; measured by assessment: AYP [Average Yearly Progress]and API [Average Percent Increase ]. Schools failing to meet the standards could have their administrative and teaching staff replaced.

you made it over here. Well, I see Mrs. Roberts has fed you. Those cookies are great! They're to seduce the visitors."

"Here! Take a seat. This is my favorite." He pointed to the couch Penny had indicted. "We're informal here." Relaxed, he waved away the tray his guest indicated. "Not for me. You'll have to punish yourself for eating some. Anyway, meeting a few people for dinner. So, relax. We're winding things up early. Some time-out before this evening. Lots of big things happening." He settled into the opposite couch. His blue eyes gleamed, always precise and calculating behind the smile.

"How you been? Kids still driving you nuts? Keeping out of trouble, I hope? Kiddies all doing their homework? Or else teacher spank?"

"I'm fine. Came to pick up Penny. Her car's in the shop. Admiring the surroundings."

Obviously in his element, the CEO of TriDelta was comfortable. Irritatingly so. "Yeah. It's nice. I like it. Designed it myself. Believe it or not. Hey. See you got a copy of the CH Chronicle. So, what do you think? Looks pretty exciting, eh? This Reform thing is blasting off. Like a rocket." He rolled himself back in the cushions, crossing one leg across his thigh to adjust a lace of the alligator shoe. "But that doesn't interest you. Forgot!"

"If you mean the Reform Plan, it interests me. It might work. Not sure I understand the motivation behind it."

"Don't understand? Lots of people seem to. Improve education. Help kids. All that good stuff. Nothing complicated. I'm not even an intellectual and I can figure that one out." He stroked his chin and neck and his eyes narrowed. "Pretty much out in the open. But you're one of those people who thinks everything's what? A conspiracy? That public education is fine the way it is. The best thing since what? Lubricated condoms?" He snorted and shook his head as if amused. "So? Get the AP job and find out if it's any good or not. Simple!"

"I'm wondering."

"About what?"

"Values. Impose corporate values. In the schools."

"Like I said: Round Two! That's bad?" He ignored Besserian's protest. "Right now? I don't see your values working. Unless you mean kids goofing off. Being pampered. Which is rejection! Being driven into gangs. To Drop-Out. They're young men. Young males. But they're treated like Pollyanna's. Dominated by females. Gangs give them some sense of validation. For being what they are. Acknowledges them as male. But you think school is helping them? School values don't need to be changed?"

"Somewhat. Yes."

"Bingo! Knew we had something in common. Dropouts? Gangs? Kids not learning enough! I agree with you!"

"Maybe."

"Dropouts?" He stabbed his finger in the air. "Here, if somebody quits—who's good—it's my loss. My failure. But you guys? You don't accept responsibility for students quitting. So, that makes my values wrong? I don't think so, pal."

"There are problems in the schools. But you're the only one in the world who knows that?"

"Give me a break. I'm offering a solution. Reality values. What're yours?"

Besserian stood up. "This 'let me tell you all about what's wrong with schools' conversation is a bore. I'll give you a break. This conversation is pointless."

"Hang on!" Buck got up, placing his hands on B's shoulders, easing him back into the couch. "I'm interested. So? There's shit about the schools I don't know? Tell me."

Besserian shook his head resignedly. "OK. Why not? I'm interested in the motivations of this 'corporate help'. I think it could be dangerous, rash, to take the failure of education—OK, I'll give you something on that; schools aren't what they should be—out of context. By that I mean apply *carte blanche* what somebody running a corporation *thinks* should happen in the school because he *imagines* it happens, works, in his own corporation. His personal interpretation of business management will work in public education."

"Shit! Context! Look at the issues! Reality! Kids aren't learning. So? Basic management? You try something else. Figure out what motivates people. And go for it." Buck walked to the expanse of glass, rubbed the back of his neck and came back. "We didn't exactly hit it off the last time. Maybe we can do better ...."

"Better?"

"Shit. Different. See, it's that superiority again. What have you got to be so GD superior about? I mean what are you doing, yourself, to help education?"

"And you're not patronizing,..."

"OK. Hold it. Let's not put the gloves on again. Yet. My point is that in my business we have zero tolerance on ...."

"Hate that expression."

"... problems. We solve them. Face them. Don't hope that if everybody smiles sweetly, problems will go away. Don't shove our heads in the sand."

"I'm not .... What's the matter?"

Buck came close, looking down. Examining. "OK. Right. I don't see any particles—sand—in your hair: what there is of it. Shoulders? Could be dandruff."

"Funny. I'm impressed." Besserian sneered.

"OK. I'll behave myself. Back to business. Point is that here people make a contribution. Your kids should. You should. Why. . ."

"They do. You think you . . "

". . .not make a bigger one? Think a minute. Maybe this AP job is the way to go. Could lead to what *you* want. Reform Plan might be looking for smart guys. And you're smart enough to make it work. Smooth over the rough spots. Who knows, I might even be able to help in the leadership-management area? For the AP job." He motioned to the expanse of the room. "This didn't all happen by itself. OK. Take it or leave it. It's an offer."

"So teaching isn't leading? Let's see, you've been a teacher for, what did you say, how many hundred years?"

Buck spread his hands, rubbing his palms together, squirming as if his clothes were a nuisance. "Buddy. Please. Please. Do me a fucking favor! Don't be so shit-assed defensive! I'm not attacking you! OK. So, it's none of my business. Did I say I know *all* about fucking teaching? Did I? Just listen? OK? A minute? I'm saying you're moving out so you can do *more.* For kids. Going into management. And I know management. So, if I can help. Clue you in on some things? From time to time? Hey, I'd be willing. To try. Nothing devious. Nothing sinister. I'm not trying to get in bed with you. Shit! Sure, teaching is leading. But a different kind of leading. And you don't want to let those dip shits screw up real reform. I manage ..."

Besserian rolled his eyes and inhaled. He sat back, obviously frustrated, rubbed his nose and scowled. "It's just possible that business and education *are* different. And you might just possibly have a myopic view of what happens in schools."

"OK, big guy! You win. I'll say just one more thing before the next round—at the risk of being 'myopic'. I'm going to guess that apart from your jealousy of corporate types, you're . . ."

"Jealous! Talk about conceited . . ."

"Smoldering hostility, then! You're not satisfied with the school. Or what you're achieving there. For kids. For yourself. And not completely sure that the AP job won't have some blind alleys you haven't been down before." He stifled a yawn and nodded his head slowly in a vertical motion. "Before you get more twisted, I'll tell you something. I used to be like that."

"Like that? Like what?"

"Like you." Besserian winced, rolled his eyes, and shook his head as Buck continued. "Then I decided I don't want to be a little nice guy, doing nice things for ass-holes, hoping some jerkoff will pat me on the head and thank me for making money for him. Doing a good job! Bull fuck! I decided I'd do a good job for myself. Stop hoping somebody will 'appreciate' me. I decided I wanted to push other guys around, give the orders, kick ass, get the big bucks, big office, car, and house. You know the scene."

Besserian's brown eyes were slits. He nodded, clenching his teeth, adjusting his tie, shifting his weight as if anticipating a punch.

"I'm good at figuring people out. It's my business." He sat forward on the couch. "Here, I have to make quick decisions about people: competence, motivation. Forget this AP crap for a minute. My guess is your kids aren't doing as much as you'd like them to. Right? But I have the impression you don't know exactly what to do about it. So you put on a 'superior' attitude ...."

"My 'superiority' bothers you a lot, doesn't it?"

".... which doesn't solve the problem. Doesn't face it. Result? Neither you nor the kids get anywhere. Or you don't get them as far as they should. And you don't get yourself where you should be-or think you should be."

"You know that teacher you told me about in the restaurant? The one you punched out? Assaulted? When you were in high school?"

"That fag? What about him? He was the Dean."

"I think I see his point." Besserian glowered petulantly.

Buck's eyes gleamed. "I didn't *assault* him. I defended myself against an idiot. A pervert. Taught him a lesson he should have learned for himself. Hey! Chill! First thing you know we'll be going at each other! Again!." He walked over to the table and took a cookie. "Want one?" He gulped it without waiting for an answer. "I'm not trying to pick a fight with you. Although that might not be a bad idea. Let me ask you something. Why don't you do something. Get involved in this?"

"What?"

"Reform? School administration. The AP job. You're smart enough to go up fast. Use school reform to help you. As well as kids. You know something? I'm going to make a guess about you and you can tell me to screw myself if you want to."

He overrode Besserian's attempted retort, making a horizontal movement with his fist. "So, you don't need my help! Your call! I won't give it. So? Do it on your own. But, at least climb down off your shelf and take a risk." Buck looked steadily at him and said nothing. He seemed to be deciding not whether the other man needed punishment but only the severity.

"My 'shelf'? Damm, man! Hung up on yourself! You've got all the answers for someone who isn't in teaching." He shook his head as if in disbelief. "What a . . ." Besserian rammed his foot into the floor, enraged. He started to get up.

"Hey, don't! Sit down. Chill out, buddy. Don't get your ass in a bind. I'm just telling you some things you already know. But don't want to hear. Relax. Because somebody makes money doesn't say he's bad."

Buck waved his hand signaling Penny who was approaching toward the glass doors, not to join them. "Listen for a minute, big guy. There are all kinds of ways you could use this AP thing to get kids excited about school work—about learning. Make education work for them. Make it exciting. You always want to know 'Why'. I'll tell you. Teach them—more than that—*show* them, how they can grab a piece of the action in the real world. For themselves. That's what I have to do here. To make my guys go from good to great."

Besserian estimated the angle of the shafts of light streaking through the narrow opening of the draperies, and turned back to the other man. "Go to any party and as soon as you say you're a teacher there're a couple of idiots who know all about problems in education and how to solve them. Sure, they're problems. Lots. But if they know so much, why don't *they* solve them? Why don't *you*? Everybody's telling teachers how bad they're doing. So you who don't know anything about education—you've already said you have no use for it—are telling me, teachers, how to do our jobs! Talk about conceit!"

"You're on the wrong track! My beef isn't with education itself, *per se*, as you would say, but with the way—the *way*—it's practiced." He brought his face close. "Big f-ing difference. The *way* its practiced. You take everything so damm personal-ly! Damm! Why do I criticize education? Because it isn't fucking working. If it were a business, people would shit-can it. And the fuck-ups running it. That's *why*! Maybe you're the one who's conceited!"

Besserian shook his head in disgust. "Mr. Perfect again. You tell me I'm doing a botched job. You don't know me. You don't know anything about me. You've never been in my class. Never met my kids. But you're sure they're not learning and I'm a failure. That I'm the problem. Well, maybe I'm not impressed with you either. But I don't tell your employees how to do their jobs when I don't know anything about them." He was incensed. "Besides, you've had all the advantages. Maybe you were 'abused' as you call it, ..."

"I didn't say I was abused. I could care less. I decked his ass. I taught him. Reality."

"... in some way at school. A lot of *my* kids are abused but the difference is they don't come from the privileged class. So they, especially males, have to accept it. They're abused more insidiously than you were: especially by being programmed into second class status, second gender status, when they don't stand a chance of getting anything like this", he raised his arm to indicate the room: "a society which makes them victims and then tells them they're failures for being the failures they're programmed to be!" He spat out the words. "And on top of that infuses them with gender inferiority. I'm not like you. I'm not Mr. Corporate Perfect. No, I don't have the world by the ass but most teachers do the best they can. With what they've got! And I don't tell everyone else he's a failure because he isn't like me. So now, you're theorizing about how your money-making skills can help the schools? You can solve all the problems in public education. Go for it!"

Buck moved in his seat inhaling the luxuriant aroma of the leather. He spoke quietly. "You don't have to be impressed with me. I only have to be impressed with me. Schools have money up the ying-yang, buddy. Believe me I know because I invest it. The problem is they don't know how to *use* it. To solve their problems. I suggested—*suggested*—that *maybe—perhaps*—the AP job might—*might*—enable you to do more for kids. Because I thought you wanted to do more. For them."

The other man moaned and shook his head in disgust. "Holy Mary help me! This is un-fucking believable."

"Forget it, then. What do I know? I'm probably way off base. Anyway, I'm not riding your ass, like you think. You're the one who's up-tight." Buck watched him closely. "You don't want them second class? Fair enough. Then don't be second class yourself. You keep trying to convince yourself that there's something wrong with getting things for yourself: the stuff you want. But won't admit. Good things. You're hung up that personal gratification can't be combined with helping other people. The Mary Worth syndrome—is a euphemism for not facing your own devils. Find out who you are and be comfortable . . even happy. . . in that. Be yourself. What do you believe in? How can you teach kids when you don't know yourself? Who you are?"

"I hate that mindless expression."

"What mindless expression?"

"Self realization."

"You got a hearing problem, buddy. I didn't say that either." Buck surveyed his own shoes approvingly. "You must be the one who's thinking it. I got the idea the other day in the restaurant, briefly, very briefly, that maybe, *maybe*, you wanted to go somewhere. In order to do more. For kids and teachers." He walked to the array of Birds of Paradise in the massive Lalique vase and inhaled deeply. "I see potential in the AP job for you. I'm not grandstanding. No need to get your ass in a sling. You can't do it? Be my guest!"

He walked back, surveying Besserian on the couch. "OK. You *might* be more than a typical Liberal: bitching but with no action except to get more government money and never take responsibility for failure."

Besserian came out of his seat, eyes dilated, fists clenched. "Do I tell you how to run your company?" He felt his own perspiration and wondered if it showed.

Buck swung around placing his face close. "No. Because you can't. Chill out, big guy. Relax. And I'm not telling you how to teach. You probably are competent. Maybe in some other areas, too."

Besserian's eyes burned. "Like what else? What's that supposed to mean?" The silence broke the wall between them and opened a chasm.

Buck ignored the question. "The people I deal with want to get something for themselves. They want to kick life in the ass and not be kicked themselves. So? They face things: their own skills. And limitations. Don't hide from them. You know what Liberal means now? Someone who can't put himself—herself I guess I have to say to you—on the line so he—or she" he sneered, "is always saying what he—or she—can't do or how he—or she—needs to be 'helped' to do it. And that, my friend, is the rut education is in now. Because it's run by welfare liberals. The curse of this country." He waited. "You know what they *really* want? But are too sniveling and whining to say so?"

"Why don't you tell me!"

"Unreality. Protection. Security. Safety. Code. For *themselves*. Give a damm about kids. What they're not smart enough to realize is that protection takes away power: their own power. And *Kids* power. Doesn't give it. They're feeding kids their own poison. Putting them in prison with themselves. You said it: second-class citizens. You didn't say that the people bitching about it are the ones doing it. You guys want . . ."

"Me?"

". . . OK other guys—and gals—in the schools want to make kids run like little piglets to the trough where they slurp up their gruel. Get fat. Not smart enough to ask *why*! Why they're being fattened. Possibly, just possibly, there could be a pay-back time?" He gulped some air between pursed lips. "My point is, as an AP, maybe, just *maybe*, you could *help* them, show them how to slurp up knowledge, power, and not poison."

Besserian moved as Buck touched his shoulder with his fist. "OK! I get carried away. I'm used to telling people about opportunities where they can make money and cash in on deals. Liberate themselves. That's what I do. Get paid a lot for that. So that's what I thought about you. Only I'm not expecting to get paid for it. This time. Reform plan? Forget that. Forget the AP. You're so snagged by my making money that you assume the worst. I'm not all that bad. Anyway, a guy needs a shot up the ass sometimes." The men glared at each other. "Public education needs an enema. You able to give it?"

Besserian stammered something unintelligible. Buck flicked his hand across the top of Besserian's slightly wet-look hair, displacing the shaft of light on the cowlick. "Think about it. How it could help kids. And you. Anyway, nothing personal. I don't have time for personal."

Besserian breathed audibly. He inclined his head back slightly. And frowned.

"Right. You've got more power than you think. We've both got things to do. Anyway I see Penny in the other office. And you two need to get some dinner. So? Chill!"

Besserian winced.

# *CHAPTER X*

## *Unexpected Advice*

That morning he found her note in his mailbox. "Please see me during your Planning Period before you leave today. Patricia Allsbury, Ed.D"

He could visualize her writing it: reaching, with the characteristically precise movements of slender hands, among the ordered stacks of papers on the desk, for those special cards reserved for troublesome staff in need of correction. The paper, linenfold bond, was a mauve tint. Snapdragons and petunias, intertwined with pastel ribbons, formed the border. The pink baroque script at the top; a convoluted flourish: 'From the Desk of Dr. Patricia Allsbury. May we talk?' The handwriting, however, was precise and deliberate; the strong vertical strokes contrasting with the filigree of the design.

She had a reputation for finding out things. In addition to being both prescient and observant, she encouraged informers, rewarding them, in the usual way of administrators currying support: 'extra duty hours': monthly stipends that, if, on occasion, actually had duties attached to them, were nominal. Being a 'team player' was financially advantageous.

In any case, what else could it be other than the students in the alley? Someone had told her. But who? He began planning his defense: essentially that he hadn't seen anything. Definite. And, in response to why he was there at all? His presence was accidental. In any case, it was what? Over three months? Possibly, this was something else?

His previous dealings with her had been infrequent: businesslike but not unpleasant. Besserian had the impression Allsbury approved of him. But if this was about the Alley, it could be serious. As an administrator, she was potentially dangerous. Inaccurate and false information, personal bias, often fueled an administrator's political aspirations.

Administrators fell into two groups, both dangerous to the unwary teacher: political and self protectionist. The former—hawks—fought to gain and maintain power: prosecute cases that enhanced their professional aspirations. Overlook the others. Self-Protectionists, chose small waves and rode them cautiously—using them to legitimize their precarious, even superfluous existences. Self-serving agendas made politicians dangerous. Caution made self-protectionists, the ostriches, fearful of pulling their heads out of the sand or, in schoolspeak, out of their asses—inclined to prosecute the weak, bypass the guilty. Ostriches were as dangerous as hawks.

In both cases, facts, truth, the personal and professional havoc inflicted on the accused, were secondary considerations. Teachers, with good reason, watched all administrators warily. Expediency characterized the Teacher versus Administrator undertow. And any matter involving sex—'morality' in eduspeak—was a buoy, warning of the current. Rumors were rife of administrators who, sublimating facts to either ambition or protection, had drowned a teacher. A vicious game.

On reflection, he may have made a mistake by not reporting the Alley incident. But what was he going to report? He hadn't actually seen anything. He was to be another Mr. Phillips with his vicarious titillations? Sexual repressions?

There was also the hazardous theory of 'Student Rights'; oozing from the equally murky quagmire of 'Due Process'. These vagaries insulated students from responsibility and consequences, anathematizing student accountability: rendering it 'gender-biased', 'mean-spirited', Fascist, chauvinist, racist, 'Traditionalist', *et al.*

It seemed to Besserian, that the Due Process mystique had grown; inversely proportional, to the decline of academics. Classics of Literature which valued obligation, loyalty and truth, were dunned into oblivion; replaced by stories depicting nebulous, meandering examples of self-indulgence, self-fulfillment, and self-aggrandizement often under the aegis of gender 'leveling'. Literature that analyzed the complexities of human commitment, conflicts of loyalty, the difficulties of fulfilling mutual obligations, and the responsibilities of social interaction, gave way, in present readings, to the isolationist philosophy of 'me', 'self', and ego: with themes like: 'Girl Power'; 'I've got to experience what it's like to be me—even at your expense'; 'I want what's best for me and I won't let you or anybody else stand in my way'.

The emphasis was on the obligations of others to me, the legitimacy of denunciation and retaliation against anyone who violated the shifting, amorphous, self-centered, politicized cultural ethic. State Standards and the reality of individual teacher classroom management of the curriculum expunged from assigned readings stories relating individual responsibility and commitment to others: of Absolutes. Of non-situational ethics. Curriculum literature, extolled simplistic, self-centered, politically correct relationships.

The demise of the study of logic, including that of mathematics and the sciences, spawned the erosion of commitment; of obligation. Few courses emphasized the substance of these disciplines, and a decreasing number of students pursued them beyond the basics. As a result, students were ignorant of the refinements of cause and effect: of objective, finite, exact solutions. They had minimal exposure to the logic of the sequence of actions—to say nothing of the sequence of tenses. Since they were not exposed to logical thinking, they had little understanding of the effects of their actions on other people. Besserian was beginning to conclude that the juxtaposition of these concepts, 'protection' in favor of 'self-reliance' and logical analysis, was a factor in the increasing recklessness of student behavior: physical, verbal, its myopic self-centeredness: cover-ups for their lack of self-confidence. Disdain of traditional values was the obvious step-child of the abandonment of them. This type of education imprisoned the individual in powerless self-pity.

The culmination of the politicized academic culture was an icon, peculiar and unassailable: the perpetual Child—the politically correct Nativity Nouveau. It was a fabrication perpetuated by its own unassailability, deemed, *ipso facto*, in any controversy, to be right. And right now, it was the source of Besserian's concern.

He recalled rumors of administration investigative tactics: 'Do you have problems accepting the sexual lives of students?'; 'Do you feel threatened by the youth of students; the rich careers opening to them, perhaps greater than what you, yourself, may have achieved?' He could also imagine the indignation of outraged parents; that their 'child' had been spied on to 'satisfy the perverted inclinations of some male'; 'So? Maybe the kids had been there! That don't mean they was doin' somethin' bad, and anyhow what was *he* doing there at that time of night, covered up in the dark, and him bein' a growed man and all?'; and 'Why was he so interested, nohow; spyn' of them and all?'

He was cognizant of the danger and havoc inflicted by shifting the burden from the culprit to the witness: aware of the financial, emotional, and professional anguish that could descend on a teacher. Under the cultural phenomena of 'student rights', 'child rights', 'political correctness', the adolescent found to be at fault, witnessed by a teacher, could, very quickly, be assisted to extricate herself—perhaps himself—by spinning a web to ensnare the witness. Obligation, consequences, even guilt were shifted from the perpetrator to the witness. The immorality of this equation, the illogic, the enmity, were not factors.

To add to the weirdness of the 'student rights' imbroglio, the witness of even possible sexual irregularity was subject—the Child Abuse Reporting Law—to fine, loss of job and imprisonment if he—she—failed to report not only what he had seen, but his suspicions: even if later, it was discovered, no crime had been committed!

As in the case of any idolatry, periodic oblations—and sacrifices—to the icon were required to reaffirm its sanctity. Besserian had a healthy trepidation of involvement in a student, 'Child Rights' issue.

***************************

They had been ignoring him. Sheila, Dr. Allsbury's secretary, away from her desk at the Principal's end of the main office, was engrossed in a conversation with Marvella. They were scrutinizing mail-order catalogues. Their muffled guffaws did not conceal comments about the most appealing items: plastic 'left over' containers; elaborately configured Bundt pans; tissue dispensers; illuminated Halloween decorations; and self-adhesive plastic hooks. Another publication offered 'Alluring Enticements for Male Arousal'.

"Mr. Besserian, I said: and did you *want something*?" Sheila repeated the question, this time without looking up. "You know good and very well, teachers only to come to main office after Three!"

"As I said, I'm here to see Mrs. Allsbury. She asked me to come."

"Then, you just going to have to wait! *Doctor's*," her emphasis was a reproach, "not here now. Might could be at a meeting. At District. Really couldn't tell you. Or when she'll be back."

She looked up bitterly at a student who, warily, had entered, uncertain where to go, and bawled: "You can just go right back out through them doors! And use the other door! To counselors!" She was enraged. "I tired o' tellen' you kids! Hollerin' over and over! Now, you jest to *git*!"

Irritably, she turned back to Besserian. "And you too: had better check with Ms. Allsbury. Later." The two women resumed their perusal of the publications.

"That jest so-o-o-o divine! I could use that beside the . . .", Sheila, her hand draped over her colleague's shoulder, pointed to an illustration, that, whatever it was, produced mutual squeals of titillation.

Besserian was meant to overhear parts of their conversation. "Could you imagine if that one was to be a Assistant Principal?"

"No way! Not going to happen. Not if I can help it."

He began to pace the area, his frustration growing.

Sheila raised her voice petulantly. "There's jest no point for you to go on wasting your time here, Mr. Besserian. I told you! She not *here*! And you *could* come back!"

He took some assignments from his briefcase. Sheila returned to her desk and the secretarial interchanges diminished. And then flared.

"Sweetie, don't you go and forget, now!" Marvella reminded her colleague, "She say you got to have the Student Lists done by end of today. You know that?"

"You menstrual, girl! Could think that!"

Marvella, looking around exasperatedly, noticed a whiteboard eraser, and, giving way to her indignation, shot it across the room, striking the other woman on the head. There was a stunned silence. Alarmed, both burst into volatile laughter. Then tears. The assailant, with intense histrionics, face in her hands, bawled, "I am so so-o-o-o-ry! I am-m-m! I jest don't know why I ever do tha-at! I don't know what come over you, girl! You is menstrual today, sure!" She pawed the air with her hands and arms.

Besserian watched the display in amazement. Marvella rushed to her *alter ego*, embracing her with tears streaming, "I am so, so, very so-o-ory! I am jest so so-o-ory! Lord be my witness!" Suffused in mutual hugs, mutual tears evolved into mutual peals of laughter.

The emotional interchange was interrupted by a flurry at the door and Patricia Allsbury swept in, wreathed in smiles. "And how's every little thing, ladies?"

Heedless or mindless of the altercation, the administrator churned through all of them. "Mr. Besserian can wait for a short minute. I'll be ready shortly. He can have a chair over there. They're provided for teachers who are waiting. And I think teachers *are* told that!"

Marvella and Sheila, vindicated—their altercation dissipated—shot aggressive looks at the teacher, and recommenced their perusal of the catalogues

"I can see you now, Mr. Besserian! Will you come in ple-e-ase!" It was not a question. Standing in her office doorway, she presented a smile which, to Besserian, approximated what in the Marine Corps he remembered was termed a 'shit-eating grin'.

The Assistant Principal's office was small and, with more than three visitors, crowded. And it was absurdly small for meetings, most of them attempts at conflict resolution: parents; students; teachers; security, community delegates. Notices, reports and directives, precisely stacked, labeled, and color-coded, were on a small round conference table, covered by a floor-length mauve, sateen skirt. He picked his way carefully around the meticulous clutter.

One of the narrow bookcase shelves was reserved for knick-knacks: crystal or painted porcelain: a trumpeting elephant, lady's shoe, hourglass, multi-faceted three-dimensional octagon, a unicorn, a crystal apple labeled: 'An Apple for Teacher', and a one-room schoolhouse, American flag flying.

There were framed testimonials. 'In appreciation'; 'Commendation for'; 'To a Dedicated Team Player'; illustrated by a lioness with her litter gazing wistfully over a verdant landscape; a polar bear crossing the ice followed by her two cubs; and facing directly into the camera, female oarsmen—oarspersons—sweating, gritting their teeth, chests overflowing their spread knees: captioned 'Enjoying the Experience'.

A carpet of Persian design graced the residual floor space. A slender vase held one long-stemmed blue rose. As indicated by her nod, he eased himself carefully into a chintz covered chair; resentful of both his size and weight.

She made motions of re-ordering her desk although it would have satisfied the most meticulous Drill Instructor. Angling her head, she attempted a smile that did not mask the pained expression. "And how are we this afternoon?"

"I'm fine. How are you?"

She ignored the impertinence. "I am sure, sir, you know why I asked you to come in today?"

"No idea."

"Oh?" She maintained her smile, and waited patiently, obviously expecting him to reconsider. "It does concern students?" She nodded.

"OK. Tell me."

She nodded again, lips pinched. "Allow me to put it this way, Mr. Besserian. And this is purely confidential and, for now, off the record." Angling her neck, eyes narrow and dark, the AP continued. "Several parents, and students, have complained. About you." Allsbury adjusted her neatly folded hands displaying the diamond ring and sapphire bracelet. "I'm sure you would want to know."

"Who? Who are they?"

"That, I'm not at liberty to say. Unfortunately." She twisted her mouth benignly. "You're familiar with student confidentiality—Student Rights?"

"So, what's bothering them?"

"Could you excuse me for a moment?" There seems to be a problem?" She edged around the diminutive desk, squeezing past his chair. "Ladies! I wonder if someone could take care of the telephones? They've been ringing for quite some time?"

Sheila disengaged herself, without acknowledging the request, and moved languidly back to her desk.

Allsbury waited. "We are here to serve students. I think we all try to remember that?"

"Was on my break?" Sheila muttered into the phone and placed her hand over the receiver. "And you could ask anybody if it's not my time!" Four fingers cavorting around a plume-tipped pen, she was covering a message pad with a flamboyant scroll. Disdaining Allsbury, she redirected her attention to the computer screen, holding the phone away from her ear.

Besserian took the opportunity to glance at the cover sheets of the precisely stacked papers on the adjacent table. Red: Lesson Plans. Blue: Security, Safety, Earthquake. Yellow: Parent/Student Conference Guidelines. Green: Disaster Intervention/Grieving. Magenta: Teacher Evaluations. Brown: Assessment.

"Excuse me, Mr. Besserian? If I might?" He adjusted his legs, moving to permit her to resume her place of authority. "We do need to come to resolution on these issues. And to hear your viewpoint?" Again, the vacant smile.

"Issues? I don't have a viewpoint on what I don't know anything about. So, why don't you tell me what's bothering them? Bothering everybody?"

She adjusted her glasses and massaged the gleaming stones of her bracelet with her thumb. With her fingers she traced the sculpted surface of the pink cameo that held the Hermès scarf. "It seems you have made personal remarks to students."

"Remarks? What, precisely?"

"That I cannot say. I explained confidentiality. And, we need to resolve issues. Not words."

"In a normal place of business, one has the right to know the specifics of an accusation."

"This is a school, Mr. Besserian! Not a business. However . . .students—and parents—are saying that you have, on occasion, made personal remarks. Ridiculed them about their personal appearance."

"Absurd! Never!"

"Did you make comments about a student's use of cosmetics?"

He glowered, wrestling with resentment. He searched his memory, to make sense of the absurdity. "I did tell one girl . . . ."

"Might I suggest, 'young lady'?"

"I told one not to put lotion on her legs and thighs during class instruction." He could feel the moisture on the back of his shirt. "You're telling me you consider—personal hygiene—acceptable? In a classroom?"

She reached over and touched the back of his hand, then waited, choosing her words carefully, checking the alignment of the two pens, precisely horizontal, in front of her.

"Mr. Besserian. I have been in education for almost thirty years. They have not always been easy years. For various reasons. Right now, I'm concerned about you. Please trust me."

"I don't follow you."

"Often in teaching, and in administration, it isn't what we think, or even what we know, that's important. We have to bend, sometimes. To politics."

She reached into her Coach handbag for some mints, took one and offered them. "The skill is when to bend. And how much. But more important? The wisdom of accepting the political reality. Not isolate ourselves from it. Not put ourselves above it. Otherwise politics can crush us. Make us useless."

"I'm not sure I follow you."

"I think you do. An example. I was the token woman administrator. In my lofty idealism, I denied the politics of my appointment. The reality.

And, refusing to see it, I became an anomaly. Of an administrator. A curiosity. Ineffective. Because I closed my eyes. Blinded, I became a true victim. Instead of a leader. A functioning anachronism. That satisfied the political quota. Refusing to accept a painful reality, I played into the hands of the 'old boys club'. In doing so, I lost my ideals to help students. And teachers. And myself." She waited, watching. "Do you know why I'm telling you this?"

"No."

"Because I don't want you to do the same thing. I want you to take the Assistant Principal job. To ensure genuine reform. And when you do that, you'll be attacked. Savagely. You won't, can't, survive. Unless you admit the politics. Unless you get help. Now, you don't have managerial experience. I can tell you what not to do. Not what to do. May I speak candidly?"

"Sure. Yes."

"Your wife is in business management? Perhaps she can help?"

"She's successful. But we don't' talk about how. How she does it."

Allsbury spread her hands. "I can only tell you what I've learned. Call me foolish. Silly. Many people do. What I mean is: don't make the mistake I did. Or you'll be unable to help students. Or teachers. Or yourself." She relaxed. "I'll smooth out these complaints. With the proper people. So you can get involved in Reform. True reform." She smiled. "Thank you for your time."

---

# CHAPTER XI

## *A Proposal*

"OK. What you're sayin' is you want us to be what—'involved'?" Aldo emitted one of his irritating, raucous horselaughs. "Mr. B, we're already 'involved' now. Sorta. Sounds like lots of more work. You should go easy on yourself, Mr. B. Give yourself a break. Don't overdo. You already got your memories. And you'll be retiring pretty soon. So you don't want to cloud up your record." His guffaw was an additional effort to attract attention.

"What you makin' this changes for, Mr. B? Was OK up to now. Kinda."

"An opportunity to analyze reality. A real event. For ourselves, not someone else's version of it. An event that hasn't been predigested...."

"Ugh! That's yuk." Griselda turned down the corners of her mouth, grasping her lower lip with her teeth.

"Won't that mean we'll have to have some ideas about it? For ourselves?"

"Precisely the point, Rigo. After you've deciphered the facts, unexpurgated, you'll draw your own conclusions. And in the process, you may devise some new concepts: of your own. Or refine some you already had."

"We not going to follow the State Standards?"

"There is no specific state Standard for this Project. So, yes, we set our own. Our own Project. How well we carry it out, is up to us." Besserian arched his eyebrows. "Does everyone have a copy?"

"A copy of what?" There was a flurry of excitement. Papers moved rapidly among the desks.

"Hey, I didn't get both pages."

"Over here, girl. You forgot me."

"I just gave you it, 'Sandro. So, you can just go look around, Mr. Big Mouth. You need to pay attention to stuff. That's why you don't know nothin'. Serve you right, boy."

Allisandro squeezed the bulk of his six-foot frame into the molded plastic desk. "I get more on testes than you do. What you get on that last one, girl?"

"Watch who you're calling girl," she hissed, "Boy!"

"Let's get organized here. Macrina, would you make sure everyone has a copy of the Project outline? Both pages?"

"Yeah. A time bomb! Hey! Mr. B! You hear about the bomb threats that's . . ."

"Let's talk about that later. Right now, we need to get the work started."

Jesus held his copy close to his eyes, grasping it firmly as if to subdue it. "Hard ass stuff, man." He furrowed his brows. "This'll wear out our brains. We got our whole lives ahead of us, Mr. B. You don't want us to have a 'total school experience'?"

"When we supposed to be able to get this done? Holy shhhh . . . t."

"Mr. B, Jesus, he said a cuss word. He's bad!"

"Jesus. Watch your language." Besserian assumed a mock solemnity. "There are ladies present."

"Where? I don't see none." Jesus twisted in his seat, surveying the room loftily, his laugh reverberating over the banter.

"He wouldn't know what to do if he did see none."

"Ladies and gentlemen. Personal remarks are out of place. As you can see, this Project requires cooperation. And respect. Everyone working together."

"Guys, let the teacher talk. Give him some air space."

Besserian waited for the restlessness to subside.

"Great. Let me explain so there won't be any confusion and everyone will understand exactly what will happen. The goal."

Griselda pulled spindly legs onto her seat. "This don't make sense to me. We're not used to this kind of stuff. We're not supposed to get work that makes us to go outside of the school. That's why we's supposed to have a classroom for us to work in. No! This is no good. Our parents won't like it. They don't want us doing this kinds of harassment. Causing us stressful. They say teachers gives too much work, anyhow. Gonna see my counselor on this. She gets after teachers who hassles kids: gives more work than kids supposed to do."

"You don't even know what it is. Let the teacher explain, like he's trying to do. Looks like something we could learn from. Could let us advance ourselves." Felipe Estrada pulled his desk closer to Sandra Guzman and jabbed at one of the paragraphs with his fist. "Looks like a plan. Let the teacher explain hisself." The young man nodded affirmatively. "Looks like we could get some special experience. Like we don't get in some other classes." He flicked the paper with his thumb and middle finger.

"Mr. B, this Project mess up football practice? 'Cause otherwise Coach McCauley's gonna' have a appendix fit. He says that any time teachers gives work that cuts into practices and makes guys work too much, he's going to the Principal. Or to the Superintendent."

"Or to the CIA! We got our rights!"

"Project will give you the chance to see politics in action. Some of you can vote already."

"I already did. For Clinton and Monica?" Francisco Mendoza whispered loudly to Marvella and they both contorted in laughter. "She said she wanted a man she could look up to."

"Gets us out of Jurassic Park. Into the here and now!"

"Francisco. You're interested in politics. What I want us to achieve here, with this Project, is your participation in the development of an historical event. Not watching: but doing. Not learning someone else's conclusions. Forming your own. In other words you analyze the documents and ask, 'What does this mean?'. Why does it mean that? Why is it important? And for whom?' You ask the questions. You give the answers. Not the text book."

"Sorta like us be writing the history book!"

"Exactly."

"Cool. I like this. Some s…stuff, man."

"School's like being caught in a loop. That's why they give us history books. They're supposed to tell us stuff and then we know what to think about stuff."

"Macrina, let me explain my thinking and you can see if you agree. You're right. We don't have access to documentation, primary sources we call them, about, for example, the Crusades, the Thirty Years War. Nor do we have the language skills. Even in U. S. History, we can't look at original documentation of historical events."

"We could do stuff on dinosaurs! I mean there's plenty of stuff on TV and the Internet and all." Aldo guffawed, looking around for corroboration of his humor, but finding none, turned back to Besserian. "Got you, man. Sorry. Go for it."

"This should be an opportunity to observe the historical process unfold." He pointed to the outline. "Reform Plan is important. And we have access to information about it. I've cleared everything with the school district. They've agreed to let us look at the documentation. Based on our analysis we'll decide for ourselves whether we think the Plan should be approved. Or not. We'll write our reports and give evidence to support our opinions. I think people will be interested in what we have to say. What we've found out. And why."

"How do we get marks for this? What about GPA?[19] I don't think my counselor's going to like this."

"Yeah. Miss Brauphman and Miss Lopez-Workman? They not like teachers messin' with students GPA's. And tellin' stuff about what they say to them. Says that's personal. Gets kids screwed up. Stresses them. Makes them paranoid."

"It's like we're looking for evidence of things, Mr. B?"

"Exactly. Evidence. Connections. And we'll be working together."

"Sounds like about a story my uncle told me? Finding out stuff? Some place in like: Iceland? People wanted some new water pipes for the city but then one guy investigated the plan? And then found out that the plan would help some people but hurt others, 'cause the pipes had dirty water? Not clean like they thought? And people was getting sick. Poisoned instead of made healthy? But if the guy hadn't investigated the Plan nobody woudda knowd. And what to do? Either way somebody would get screwed. The investigating guy was like torturing himself what to do."[20]

"You do that, Jesus. To people. Jest by lookin' at them. What you complaining about?" Veronica Valdez seemed bored. "Mr. B what about credit? We're gonna' be marked on this, right?"

---

19 GPA: Grade Point Average: A=4; B=3; C=2; D=1; F=0. Add letter grade values and divide by four.

20 Ibsen, H. *An Enemy of the People.*

"This will be Extra Credit. Raise your GPA because it will be extra points. How many people ever get a chance to do original historical research? Not many."

"Supposin' some of us don't want to? Do this?"

"You don't have to, Gloria. Completely voluntary. Nothing will count against you if you don't want to. But, I think, once you start, you'll find it interesting. And want to continue. The point is to find out for yourselves. The reality of a political event."

"But, Mr. B., how about if the records we'll be reading don't tell us the right stuff?"

"That's for you to decide. If you think the information is slanted or incomplete, then you'll include that in your final report. If you think the records are trying to hide something."

"So, when's our class time? For this?"

"Mostly after school. Three hours a week. You divide yourselves into groups: four or five per group? We'll go to the school district after school. Tuesdays and Thursdays. I've arranged transportation. And also, we can do some work here, in our regular class to compile notes, write reports, that sort of thing. Occasionally we may be able to go during class time. Mr. Baques has approved that. As I said, I'll be working with you."

"I don't think my mom's gonna' go for this. She wants me in school all day."

"Again, this is voluntary. In that case, Rigo, you can do another extra credit project: Ms. Weatherby's class, if you prefer. Project is completely voluntary. If you don't participate, it won't hurt your grade. You decide."

"How about if before we jump into this we try it out first? See if it works? My uncle sad that when he was in RECON, in Nam? That's what they did. Not jump into a hole without checking out what's in it. First. I mean you can't never tell. Could be snakes and all."

"Or big ass ole' poisonous frogs. Like the ones in Tasmalia...or some place. You can tell! The brighter they are is how poisonous they are. And lemme tell you. Some of them's flaming! And those guys can kill you!" Francisco reiterated the danger.

"We gonna' overdose on information! Cool."

"Mr. B. I seen this movie once where these people went into this, like big ass ole' dark, stone castle? It had big ole' high walls, barb wire, and prison cells, and torture rooms? And these guys found old papers in some wood chests? And then these other guys came in and tied them up and stuck stuff in them to torture them. There was lots of blood and they was screaming."

"I don't think any of us will be in physical danger, Jeffrey. Obviously, you can help us out. Should that occur."

"Cool." Francisco gave the thumbs-up sign. "You be our leader, Mr. B. We straighten 'em out. Good. For you."

"Mr. B, you can't never tell. About who might cause trouble? My uncle was in 'Nam? A Navy Seal?"

"You said RECON before."

"Let Jesus talk, Monica."

"And he said that our army guys, they used to torture people there. But nobody didn't say nothin' about it. He said it wouldn't matter nohow, 'cause nobody would do nothing' even if they was to find out."

"He was probably the one doin' it. Else, how'd he know about it? Like you would, Jesus. Bet you'd *like* that. Totally. Perverted stuff. Like that. Ugh!"

"Hey girl, you better watch your ...."

"Griselda, Jesus is giving us the benefit of his uncle's experience: first-hand information. Let's accept it as such. He knows and we don't. Case in point: with this Project, we find out for ourselves. First hand information. About the reform plan. Like Jesus' uncle did about the Vietnam war. As you say, Griselda, there's the possibility that people won't want to hear the information. It's a risk we take."

"What you want to do this for, Mr. B? I mean you never did this in other years?"

"Good point, Rigo." Besserian rubbed the thin spot on the top of his head and paced the front of the room. "No, I didn't do it with other classes. It's new. For me. We'll discover new information. Think for ourselves ..."

"Like outside the box, Mr. B?"

"Exactly. Learn to respect each other's ideas: to pursue avenues of inquiry that otherwise we might not have considered; get ideas from each other. New information. Learn how to disagree. Because we're not all going to react the same way to the information. Whatever we find."

"Cool, man."

"So, it's like we're Historians, ourselves?"

"Exactly. Researching something that's important to us. Each of us. Somewhat like playing a role: of detective."

"Sounds like a winner, sir."

"Isn't History supposed to be all about kings and queens and wars and dates and stuff? And dead people?"

"Most people only know what's told to them. If what they're taught in school, newspapers, TV is distorted, or incomplete, there's no way they can challenge the distortions. Even be aware of them." He continued pacing, thinking aloud. "Now, how do you think you might be using the information you'll be getting?"

"To pass your tests?"

"More than tests, Alessandro, I hope."

"So everybody gets a 'A'? Hey, a winner. Cool."

"Here's where it gets interesting. You'll compile your information, analyze it, and make conclusions: decide if Reform Plan will benefit Cathedral Heights in general and our school in particular."

"Then we'll all get a 'A'?"

"Maybe we could sell it? The information?" Rigo was excited.

"You sell it on the street, man! And Mr. B, he's gay."

"How do you know Allisandro?" Besserian accepted the invitation to join the game.

"Look! Look at him! Can't you tell!"

"Watch that." Rigo glared at Allisandro, exchanging laughter, feinting punches at each other.

"Guys. You'll be responsible for accuracy and completeness. That's essential. If you don't have time to check everything, then record what you didn't have time to look at."

"Not the way it works in Mr. Warfles History class. Kids has to say the way it is in the book or else he don't like it. Yells at them."

"So, after your research you have several choices: a report to the School Board, an article for the newspaper, organize a public discussion forum. Who knows? We'll see after we get the information."

"Hey, we could have a senate investigation. Cool!"

"Possibly. Or you might discover leads to other sources of information. It's up to you."

"Mr. B, seems like you be puttin' lots of work on yourself. You sure you want to do this? I mean you're not as young as you used to be. Like you say, you didn't do nothin' like this before. I mean we didn't."

"It will mean some more work, yes, Marco. For all of us. But you'll be reaching a goal."

"What's that?"

"Finding out the facts: the reality. Of the Reform Plan. Allow us to see things we might not have seen before. That's what school, what learning, our relationships in this class, should be."

"But, Mr. B? How about if something gets screwed up? Mr. B, I seen this movie where this guy never thought he could do nothin', and that his ole man and his brother didn't think he was any good: that he was, like bad, and so he wanted to prove he was as good as they was, and he grew up some lettuce to send back east for some war, but the lettuce rotted in the train cars and he was worse off than he was to begin with. And they still didn't like him. And then he found his mom. In a different town? And she sorta ran a . . . special kind of house? With ladies. And he knew he wasn't bad. And she wasn't bad. They was the same. Then both of them figured out they had to be like they really was. Not like what other people said they should be."

"Acceptance of the reality of another person? Isn't that love? Strength? When it doesn't hurt anyone else. Robert?"

"He was cool."

"Well, maybe he shouldn't of tried at all. Might of been better off before when he didn't find out nothin'?"

"Maybe. Perhaps, Gloria. Remember he found out he wasn't bad. Nor was his mother. When you face reality, honestly, you're good."

"Sounds like he got to like himself? Mr. B? When's it OK to like yourself?"

"My opinion, Allisandro? When we're doing something we believe in. Not because somebody told us it *should* be important to us. And we don't hurt anyone else in the process."

"So, like feel good about our work? You feel good about your work, Mr. B? About being a teacher?"

He waited. The room was silent. They waited. "I feel good. About this Project."

"Mr. B, this is like 'hands-on' for us?"

"Exactly. See it happen. As it happens."

"Cool shit, man!"

"Hector, inappropriate talk in a classroom. Guadalupe, you have a question?"

"Sure do. We're not supposed to be doing stuff like this. We're supposed to be reading from the book and learning like they do in other classes? I don't like this. I don't see that this is the purpose of school. Miss Cort-yair? She's my French teacher? She says that lots of kids get screwed up if somebody tells them languages comes from dead stuff like Latin or Greek, and that ain't true and that's why we not supposed to learn old languages and stuff. Don't need lots of complicated rules. Grammar? She says grammar comes from the present. Whatever way people talk now is the way they should talk. She says we should stay in the present time because that's where the only important things come from. Learn from what you can see going on around you. Not from past stuff."

"My uncle said that when they was in 'Nam, one time he had to lead his patrol across this big ole river, the Nile, ...."

"That's in India, creep!"

"Go on Jesus. But could you make it brief? We're running out of time?"

"OK. Well, when they got in the water, they couldn't turn back because there was crocodiles in the river and they came swimmin' after them, fast as they could. And you know what Mr. B? He said crocodile's jaws works the opposite to the way alligators' jaws works, they open ..."

"Fascinating. Totally!" Gloria yawned.

"What could you know? Was you there?"

"No, and I don't wanna be."

"And the only thing the Marines could do was think about gettin' to the other side, fast as they could. And one of them had his foot bit off and there was blood all over and ..."

"Stop! That's yukkie! Tell him to sto-o-o-p Mr. B! And that never happened anyway."

"Your point Jesus is well taken: the Marines suffered incredibly severe hardships, for what they were told they should believe in. Everyone doesn't have that: heroism. Were their leaders worthy? Of that trust? And I agree. Finding your own ideals? What's *right* for you, and living up to them: that's also heroism."

"What if, maybe, you have too high anticipations about this, us, Mr. B?" Jesus lounged in his seat. "I mean it probably looks good and all, but you know the old saying: the higher you fly, the further down you have to fall?"

"So, if you don't fly, you won't fall and get hurt? But the bird who doesn't try to get off the ground is more vulnerable. The bird needs to know that."

"But we're not birds."

Besserian nodded agreement to Gloria and noted another hand. "Sandra. Yes."

"It seems to me that if we want to learn how to take control of city government and business and all, we'll we need to begin that now. Where else can we start? This looks like a Plan to me. Go for it! Gives us a chance to find out about how schools work behind the scenes."

Besserian nodded. "I think so, Sandra."

Marco sauntered to the pencil sharpener, watched intently by several girls. "Hey, boy, you're standing at that sharpener for a long time. And you don't have a pencil in your hand. What you going to stick in there?"

"Griselda, you need to avoid personal remarks. In the classroom."

"My uncle ..."

"No, not again. Save us!"

"Go on Jesus but they're only a few minutes before the bell."

"My uncle told me about this story of a guy in like ancient times who was pushing a big rock up a hill? And every time he got right up to the top, some bad guy came along and made it to roll back down to the bottom and he had to start over pushing it up again. And he had to do this for lots of years. Like forever?"

"And?"

"So, for a long time I didn't really like that story? Then I began to think? That lots of stuff in life's not so easy? That maybe what life's all about is problems. How to deal with them. Best as you can. They just keep happening. You might to wish they'd stop. Sure. But they don't."

"Sounds like a good observation, Jesus."

"And we figured out when we was talkin'? Me and my uncle? That there's personal stones to keep pushin' up the hill? And other stones that everybody should have to push up together? Or they could be run over?"

"I agree. As you imply pushing that stone up the hill over and over gave him more dignity than the people who didn't struggle to push anything at all? Who just watched?"

"See what you mean, sir."

"Moral of your uncle's story might be that success comes from the dignity of the effort itself. The risk? The actual rock, getting it to the top was incidental to the fundamental issue of his own determination and courage. Maybe a lot of us have a 'rock' in our lives?"

"Maybe life, just living, is the rock?"

"Good point, Rigo. Are we going to cry 'victim'? The reality, like it or not, is the rock. Are we going to let it roll back? Crush us? Not try to push it up again? Expect—wait for—somebody else to push it up for us? Because that's easier? In the process of pushing, we can learn about ourselves. Achieve dignity."

"Go for it, Mr. B. I have confidence in you."

"On a roll, man." Felipe grinned. "That's a pun?"

"All of us need to trust our inclinations. And then test them."

"We'll follow in your footsteps, Mr. B."

"More like walking together, Felipe. Pushing together. Our own rock."

# *CHAPTER XII*

## *Mutual Needs*

Besserian had seen Buck even before the other man shouted to him over the hysteria of the crowd, the screeching coaches and players; the blaring loud speakers.

"Hey. Over here!" Buck gave the 'thumbs up' sign and pointed to an empty place. Manipulating his way up the steps, Besserian sidestepped misplaced fingers and hands. He heard his name called and waved: students, parents, some teachers.

Buck's attention was divided between the game and emphatic interchanges with neighboring fans. In the row in front of him, someone pushed over and pointed to a spot for Besserian.

A piercing blast from the referee's whistle. The attention of the enormous room shifted instantly from the limitless distractions, coalescing on center court. The players swarmed over each other chasing the ball, darting, turning, jumping: arms up, arms down, arms extended. One, wrenching the ball, sprinted to the opposite end of the court. A breakaway! The crowd was catapulted into an emotional frenzy—a collective clarion call as it detonated its surfeit of emotion and physical exuberance. They stamped their feet, whistled, shouted for their team, bawled against their opponents, twirled their noise-makers desperately—as quickly as the stubby little hand grips would permit—waved their arms deliriously, kicked their legs, rang cow bells, emitted blasts from compressed air foghorns, booed, prayed, cajoled, pleaded, and praised. Their ecstasy was irrepressible: affirmative, negative, directionless.

The screaming of the players on the court was amplified by their comrades along the sidelines who exploded like frenzied banshees, running, jumping, grasping each other frantically and desperately, as they screeched encouragement to their own team and imprecations against their adversaries.

Besserian looked over his shoulder several times. Buck was caught up in an animated discussion about the motives and competency of the referee. "God-damm bummer! That guy must hate our asses. What the hell is the matter with him? Sexist bastard." But he was in his element. His outpouring led to an enthusiastic and heated exchange with another fan, emphasizing his point by grasping the man's shoulder, although he addressed his remarks to the wife, who, relishing the attention, nonetheless kept her eyes fastened on the game.

Play was interrupted: punctuated on all sides by accusations and gesticulations of resentment, petulance, outrage, or exuberance. And always: noise. Bellowing. Rage.

Penny had relayed Buck's suggestion about the game.

At the edge of the court, two tuba players um-phed out of unison, augmenting the overall cacophony. It heralded the appearance of the *Adorables*, who made a vaudeville type entrance, arms entwined behind waists, and kicking high—as high as possible—with varying degrees of skill. The movements of their 'routine' were disjointed: legs widespread, crouching low on the floor in a masquerade of sultriness, twirling, high-stepping, then, inelegant leaping. Their efforts were sporadic as they tired quickly, especially those who were 'large'.

Each was clad in a 'low rise' mini-skirt. Their mid-sections, exposed from far below the navel to just beneath artificially upturned breasts, were painted either brown or yellow, and imprinted with a brown or yellow contrasting letter. The intended composite was 'Knights'. In the excitement, however, pawing each other petulantly, the letters were rearranged: 'KNIGHTS' became 'KNGSHIT'. Unaware or unperturbed, the young ladies completed each 'routine' by wildly embracing one another, touching their toes, backs toward the audience, kicking out their legs in paroxysms of gleeful self-satisfaction. Signaling the climax of their importunities, swirling their miniscule skirts—revealing their panties—they tumbled into kneeling positions, to watch, squint-eyed, sweating, with baffled expressions, the desperate movements of the players on the court. 'Our young ladies' as Mr. Baques styled them at the weekly Pep Rallies, were disorientated and fatigued.

To Besserian's analytical eye their role was unclear. Traditionally, their gyrations would have complimented the players. Now, because the players were female, their blatant sexuality was what? Surfeit? Compensation?

The Knight coach, exhibited another form of aggression. In skintight, fawn-colored, polyester pantsuit, she checked and rechecked her clipboard, pounding it with the end of her pen, screwing up her mouth in consternation. She had thrown off the jacket, revealing the "S" shape of her slim figure, rolled up her sleeves and loosened her regimental tie. The tailored shirt emphasized her protruding mid section and narrow shoulders. She strutted, paced, and stomped on the sidelines, shouting shrilly at her players, who, when summoned, either from the floor or the bench, crept to her, and crouched like terrorized Neiblungs at her ankles, watching with adoring but fearful expressions, until, having vented her spleen at the other team, the referee, or, as was usually the case, one of her own, ordered the replacement onto the court; her staccato directives, alternatively registering disgust, anger, rage, and resentment. She strutted with huge strides and turned intermittently, legs spread exaggeratedly, banging one fist into the other, to display her fury to the crowd, epitomizing the requisite level of indignation.

Indeed, the rival coach was cast from the same mould: trotting up and down the sidelines, grabbing players by the shoulders, arms or necks, pushing others with a slap on the seat of their long, billowing, skirt-like 'shorts'; remonstrating, cajoling, condemning, executions of play. Beside herself with emotion, positive or negative, lauding or reviling, she leaned forward, teetering; toes precisely on the colored line, thrusting back her posterior, magnificently outlined by the synthetic fabric stretched to breaking point, arms extended wide on either side, hurling indiscriminate invective. She looked to be poised to execute a fantastically unorthodox dive, so that possibly, under the excruciating pressure of the moment, unable to endure her own spleen for one additional millisecond, she might actually catapult herself physically, as well as verbally, into the maelstrom on the court.

The reaction of the players to their coaches was the same. Besserian recalled the dog fight, behind someone's garage, he had unwittingly attended at the urging of Jesus Gutierrez: the expression of dread shown by the Pit Bull, immediately prior to being released into the ring, as it comprehended the steel in the eye of its owner, resolutely tapping the butt of the heavy whip against his boot, warning the animal of the consequences of defeat.

The gymnasium was a bewilderment of resonant buzzers, whistles, garbled announcements, trombones, tubas, coronets, frenzied shouts, the entire deafening din exacerbated by reverberations against the steel girders high above—crisscrossed with pipes and ducts.

"You having the best time of your life? Here, scoot over." Buck was beside him, angling into the next spot, calming the objections of the adjacent spectator with his self-confident smile and a caressing pat on the back punctuated with, "Great game, eh? Our gals sure showing 'em! Looking good! Damm good! Should ace the championship this year." He spoke without taking his eyes from the binoculars with which he surveyed the players and the spectators. "Here, have a look."

Besserian swung the glasses over the court. He was struck by the near exhaustion of the players, stooping, hands on their knees, or, gulping huge mouthfuls of air, hands behind their necks, weakly calling encouragement to one another.

From the other team, came remarks of deprecation to the girl, steadying herself, hyperventilating. Having run both hands through drenched hair, she wiped them on the back of her billowing shorts, grasped the ball and analyzed the basket with the scrutiny of a diamond cutter poised to strike the critical blow. Mouth hanging wide, her face a study of total concentration, she crouched into a near kneeling position. And released the ball.

Soaring high, obviously euphoric in the mission entrusted to it, the sphere rose gracefully and slowly into a beautifully formed parabolic arc. Hovering at the vertex, suspended, reluctant to complete its task, it was the cynosure of eighteen hundred eyes. Silence gripped the vast, sweat-drenched room. Every eye riveted on the descent. The beautiful precision of the downward completion of the arc: the absolute self-confidence of the sphere. Slowly. Precisely. Resolutely. Basking in the total attention, it prolonged the final moment of ecstasy as nine hundred mouths sucked in air, breathless at the agonizingly beautiful delay.

Finally: the consummate logic: the irrefutable, inevitable, magnificent mathematics. Eighteen hundred ears heard with astonishing clarity the music of the 'swish' as the ball, completing its downward path, the achievement of its arc, caught the net and rested inside the metal hoop just long enough for every eye to savor the precision of the placement. . . and fell to the floor with an audible bounce: spent, exhausted, totally self-satisfied that it had accomplished something perfect.

The crowd erupted. Players ran together and enveloped each other in a surfeit of hugs and kisses, shrieks and screams. Their coach, however, disdained this outpouring. She strutted, mimicking, probably unintentionally, Mussolini reviewing adoring troops from the loggia of the Victor Emmanuel monument. She confronted the crowd disdainfully. Grasping her waist with both hands, lower jaw thrust forward, she threw back her head, shoulders gyrating, and stood, legs widespread, consumed by the mindless adulation that drenched her.

Buck, caught in the emotion, clamped Besserian heavily on the back. He turned to several others exchanging various kinds of physical contact to reaffirm mutual values. "Great game. Get a load of Twenty-One, the way he handled the ball? Spectacular!"

The woman near him interjected, "They happen to be a *girls* team, sir."

Apparently, Buck didn't hear. "These guys should go the whole nine yards to the finals. Great!"

He brought his face close, within inches of Besserian's. "Say. Surprised you made it. Glad you did." Buck scrutinized him. "You don't like this do you? Too much 'hands on'? Not intellectual enough?"

"I like it OK. Anyway, part of my 'extra duty' assignment. I have to. And it shows support for the kids. They appreciate it. I promised them I'd be here. Important to them. These girls are putting out a hell of an effort."

"Tell you what. Almost over. Let's get out of here. How about it?"

Besserian nodded and they picked their way down the steps, Aldo, Jesus and Rigo spotted him. "Hey, Mr. B. We already got our homework done." They slapped one another on the back, laughing exuberantly, acknowledging their teacher to associates. Besserian waved, almost losing his balance. "Sorry, Miss. Thank you. Excuse me." The two men made their way to the main doors and into the relief of the relative quiet outside.

"Gets a little stressful. But it's important to support the kids."

"Good politics. Me too. Doesn't hurt. Except the eardrums. Where you parked?"

"Teachers' lot. How about you?"

"You can give me a ride to my car."

They edged through the outside throng.

"Hey, Mr. B. Catch you tomorrow, man."

He gave the 'thumbs up' sign to a student he didn't recognize.

"Good game, eh?"

"Very good. Excellent. Commitment. Motivation. Conditioning. Skill. They've got it all."

They were at the side entrance to the parking structure. "Watch those loose gates," Buck observed indifferently. "Screwed up security here. Bad management. Typical." He shook his head in disgust.

Besserian found the car and maneuvered up the ramp slowly. Others were leaving early, as well.

"So, you liked it?"

"Sure, I liked it. It was interesting."

"That coach? She knows what she's doing."

"She does?"

"Look at the results."

"Results? OK. What are they?"

Buck was drumming the edge of the seat, hands between his legs. He watched out the window moving his head methodically. "What do you mean, what are . . .? He catapulted out of his slouching. "Shit!" He banged the windshield. "Over there!"

"What?"

"That's where my car is. Supposed to be." Then he exploded. "Why that cunt! She took my car. I'll be fucked! God damm!"

Besserian looked at him incredulously. "What's the matter?"

"Shit. Car's been stolen. That's *what*!" He gulped a huge mouthful of air, striking the dashboard with his fist.

"I'll get Security."

"No, you won't get fuckin' Security."

"If somebody stole your . . ."

"If somebody stole my asshole. Shit! Nobody stole my fuckin' car. She's just getting back at me."

"Who? What do you . . .?"

"Forget it. Sort it out tomorrow. She just wants attention. Should never have given her they keys." He punched the seat between his legs several times, shaking his head at the absurdity of the situation. "Shit, now what?" He slapped a fist into his left palm. "Hate being dependent on people. Now, I don't have a car. I need a drink. Beer?"

"Sure, OK. Maybe. Where?"

"Any place. I give a rat's ass. I'll show you."

*******************************************

"Well! My, my, my! If it isn't our little wandering boy! Bucky! Wonders never do cease! Come to get your car?" Pushing forty, her black rayon dress boasted a flashing rhinestone broach. She put the drink down in front of him displaying deep cleavage—a movement with which her dress cooperated fully. "How about your friend? What'll it be, muscles? You look like you could use a shave."

"OK. You got back at me. We're even. And yeah! He could use a bourbon on the rocks and some quiet."

"No need to get your ass in a sling about it. You in a bad mood, sweetie? Car? Got you over here!"

"Hey, Arlene, you got me, OK? Now lay off! I got a couple of things to think about right now."

"Like that dinner somebody promised me?" She scrutinized Besserian, jangling ice cubes in a glass and reached for a bottle in the well. "Seems like somebody doesn't want to remember."

"Some fruit juice will be fine for me, Miss."

She sucked her teeth loudly, dumped the ice out of the glass and reached for another container. "Here you go, sweetie. Take it slow." She pushed two glasses on their useless postage stamp napkins, scrutinizing Besserian carefully. "You got big wrists. You a trucker?"

"No, he's not a trucker. He's a animal trainer."

"OK. OK. The dominant type. Interesting. OK. Sure! I can live with that." She nodded appreciatively.

"Say, Arlene, why don't you take care of those guys at the other end of the bar? What time you get off? Tomorrow?"

"How about ten?"

"I'll pick you up."

"Go to your club?"

"Yup. So wear something nice. Give those old fuckers something to get excited about. Not that most of them could do anything about it anyway."

She slid a thumbnail against lower front teeth. "OK. Make sure you don't forget! This time—especially with anybody in your office? If you take my meaning? Huh!"

Buck gulped and splashed his drink on the front of his shirt.

"Did I say somethin'?"

"Other end of the bar, *rapido*, or no dinner tomorrow."

"OK! OK! Just, gimme a break! Some people! Talk about *controlling*!"

Buck winced, stared into his glass, then looked slowly at Besserian. "She doesn't know what she's talkin' about. Not all there." He rubbed his palms across his forehead, wetting his elbows from the spilled drink. "Shit!

Can't even wipe the counter." He turned and looked up. "Give me a couple of napkins, will you? You OK?"

"I'm OK."

Buck squinted, inhaled deeply, moped the liquid, and flicked the napkins into the well behind the counter. He ran one finger inside his collar. Neither man spoke. They listed to the murmur of seductive laughter from the other end of the bar.

"Penny's got a good future with Tri-Delt. Works hard. Professional. All the way. And the company's going places. Into the big time. It's possible this Reform Plan can work for TriDelt. She'll move with it."

"How?"

Buck tugged at his loosened tie, stuffing it into his jacket pocket. "Get school district into more investments. Bond issues, mostly. For reform programs."

"Doesn't Pritchard do investments? Bonds?"

Buck stood and adjusted the bar stool as if it were an irritating competitor. "Not really. Right now, buddy, it's how Reform Plan can help you." He gulped his drink. "And back to what we were talking about before. What do you think of the team? The girls? Pretty good? No? Yes?"

"Very good."

"But you don't like them?"

"I admire their skill. They're obviously talented. Obviously work hard. Very hard. Committed to each other. Probably to the coach, too."

"You didn't like her, did you?"

"She's a bully."

"She pissed you off. Obvious. Why? She's a teacher. Like you."

"Not like that."

"Maybe you should be. Instead of bitching about her, why not learn something from her?"

"I'm supposed to learn from that ranting? So once again! Here we go! You know all about teaching! Is there anything you don't know? Damm! Give me a break, man!"

"You're hung up on her style. So you can't see what she's doing. That maybe, just maybe, she's got her head twisted on right. That she knows what she wants. What they want. What she needs. What they need. And she's providing it. Maybe she's figured out that in order to meet their needs, she has to meet her own. First. And she's not afraid to say so. That's what pisses you off."

"What the hell are you talking about? So, now I'm afraid? Wonderful! What am I doing here?"

"Hold on a minute. Maybe she understands something you don't. Sure, they're worth a lot to her. But she's not just taking. She's giving. Giving them something they need: develop their skills. She's letting them be the winners they are. But didn't know how to be on their own. What pisses you off the most? She's figured out about needs: theirs and hers."

"But I haven't! Great!"

"Hang on, buddy. Before you get your ass twisted into a knot. Again. No. I don't think you've figured out about Needs. Yours. Or the kids. You haven't taken the first swig. Not at all. She's way ahead of you boy. Your problem? I . . .

"Now, you're going to tell me." Besserian dripped sarcasm.

"You know something? I think you're afraid to do what that lady figured out a long time ago: how to be a good teacher. Sure . . .

"I got to get going."

". . . she rants, and struts. Forget that. That's style. Look at content. Maybe she can teach you something. Something you didn't know."

"Right." Besserian scowled and shook his head. "But you do."

"C'mon. Sit back down. It's like sex. Take it wherever it happens. Even if it's not exactly what you're looking for. Shit! Improve your technique. Satisfy your needs. It's not a marriage! Not permanent. Big fuckin' deal, guy!"

He rubbed the back of his neck. "And this. It's about needs: theirs and hers. What you don't like is that they meet her needs: more money, lead to a better job. But? it's mutual. She meets theirs too. College scholarship? Maybe professional basketball? Coaching? Endorsements? Public accolades. Success. Big bucks."

"I know that."

"Right. You do. For them. But what irritates you is that you're not bound together with your kids. Like she is. With hers."

Besserian watched him saying nothing. Scowling.

"Problem you have, that the lady coach doesn't have—and that's why, really why, she pisses you off—is that the culture doesn't validate what you want for your kids. The way it does her."

"The gushing fount of wisdom. Never stops. So?"

"She gets the accolades. You don't. But! She works for them. She's got a realistic relationship with her gals. Not an imitation relationship."

"John Dewey the second! Wonderful. You know everything."

"Perhaps, *maybe*, you might be able to learn something from her. Even you."

"Me? Learn from her? About teaching? I can worship at the female temple.""

"Right. You can. You should, really. How do I know? Because she's like me. That's why I piss you off too. People who work for me fulfill my needs: money and power. Same time they fulfill their own needs."

"So, you're a bully, too. In your work? In social conversation. I would never have figured that out."

"Fuck bully! It's about results. I get my needs met. My people . . ."

"*My* people! Wonderful!"

"They get theirs. I'd be a bully only if they *didn't* get anything out of it. But they do. They get a lot. No. She's not a bully."

Besserian glared at the glass and twisted the useless napkin. "I already . . ."

"Your problem? You don't like that lady's style. She's aggressive. But—and it's a big but—she's reaching them. Giving them something. And you're not. And that bothers you. So much that you can't see beyond her tactics. They irritate you. That lady's got a strategy going there, buddy."

Besserian watched him; searching for the appropriate response. He scrambled . . . "I already started a . . ."

"Started! But not going yet. And I piss you off. Because I'm aggressive. And successful. Look at the money Penny's making! My people make . . ."

"*My* people! *My people*! They're your servants?"

"Shit! I give them a place to make money. Sure, for me. But, for themselves, too. That's my end of the bargain. It works two ways. For me. And for them. Where me and you are different . . ."

"May I suggest 'you and I'?"

"Fuck! Suggest whatever you want, if you want to be a dip shit about it. I'm leveling with you, buddy. How many people ever do that? Telling you what they've found out that works? If you don't want to hear it, get it, stay stuck in your hole, then fuckin' be my guest. Stay in your idealistic world of unreality. But don't keep kids in it."

Buck glared at him. "You know, buddy, you got yourself so wrapped up in that lady coach's 'style' that you've decided you don't like, that's somehow got to be inferior to yours, that you got fucking constipation of the brain. That you can't see what she's doing. For those girls. You need to give yourself a mind enema. Or get somebody give it to you."

Besserian slammed back off the bar stool, knowing he should do something drastic. But what? He tried glaring indignantly.

Buck stood up and backed away from him.

Arlene and her admirers glanced over from the other end of the bar. She laughed loudly and emptily. "Hey, you guys keep the noise down over there. We're trying to have a respectable conversation over here."

"Tell 'em, sweetie?" One of her associates jostled the other.

"OK. You're pissed. I was out of line. I can be an asshole at times. Here!" He held out his hand. Besserian looked at it. At him. Scowling, he took it reluctantly.

"Come on. Sit back down. OK. Right. In fact, you've got a bigger problem than Coach Superwoman does. You got to define kids needs. For them. She doesn't. And your kids can't tell you because they don't know. The culture doesn't validate academics. Like athletics. Athletic needs are built into the culture. Academics don't have stadiums—stadia, sorry—of eighty thousand all over the country. So? You got to show them? Am I right?"

Besserian remained sullen. He snorted reluctantly. "You said one thing right. Intentionally or unintentionally, you tied it to the essence of the reform problem: Reform has to decode the culture to find its real values. It says it values academics. That's the code. But it doesn't. It values self-preservation. Of the cultural institution. Public education."

There was only the drone from the other end of the bar with the occasional raucous interjection.

"We've talked long enough. Glad you didn't land me one in the teeth. You got to get home. Penny'll think you're up to something. You get out of here. Arlene'll give me a ride. Or my car. Enjoyed it. So? Both of us, *you and I,* aren't so different? After all?"

# *CHAPTER XIII*

## *Discussion*

"OK, folks. Thanks just a whole lot to all you for your turnout? Here? This afternoon? Team Fillmore! A Wow factor! Got to be, well, forty, maybe more, of you? Just a great turnout. And on your own time. Show your commitment. To Team. Well, I guess we all know why we're here...."

"Maybe you'd better clue us in Jose?"

"Right on Brember . . . "

"We need to recreate ourselves."

"Always, Laura. What we need to talk about today is some of the details of the Reform Plan. Its future. For us. There's some complaints with people sayin' they don't have a clue. So, the idea is we figure out how Plan will help us. What stays! What goes! So we reach in the barrel and come up with the right decision. For down the road. And right now, let's see, that's about seven months away. To finalize?"

Baques beamed. "So? Let's cut to the quick! Seems Señora Alma Arcáña, Board President elect and community liaison won't be able to be with us due to a previous conflict. So? Let's us to do a quick 'round robin' so's we can all know each other."

"Hey Joe! We already know each other. How about us play teacher some other time. Not on school time! Some of us got to watch *Sex in the City*, tonight!"

Either Baques chose to ignore Blaise Jackson, Computer Graphics, or he didn't hear. He was absorbed with Peter Pritchard who had just entered, shaking his hand warmly. "Always a pleasure Mr. Pritchard." He turned back to the audience. "But OK, then. We'll bypass the formalities for today so's we can move on. Mr. Pritchard? He'll be giving us the inside skinny."

"My pleasure, Mr. Baques. This will be a learning experience for me. I will learn teacher Needs."

"You'll sure learn that." Baques laughed self-consciously and turned to the other committee members. "Mr. Prichard'll see Team in action. And just a great Team. A super Team. Team Fillmore."

"He'll sure see somthin', that's for sure. Around here." Blaise batted his eyes. "No tellin' what, though, exactly!"

"Agenda?" Bruce Warfles emitted a horselaugh.

"I believe Marvella is ready to pass them out now. Let's move on folks." The principal exhaled a sigh of relief. "Everybody knows everybody else."

"I wish I didn't know him!" Brember Bathersea, Geography, smirked at AP Marvin Johansson."

"Hey, boy. Just don't you go baggin' on me! Jest wait 'till your next extra duty assignment. You'll find out, g'buddy!"

"Guys, I know you love each other. But for now, let me re-introduce two other guests. Probably you all know, Ms., i.e. Dr. Claudia Obesso from District? In charge of the all-important Bi-lingual/Bi-cultural programs. Very, very high priority, in our District to promote Diversity: I'm proud to say, of our esteemed Superintendent. And welcome to you, Ms. Obesso. Always our intense pleasure." He nodded his head slowly. "Also, Claudia is here also representing Dr. Jones-Laporte, our Superintendent who is, I believe on a teacher recruitment trip. I'm not sure just to where . . .."

"Just a fab itinerary, Mr. Baques: New York; London, England; Madrid, Spain; Paris, France; Nigeria, Africa; Jamaica, South America. She's determined to bring back the very best teaching talent back to us here in our District and to Fillmore. And I know we all appreciate that. She was just telling me before her departure on, get this: *Concorde*! Wow! What is it? Three hours JFK to Paris, France? Just the other day: in her so-beautiful office?" There was a smattering of applause.

Agnes Leavering, General Math, observed dryly, "Kind of far to go look for teachers, isn't it? I mean how many teacher training colleges are there right here in the Los Altos area? Fifteen? Twenty? And each of them with thirty plus graduates a year! They're not looking for jobs? They don't want to teach? And we need to spend that kind of money to bring in outsiders! From eight thousand miles away! Besides, I hear Jones goes first class everywhere! Hotels? Restaurants? Isn't *Concorde*, what? Minimum of $8,000 one way? And she went with three board members? That's what? Way over forty grand! Before expenses! Minimum. OK. Go for it. Local teachers are substandard? We need to bring in outsiders? Pay for their travel and expenses from Europe or Africa to here? People who don't know about our kids' culture? Say our kids speak low class Spanish. Not real Spanish like in Spain. And they supposed to promote Diversity?"

"And I hear those from Spain and Africa don't like our kids too much. Say kids not respectful enough. Not disciplined. Don't do their work. Got attitude."

"Folks, I won't lie to you. Relax. Nobody is saying local individuals are less than. Certainly not Dr. Jones-Laporte. She's determined to have only the very *best* for this District. The best ridership possible. Diversity is what it's all about. Let's not to forget that. We may need to remind ourselves. Each and every one of us know that Dr. Jones-Laporte is just super conscientious: an absolutely incredible person! And, she just might even be extending her trip, in that regard?"

"I heard French Riviera."

"You said about Bi-lingual? Diversity?"

"Miss Cortère? Our most recent acquisition. Yes, we need to hear a new viewpoint. Yours?"

"You should learn a lesson from us. Hinglish conquered us in 1760: let us keep our language, schools, French law. Our priests told us was OK because Hinglish let us keep Cadolic religion that was illegal in Hingland. *Quelle grandeur!* [21] Priests used us to protect der *institution*: not us. And Hinglish used priests to keep us quiet. Hinglish deceived us, true. But not so bad as our priests did. We trusted dem. You have a good expression: screwed without even a kiss."

Several in the audience smiled uncomfortably.

"So? What happ-én? French language, schools, law, religion: all keep us *sep-ar-ate*: second class citizens: tolerated so long as we behave ourselves. And we never had French culture to begin wid—we were laborers, immigrants—and Hinglish not allow us to have ders. We became what? No-ting. Frenglish. French laughed at our old fashioned pronun-ci-ation and expressions. Still do. And we couldn't understand the Hinglish. We were excluded by education, language from government, management,

21 *Quelle grandeur*! What munificence!

universities. Except on da lowest levels. Exactly what Hinglish wanted. And what Church wanted. Same purpose. Reasons diff-er-aunt."

"Your Diversity? Bi-lingual? Beats me! You do same ting to dees kids. Det Hinglish do to us. Best ting you do for dees kids is to sink em: in Hinglish. Lose der cul-ture? I give you some news. Dey lose it before dey get here. And Bi-lingual keep it lost. And not get dem what dey really need to survive here: your culture. And you say you helping dem! Helping dem do what?" She laughed sardonically.

"Why you tink we leave France? In da first place? Were low class. French not like us. Still don't. Same ting for dees kids. Dey got not-ing in common wid Spain. Or educated Mexicans. What culture you trying to preserve? And worst ting? You guys fooling yourselves: culture you say, you pretend, you want to give em? Not true. Bi-lingual give em a barrio culture det not help dem: make dem neider Mexicans nor Americans. I already said: make dem second class. You deny dem what dey need to be equal: your culture. Specially Hinglish language. Bi-lingual not 'transition' dem into Hinglish. Keep dem out of Hinglish. Bi-lingual is a myd. Not happen. You guys need what you call 'reality check'. About facts. On yourselfs. Do you—schools—want dees kids to be equals? Or not? Or you doin' it for political?"

Baques smiled uncomfortably. "OK. Ladies and gentlemen. Need to move on. Let's us do a follow-up on the Agenda or Mr. Pritchard might think we don't know what it is we do want." He chuckled and Peter Pritchard inclined his head toward his right shoulder, moving his hands laterally, palms down, fingers raised, an odd gesture, perhaps to ensure his detachment from the teacher-recruiting project.

Baques flashed his smile. "Mr. Pritchard? Perhaps you would start us off by clueing us in on any matters? Reform Plan? Reform might just be the 'handwriting on the wall' that we need."

"Mr. Baques, thank you. I appreciate the extent to which you are dedicated to community involvement. Permitting community members to participate. I think the best thing is for our group here, your team, to offer their observations and, if at any point I can help to clarify, well, I'll do my best. But no! It is your meeting. I am your guest. I want to hear *your* needs. And then work with Dr. Jones-Laporte and your Board to tailor our Reform Plan to meet them." He paused. "To reiterate, I do thank you for allowing me to attend."

"We get credit for being here, Jose?"

"You'll be remembered in my will, Agnes. Don't worry." Baques laughed weakly. "Anyway, I know it's late and you've all had a typically stressful day. Wow! You slugging it out in the trenches! And you have your families. Or your significant others! So let's all keep this as painless as possible here today, folks. And we can do that if we work together—pull as Team. And I do think we're a pretty special Team in that respect. Here, at Fillmore. I mean, if we can't do it together, well, I guess nobody can." He moved his head slowly in introspection, squinting. "Super staff. The best!"

Instead of the usual camel hair, Baques was sporting a voluminous, hooded, brown and gold nylon stadium coat that reached to his knees, sleeves covering his knuckles. On the front was emblazoned 'Fillmore Knights: Mr. Baques, Principal Cheerleader'. On the back was the emblem of a white knight: charging: lance at the ready.

"Bruce? Everybody? As you can see Agenda's pretty straightforward: Reform Plan: the Future of Fillmore. And the reason for leaving it in generalities everybody, was so's anybody who wants to, can just chime in and say what she or he thinks?"

Rayella Brauphman emitted twittering sounds and adjusted her oversized pink and white sweat shirt, with 'Love and Rainbows' chiseled across the front, as if to seat herself, but immediately had second thoughts. "Just to hold on a New York minute! Now, I just know Arnida's not expecting this, and I won't lie to you, but, well, it would be just real nice, if *some* of us could sorta', well, pitch in?" She was unsure whether to wait for a response. Blank stares responded to her entreaty. "Put a 'little something' in the jar on the counter? To thank her? I mean, after all, this *is her* Science classroom and these *would* be her cake and sodas? Gotten by her for her very own kids? But you guys recreate yourselves. Come to your own fullness! I just think it was real dixie of her to do it, that's all. For us!" She was on the verge of tears, contorting her bulk compulsively, corners of her mouth drawn down, eyes squeezed. "I'm sorry!" Narda Teklebrahan reached over and squeezed her forearm reassuringly, smiling benignly, offering the perennial 'tissue', guiding her into an adjoining chair.

"We do need to take things slow, guys. Qu-Yahni? Ms. Lewis?"

"Salaries? Will we be getting the kind of money we should be? Skip the BS. Let's talk turkey!" Her sweat shirt, with the letters O.L.L.4.O.P.P was mauve with pink lettering. [22]

"Super point. But before we get into this too far, I need to say that what we're doing here, is sorta 'makin' a list and checkin' it twice'? At this

22 O.L.L.4.O.P.P: Out Late Looking for Other Party People

point? The actual program, again and here's how I understand it, folks, will be a meltdown of what's on your needs assortments."

"So, really, we don't know what this Reform Plan is? Or will be? Correct?"

Baques hunched his shoulders and dug his hands deep into the jacket's bottomless pockets. He winced as if unexpectedly biting into a lemon. "Well, we're all sorta feeling our way, on that element, Narda. Still. But I can tell you it's not set in concrete. Leastways, not as yet. In all the details. So, once again. We're here today, and Marvella is right here beside me writing it all down—and just a super duper thanks to her on that?"

"Sort of a shopping mall list?"

"Right. To be forwarded to Elayne: Dr. Jones-Laporte, and the Board."

"So, an actual Plan, *per se*, is a nugatory—at this point, Jose?"

"Sandy! As per usual! In there slugging! Once again! We're here to make out our 'shopping list'? So the Plan, when it's completed, will have all of your items filling up the bag. The Reform shopping bag." Baques shook his head reassuringly. "And, I know Claudia will be partnering with us and the Board to bring our shopping bag into a fulfillment mode. We're still selecting from the medley."

"How is Plan going to resolve Dropouts? Of good students? And teachers? Or the non-working Discipline Policies. Drugs? Gangs? Physical and verbal violence?"

"Mr. Mugwabe, always in there pitching! Too! Right. Let me do a backstep on that for a minute. Today. Here. Right now. How about if we could make our list of items we want in the Reform Plan ...

"The Reform bag?"

"What about Teacher evaluations? Illegal Focus Walks that has teachers spyin' on each other?"

"Well, just make sure salaries at the top of anybody's list: all's I got to say."

"Thanks Arvetis. Sandy? Ms. Weatherby?"

"How about students roaming the campus every day? Must be over a hundred?"

"What about putting kids in classes they like and have skills for: auto, computers, woodshop, hair styling, electrical? Instead of keeping them failing Algebra, literature, science? What difference does it make whether they *can't or won't*? Bottom line? *Not!* Doing the work. Dropping out! Opting out!"

"I agree with her. That's why they're continuous problems to themselves. And to others. How's Reform going to change that? Help them?"

"Anybody ever think that maybe *Dropout's* not correct? Maybe should be *Pushed Out?* By us?"

"And I got kids who's on parole. In my Period Three? Parole? That means they were convicted of a serious crime. And I'm told I can't refer them for discipline problems. Parole Officer forced her way into my class; even though state law says not have to admit anyone except the Administrator. *She* said Parole Officer was 'special' and *I* couldn't *interfere* with *her* student!"

"I still say teacher salaries, all the way. Pay us what we're worth and the problems will go away."

"Somebody said kids roamin'? Out of class? So, try this on for size. I find out that those kids, out of class, are still carried on the school attendance roster. So school gets paid the same as if was in class."

"You're right, Mr. Huerta. I hear we show ninety-four percent in attendance but at the same time we got twenty percent plus out of class? Tax-payers know that we Mickey-mouse around with attendance? And that's big bucks! And administration allows it?"

"How about this! After ten consecutive absences, rules say we supposed to drop the kid permanently from the class rolls. So? I reported Alonso Sullivan to the counselor? Guess what? Kid stays on my class roster! Still not coming to class! No difference if I mark him absent. More than thirty days now! In effect, taxpayers are paying for a non-existent student! Multiply that by what? A couple hundred? Every day? That's how many thousand tax payer bucks? Five, six thousand? Per day?"

"Everybody knows Grade Twelve competency level for most kids is Grade Five through Seven. Right? What's Reform gonna do about that?"

"And let me piggy back on your thought, Cindye if I might. You know! You're in Special Ed. There's just lots of kids going into the army? Marines? Can't get jobs. Been messed up with the law? My question is we're training them for that? For cannon fodder?"

"Hey sit down, Fascistic! Go to another country if you hate this one: our Democracy! Anyway this still best country in the world. Don't care what Communistic says."

"No, I won't." The speaker, smoldering, abandoned his customary diffidence. "I'm not mouthing the political spiel. That's what's bothering you. My point is that some of these young males, already alienated, come out of gangs, that they joined here in this school. And got training in violence. From here, they go into the military: a military which increasingly, is finding it difficult to recruit. And therefore lowers its admission standards. Another factor: these young men want to legitimize their sex: by learning they don't have to be subservient. Don't have to be weak. That they're not inherently inferior. So, what happens? The military teaches them, as I said, weapons, fighting techniques, interrogations that include torture. And drugs. Tells them the rule of law is meaningless without power—guns—to enforce it. That power makes right! Taking control into their own hands, deciding on their own who gets killed and why. Deciding who, among the civilian population, is *their* personal enemy. They waged a personal war there. Now, doing it here."

"Those who aren't killed in the process, and many are, come back, and return to the gangs. Now, they're *senior* gang members, graduate students in violence, ready to train recruits, from this school, in violence: criminal activity."

"BS! Shut the f-up, guy! Who is this wierdo ...?"

"Sure, no one wants to hear this. It reverberates back on our present cultural values. On what we're doing or not doing in our schools. In this school! Shouldn't Reform at least *consider* strategies to involve our young men in learning, in utilizing their talents: academic and vocational so they *can* succeed *here*? Do we want to continue to live in a vacuum? Continue to deny that we're *not* preparing them to be self-sufficient, productive members of society? *Driving them out of the education we're supposed to be giving them*? Proof? Look at the number of gangbangers here at Fillmore! Those that we know about! Then look at our prisons! Reform? Needs to look at our part in channeling them into gangs? Into the military? Into prison! Shouldn't we acknowledge the reality of the problem? *Our* problem? That becomes *their* problem? Work with them? Not relegate them to second class status? Cut them off from the opportunities available to our gender-correct students? And you know what I mean by 'gender correct'! Give them the opportunity to succeed here so gang membership is an unnecessary option."

"Sit down!"

"Mr. Huerta. We need to stop. Frankly, I don't see how what you seem to be saying fits into school reform. But deal with that later. Let's wind down. And a report will go on to the Board. Bottom line, folks: if we don't protect ourselves? Then we can't protect students. In the meantime we'll be working with Mr. Pritchard to iron out all the tangles so we get the best possible Plan for each and every Fillmore Knight. Thanks again to our team—leastways those on it."

As Baques moved toward Warfles and Pritchard he called over his shoulder, "And Mr. Huerta, I *will* need to conference with you tomorrow during your conference period?"

# *CHAPTER XIV*

## *A Workout*

Pushing against the glass doors, he was struck both by the immensity and the noise. The entrance, a gleaming hexagon, must have soared thirty-five feet—an expanse of neon-filtered glass block: green, red, and blue. Thin tubes of pink outlined the registration desk and Health Bar. The latter, with its 50's chrome and orange leatherette stools, Formica counter and mirror engraved with palm trees, offered milk, banana, ice cream and egg 'health' drinks, all of which could be enhanced with a variety of multi-colored toppings and syrups. Sound billowed—thumping, blaring—reverberating from the cavernous main room. A female vocalist warbled a shrill descant:

> *For all eter-ni-ty-y-y, eter-ni-ty-y-y,*
> *I will sta-a-a-and by yo-u-u-u,*
> *You are my ever-ry-th-an-an-aang . . .*
> *Al-wa-y-y-y-s and for-aav-aavv-aav-aa-verrr.*

"I said and jest where you think you goin', bro?"

"Are you speaking to me?"

The attendant, in his twenties, responded with grating laughter directed to a coworker behind the counter. "Am I speakin' to you?", he snorted.

"Am I speakin' to you?" He rolled his eyes balefully. "I guess I *speakin'* to you. Don't see no one else standin' there! Does you? I sure don't! Unless maybe you got Superman vision!"

Besserian ignored the insult. "I have a Pass. A member gave it to me."

"Well, now you just better let me to see that Permit, then." His laughter was sardonic, confirming Besserian's initial impression. "Hey! Listen up, over here, Baja, sugar? We still honorin' them green passes? Or they expired?" He called to his colleague, twisting the card in his hand, fingering it cautiously, a possible incendiary device. "Now, you jest could stand back over there. Sir! By the wall. Out the way."

Obviously a multi-tasked person, Baja, hand-set pressed into her shoulder, slapped one hand repeatedly on the counter to emphasize alternatively agreement then challenge to the voice on the phone. "You gimme a minute, boy! Lemme run a check on that," as she finished counting a stack of bills, snapped a rubber band around them, flung the bundle into a lower drawer and locked it. In her consternation, she smashed down the receiver, probably negating the "Catch you later, girl!" with her telephone acquaintance. Black eyes hurling enmity at Besserian, she pivoted and disappeared into a back office.

Besserian moved back to allow new arrivals to present their 'Permits' to his interrogator. The badge on his red T-shirt stated:

ME FITNESS
Welcome
LaVerne: Assistant Manager
My Pleasure Is Having You Meet Your Max
Have A Nice Day

It was outlined in red, white, and blue with an American flag design. LaVerne scanned member cards perfunctorily, keeping a malevolent eye on Besserian.

"Probably thinks you're a terrorist." Coming from behind, Buck startled Besserian, slapping him on the shoulder. "Come on: let's get going: you're late!", pointing him in the direction of the locker room. "I've been here for thirty minutes! All warmed up! That guy? LaVerne?" He spoke loudly, punching LaVerne playfully on the shoulder. "Dude needs his ass decked. Tried the same shit with me once."

Buck laughed, nudging LaVerne. "He's cool, buddy!" LaVerne nodded doubtfully, gave a half-smile and returned Buck's 'high-five'.

Buck elbowed Besserian, "He's like that because they're afraid of kids in the schools. But I'm not telling you anything. Some kids need a good ass whipping. Probably wouldn't be in a dead-end job like this if a teacher had straightened him out." Buck seemed preoccupied. "Anyway. Turn right there to the Locker Room. You bring a lock, like I told you? Good. I'll be in the weight area. Make it quick. Glad you're here."

Changing into loose sweats and T-shirt that he covered with a baggy sweatshirt, he located Buck assembling an assortment of weights, watched by a muscular Asian. "Mike, buddy! Thanks for the help. Yeah. A couple of hundred crunches. At least! Got to. How many you been doing?" The answer was lost in the noise as Mike gave the 'thumbs up' sign and moved off.

Buck had no sweats. He was in stretch shorts. Russet hair extended from his neck to below the deeply scooped red, yellow and black tank top. The shadow on his face was the same ginger hue. Energized, stacking plates on either side of the bench, he didn't look up. "You do your warm-ups? We need to get a routine going. Need to hang loose, guy."

"You want some help?"

"How about grabbing some twenty-fives? I'll set this up for us."

Besserian thought they must look an odd pair: he in sweats, pullover and tennis shoes; contrasting with Buck's square-cut shorts: the white fabric defining his jock, the auburn covering of his legs and thighs, shoes with translucent gel-like soles. Buck moved nimbly over and around the bench, positioning the weights.

"You're being watched." Besserian motioned with his head at two females at the far side of the weight area. Behind them was an entry marked, 'Private. Ladies Only Work Out Area'.

Buck finished stacking the weights. "You say something? Oh, them? Checked them out already. They're here for the sights. The usual."

"They're watching?"

"Of course! That's why they're here. You can always tell. When they talk loud to each other, like that, so you'll hear them, and keep slapping each other and giggling? Most definitely checking us out. Get a load of that wet deck! Shit!"

He positioned the bar over the bench. "Want to have some fun? Keep moving around. Turns them on. They like to watch guys lifting. Spotting.

That's why they're out here and not in the girl's area. You start? Eighty-five OK? To warm up?"

They spotted each other, adding weights as they moved through he sets. "That's good. You've been doing your homework. Make it easier if you'd take off that sweatshirt. Say, how many shirts you got on?"

"My homework?" Besserian struggled with the outer shirt, laying it on the weight rack. His T-shirt didn't conceal a trim torso, already beginning to glisten.

"Didn't you say you had weights at home?"

"Right. Work out most days."

"We can handle more, then. You got good definition. Don't need a sweatshirt. OK with one-fifty, now?"

"Sounds good."

Buck stood behind him placing two fingers under the bar as Besserian completed his last two reps.

"My regular work out buddy fagged out on me. His girlfriend says he spends too much time here. Typical control freak. So, I shot you a call. Glad you could make it." He nodded admiringly. "Good. You got that last one by yourself. I was barely touching the bar. Looks like we can move up. Need some more twenty-fives. See any? Hey! They're some over there. Where those girls are. Give 'em a thrill."

Besserian, already enjoying the tightness in his chest, shoulders, and biceps, moved toward the two women. One, in a lycra body-suit, turquoise, cut above the waist, lay back on the bench half watching her companion who was shaking out clotted strands of bleached hair, patting her scalp slowly with a canary colored towel, and whose bikini displayed lettering across the back: 'Lifestyles'. Bikini was thin with protruding clavicles whereas Body Suit was what fitness commercials would call 'Before': hefty breasts and thick, potted thighs.

"Ladies. If you're not using those twenty-fives? Could I? Take them?"

"Ladies?" They exchanged glances and snickered. Body Suit spread her legs wider, then drew one foot languidly onto the bench, arm resting on her knee. "Why not? Help yourself. They don't belong to us." She leered, "Sir." They twittered at each other.

Bikini observed insolently, "Your 'friend'", she paused at the word, "send you over, guy?"

The music was experiencing another sporadic interruption: Baja commanding her staff. "Terrance! Front of-fi-ii-ce! Once ag-ai-ai-n! That would be," Baja giggled intimately, "Terrance? Now or so-o-o-neeer!"

She gurgled deeply, gushingly, into the microphone. "Better step on it, Terrance: home boy! Or else! Mama spank!"

She waited a minute. The announcement resonated as, piqued at the delayed response, she increased her tone by five decibels: "Now, that would be: once again! Terrance! Reception! A-S-A-P! Client call! On the double, boy! NOW!" Reaffirming her consternation, the music howled, bass thumping, clarinets squealing.

"Get a good look?" Both of the women surveyed Besserian, on his haunches, checking the numbers on several stacks of plates.

"Good look? Looking for twenty-fives."

Body suit drew her other leg onto the bench clasping her knees. "You sure you know what it is you're looking for, hot stuff? You know, DJ, I maybe think he really was: checking out them weights." She sniggered knowingly. "You and Spiderman over there? You two real good friends? Or what? Partners?"

"We work out together."

DJ recommenced the hair shaking, corners of her mouth drooping. "Sure. Bet you do! OK, Honey. You're cute. We won't hassle you. Leave you to be."

Besserian made an effort to smile. "OK? If I take these?"

"Already told you, fellah! Don't belong to us." DJ was arch: "Sir."

Body Suit sneered as Besserian moved away.

Buck was ready."Hey! Hot stuff? Back there?"

"I guess."

"They're wondering if you're Clark Kent. When you'll turn into Superman." He moved to the end of the bench. "Your set. Let's see those plates. See what we can do now. How much we can get up."

Besserian positioned himself under the bar, rearranging his hands for a stronger grip. Inhaling, he dug his feet into the rubber matting. "You ready?"

"Sure. Not going anywhere." Buck looked down as he positioned his feet firmly, thighs bent in anticipation, torso leaning close into the bar. "Go for it. Give it all you've got."

Besserian lifted the bar cleanly and completed seven reps. On the last he filled his lungs to capacity, thigh muscles straining, body arched.

"That's it, boy! Push it out! Push! Go! Go! You got it!" Buck was bending low over the bar, legs wide, fingers barely touching it. "Good. Real good. Keep your back flat on the bench. We're getting there, buddy.

That was good. Now, see what I can do. Watch me on these. And then we can step up."

They settled into a routine, exchanging and adjusting the plates, complimenting and assisting each other.

"You do pretty good. For a teacher!"

Besserian ignored the remark. "Twenty more?"

"Sounds good. Keep going."

Exchanging places, they continued the intermittent dialogue.

"How're you're classes going? Got some ideas? To turn kids on? And that AP application? Heard anything?"

"The Project. Just getting it organized. What I told you the other night. The AP? Principal told me they'd be an interview in a month or so."

"You think Pritchard's Reform Plan's going to stop the problems in your school? Hey! Back flat on the bench. Always!"

"That's the unanswered question right now."

"Ever think that maybe there could be a private agenda?"

Besserian shrugged. "Maybe. Why? You have some ideas?"

"I'm like you. Interested in seeing what the Plan comes up with. You? You'll be hearing stuff. As AP. Be in the center of the Reform action."

"I don't have the job yet. You're probably closer to information than I am. You've got connections at the District."

Buck wiped his chest with the towel. "Not really. Problem is people speak in code. Say they want high academic level. But they don't want to risk the political repercussions. Look at you. You got good definition. But you know you have to work for it. Education doesn't teach that now. So? People don't want the reality of unequal. So? Code. To hide reality. Hide the differences they say are so wonderful. Example? Democracy. Means different things. To different people. For different reasons. Like the Bible: means anything you want it to."

"Do you think this Reform Plan will actually make changes? Needed changes?"

"If there's somebody in administration to make it happen. Sure, it will. Need somebody in administration to define the 'needed changes'. You, for example."

"I heard Baques' been seen a lot at Pritchard's office. He's been talking to a number of teachers privately. About Reform."

"He and Pritchard make time for people who'll be useful."

Besserian assumed the Spotting position. "Sure helps to have a spot. Don't have it at home. Appreciate it." He watched his partner squeeze out the last reps. "Hey! Just thought of something. Maybe we could . . . there you go. One more."

"Wow! Did it! Can sure feel it. You too? Good pump! And what's that? That you were saying? Maybe we do something?"

"Was thinking if we could spot each other? Maybe one or two times a week? We'd get more out of it. Both of us. I can't do it at home."

Buck nodded gravely. "Why not? Sounds like a plan." They changed places. "You know? Something bothers me about you."

Besserian, moving his fists along the bar, feeling for the correct placement, looked up.

"Go ahead. Don't stop. Keep your grip. You said your Project with kids? It's going to investigate Reform? Might be risky. For you. Kids too."

Besserian strained through the last two repetitions. "Risky? You mean dangerous? In a school?"

"Never know. I'd be interested in what kind of stuff you uncover. How you deal with it."

"How I deal with it? Probably will be routine. No reason to think anything else. Is there?"

"Beats the shit out of me. Hell, man! That's your job. I don't know diddly about teaching."

The announcements were intermittent, constantly interrupting the caterwauling vocalists. "Once again, folks! Guests *are* reminded! Please! To stack your weights! And no bags on the floor! Do not hog benches and exercise machines! And twenty minutes on treadmills! Max! Remember: wipe down benches and equipment after each usage. Each guest must have a towel while on the floor. So, just a friendly reminder, folks: guests *not* observing these requirements for your own safety, *will* be cited! Rules is for the benefit of everybody! Once again! Enjoy your workout!" The music recommenced, decibels soaring.

"Here you go! Let's add some tens. You're structured. Need a definite plan about stuff. Careful. But don't be too careful."

"Being careful? That's bad?"

"I didn't say anything about bad. Don't get your ass in a spin! Every time anybody says something. They'll be some on-the-spot decisions. That's management. What you're going to be an expert in. Good news is that you're not following a script. Somebody else's script. You'll be writing it." He helped Besserian with the last rep. "Make you look good for the AP job."

"That's one-eighty! Watch it." Buck commented between sets of five reps each. "It's risky when somebody, you, for example, starts looking for the facts. Not playing the CYA game. True in any business."

"You think everybody wants their eyes opened?"

"No. Isn't that what education's supposed to do? Here you go. I'm watching. Careful. Big one here, buddy!" He was satisfied with Besserian's control. "You know, I'm glad Penny's at Tri-Delt. She's got a lot of drive. And she pushes herself. Soaks up stuff like a sponge." He smiled watching the rhythmical movement of the bar. "That's the tricky part about a relationship. Any relationship. Change. Not play CYA. It's got to be there or both people stagnate. But it's risky."

"Risky?"

"No gain in anything unless there's risk. Shit! You might drop that bar on yourself! Say you were to get distracted looking at those two girls? And now? What you're really planning is a new relationship: with your kids in your Project. Whatever it turns out to be. So it's a risk. For you! For them! Just like I took a risk with Penny." He laughed. "Of course, so did she. Anyway, everybody needs a jolt up the ass sometimes. I sure do. She tells me things I might have overlooked. What to stop. What to start. Even where to readjust my planning so I keep my expectations in focus. Guess you could say, she's my 'spot'! At work."

"You think schools should be run more like a business?"

"There're businesses and businesses. Good ones like mine. And screwed up ones. Same as schools."

Besserian, straining, rolled the bar back on to the uprights. He sat on the bench, savoring the moment of relaxation.

Buck seemed in no mood to change places. "Management? Look at your school. A budget of a couple of million? Tax payer money. With an unbelievably high drop-out rate: what? Over fifty percent? And most of the remaining kids below average in reading and math! Where's the accountability there? The only thing I ever hear is 'more money' and 'we can't help it that kids don't want to learn!' Shit! Show me a business where 'I can't' is accepted as management. Leadership. Yet, school is paid big bucks, millions of them, to 'can'. Screwed up, man! Blame is shifted from the people who're paid to help kids—teachers and administrators, school board members—to the kids needing the help! Seems to me that's what reform needs to look at. CEO in a business who can't deal with the 'bottom line'? Chuck his ass out."

Buck continued. "You guys *have* a bottom line? Anyway: one eighty-five! Damm good, man! We're both pretty good. But tell me something. You've done the school administration courses?"

"Right. Otherwise I couldn't apply for the AP."

"Seems to me, well, put it this way: aren't those administration courses supposed to prepare a teacher to run a school? Teach teachers to be managers? Sort of a MBA to change teachers into managers? Into administrators? Principals and shit?"

"A reasonable question. Put it this way, the courses are theory: strained through political correctness. And given by people who couldn't remember the last time they were in a classroom. Or a school. If they ever were."

"Not too exciting, then?"

"Try useless? Accounting, budgeting, forecasting, statistical analyses, dealing with unions, contracts, unsatisfactory employees, community accountability, incorporating parents and community into the school managerial plan? Wish again! None of that. You try a few. Same weight."

"Then, what the hell did you do? For administration classes? Anything?"

"Listened to the theory of Special Education, of Diversity, of Bi-lingual education."

"Why?"

"Because education is political. Let somebody use word 'oriental' instead of 'Asian'? All hell breaks loose. You can get thrown out of an administration program for that."

"Shit, man! If they taught you guys real management skills? Shit! I'd be out of a job! That's why they pay me big bucks as a consultant."

"There's a lot of bitching in administration classes about how 'unfair' NCLB is for kids—read: unfair to incompetent teachers and administrators.

"Seems we both agree on one thing: find out about this Reform Plan. What it's up to. What it's worth to us?"

"Worth?"

"Right. You get the AP job and find out if the Reform plan's on the level. For me: more bond issues. More investment counseling. For whatever projects they want to reform: need money for."

"You know, if we *were* to find out anything, say underhanded, about Reform, it could, as you say have some risk. Danger, I think you said."

"Sure. You can bet your ass with that queen, Pritchard involved, money's involved. Physical danger? I heard it's happened before. In this school district?"

"There was that Principal who was murdered a couple of years before I got here. Never found out who did it. People think he probably found some payoffs."

"And career danger. To you. You say the wrong thing, find out the wrong thing. You'll be in serious trouble. Not get the AP job. There's danger in rocking the boat. Bad guys might win out in the end anyway."

"So?"

"So, the moral of the story is watch out. Don't let your student Project backfire. On you. You could do more than stub your toe."

"Hey, just thought of something. Why not try more reps and use tens instead of twenties? Might get more out of it. Both of us."

The music cascaded over the room, subduing the occupants:

*"You are the riv-er of the Ni-i-i-le, the Ni-i-i-le;*
*The ri-ve-er, the ri-ver-er of the Ni-i-i-le;*
*The Ni-i-le."*

"Actually this place is a case in point."

"Of what?"

"Of political correctness."

"How's that, Teach?"

"I don't see a Men Only Work Out Area. And you heard about a guy thrown out when a woman reported him for making 'provocative noises'? Doing bench presses."

Buck surveyed him carefully. "Maybe. Anyway, we've been talking too much. Working out our brains more than our abs and delts. Let's get in some leg work. Jump in the shower. Then get our asses out of this zoo."

# *CHAPTER XV*

## *Non Judgmental*

"Now, ladies and gentlemen! We *do* need to remember the concept: Non Judgmental! Never. We are not here for that. What we do is, we make comments and observations: about what we see and what we observe. *Not* what we *think*!" She smiled and reached under her blouse to adjust a bra strap. "It's important that the teacher feel good about the experience. The teacher can't savor the experience, if there's Judgmentalism."

"Maybe you could go over what we're supposed to do? Again? Except, of course, to avoid Judgmentalism?" Sandra Weatherby inquired.

"Like education in general, the Focus Walk Concept is not an exact science. To address your question—and I do appreciate your interest, Miss—we are *observing*, let me repeat, *observing*, areas of instructional activity. In some cases, we may wish to offer those observations, *if*, and that's a *if*, mind you, the teacher requests it. But I don't think they will. But, first and foremost, always, always, in a totally *non-Judgmental* way."

"Maybe you could run that by us again? To make sure we got it, please? Non-Judgmental?"

Again the tugging gesture with the bra strap, as if somehow, possibly, it held the answer to the vexing question. Dr. Sanchez-Mullen, District Director of Secondary Education, was effusive. "Our visits are quick: in and out! Six minutes max: *observe*, what's happening. Afterwards, we conference. Together. And at that strategy we start off our comments with 'I saw . . .', 'Students were . . .', 'teacher was ...', 'there was ...' kinds of expressions. Under no circumstances do we say, 'I *thought*'! Never that. We do *not*, underline *not*, say stuff like, 'I liked/disliked the way . . . bla, bla, bla'. We do not say 'That was a excellent yakkety, yakkety', or 'that was a bad presentation of ... you name it', because that would be a Judgmental. We do not say 'There was only ...'; 'I don't think...'; I didn't see . . . those kinds of negativities. Because those are Judgmental. Avoid the words 'not', 'good', 'think', 'wonder why they didn't or did', bla, bla, bla. And we must avoid . . ."

"Judgmental. So, we are supposed to . . .?"

"Observe! Observe! Name of the game! No value judgments. But, not to worry, we'll get used to it as it comes out in the wash." She turned down the corners of her shiny lips and thrust her head forward. "Another quay-stion? We *are* behind schedule—but, of course, . . ."

"Frankly, I don't see how the teacher and students benefit from this *observation* without telling them specific . . .."

"Might I just suggest, 'visitation'?" Sanchez nodded affirmatively, aggressively.

"OK. But shouldn't we say what . . ."

"Should? Should? I'm afraid I have to back away from that word." Sanchez shook her head negatively. "Should is Judgmental. The name of the game is *avoid,* Miss. Avoid J*udgmental.* Nada."

"Kids throwing books, not doing work . . ."

"Sir! If I could do a backup so as to do a refresh on this? We look at the 'is'. The 'inner depth'. Mr. Besserian, the Focus Walk benefit concept, will be derived to them, as *they*, not us, uncover areas in which *they*, teacher and students, could—never should—redirect their attention: their own paws-ability of doing more of, less than. Whatever! Through our observation, once again and, always *along Non-Judgmental lines*, they uncover benefit areas of exploration: the 'Two To Glow On: One to Grow On' feedback situation we try to implement in any conferencing module. Always. With any teacher."

"Doesn't that presuppose a great deal?"

"A great deal? I don't follow you. Of what?"

"Of objectivity? About themselves? On the part of the teacher? And the students?"

"You know, Mr. Besserian, I'm going to suggest that we do suppose that? That our teachers *are* pro-*fay*-shon-al." She paused, nodding affirmatively, to savor the impact of her thought, "and who know the *best* interests of their students? To heart?" She peered over the top of her beveled glasses, eyes wide, head inclined, lower teeth grasping upper lip. "Frankly, sir, I'm picking up that you seem to think our teachers aren't? Don't?"

"Aren't what? Don't what?"

"Don't like kids! Aren't pro-*fay*-shon-al". She articulated carefully.

Dr. Allsbury broke in. "He didn't say that nor should that be prognosticated."

Sanchez-Mullen smiled painfully and bushed back her bobbed hair with the back of her hand. "OK! Let's move on! Ladies and gentlemen! If I might have your attention! We'll be in two groups. Group A would be me, as leadership, Ms. Weatherby, and Mr. Besserian. Group B, now that would be Ms. Cortère with Mr. McCauley with Ms. er *Dr.* Allsbury as leader in charge. Group B will cover the English classes on this side of the passageway and Group A, us, will, obviously, cover the ones on the other side. Remember, no more than six, repeat *six*, minutes per each classroom, then: back outside. To match up observations. And once again! Observations! Never Judgmental! Avoid the 'feel' words: 'upset', 'bothered by', 'wondered why/why not', 'liked/disliked', 'glad/not glad', 'concerned'! Those sorts of things. Replace those negativities by 'saw', 'noticed', 'glimpsed', 'observed', 'spotted', 'witnessed', 'tracked', 'viewed'. Everybody on the same side of the coin. So as to be with them: in their pods."

************************************************

Confusion exacerbated the clutter of the room. Some were in small groups, others were moving spontaneously. Besserian 'observed' one girl sitting on the floor, under several desks pushed together, slapping pieces of clay noisily. The finished product seemed irrelevant. When asked what she was doing and why she was sitting on the floor, alone, under the desks, she looked at Besserian insolently and let him repeat the question three times. Finally, she twisted her neck and head, screwed up her mouth, looked away and murmured petulantly, "Mod'lin'". Besserian ruminated, "In this English class, I observed a student, seated on the floor, under a desk: modeling. Clay."

In another part of the room, five students were coloring numbered pictures. The crayons were also numbered.

Theresa Roehampton, Grade Eleven English, at her desk in the back corner, had pushed some of the clutter aside and was locked in an earnest conversation with a student who, she later revealed, had 'parent issues' and needed immediate 'intervention'. "I'm tellin' you! It's all the time! Lots and lots of my kids has problems at home. Especially when it's a parent. They get a raw deal. Need help. They got issues, man! And nobody's here to give it to them! School counselors? Take a number! Our kids need 'now' help. Parents don't understand their lives. Stress they're under. And no wonder! They shouldn't even be here. Most of them."

Student psychological 'issues' were, apparently, the main reason, she emphasized 'Activity' instruction, rather than writing, grammar, reading, textual analysis. She explained to Besserian and Weatherby that she preferred, "for kids to get out of their issues, through togetherness." Apparently, she meant socializing: working jointly to solve what she called 'right brain' issues rather than 'left brain stuff' of academics which, after all, she opined, only 'screw them up worse than'. Also, that instructional device gave her additional 'privatized time' for needy students.

Besserian observed some students grouped around a computer, 'surfing' bridal gowns and Screen Savers. He also observed photographs dangling over Learning Centers: 'The Family', a lioness followed by two cubs; 'Party Time', a female in formal gown; 'Extacy'[sic] was a sequined-suited male rock star depicted with bulging sexuality.

The classroom walls were cluttered with pictures, drawings, newspaper cutouts, and three-dimensional collages. Several depicted footprints in the sand. Others showed females in bikinis or sculpted body suits. Those taken in an amusement park exhibited individuals, hair streaming in the wind or blowing back in their faces, howling with 'ecstasy' as the 'Zipper' plummeted into an eighty-degree turn or the extended arm of the 'Whipper', hurtled its occupants laterally and vertically.

There were multiple scenes of female animals with their young. Other photos showed police apprehending criminals, smashed cars and mangled bodies in freeway accidents, and suburban bar-b-ques: supervisory females in earnest conversation, males tending the grill, holding the *de rigueur* can of beer

There was a time-line banner illustrating contemporaneous historical events. Non-western cultural achievements were brightly colored. For example, one could see that prior to the construction of the cathedral of Chartres—not colored—the Aztecs already had completed their monumental achievements at Chichén Itzá and Uxmal; the Pueblo Indians, their terraced housing; the Khmers, their temple at Angkor-Wat; and the Alaskan Inuit, their ice dwellings.

Ms. Roehampton seemed unconcerned, if not oblivious to the progress of her students in their Projects. Besserian caught her eye and smiled. Nodding curtly, she shook her streaming hair, and blinking, pushed with the back of her wrists those strands that impeded her vision.

"Good morning, Ms. Roehampton. Some of us are being taken out of our regular classes for Focus Walks. I think it's supposed to help us as much as the teacher visited."

"You didn't do your teacher training? For your credential? Anyhow, a total bomb. Whatever. I guess. Do what you have to do."

"Could you point out where the Standards are displayed? And how they're incorporated into your Lesson Plan? Where your Lesson Plan is displayed? Classroom Management Policy? Homework policy? Grading policy? If you don't mind, your Attendance and Student Assignment Book? You know. The regular things required of all teachers?"

"Not for other teachers, we aren't. And no, I won't. No way! Un-un! No sir-re-e! You're a violation of the Union Contract that says we don't have to show what we do to anybody! 'cept to the site administrator! And even there, it's 'ify'. Other teachers not allowed to do observations." She shrugged. "But then, who cares? Warfles is filing a Grievance about all this. It's Mickey Mouse! Against Ed Code to have anybody else see student grades. Violates their privacy. And teacher privacy: to make us show class policies!"

She shuffled some of the clutter of papers and books on her desk and bent to look in a side drawer. Not finding what she wanted, she went to a filing cabinet. Besserian observed that she was dressed in low-cut, cream colored Pedal Pushers, with a short-sleeve purplish shirt of crinkled fabric that occasionally hid her navel. Her bare feet were in tire-tread sandals. A plastic barrette in the design of a hot-dog, colored with mustard and relish, secured some of the straggling strands of hair.

Even from a distance, Besserian could see that the files were crammed indiscriminately with papers, books, folders, candy, cake, drinks and plastic eating utensils. She rummaged for a short time and turned around.

"Hey, Laura! Sweetie? Just to come over here! A quick min-ute! If you would? Have a look where's that roll book—you know the grade book—and the rest of that stuff? Did you put it somewheres?"

The student—interrupted from an earnest discussion with co-workers: all of them whispering, giggling, protesting affection: arms, hands, shoulders thrust up against one another—nudged by her companions, disengaged herself, and whispered desperately, mouth gaping, in the teacher's ear:

"N-o-o-o-o! I d-n-n-n-t. It's not they-er-errre, Miss Roehampton! No-o-o-o! Not-iny-mo-or-or! I already told you! 'Member? How you gave it to Debby? To take to Ms. Hollyfield!" Laura managed to combine indignation with panic: desperate incredulity. "And that was awhile ba-ack. Maybe last week? Don't you ee-*mem-em*-em-ber?" Laura's eyes glistened, almost protruding. Her mouth hung open. "Totally?"

"What about that stuff on Standards? Did we ever get that finished? Last week?"

"No-o-o-o—o! Ee-*mem*-em-ber? Not ev-e-e-veen." Irritated, Roehampton turned to Besserian.

"OK. Well, this is our busy time? Students are all focusing on their Activities. And getting ready for state tests. You know, end of quarter, end of semester. The usual? Gar-báge? Play catch-up?" She slouched on the stained polyester chair cushion. "And we're supposed to be *teaching*? With all these interruptions? No way, José!"

"Could you tell me this, Ms. Roehampton? And, again I know how busy you are." The pedagogue remained sullen. "Since they seem to be occupying your students' time, what are these Activities? Who designs them and how are they integrated into the subject of English literature? And grammar?"

"OK. I guess. They're studying about Ancient Egypt and the Sumerians? And Babylonians? The projects match up to them." She bobbed her head in agreement.

"How does that work? In an English class?"

"If you know anything about the book, you'd know there's a couple of stories—here, let me show you—about kids in the time of ancient Egypt?" She rustled among the desktop clutter, not finding what she was looking for. "Chandelle, let's have a look at your book, baby-girl?"

Chandelle stretched languidly, and walked slowly to the teacher's desk dangling a heavy text that she deposited with a thud. She shook long, black hair and scrutinized Besserian: languidly, disdainfully, approvingly? Her tongue moistened the corners of her mouth and she twisted her shoulders slowly.

Roehampton impatiently rustling the pages, found the stories. The first was entitled, "Aida's Search for Her Personal Light." The second, "Two Teens in the Time of the Pharaohs: Kamenwati and Tamafriti."

"Do your students enjoy reading these stories?"

"I guess. But usually not too much. That's why I have to have the Activities to keep their interests up? Actually, this stuff is pretty far out from their livelihood. So, Activities help those who's having difficulty—just about everybody—reading. The stories?"

"But all the students do actually *read* the stories?"

"Well. You *could* say that. More or less." She rummaged through the desk clutter. "Now, where are those? Murphye, did you put the Progress Report Cards back? After you finished, sweetie?"

"In your bottom drawer, Miss."

"Anyway, lots of the kids *do* read the stories. But the problem is that these stories are written at a too high reading level standard. For them. It's all come about with that Standardized Tests gobbledy-gook. That mish-mash! Another part of that stupid 'No Child Left Behind' law. Sure, kids in rich areas, white kids, Traditionalist kids, can handle it but . . . our kids? No way! They're reading three . . . four . . . sometimes five or six grade levels below Standards when they get here. There's no way they can understand this stuff. And, if you really want to know the truth? Some of the teachers have a hard time with them theirselves! I mean look at those names? Who can know how to pronounce what: *Nafretiri?* Or some such! I mean give me a break! Nobody could pronounce them. Even a college-educated. And if they could? So what? Just you tell me one kid that's got a name like, well, look here on this page: *Hatshepsa*? Or *Nephthys*? You figure it out. No, Activities aren't about reading exactly but it could help kids to at least *hear* about *parts* of the stories. When the reading is just too darn tough."

Across the room, Weatherby smiled and moved to a group of students. "I'm Miss Weatherby. Could you tell me your names?"

"I'm Madison?"

"I'm Morgan. And these here are Geoffrey, Tomas, and Cyndie?"

"Young ladies. Gentlemen. What are you working on now? What is today's lesson?"

They scrambled to reply with excessive assertiveness, "Let me!" "Me first!" "Here!" "You got it, lady."

"Such enthusiasm! I'm impressed! Morgan? I like the way you have your crayons and colored pencils so well organized."

The girl giggled shyly and turning to a page in her folder, read dutifully but haltingly from a typed script. "We are studying according to the state standards. Today's standard is Number forty-one: com-per-hen-si-on? And a-a-a-per-er-ci-ci-ation? Of other cul-shures? 'specially sen-ce structure and gra-merr?" She watched Weatherby intently for approval, speaking slowly. "In our class we allays follow State Standards?" Without being asked she moved into the second paragraph of the typed text. "And Ms.

Roehampton, could you explain the Predicate Nom-in-at-t-at-at-tive", she stumbled over the word, "again? I-think-I-was-absent-for-you-teaching-of-it? Jesterday?" She looked up, pleased but breathless, reaffirming that her colleagues were following the same script in their own folders.

"Thank you, Morgon. Could I see some of your corrected assignments?"

Immediately, they exploded into action, scrambling, electrified, as if responding to a cue: "Mine! Mine, Miss! Look! Look here!"

"Wonderful! How about Tomas? Could I see yours?"

"Sure." Proudly, he displayed a list of synonyms and antonyms. It was marked A+ with a penciled Happy Face at the top and each word bore a huge red check. It was dated six weeks prior.

"Do you have anything more recent? Any of you?"

They looked at each other, giggling conspiratorially. "Well, not rally! Miss Roehampton is just real busy with stuff. We turn in our stuff and when she has the time to look at it? We could get to do some of them over? So we can put it in our folders? Like this one."

"When will your next assignment be due?"

Cyndie giggled. "We don't know. When Miss gets around to it. I guess it's not all that often? You know?"

"Are there remedial programs available? After school? In reading? Writing? Should any of you want it?"

"Yes, sure." Geoffrey spoke positively.

"Do you go every day?"

"Not really. Sometimes teacher's real busy? Overworked?"

"But you get credit?"

"Sure. Anyhow, Ms. Roehampton, she gives extra, *extra* credit when we read stuff she gives us. To Focus Walk visitors?"

Besserian was concluding his conversation with Roehampton. "Are student reading levels improving?"

The teacher brushed two loose strands of hair from her eyes. "Some. Problem is these kids don't want to read. Or do Math for that matter. And let me say, if they're like me, they could never learn Math anyhow. Anyway, kids can't read and they don't want to. Got a steady diet of TV: MTV, and 'Munster' type programs. And porno. More interesting to them than reading."

"Wouldn't that make classroom reading that much more important?" Weatherby watched Besserian as she approached and caught the end of the interchange.

"Could."

Sanchez-Mullen interrupted. "Six minutes is long past due, ladies! Can we end this really exciting conversation? And great class, 'Resa! So! We ready to crunch some facts outside? Now?"

"Thank you Ms. Roehampton for your time. Sorry for the inconvenience." Weatherby corroborated Besserian's remark with a smile.

"Be my guest! It's all about kids. We'll see what Warfles can do to stop all this. Focus Walks nonsense! I mean what about teachers rights? The pits!"

********************************

Focus Walk Triumvirate, Group A, reconvened in the hallway. "Sure don't see Ms. Allsbury's group? Probably moved on to their second observation. Less dawdlesome than us. Anyhow! We can conference right here. So? How about if you started us off? Mr. Besserian?"

"I was not impressed with the . . .".

"A No-No! You for-ge-e-e-t! What did we agree on?"

Sandra interjected, touching Besserian's arm reassuringly. "I'll bite. Non-Judgmental?"

"Ab-so-lu-tely. Now, in that mentality would you care to rephrase your observation, Mr. Besserian?" She grinned.

Sandra could feel the tension mounting in him. She picked a thread from the upper arm of his jacket.

"I saw students working on Activities. Some students."

"Yes." Sanchez-Mullen adjusted a bra strap. "And observations? Sir?"

"Maybe it's what we *don't* observe, that's important?"

"How's that Mr. B?" Weatherby caught Besserian's eye. Sanchez, scowling, stared at him. "Sir?"

"We didn't observe what might happen to kids in the future. Based on what we see happening or not happening now. Maybe we should try to do that."

"Can't say that I follow your drift. Sir!"

"Ms. Sanchez, we're looking at the classroom as an end in itself. I'm suggesting that it might not be. An end in itself. What if we considered the classroom as a road? A transition. To what we want the students to achieve. In the future. For themselves? The extent to which we empower them now, in the classroom, to make a success of their future lives?"

Weatherby was intrigued. "So, if we're not giving them the tools, we're deluding students that they have a choice about their future lives."

"Mr. Besserian, observations like that reminds me of a racist or a Gender Opposed commentary? Traditionalist?"

"Ms. Sanchez, let's not be Judgmental about Mr. Besserian. He's giving an opinion. . . "

"Ms. Weatherby, I really don't think Mr. Baques or Dr. Jones-LaPorte would appreciate . . ."

"As a teacher myself, I have to say I was confused by the use of Activities to replace the mandated course content. I . . ."

Sanchez-Mullen twisted her liquid sepia-colored lips into a pained expression of reprimand, but Weatherby continued... "I didn't *judge* what I saw. I said I was *confused*: by what I saw. Let me *observe* this: I did not *observe* students reading. Did not *observe* them writing. Did not *observe* examples of student work. Did not *observe* student grades, or lesson plans. Did not *observe* student involvement: in learning course content. Did not observe teacher interacting with students to explain the Standards. The mandated Standards. Did not observe the teacher's instruction."

Releasing pent-up frustration, she continued. "However, I did *observe* Activities, not related to English grammar, writing, or reading of the English language. As a result of my *observations*, I do not have evidence of student reading or writing proficiency as mandated by State Standards. Or their proficiency as evidenced by corrected assignments returned to them."

"Now, I *have* asked you! *Please*!" Sanchez-Mullen was peevish. "You were, both of you, taken out of your classes, with the cost of substitutes provided. To contribute to the Focus Walk Process. Not bad mouth it. And, Mr. Besserian, I think Focus Walk is a tool Mr. Baques expects every future administrator to have in their tool boxes."

"Ms. Sanchez? Regarding activities? If teachers are evaluated *de facto* on student scores?"

"How do you mean?"

"Class average is 'B' than that's a 'B' teacher? Then the teacher has an incentive to assign what? Easier work?"

"Easier? Better? Mr. Besserian? Ms. Weatherby? I think we agreed to veer away from judgmental?"

---

# *CHAPTER XVI*

## *Friendly Competition*

"Here you go. Take it." He flicked the small, hard ball to Besserian who, surprised, side-stepped deftly, and using a powerful backhand, swatted it into the front corner.

"Shit, man!" Buck lunged forward, making a complete turn high off the floor, brought the full force of his shoulder and forearm into the swing, catching the ball with the center of his racket before it completed its perpendicular drop. The pellet shot straight into the backcourt, exploding past his opponent.

Besserian's reflexes, were primed. Crouching low, he ducked, the muscles in his thighs and back rigid, distended. He exhaled and, judging the speed of the projectile correctly, sprang out of the crouch, and raced to the forecourt. Pivoting, he smashed his return into the front wall behind him. He had caught the ball cleanly with the power of his thighs and shoulders: sent it whistling, jettisoned, where, compacted by the force, it was flattened: a two-dimensional object. As if petrified, it clung to the wall for an eternity of seconds then, recovering, rebounded frantically into center court. Besserian shouted in desperation and triumph.

Both men were transfixed. Each riveted one eye on the irascible black projectile and the other on his opponent. Gauging his opponent's next move, Besserian was poised for the return, desperate to meet it. Mind racing, he calculated that Buck would catch the ball easily and lob it to the front—his favorite trick—arch it to the back wall, high, requiring his opponent to reverse his direction, scrambling desperately.

Besserian sprinted to the forecourt, careening hard against his rival's torso, crouched, preparing to make his shot. Each was totally absorbed, completely tensed, eyes flashing, muscles swollen, glistening.

Buck outwitted him. He pushed back hard, knocking Besserian to the floor and, seizing his advantage, savagely whacked the ball directly into the front wall. It ricocheted to the side, lost its force, and slowly, even languidly, reached the back wall as if indifferent, savoring the frenzy it was causing below. Besserian, watching in amazement and anger, enticed by its diminished speed, collected himself, scrambled to his feet, and hurtled forward. Too late. The elusive object, now vengeful, dropped petulantly to the ground, mocking Besserian's savage swing. The racket shattered into the floor, the sound reverberating crazily because of the exaggerated acoustics, and hung stupidly and limply, two useless pieces.

"Had enough?"

Besserian was bent over, hyperventilating. He watched his opponent with a combination of resentment and relief. "Good play. Shit!"

"Right! Hey, you OK?"

"Yes. I'm OK."

"Don't look it. Sorry about that last shot."

Besserian pulled himself upright still breathing heavily. "What? Why the *sorry* shit? It was a good shot. I'm the one who missed it."

"Sorta blocked you." The self-confident laugh. "The breaks. Grab my other racket? Over there in the corner?"

Besserian shook it a few times to get the feel, using the opportunity to mop his head, face, and neck.

"Your serve, buddy! Let's go!"

Besserian slapped it hard, close to the corner. Buck catapulted forward and swung powerfully, catching the ball squarely. Not three feet from the wall, he slashed it forward and ducked as the return hurtled past him. Catching his breath, Besserian gauged the distance and started his run forward, intercepting the ball at center forecourt. His arm, already in motion, came around in a full swing and he caught it squarely, propelling it down onto the front wall at an angle. It arched back, high but slow, and both men were mesmerized, mouths open, one crouching in a near sitting position, the other leaning far back, following the unhurried, lofty arc of their quarry.

Buck realizing the trajectory, scrambled several large steps toward the back wall, spun and caught it with a forehand, outwitting its effort to elude him. It hurtled into the center front wall where Besserian caught it neatly. It was a powerful side shot, and the ball tore directly into the other man.

Buck swinging in self defense, jumped high, lunging, shouting in rage and confusion, brought the considerable force of his chest, back and forearm into what could have been an amazing return shot.

But the ball was too close: inches from his face: much too fast. His mid-air swing whistled. The ball shot behind him, ricocheted disdainfully off the back wall, veered into the side and dropped triumphantly. Insolently.

"You OK?" Besserian, himself gulping for air, trotted over. Buck was face down on the floor. A trickle of blood meandered from somewhere under him and began a lazy course towards the center of the court.

"You sure?" he repeated.

Except for Besserian's breathing and the thump of the rock music from the main room, there was silence.

Buck turned over slowly, rotating his shoulder and back muscles, squinted and wiped his jaw and cheek with the back of his hand, discoloring the russet stubble. Dazed, he looked at Besserian peevishly. "What? Sure, I'm OK. Made a stupid shot."

"I shouldn't have . . .."

"Fuck. That apologizing shit. Need a towel. It was my own dumb ass fault." He started to get up, obviously in some pain, grabbing the towel from Besserian.

"You want yours? That's mine."

Confusion compounded Buck's general consternation. "What?" Mopping his chest and face, he inhaled deeply.

"Yours is over there. I'll get it."

"Hey. Forget it, man! This is OK." He rubbed the cloth over his torn shirt, glistening hair, soaking neck, thighs and arms. "You probably don't have any diseases. At least any I don't already have. Probably take a shower most days."

"Want some water?"

"No. I don't want any fuckin' water. It'll stop in a minute." He shook his head as if to turn off blood trickling from his nose.

"You sure walloped that ball . . .."

"I didn't hit the fuckin' ball. I screwed up. So? That's the problem."

The rumbling music echoed from the next room increasing the silence between them. Besserian heard the jump of the minute hand of the clock above the door.

"OK. Big Guy. Let's call it a game. Give you that one. Get your ass next time." He began an awkward scramble to get to his feet.

"I need to tell you something. Before we go out."

Buck turned impatiently, eyes suspicious, scowling under the overhang of his forehead.

"Your shorts ripped. On that last shot. Might want to throw a towel around you when we go out."

"What? What happened?"

"When you made that lunge. Shorts ripped. Down the back. I can get you another pair. LaVerne might keep some?"

Buck reached behind, verifying the situation, making a partial gesture of pulling together the ripped cloth. "I'll be shit! Bummer! And no, I don't want you to get me a pair from fuckin' LaVerne. Towel will be OK. Let's head for the locker room. Give everybody a cheap thrill. They've never seen a guy in a jock before?"

He moved to get up and sat back, obviously in pain. Besserian sat on the floor watching.

"I'm pissed. Look at me. Made a stupid play."

"It wasn't so.... ."

He scrutinized Besserian and there was a glint in his eyes. "But I'm not so pissed off as you are."

"Me?"

Buck, wiping the back of his hand across his nose, several time, surveyed the result, defying the flow to start again.

"You're angry. About stuff. About everything. You hide it—or think you hide—it by intellectualizing about whatever happens. And about people. By being 'abstract'. Tangents. Not direct hits. That's the way you work. Then you know what? You get even more pissed because your technique, and it is a technique, doesn't work. So lots of times, you're frustrated, thinking you're supposed to be patient, a good little boy, and hating yourself, getting pissed off. Because you're not." He shook his head and grimaced. "Shit, man! Be like me. Admit you're pissed. Life's a bitch. Keeps hitting you on the rebound. Where you don't expect it. Accept it that way. Quit wondering what's wrong. With you. Life's a game. You gotta see it that way. Or it'll drive you nuts. Or you'll never do anything."

"You . . . "

"I used to be like you. Until I wised up. And with a little help from my DI, as I told you."

"I don't . . ."

"Yes, you do. I was like you. Until I decided I was going to kick some ass instead of getting mine kicked." He scowled, tugging at the obdurate cloth in its determination not to cover him. He attempted to pull part of the towel around him then abandoned the effort. "You need to get angry. Start smashing stuff. You see what you did today? You got pissed off as hell and then you hit that ball. You were good. Need to do it more often. You anticipated what I was going to do. Countered it. Do it in your work, buddy! And lifting—weights—isn't the same thing. Not enough. Doesn't do it."

"Do you know so much about everybody? Or is it only me?"

Buck clenched his teeth, pursed his lips, and scowled. "I do know a lot. That's why I'm where I am. Shit, man. I'm not here to play games with you. I'm not raggin' you!"

Besserian opened his mouth to make an observation and thought better of it.

"OK. So, I fucked up that shot. Doesn't mean I don't know what I'm talking about. And you got lucky. Next time? I'll take your ass." Shaking his head vigorously, spraying out a stream of moisture: a pungent musk. The thinning hair was curling aggressively in the cloying humidity of the court.

"You had an idea. The other night. In that bar. To get your classes in line. Get your kids jacked up. Get yourself jacked up. To jockey yourself into school administration. The AP job. Turn this Reform shit to your advantage."

Buck bit his lower lip and scrutinized his companion, flicking his finger dismissively at the pieces of cloth. "You're looking for something about yourself. I'm not. I've found what I want. About me. Trouble is you just might find what it is you're looking for. Then you wouldn't know what to do. And you're afraid you might screw up, get hurt looking for it. So you don't do anything. Makes you unreliable."

"Unreliable!" Besserian stepped back, scalded by the remark.

"People pick up on that. In any relationship. Personal. Or business. They'd prefer a pain in the ass like me. Why? They know where they stand. What I'll do. What I can do. To help them. That's what people want. Help. You're a teacher. You should know that. As I said, in any relationship: don't know or won't admit it. Help. Me? I'm helpful. People like that. Sometimes they get too close. But, well, that's another chapter. In my book."

"Relationship?"

"Right. We have a relationship."

"Well, I . . ."

"Why be so afraid? Admit it. It's pretty straightforward, nothing complicated. We like doing shit together. Some stuff, anyway. So? We should do what we like and fuck the stuff we don't like. Easy. I help you. You help me. Relationship's a game. One guy doesn't win all the time. Like today? You whipped my ass. So?"

"Relationships are serious. Have to evolve. Be tested."

"Relationships aren't theory. They're trust. You play a hunch. Then do some testing. If it seems OK, it probably is. Go for it. You're looking for the pot in the rainbow, buddy. Guess what? It's not there. And you're not going to find it even if it was there. What are you afraid of?"

"Afraid? You think I'm afraid of something? You?"

"Premonitions? I get them about people. About relationships. Usually right. I had it about Penny. Was right about her. Her potential. And, I got a good relationship with her. She learns. And when I can't learn from somebody, shit, there's no more relationship. You should do that. Look at people. Don't expect them to look at you. Play your hunches."

"I prefer to ..."

"Forget prefer. Forget being careful. Risk stuff. You did that in a couple of those shots today. Forgot yourself. Blasted that ball. Knocked my shorts off! We were together. Using each other. Helping each other. How much more of a relationship do you want? Shit, man! We're not going to bed together."

"Help me up. Let's get out of here. You know, it's intellectuals, theorists, like you who make it possible for all those creeps to get control of public education and screw it up. People like that moron Baques , Bacon-Gaither. . . what an ass-hole name. . . Jones-LaFork and the rest of those dorks. You're playing right into their hands.

"You know they're creeps?"

"You know anybody's a creep: when you can't have confidence in them. Trust them. About whatever is serious. No confidence? No trust? When a guy doesn't face that, he's worse than they are." Buck chortled. "You know, good and God Dam well. OK. Mr. Wise Ass." He shifted, irritated at the persistence of the competition from the ripped material. "OK. Prove me wrong. I'll bet you . . . what . . . a new jock strap, I'm right."

"About?"

"There you go again." He shook his head disdainfully. "About Reform Plan being a cover. For something. That it's phony. You care about kids? OK. You need to find out. You coming?"

Besserian seemed to be pondering something. "What? Right."

"Like I said. Phony reform means a dead end for most of these kids. School's not doing its job. They'll be trapped in the second class citizenship hole. Take that back. Third class. But the worst thing? Kids will actually believe they're lucky to be getting 'educated'. And all this talk about 'change'? Point is what kind of change? Any jackass can 'change'. It just might not be change for the better. Phony reform will turn kids into drones—the gammas. And all because they won't, can't, really, see what the System is doing to them. So? Don't know who to trust." He nodded and stared at him directly. "You need to ask yourself: do the kids trust me? Bigger question. Do I trust them? Respect them? It's a relationship, guy!"

Besserian was uncomfortable: his dripping shirt feeling cold, clinging to pecs, biceps and abs.

Buck watched him. "See, you're caught. Ever been hunting?"

"No."

"You know those blinds? You get in them and watch? For something to come along? Deer? Moose? Same with you. You're in a blind. But nothing's coming along. You're a hunter with nothing to hunt. I was like that. Like you. Until I started TriDelt. Built myself a real team. Didn't wait for what I wanted; to come alone. You're in such a 'blind', you don't even know what you want to come along. But, if it did, you'd deny it. And another thing."

"Why don't you tell me."

"If you stay in the blind something might come along. But? It might not be fooled! Moose might sense you. Then charge. Tear into you. You could be the one hunted. Actually, you're more vulnerable in the blind than out of it. But you, most people, don't know that."

The shorts were a dead issue, irrelevant to both of them. "You don't want to get your shorts ripped: somebody might see what you got? What you are? OK. Safer, sure! But you won't get anywhere. Sure, you can stay in a safe place! Never get hurt. But, that safe place? Might not be as safe as you think. And? You don't have a relationship. Except with yourself. Learning? Impossible without an honest relationship. You need a relationship with your kids."

"And that's why you think I'm angry? I'm hiding?"

Irritated, Buck tugged at the towel. "That's why I *know* you're angry." He shrugged his shoulders and shifted his torso and shoulders in time to the rock music from the other room, heedless of the slipping towel. "This is funny. Sometimes you got to stick your ass out. Or realize it's showing. And then decide what you want to do about it. There are lots of possibilities." He slapped his companion on the back. "Let's get dressed. LaVerne and, who's his friend? Baja? They'll probably think we got a thing for each other in here." They opened the door to the cavernous main room. The volume of the sound almost knocked them over:

*You are my ev'ry-y-y-th-a-a-ng.*
*And I wi-i-i-ll st-a-a-nd by yo-u-u-u.*

# *CHAPTER XVII*

## *Showcase Time*

The hemline of her navy blue accordion-pleated skirt dipped in front, below the knees. But now, the dip was more pronounced because she had to lean into the still-too-low microphone. Platinum hair fell in stiff tresses over her shoulders. Metallic, gilt-framed glasses, inlaid with plastic tortoise, were poised in her left hand. She surveyed the half-filled room with a tolerant smile. Once again, she swiveled to check the dignitaries seated behind her.

Reassured, she smiled a return to the audience. "What brings us here today, as I am sure you are well aware of, is the just outstanding achievements of our Fillmore GATE program. That's right, there's threats out there. Nowadays, single race schools, Traditionalists, growl at us when we come up to the starting line alongside of them. And you know why?" She bobbed her head in agreement. "Scared: blank-blank: that we'll beat 'em! But, well, let 'em eat their hearts out! We should worry! And this show-case for our GATE students today will prove that our kids are just as good as at any of Their schools."

Obviously self-satisfied, she became less acerbic. "Well, I'm just so happy to be with you here today? But I might ask for your attention, please? And may we to begin? Thank you."

Executing another pirouette to reassure herself that the dignitaries were still there, she beamed a closed-lip smile to the audience, eyes clenched. "Now, as you know, I'm Ms. Rhonda Davenport? GATE coordinator? Gifted and Talented Students? And I'm just super excited to have you here with me today? On this shining occasion?"

Sneaking another glance behind her, she continued, lower jaw thrust forward. "And, once again. Realize, these are your top academic student achievers! They're the ones giving the lie to Traditionalists who says we're 'less than'."

"But, first along, I know you want to meet our dignitaries. So, to lead off we have that just super leader of distinction, our Superintendent, Dr. Elayne Jones-Laporte who has been a real straight-shooter for GATE program these donkey's years: that has made GATE such a outstanding success the years I've been Coordinator?" She beamed effusively. "And before we hear from you, just let me say, here and now, how just on yesterday I told her how very much we do appreciate all the benefits she imposes on our students. Dr. Laporte?"

The dignitary in question nodded brisk concurrence with Pritchard. Their shoulders touching, he arched his eyebrows and smiled broadly. She untwisted long legs, moving her head gravely in unison with Pritchard, then, scowling, placed her Coach handbag on the floor beside the chair, and moved to the podium.

"And thank you so very much, Ms. Davenport. What could we ever do without you? A Fillmore icon!"

Her severely tailored suit exemplified appropriate female executive attire. A brown pin-stripe, with short, tight-fitting skirt; it was a backdrop for the gold, red, and blue Givenchy scarf trailing over one shoulder and secured by a prominent circular gold medallion: intertwined script 'J-L' in diamonds. From the gold rope chain around her neck, glimmered a gold Mercedes-Benz emblem. Her gold Rolex was also diamond-studded and Italian calf shoes complimented the bag. A grin hesitated on the face, militating somewhat, the hawk-like features and glistening sheet of seamless black hair.

"We, in our District, and probably especially with Fillmore, have so very much to be proud of with our achievements. And especially our GATE achievers. So, thank you, Ms. Davenport. So very much. You are a inspiration, a blessing, to us all in your attainment."

Her face narrowed. "GATE showcase gives me the capability to say two critical ideas. First and obvious: Reform has already started in our district. And we'll have more of it. So Others when they try to parade their superiority at us will find out! We see the proof right here in front of us: our GATE students! And I'm sure, many years from now, these young ladies will not look back in rage, but with pride, at the blessings they achieved. Here, at Fillmore."

Laporte nodded gravely to the audience. "And second? What GATE does? It evidences my unerring belief: that we don't have 'at risk' youngsters in our district! Anywhere! No! I won't allow that terminology to be used! By anyone! Ever! It's another way Traditionalists have of trying to scare us into thinking we're 'less than'."

"Say it, girl. Doctor."

She accepted the accolade jettisoned from the audience. "GATE proves the lie of Traditionalists: that our kids are as good as any. And with the proposed Reform Plan? We'll be just a whole lot better." She swiveled abruptly, paused, and re-encountered the audience. "Reform Plan? Will give us more betterment. So, I'm going to call on Mr. Pritchard to illuminate us on that? Mr. Pritchard? If you would, sir?"

Pritchard smiled somewhat, and grasped Davenport's extended hand. "It is a special pleasure to see the work of a dedicated leader like Ms. Davenport, who puts students first: helping them achieve. GATE is the proof of Dr. Laporte's testimony that we are not 'at risk'. No. That we have made, already, great strides. And that is the purpose of Reform: to continue that forward momentum. Not to disrupt. Not to undo. Let me reassure you that there are certain things we do not want Reform to do."

He spread his hands to quiet the possibility of applause. "Accountability? People say our Reform doesn't want it! Not true! We do. But not Accountability that expects students to reach impossible educational levels. Dooming them to failure before they start! Our Reform will hold teachers accountable for interpreting the curriculum according to the special needs of their own students: that *they* know best."

"Accountable for test results? Of course! But, for now, teacher made tests. Reform Accountability will not mean an outside consultant spying on your teaching through a computer system, saying a certain teacher's students, based on test results, do not measure up! To what that outsider, probably not even an educator, thinks they should be! Based on *his* outside 'norm'! Castigating that teacher as incompetent: refusing to allow *her* to consider special student needs."

He continued, interrupting the applause. "My friends, our Reform Plan will not jeopardize the role of the Teachers' Union. And Reform will be local, designed *by* us, not *for* us! Our Reform will be *listening*! Hearing *your* needs in the classroom. *Your* dedication to students. Our Reform will not be designed in the marble halls of the state or national capitol. It will be designed here. By you! So that you create the future of education. As you, the professionals, know best. Making public education the fulcrum of our God-given democracy." He waved aside their applause and accepted a hug from Ms. Davenport.

"And thank you so very much, sir, for the benefit of your words. Your wholesome message. Personally, I feel that you are anointed to guide our school district to the Garden. That the Lo-ord will provide a safe harbor for our students here at Fillmore."

Smiling hugely, adjusting her spectacles, Davenport continued. "And now! This is what it's all about. We'll just to ask our GATE *Fillmorians* to demonstrate on their own behalf? Exhibit their accomplishments! So! Without further ado, I will invite Ms. Shernise Bigby and Ms. Lorayne Twiller, both Grade Twelve? Seniors? To please to step forward? Here? At this time? And ladies and gentlemen please to put your hands, and hearts, together for these two young ladies as they will give a rendition of a world-class poetry."

She beamed as the girls, doubled over in laughter pointed at one another. Shernise struggled keeping one palm over her mouth, but at a nod from Davenport, Lorayne was able to modulate her own giggling. "The title of our rendition is," she struggled to contain her tittering, *Yet, You Worship Me.* But we'll be saying it together?" Another Davenport nod and each produced a written text. They read in unison.

"You fear my pow-er,
    Yet, you worship me!
You castrate my men,
    Yet, you worship me!
You suffer my wisdom.
You refuse to honor Krishna, while
You remake me with missionaries!
    Yet, you worship me!"

Gaining confidence, they continued.

"You are all in my Blackness;
And my Blackness is all in you.

The Pope kisses my feet;
    I am the Black Madonna.
I dance in my own temple;
    I am the Black Tie ball.
    I am larger than life:
    I am the Black Sea.
    I am incomprehensible:
    I am the Black Forest.
    I ride the fierce wind of rebellion:
    I am the Black Stallion.

The students gestured dramatically for the final verse, pointing accusatory fingers at the audience to emphasize second person pronouns:

"*You* are all in my blackness:
And my blackness is all in *you*.
I am the wine *you* prize:
    I am 'the darker the berry'.
I gamble with *your* sincerity:
    I am the Black Jack dealer.
I am 9/10ths of *your* seed:
    I am the Black child.
I am the first world out of place:
    I am *your* third eye.
I am *your* classiest color:
    I am basic Black.
And *you* worship me!
So: what *is* the problem?"

The applause was scattered. "Thank you so *very* much, young ladies! I know we all derived a blessing from their intonation. To witness what our students could do? I always think poems should put things in the right place for where we're headed, not for some ancient time in the past."

Struck by a thought, she interpolated. "As you could tell, in my English classes, we have writers that talk about important things that's happening in the here and now? Not have outsiders tellin' us that new writers are 'less than'. That we need old writers: back from some Jurassic Park time! Anyway, my kids always get a good chuckle when we reference 'D-E-M's': Dead European Male writers. They've decided that D-E-M's don't have a message for them so we don't need to keep on tryin' to concentrate on their by-gone writing and prejudices: tryin' to menace us, tryin' to demand that we accept *their* culture. Make us try to figure out what they're talkin' about. No, I have to tell you, our kids don't appreciate being told they're supposed to have to wander around in '18th century Country Churchyards' or be thinking about stuff like standing on 'Waterloo Bridge'—wherever that is—and all such like that. No! They like to find out about today issues. The here and now? That today writers talk about. That matter to kids. For their futures. Because they're finding out how prejudiced the 'before system' was toward them. Not allowing for them to express their own culture! So, yes! Let's move our school District forward to stamp out the threat of the unequal. Like Mr. Pritchard says."

"I'd like to make a agreement? With Reform?"

"And you are?" Davenport turned down the corners of her mouth and gestured with a gold roller pen.

"Cherry Hamilton. County Parole Officer: Fillmore permanent detachment. I don't want Reform that's soft on crime and criminals! We need the out-of control guys locked up. Not paroled. And yeah: jack'em around: hard! That'll get their attention. Sure, it could be harsh on them. So? We need harsh detentions. But, hey! Life's a B! They gotta learn. Guys has to be put away. No more yakkety-yakkety about 'rights'! No! Step on 'em. And hard! Power punch 'em! And sure, it might could cause some discomfort! But so does renditions! So does Gitmo! Same for Abu! Teach 'em who's boss. Now. Not for the future."

"And you have your hand up? You would be Mr. Huerta, I believe?"

"Affirmative. I think Reform should set up a five path educational system—not tiers, not levels. Recognize that everyone is *not* the same: sameness is the albatross around our necks. Legitimize different interests. Different skills."

"About what?"

"Education can't be the same for everyone. Because people have different abilities. Different interests. Different psychological make-up. Different backgrounds."

"So, you believe in unequal? And you say you're for kids?"

"We need to redefine our educational system: so that we can offer equal opportunity to different people. Repeat: different is *not* unequal. It's Reality. Reform has to face that."

"Say what you got to say, man! Then sit down."

"Education needs five branches: equal but different. One: academic preparation for academic college courses: chemistry, math, literature, languages sorts of things. Second: non academic high school courses in preparation for non-academic college courses: sexuality, Chicana Studies, Social Diversity, for example. Third: technical high school courses—electricity, computers, as examples—to prepare for technical college courses or as an end in themselves: for job preparation. Four: train our students in jobs and skills: plumbing, tile setting, carpentry, auto repair, hair stylist. Teach them a skill so they can earn a living. And Five: a Supervised Learning tier where those who cannot adjust to courses of any kind, don't accept normal constructive social interactions, are given a uniform, assigned work, paid a minimum wage—forestry, infra structure repair, for example—until they acquire the social skills necessary to be in a program where they learn a trade or do academic work. After they have learned accountability. Consequences."

"Hey, geek! Stuff it! You don't like our kids? Then go to a Traditionalist school where you'll be happy. Not try to put your racism on us."

Davenport noticed another hand. "Yes? You are?"

"I'm Vangi Stillcart? Journalism and Year Book." Large white letters: W.Y.N.A.M.F.T.J.-A.W.W.D.I, were emblazoned on the baby blue background of her voluminous sweat shirt.[23] "Everybody keeps on blabbing on about how our kids in senior high school can't read, or write? Not do math? Well, why not have Reform to go back to the alementary and junior high feeder schools and find out why those schools, teachers and administrators, didn't do *their* jobs? Reform *them*? See why their teachers not teaching. Not act like it was all our faults. Why kids didn't learn *before* they get here." She muffled a sneeze. "We can reform ourselves to death. If kids get here unprepared, our Reform is wasted time. That's all I got to say."

"What about if we 'reform' all our teachers that's taking kids to private clubs, to swimming parties, and even dating them? Was a time, least ways some of us could remember, that teachers had a dress code and a moral code that made it so they didn't do their private lives with kids."

"I don't think we need to get into personal morality issues here, sir. Ms. Weatherby?"

"I think Sgt. Hershey has a good point. Personally I would expect Reform Plan to follow up on that. I was going to say that whatever Reform

23 W.Y.N.A.M.F.T.J: -A.W.W.D.I. When you need a man for the job: a woman will do it.

we do, it needs to have built in monitoring, so we keep tabs on our progress: what's working: what isn't sort of thing. Revise. Adjust. Periodic review of goals. So we meet them."

"That lady's got a hellava good point. Go for it."

"Mr. Dimmock, please! Language! Let me remind you! There are young people here, after all!"

"Sorry, Ms. Davenport!"

"How about if Reform was to cut back on the number of days we have kids out of class for assemblies, pep rallies, informationals, cultural learning days, field trips to the Petting Farm? Stuff like that?"

"And your name would be?"

"Chandra Rajogopalachari, Algebra II. Why not do Reform ourselves? We know the problems. We can construct the solutions. Teachers will be more likely to accept it if they've designed it. Not outsiders."

"Get with it you guys! Who's all the ones sayin' everthangs so bad! I think we're doing pretty darn good. Right now! GATE is proving the point. We'll get there. Just give us a tad more time to do it in. And more money! Let us find our own way. Sure, we might have a few wrinkles. But we can iron them out. We're OK. GATE proves it."

"Right! And sure; sure we got a few problems. Sure we do!"

"And you might be, sir?"

"Blaise Martyn-West: Driver-Ed? Everybody knows me. My thought is taken from that guy in the Cadolic Church? In the red silk? I mean he's got it on right side around: Sure, they'res some problems! He admits it in his Church! Like he said, a few bad apples in the barrel? So? No big deal! Don't mean the whole barrel-fuls bad! I won't lie to you!"

"Your point, sir?"

"We got a few cracks in our dam too! No big deal! Just ignore the rotten ones. Don't eat 'em. Then we'll be fine. Don't have to throw out the whole barrel. That guy not sayin' his whole Church is bad, just 'cause of some goofosities. In it. No, way! Same goes for us! Not say all about schools is bad 'cause of maybe a few bad apples. Happens all the time. I mean look at some of the goofeses in government? Sex, drugs, lying, gay rest rooms? Are we goin' to throw out the whole government? No way, Jose! No big deal. Sh . . .stuff happens. Everywhere. We'll get there."

"Hello! Everyone? I mean I'm Nancy Toomey: woodshop? I'm for Reform that keeps us on our track? Now, we got sixty percent gender superiority in woodshop, now. And upping! Be eighty percent not before long down the road. I'll go for Reform that supports gender-specifics like what we're doin' in Wood Shop. Change the see-saw. So the bottom goes up. It's our chance now."

"This meeting has indeed been a blessing! We're about to end but let me just to say, before? That our Reform will be looking at the future? Not just at the here and now? And, folks, let's just to relax! About it! Chill, as the kids would say. We need to 'roll with the flo'. Muddle through. We'll make it. As that man just said. Somehow. We always do. Let's rock and roll. It's gotten us this far. Thank you for supporting our GATE kids. They're a blessing. And so are you." Ms. Davenport swirled and bowed to the dignitaries.

# *CHAPTER XVIII*

## *Deuce is Wild*

Besserian crouched low, pivoted and sent his right fist solidly into the padded mitt.

"One! Two! Hook! Right! C'mon—sit on it!" Buck shouted at him over the din, "Doin' it now, boy!"

Besserian danced back, kept his fists high, breathing hard. He was exhilarated. He came in low and sent a left jab straight into the mitt.

"Double jab! Left hook! Hurt me!"

Jabbing, pivoting to his right, he shot the hook. Buck moved the mitt higher, taking the punch. Besserian followed with a left upper cut, then a right combination. Both men laughed. "Not so fast there, big guy! Not in The Center yet! A hook. Try it again. And don't think so much. Just do it!"

The noise at *Deuce Is Wild* Boxing Club seemed louder than usual. Blaring Rap. Three speed bags banging: bullet-like staccato rhythms. Shouting, cursing, laughing. The three-minute buzzer. The one minute buzzer. Thirty-second buzzer flashing its white warning; two minute green light.

"Hey Lobo! Over here, man! Phone. Step on it! You want that fight? Next month? Vegas? You ready?"

"Hold it! Yeah! Be right there." The two trainers yelled; partly because of the din, partly though habit.

In front of a wall of mirrors were three rope jumpers, energized into their individual rhythms, each counting his own time, lost in his unique rhythm. The cadences were altered by gracefully executed cross-overs, turns and double jumps, whirling movements; dancing with themselves, relishing the fluidity of their own gleaming bodies, mesmerized, liberated into their own unabashed physicality. At the signal from the blinking white light, shouting the command to himself, one of them, a Nureyev prototype, leapt into double jumps, knees to midsection: for thirty seconds the leather cord was a blur.

Besserian , drenched in sweat, T-shirt glued to his trim torso, moved in an intermittent shower of moisture. Buck, calling out commands, bounded aggressively and gracefully: right, left, forward, back. It was their fourth round. When, finally, the white light blinked, Besserian was heaving. Buck was euphoric, "Thirty seconds, buddy. Don't let up! Give it all you got! You got the strength, son. One! Two! Get under! Hook! Right! Keep low. Straight from the shoulder. Come at me! Come at me! Come on! Don't get wild. Keep your stance. You can do it. You got it, boy!"

Besserian followed the other man's movements, shooting out his fists: clean, hard—beyond what he could do. The banshee screech of the buzzer: the green light glowered as he threw his last punch. Misjudging the distance, he was hurtled, careening onto Buck and then into the ropes which bounced him resentfully.

Buck exploded in laughter. "Hey, you trying to kill me!"

Cyril, their occasional sparring partner, shouted energetically to make sure everyone was aware of the mishap, himself doubling over in laughter. "He's down! That boy's down for the count! Be lookin' up at them lights, now." He pranced around the outside of the ring. "See, that's what happens. You ain't some nineteen years old kid. No. Not'ny more, you ain't. Got to realize, guys over a certain age? They get older. Not younger." He was sated with his own laughter. "And they got trouble keeping up more than their gloves."

"Don't tell us your problems, Cyril." Buck pummeled Besserian's head with a towel, who, head thrown back instinctively, mouth open, took the jet of water squirted into his mouth and spat into the funneled container.

Buck shot another stream of water over the glistening scalp. "Good job, guy. Real good. Take it slow. Don't gulp. We already got our speed bag work. Get on the heavy bag. Then we'll call it a day."

"Got it." Exhausted, Besserian stepped between the ropes and grabbed a towel from his bag, wiping head, face, and upper body. Buck, his energy boundless, was in the ring sparring with Cyril, circling around his target, dodging, weaving, keeping his head out of the line of fire. Bear, another trainer, watched from the floor. "Hey, man. Straight from the shoulder, boy! Snap it out! Don't lean." The buzzer clattered. Buck threw a final right hook, clamped Cyril firmly on the back and called over to Besserian.

"You ready? To leave?"

"Just about."

"Looking good. Like you know what you're doing." Move up to working out with Bear pretty soon. Got more ring experience. Than me."

"You handle those mitts like you're sparring with me."

There was no one else in the miniscule changing room: combination broom closet, gear locker, and equipment storage area. Besides the painted, scarred, bench, there was a discarded desk chair, back careening awkwardly as if dropped from a third-story window. A dented scale was canted, missing one of its tiny wheels. Bear claimed it was as accurate as any of the more "fancy" models at The Center. "Weigh a boy here on this one. Always be most one pound of difference. No, this is good! Don't measure height too good but we can see what that is."

There was a plastic container on the counter: shirts, towels, jocks, shorts, socks; dirty or stiff with sweat and salt. It bore a crudely lettered sign: 'Lost and Found. All gear not removed by Tuesday will be throwd.' Besserian could identify several articles he knew had been there for at least two months. It was useful if you forgot your shorts, shirt, or towel. By the door beside the bench, were two jagged holes in the wallboard: irritation, anger, energy, exhilaration, frustration? Under the bench was a jumble of foot gear: jogging, boxing, Nikes, street shoes, some with a mate. Lacking a window, a six-inch diameter fan struggled heroically to circulate the viscous air. Besserian, to himself, had named it Sisyphus.

Privacy and space were not priorities. The battered door was often stuck, partially open. Occupancy by more than four necessitated stumbling, blocking, side-stepping, bending, pushing, rearranging of gear.

And boxing gym bags were enormous. Besserian was struck by the amount of gear guys lugged with them: street shoes, gym shoes, shirts, shorts; sweaters, one, probably two pairs of gloves; mitts, towels, interminable lengths of tangled hand wraps, jocks, groin protectors, Vaseline, lineament, head protector, tape, scissors, several ropes, mouth pieces, vitamins, training guides, CD's, boxing magazines, vitamins, training videos. Quite different from the clean, compact, little bags appropriate for Me Fitness.

The usable space might have been four by sex. On the floor were two five-gallon plastic buckets filled with lengths of chain, nails, screws, locks, hooks, bolts, bag swivels, screwdrivers, hammers, pliers, wrenches. Long-handled bolt cutters, rested against a bank of nine small lockers, badly dented which Besserian had never seen anyone use.

"Looking good today! Better! Good stamina! Good recovery. Landed some clean punches. I got you a couple of times with the mitts, too. Hard." Buck slapped him lightly on the back, enjoying his own observations. "One thing I noticed. You need to keep moving on the heavy bag; ducking, weaving, moving like you had a real target. I told you that! Anyway, you're getting there. Never going to be a boxer. I mean these guys been doing this since they were ten. And they got natural coordination. But you're moving along. Once you make up your mind, you stick to it. No telling what you might do."

"You look like you were doing pretty good with Bear yourself. Sparring? Next time? Us? See how much we've learned."

Buck shrugged. "Maybe." He was busy with his bag. "OK. I got extra head gear. So you don't have to get any. Got the mouth piece? Like I told you?"

"Got it."

"Don't want you losing any teeth. What'll the kids say? Teacher got jumped! Punked! Hanging out at *Conquistador*!" He was exuberant. "Just kidding. Anyway you'll probably knock me on my ass. Next time." Buck, kicking off his drenched shorts, balanced on one foot, holing out his hand, and they mechanically touched fists to confirm the next meeting as well as for support.

Besserian zipped his bag. "About ready?"

"Sure. One minute. Glad you like this place." He tugged the large bag, *Everlast Boxing* prominently marked in red letters, between his feet. "I thought you would. I'm pretty accurate in figuring people out. I figured you'd like the exercise. Makes you feel great. One thing I noticed?"

"What's that?"

"You hold yourself back. Careful. Afraid to let yourself go. Like you might run out of steam. And then you'd be fucked. Don't hold back. It's just like Bear said. The biggest muscle you got?"

Besserian scowled, rummaging in his own bag.

"Is in your head. That's what makes you finish the round. Throw another punch. When you think you can't. And another thing?"

"Tell me."

"It's like sometimes you're thinking 'what if'. Trying to plan every punch from the beginning. Can't do that. Roll with the punches however they come. Sure, you got your plan. But you can't iron out all the wrinkles before you start. Like you have to be perfect in everything. All the time. You screw yourself up that way. Need to relax. Shit, man! We're here to have some fun! Play some games! Get rid of tension. Sweat. Hit the bag. Feel good. Roll with it! But you're OK. You follow directions. Listen to the teacher."

"You notice a lot."

"I get paid for noticing. People. The better they do their jobs, the more money they make for me. I tell them: you don't have to hit it right on every time. Like Bear says, even the pros fuck up sometimes. Throw a bad punch. You're not the only one! Even me. Need some help, sometimes. Point is to just do it! Don't worry about what you look like! Don't beat yourself up. And sure, it can be intimidating here. Everybody's evaluating everybody else. It's all about appraising the other guy. As a potential opponent. So? Screw them! Worry about what you want to achieve. Not them. Don't worry about running out of energy. Or you will. And you're not flailing. Like you used to. Getting so you back off, now. Take a bearing on the other guy. Get your breath. Not panicking like when we started."

"Got your bag. Ready?"

The gym was filling up. Buck slapped various shoulders and backs, nodding, smiling broadly. The exchanges were ubiquitous, punctuated with hugs, touching fists:

"Good to see you, man."

"Looking good, buddy."

"Stay out of trouble."

"Watch your ass, man."

"Thanks Bear. See you when? Friday?"

"You got it, buddy."

There was the gambit of obligatory 'high-fives' and complimentary sexual insults.

"Lucked out getting a parking space. Not safe to park on the street. Not in this area. And this is a good time. Not so crowded as later."

"Door's unlocked. Your side."

"You got your Project. Need to make it work."

"Starts Monday."

"Good. Score a knockout with this one. Knock that place on its ass. That's what it needs. For the kids. For you, too. Anyway, let's get rolling. Have to get back to the office. Make some more money. And you got to watch your ass. All the time. Anticipate the other guy's move. Look away for a second, and you'll be decked. As Cyril says, 'looking up at them lights'." He mimicked the accent.

"And?"

"In the ring? That's reality. Like a model of life. Guy decks your ass. So? You get up and what? Try again. Winner is the one who conditions himself; improve his strategy, so he lands more than he gets. Pretty simple really. Most people? Bitch 'cause they get hit. Crying 'cause nobody should have hit me'," he imitated a whining child. "Like getting in the ring and expecting the other guy to what? Sing me a song! Don't work that way, buddy boy. Anyway turn right here! In this alley. I got my own elevator. Up to the office. Don't forget! Friday! Enjoyed it."

# *CHAPTER XIX*

## *Opinions*

"Well, this is simply wooonn-der-*ful*. Ab-so-*lut*-a-ly! Oh! And I am just so-oo glad all of you could all make it here today—be my guests here with us today?" There was giggling assent from the restive audience. "No. I mean it. Really!" She shook her glistening black tresses, a twisted truncheon, held by a rhinestone clip. "This is *très* cool. Ah-some! I am simply just so ex-*ci*-ted about what is going to be transfixing on the show here today!" She untwisted her legs, extricating herself from a rose-colored divan, gold tassels dangling from the armrests. Three steps below, two smaller couches, blue brocade with silver tassels, accommodated four guests.

Adjusting her profile, descending the mirrored steps, she centered herself between the divans, rotating on one stiletto heel, smiling acknowledgement to the overloud, recorded, applause. Mesmerized by the camera, the MC displayed a strapping silhouette, outlined by the black jersey dress, highlighted on the right hip, by a rhinestone and citrine broach. A saffron, blue and green Gucci scarf draped itself over the right shoulder. The signature devices were prominent: clipboard clasped over the prominent chest, and diamond encrusted rollerball suspended on a retractable chain from an enameled pink ribbon.

Overhead, the source of the dazzling spots that spun over the walls, was an enormous revolving mobile. Surmounting the couches, was a marquee, white lights racing around the perimeter, proclaiming: *Hit it Now—With Denise. The Denise Show!*

"Good morning, buenas días,. . . bon giourno,. . . Shalom, everybody! And how *are* we all? This screechingly beautiful day? Welcome to yet another *sparkling* edition of the: Denise Show." Her daunting smile widened. "Yes, I'm Denise Sellwyn-Lloyd, as you know," she grinned coyly, "and I am just so-o-oo happy—ecstatic really—to be here with you again on this glorious Cloud Nine day! And, Oh! Praise be! You're just going to really *love* the show today! We have some just *super* exciting guests and I just know they'll arouse you: all talented, successful, professional women! Who comprehend the score on educational issues. All community and business leaders! All examples of women on the move—in a take-over mode of progressive gender equality." She nodded solemn assent. "Ah-some!"

She twisted gleaming lips and waited. The daunting bass of the rock music gave way to a Joan Baez type voice keening, in an off pitch minor key, "*...love is a fleeting mist—a shadow which can never be held*" with a zither and harp accompaniment. Stealthily, the camera drew closer, and her large features gradually consumed more of each TV monitor.

"Ladies—and we will be deemphasizing the gentlemen here today?" She nodded solemnly, "And there are some mounting concerns in our community? About the future role of public education? And right here? In one of our Los Altos subdivisions: Cathedral Heights? And something you need to be aware of folks: things! Exciting things, are occurring in this up-swing minority-based community! It's on the move! And we'll be netting that out today. For you."

Immediately, her voice was hushed with dreadful concern. "So, education Reform, is the vital concern that the show will be highlighting this day. We're all down with that. A issue that proves how our minority cultures are on the cutting edge of solutions. Not problems." She nodded in somber self re-agreement, allowing the gravity of the situation to be appreciated. "So? Alora: here today we'll be exploring the innermost details of this critical education issue and considering what *each* of us, as concerned mothers, daughters, sisters, wives, significant others, can do to deflect it." Her head vibrated gravely in self-affirmation; claret lips downturned, eyes dilated, legs spread somewhat wider than she realized.

Her jubilant mood reappeared. "But before I introduce our lovely and scintillating studio *guests*, our panelists, I need to take just a brief moment in time to thank our just super studio *audience*: for joining us here, today?"

The camera swung over two four-tiered benches. The audience, as if on cue, shouted and screamed their enthusiasm. Undeterred, those nursing infants jumped to embrace one another. All wore voluminous T-shirts: "We love you, Denise"; "Girls Rule," and "Behind Every Successful Woman, There's A Man—In Need."

Denise blew kisses. "I just *love* you all so much. Thank you so *very* much. . . your struggle. . . your wholeness. . . your selfhood." Waving to them, smile flashing, swiveling again, she confronted the panelists.

"OK! So! Let's rock and roll! We have just a enormity of so thrilling guests here with us here today. And, I'm just *dying* to meet each and every one of you! So? Who shall we start with? I just feel like a kid in a candy store, don't you know!" She approached a blue couch and keeping her profile to the camera, squeezed herself between two of the guests. To the lady on her right, she blew a perfunctory kiss. "Thank you so very much? We'll be with you in just a petite min-ute? OK, sweetie?"

Rotating to her left, she confronted the interviewee. "Now, and Oh! You look so-oo ravishing! Intensifying! And could you give us *your* name?" She smirked into the camera. "As if I didn't already know! Ha! Ha!"

"With exuberance, Denise!" I am Sushana Boyce-Gonzalez? And I *am* absolutely *spellbound* to be here!" She grimaced, adjusted the pink and blue sari over her left shoulder, and tossed a tousled heap of blonde-like crimped hair.

"And don't you know, we're so totally delighted to *have* you here? Thank you so *very* much. And could you please to tell us your spec-i-al-ity?"

"Delighted, Denise. I'm a certified neurophysiologist—educator? And counselor? And school consultant?"

"Anything else? There's more, I know. This is one lady who has just a plentitude of talents."

"And author?" Sushana reflected and then smiled with mock diffidence. "And lecturer." She waited. "And political activist; slash docent."

"Wow! That's quite a designation! Far out!" Denise drew back and cocked her wrist. "Isn't it just *stunning* the way women are entering into these exotic and intellectual pursuits which were formerly reservist? Traditionalist! Breathtaking! And I'm vibing on how you're a strong child's advocate, Sushana? Based on your recent book that I'm so looking forward to hearing just a whole *lot* more about. It's, let's see, uh!" Denise glanced at notes over half-glasses. "*Beyond the Classroom: Mind Robotics, the Supra Learning Methodology*. And recently out by, uh, New York . . .?"

"Eastland Press."

"Of course. Typo here. Now, your penetration into . . . what? . . . well, the scholastic education of children? Will fascinate us. . ."

"Child learning modalities: Dream and Play Therapies."

"Whatever. Movie rights? In the offing?" Denise smiled gushingly. "You've got it going, girl!" She caressed Sushana's hand, avoiding most of the tourmaline, smoky quartz and turquoise rings. Head tilted to the side, she smiled wistfully, "I know ever so many school districts are experiencing your modalities. Having you to assist their teachers to be more caring? In the classroom? So, we *really do* need to hear about your help mode. We need you, Sushana! You're a beacon. For kids."

With a toss of the truncheon, she swung to the guest on her right, glancing to make sure the camera was following.

"Oh my! *Quelle plaisire!"* Clipboard high on her breast, arms crossed, a solicitous Jan Crouch clutching her bible, she exuded sincerity. "And *you* might be?" She gazed earnestly into the face of her second guest. Sensing apprehension, Denise took her hand in a comforting gesture, and beamed patronizing sympathy.

"We're all friends here and we are just so *very* happy to have this lady here with us here today; don't you know! And again? If you would?"

There was an awkward pause indicating the guest did not understood the question.

"There, there. . . it's going to be . . . *Su nombre*?"

*"¿Que pasó? Me llamo Dolorosa Sanchez."*

"Thank you just so *very* much, Ms. Sanchez. And your interest in our program is . . .?"

Sanchez looked inquiringly, mutely, at the other guests.

"I believe you-have-children-in-our-high-school ...? You-are-a-concerned-par-ent?" Denise enunciated with excruciating care, the overly solicitous kindergarten instructor.

"Got four childs in school now. Two in high school."

"Well, that is just so *super.* Won-der-*ful*! Grey-eat! And I believe you *are* active in the Fillmore School Community Advisory Board? Have assisted on some interview committees for teachers?" Denise ruffled her notes. "That is just so ah-some to have parents involved in running our schools! And we'll be talking a little later on about how important it *is* for parents to be *included*? In school governance. And if there's any problems with that." She patted her guest's knee reassuringly, moving her head in self-agreement. "So, we'll *definitely* be back to *you*, Señora. *Qué Dios te guarde!*"[24]

A studio attendant had wheeled a fuchsia upholstered chair opposite the other couch. She settled into it, drawing close to her next guest, giving the camera a clear frontal shot. Crossing her legs elaborately, her muscular thighs caressed the ridges of black stockings.

"Oh my! And who is this?" Denise was gushing. "Sweetie, you are just *so lovely*! This is a revelation! To be your age again! With that 'peaches 'n cream complexion'! And that simply *gorgeous* hair! To die for!" Denise was keening. "Well, we're just so *very* happy to have *you* with us here on the show today?" She analyzed the interviewee: tight, low-rise distressed jeans, badly torn on one knee, wide belt: the buckle, a brass six-shooter aimed downwards. A pink tank top did not hide the bare midriff. Denise reached over, touching the hair reverentially, swept carelessly over one eye in a Princess Di style. "And *your* name would be?"

"Kasidye? And I'm a 12th grai-der at Fillmore High?" She spoke in a monotone, barely audible, slurring the words.

"You're going to have to open your mouth up just a wee bit wider, sweetie, and speak up so all of us could hear?"

Kasidye giggled, twisting, biting a thumbnail. "I'm a strai-ht 'Ay' stu'ent. All my teachers can reference that. I plan on attending a four year university? Major in, dunno for sure yet?" She giggled coyly. "Cinema? Politics? Double major. Minor in. . .," she giggled, "Well, I'll have to let you know about that?" She tossed her hair, eyes shut.

"Fab! So education, higher education, is *definitely* in a affirmative mode for *you*!"

Kasidye sniggered, re-tossing her hair, twisting energetically on the divan, drawing up one boot and sitting on it. "Emphasis on Women Movie Directors? Dunno."

Denise drew back, her mouth gaping. "Spec-*tac*-u-*ler*!

Fab-uu-*lus.* And how about personal? I'm sure a young lady as *gorgeous* as you are has *no* problem what-so-ev-er! Fight 'em off, right?" She chortled knowingly. "Anybody serious?" Denise extended her tongue through parted teeth. "On the horizon? You'd care to tell us about? Any Family plans? In the offing?" Denise winked to the camera and smirked, lips turned down.

The young guest twisted bashfully and threw her hands over her face, hair flinging wildly. "Help! E-e-e-k!" She bit her lower lip, tugging at her

24 May God watch over you!

socks, pink lace with pom-poms, encircling the tops of thick-soled hiking boots. "I dunno? Sorta? Well, that's still down the road. Maybe? But nowdays, it's like totally about *personal*? Like your career? Always! I mean re-ally? Super bottom line." She screeched, a strident falsetto, chomping brutally on the other thumb nail.

"We need you to just to tell us, sweetie?"

"OK. But, I'm so totally *ner*-vus! Re-a-ll-y! Everybody looking at me? All my friends?" Flipping her hair over her shoulder several times, once again she snapped her eyes shut, face buried in hands.

"They're all loving you, sweetheart. And I just know they're as impressed as we are right here in the studio!"

Lifting her head, she managed to speak, "I volunteer? For battered women?" Buoyed, apparently by Denise's encouragement, Kasidye now, unexpectedly, found herself racing down a verbal ski jump; arcing high and then plummeting with unstoppable momentum. The pace of her speech increased exponentially. She was breathless. "And I play Varsity soccer and I'm on the Mock Trial team? Oh yeah! And I play *dee*-fence on the Broomball team; Powder Puff League? Went on to state finals last year, too? And I signed up for varsity football squad. De-fense Kick-Off?" She threw back her hands and gesticulated, breathing heavily. "And it really totally freaked me out! I mean totally! I'm like tryin' to kick the ball? And I could just *feel* all their rage! I just *know*? It's totally there!"

Denise, head tilted, squeezed Kasidye's hand, beaming commiseration, exuding the requisite support, as the girl breathlessly continued. "And I'm a finalist for Cinco de Maio queen? So, wow! There's just so much *stuff* going on! In my life! Totally can't believe it! Ah-some! In my existence!" Overcome, she covered her face, tossing her hair, desperate for respite from, at least, the weightiest of her accomplishments.

"Now, sweetie, we can appreciate how you're maxing yourself? A young lady with your strengths, and courage, but we do need to move forward."

"O-o-h!" She looked up, eyes blurred, still plummeting, still unstoppable. "And I'm applying for a couple a scholarships?" She bit her lower lip savagely. "Di'I say that? Anyways, I'm what you should call totally success motivated? I have a motivation-driven personal life-agenda. My counselor? Ms. Brauphman? She says I'm Type-A? Directed?"

"I'm sure you're a *very* active young lady." Denise beamed encouragement, twisting her lips.

"Well, Miss I just . . ."

"Someday, later on, we'll need to have you back on the show to tell us what it's like to break down the gender barrier on a formerly Traditionalist athletic team. Beat down that locker room door! Crusade for gender equality? Exploit the pink ribbon? So now, in addition to being very attractive . . . and by the way, I just *love* your outfit, you're a, let me guess . . . 'size five?"

"Four. Petit." Kasidye was ebullient.

"To die for! Oh!" Denise tapped both sides of her face with the tips of her nails, avoiding the dangling, rhinestone earrings, mouth drooping.

"And now! Our *next* guest is very *dignified* lady. I love the way she just sits there! So terribly, *correct*! Like in olden times! Like in that picture: *Somebody's Mother*? Whatever! Anyhow, I see you are . . . a Ms. Penny Besserian and *please*—do correct me if I get the pro-noun-ciation wrong. . .?"

"Correct."

"Now, you are *also* a very successful, and I might add, a very attractive, youngish career exec? So, could you to give us just a quick check list: an intro-bio to your career? I know you're on an career up-swing."

"Thank you, Ms. Sellwyn-Lloyd. I'm the Assistant Vice President of the TriDelta Corporation. I . .."

"Denise, . . . please, . . . sweetie." She was gushing. "And that *dress!* To die for! Picks up your coloring! *Sest cute*! We're not supposed to mention brand names on here, but I'm going to throw out caution into the winds? Here, for a minute? A Hazel Brooks?"

"No, it isn't. TriDelta, possibly you know, is a corporation that provides financial consulting and analysis to school districts: investments, budgeting, forecasting. So I can comment on financial matters. Relating to public education."

"Far out! Sounds intellectual. So, you're in a help mode—energetically involved in reform strategies? For schools? Ah-sum."

"Public schools. We are eager to support their reform efforts. Yes."

"That is just *so* exciting. And there's plenty of our listeners, and viewers who will want to learn your secrets for breaking that glass ceiling into top management. In that lion's den Traditionalist corporate world. We'll be coming back to you for sure, Penny." She nodded vigorously patting Penny's hand. "And thank you so *very* much for your input."

Denise moved to the días above the couches, and, seating herself behind the mirrored desk, turned into the camera and read from note cards. "Let's cut to the nuts and bolts of our diatribe, here today. So we can involve all our excellent panelists?" She spoke gravely, reading haltingly. "Now, in the interest of our peek into the 'how' of making public education better for our kids and especially with recent developments regarding a proposed Reform Plan? I'm going to toss out some hypos, and you can just jump in and . . . well . . . just say what you got to say." She smiled hugely and swiveled, now in a high-backed, tufted, pink naugahide chair.

"OK. Let's hit it!" She slurred the 's' and 'h' causing Kasidye to throw back her head, shake her hair violently, and grimace as if tasered. She sat yoga-style, head in hands, convulsing.

Denise ignored her. "Get our feet wet! And here's a biggie! A generic concern. How about that all-impor-ent issue? And that I know is so *very* critical? To public education? Let's hear it! How about: Salaries?"

The audience exploded as if on cue, and the camera fanned over their corroboration of the importance of salaries. Eating, drinking escalated: the subject distracted them from the children crawling and running on the benches.

Several shouted invectives. "That's the whole problem with schools! Don't help our kids: 'cuse not enough money. For kids!" The speakers held note cards. "State legislature keeps cutting back. While they fill up their own wallets with fat increases. And trips to foreign lands. I mean it's no wonder there's defailures, and all!"

"OK. Now, ladies, let's hold back. If we could. This is obviously a *very* sensitive area. But it's *really impor-ant?* Ms. Besserian*?"*

"Since school districts can't educate now with annual budgets in the millions, even billions, we're supposed to give them still more money? Fill a bottomless pit?"

"Wow! That's ripe! Do I hear Fascistic! So you're wanting to cut back? Take away? Steal from kids? And you're supposed to be a kid-centric!" Sushana was unable to subdue her outrage.

"I didn't say that. My meaning is perfectly clear. And Ms. Boyce, you know it. The issue is accountability. Results."

"What a 'b'! You're getting the big bucks yourself from consulting. And you want to cut back? What planet you living on, girl?"

"And let's try to tip-toe a little bit, all of us, from personals? I know we're all amped. These are just *super* important issues." Denise nodded, lips clenched. "I mean that's how you ladies reached your pinnacles. By stating your op-eds?"

She became meditative. "Here's something that interests us just a whole lot?" Denise swiveled on her chair. "Ms, Sen-yora? You're on the cutting edge of making schools accountable to and reflect the needs of the communities they serve? How well is that working? For Cathedral Heights? I know the law requires school-community interaction? Accountability."

"How what working?"

"School's accountability? To the community? School principal informs parents and community leaders what the goals of the school are? How kids are improving. How school problems being solved. Discuss teachers as leaders for the kids. Home-school interactions? Budgets? Teacher issues? Priorities? Planning? Academics?"

"Nada. Principal have a meeting maybe one time. A year. Don't know when? Maybe there's five? Six? People to come? And we don't know nothin' about money. How much? Spent on what for?"

"Did you ask?"

"Sure we ask! Lots of times. Mucho! She say that money is like a secret?"

"Tax-payer money a secret?"

"He say it to do with confidence maters: And 'nother else."

"Di me, senorina!"

"She say teachers knows how to teach. They's professionalisms. So don't nobody need to ask them nothin' about what they do. And 'nother thing."

"Please."

"We got teachers that's touching kids. And not only PE teachers, too. And some that's tellin' them 'bout private clubs. And some that's takin' them there. And all."

"Did you raise those points at the community meeting?"

"Ones we get to. Sure, we did. Principal say that go against union rules to tell people about teachers."

Penny was inquisitive. "Señora, what discussions are there at your community meetings about academic standards? Raising the intellectual level of students?"

Denise and the panelists watched carefully, unsure that Penny hadn't lit a fuse. Indeed, Señora Sanchez seemed puzzled. "Nada. Not really. Principal say they's the professionals. Teachers doin' as best as they can. Too many testes all the time."

"Well! That's the problems in the schools! They're you got it!" Sushana shook her head forlornly. "I been sayin' all along that we got to bring the metaphysics of *Mind Robotics* into the community as well as into the schools. And I'm available to do that. For them. Let me spread the word of *Mind Robotics* into the communities. Dumpster all this testing stuff!"

Denise became speculative. "Maybe schools should stop looking to the surrounding culture to tell them what to do. Reassert their own values? *For* the community."

"I agree with you Denise. Schools need to clarify their own values. Then assert them. Be leaders. Not followers. Until public education does that, our youngsters will retrogress according to the declining and fluctuating popular cultural value system, the cultural weathervane, in which they are now enmeshed. And public education will continue to have ineffective goals."

"Zero. A negativity on that. You from France, lady? Totally mind-splitting. Why you think we got consultant specialists? Out there?" Sushana was furious. "Schools got to reflect the culture. Not change it! Help! More off of the wall Fashistic gobbeldy-gook. Communism." Penny was the target of her rage.

The music blared. The audience howled as if on cue. "Ladies! This has been a scintillating meeting. We sure did hit it today! Wow! And how!" The camera pulled back, revealing the background lighting, cameras, microphones, technicians gesticulating and signaling from the banks of control panels.

"Reminds me of that song about how teachers to learn from their students! Yes, I think it's clear that 'Hit It With Denise', is the name of the game! For sure! Ladies! And we'll be back again with you on tomorrow. To explore more illuminating topics with just another super group of distinguished panelists."

She smiled hugely, lips turned down, and bowed low into the camera. "Good bye. God love! God keep! Our democracy! Forever." The background music wafted into silky strains of *Columbia, the Gem of the Ocean: Columbia, the Land of the Free.*

# *CHAPTER XX*

## *Altercation and Conversation*

"This area bothers me." He was tugging at his gym bag, pulling out a sweater. "Cold for January. Must be forty-five." Besserian appraised the street critically. "Good workout."

"Outta here." The jostling crowd, garish neon, thumping reverberations bellowing into the street were irritating. "You're doing pretty good on benches. And abs." Buck inhaled a huge gulp of air. "On our way!" He opened his jacket. "Where are you?"

"On the street. Lot was full. You?"

"In the lot."

"Give you a ride to your car."

Buck ran his finger inside his collar. "Why not? Give us a chance to loosen up. Bad area here. Getting worse."

No longer an exclusive residential area, the potholes were dangerous. Roots of Jacaranda and Chinese elms, unsightly and hazardous, jutted through upended sections of sidewalk.

With red and yellow neon outlining its concrete high tech—Neo Prison style, *Me Fitness* mocked the decline of the neighborhood: vacant or converted mansions, once the sumptuous residences of the cultural and financial *selecti quidem.*

"That's an impressive old house."

"Where?"

"Next one. On the right." He slowed their pace. "Built by Jason Audley, founder of the Audley Real Estate empire. The first Pritchard's brother-in-law. Murdered in the Billiard Room. Never solved. Some kind of investment scandal. Hey! Imagine the other stories, the secrets, these houses could tell."

"Could be. Especially the bedrooms. These look dark. Morbid. Empty. Shells. Only value lies in tearing them down. Area will be re-zoned in Phase Two of Reform Plan. I'll let you in on a secret about that: won't be low cost housing."

"Figures. I hate to see these go. Look at that port-cochère. On the side. Unusual in neo-Romanesque design. Imagine the gleaming Packards, Rolls, and Isotta-Fraschinis gliding up under it? Uniformed chauffeurs, ladies in furs and jewels. And their escorts, mysterious, even sinister, manipulating from the background."

"Maybe. You got quite an imagination there, Teach."

"Not entirely imagination. I took a tour last year. Mahogany paneling; marble, walnut, cherry floors; Tiffany glass; frescoed ceilings; bronze doors. Actually, deterioration is minimal. They were built to last. But nobody wants them."

"Built to last? But what they stood for didn't. So? They're relics. Beautiful, sure but now? Only interesting curiosities. Speaking of that, how's your Project going? To zip up your classes?"

"Got something started. It's going to be . . ."

"Hold it! What's that? God *damm* . . . !"

"Hey, what those two doin'? That's the 'shy one'. Afraid to speak up. For hisself?" Lycra and Bikini who, Buck had learned, were Lynn and DJ, called from across the street, tossing their hair and sniggering. "Like I thought! And them thinking they was acting so butch! And all! In the gym."

"Butch as a couple of tampons." Lynn slapped her companion on the arm. "Probably havin' a lover's spat?"

Pushing each other aggressively, swaggering, DJ laughed, "And if you want to know how to do it, fellah, I can teach you. Give you some lessons?"

"Don't worry, they know. With guys." Lynn answered her observation. "Done it lots of times. Probably goin' home now to do it!"

The men watched as they moved out of the light into the semidarkness.

Besserian shook his head ruefully. "The end of a perfect workout. My car's over there. Let's go." He muttered something to himself.

The scream was piercing: high-pitched and desperate. It was followed by loud shouts, scuffling, running. "You jest to come over here! Bitch! Get your ass back here, girl! I get you good! Slut!" He yelled an oath. "Get her, Jamesey! Hey, back here, cunt! Only want to play some games wid youns. Show you good time."

Besserian and Buck shot glances at each other, stepping back from the car and moving together to the middle of the street. "What the hell? Looks like two punks are on those girls? Where'd they come from?" Buck took long strides toward the sounds, motioning to Besserian. "Hey, grab my bag."

Tossing it beside the car, Besserian moved with him closer to the scuffling. "You're right. They're after those girls."

"Hey! You assholes! Screw off! Get lost, jerkoffs." Buck had moved into the commotion.

"Leroy! Get a load of that college mother. Wants to fuck wid us." Leroy had DJ by the sleeve, pulling her towards their truck; a gleaming Ram on chrome lifters. He glared at Buck. "Get lost, fag. You might to get yourself hurt?"

"You get ahold of that other one! Now, Jamesey! I got this one good." Struggling with Lycra, who was writhing fiercely, tearing at him with her nails, Jamesey was twisting his head away from the woman's flailing arms. There were gashes on his face, neck and forearms.

"You poufters better clear outta here. Don't concern youns. Screw off! You might to get hurt, younselves." Jamesey swung the woman around fiercely and brought one forearm across her neck, striking her hard in the face with his other palm.

"Hey! Wait a minute. What do you think you're . . . ?"

Besserian hesitated, considering his move. Leroy tightened his hold on 'Lifestyles' neck, half dragging, half pushing her in the direction of the truck.

Besserian froze. "Now, wait a . . ."

"Screw you, you white ass mother! You gonna try to be a little momma's boy hero? I bust you pussy ass!" Leroy, enraged, eyes dilated, tossed the woman to the pavement, gashing her face on the cement.

The man's huge hand doubled into a fist and Besserian felt the whistle of the leather sleeve across the front of his jacket. He ducked. Not quickly enough. It caught him on the side of the face, above the eye, a stinging blow that sent him reeling, dazed, struggling to maintain his balance. Caught off balance, stumbling backwards, he struggled to jerk himself out of the way. Wind knocked out, he was gasping. He saw the man's boot raised above him.

Then he heard it. A reverberating crunch followed by a savage snap. "Asshole!" Buck was crouched low, in a wide stance, and Leroy was on the ground, writhing in pain. In two bounds, Buck had sprung and shot his fist into the back of the man's skull: driving his nose into his chest. Infuriated, out of control, Buck sent a right hook into Leroy's kidney.

Jamesey, calculating, charged Besserian again, who, seeing the knife flash, drew himself up, face contorted in confusion and fear. "Fucking bastard." The searing pain in his face forgotten, Besserian sprang from below his assailant, catching the downward slash as the knife sliced into the upper thigh.

His own momentum was unstoppable. Crouching, he tossed Jamesey onto his shoulders, grabbed a wrist, yanked down on it desperately, twisting it hard, and stooping lower, slammed his assailant over his shoulder into the concrete. Frenzied, Besserian tore into him, chopping and hammering his face with the full force of his back and shoulder muscles until he felt himself jerked back.

"Don't kill him, buddy. He's done for. You got him, boy." Buck, wheezing, his face running with sweat, bleeding, had his hands and forearms under Besserian's shoulders, dragging him off the man. They lay in the street, exhausted, one cradling the head of the other in mutual defense. Mutual exhaustion.

Jamesey, groaning, was crawling to the opposite curb. "Wait! Damm you! Hold on there! I'm still a-comin'. Fucker! You bastard! Leavin' my ass?" The motor was churning; Leroy, slumped at the wheel, was fumbling with the gear lever. Without warning, the truck heaved back, missing Jamesey by inches, nevertheless enabling him to reach for the flailing door. He lurched upward, grappling with the inside handle, holding for support, got his knees on the running board, as the truck was raked into the forward gear. It shuddered, then, with spinning off-road treads screeching, shot forward. Out of sight.

Buck, lying on Besserian, his arm around his neck as much to receive support as to give it, felt his own head throbbing. He winced with the pain. He wished it would explode if that would release the throbbing. He breathed a prayer to the Holy Virgin.

Besserian gasped for air, choking at the claustrophobia of the nauseating smell of the leather jacket pressed into his face. Struggling, he lifted one arm, weakly. "You trying to kill me too?" He groaned. "I got it bad." His head fell back. "Thanks. You saved my ass."

A scenario enacted about seventy-five feet away emerged into their view. They watched through puffed eyes. Two figures were standing apart. "Hey, girl! Get your act together." Lycra, Body Suit, brushed herself with the back of her hand, contemptuous of her companion. Bikini, Lifestyles, stood gingerly mopping a bloodied face with her palm. Disgusted, she shook her head resolutely. "Gettin' my ass out of here. Them punks? I coudda had 'em too." She kicked one heavy boot into the pavement. "And you wasn't no help-out neither, girl! Not for me, you wasn't! Anyhow. Guess my ass is OK. C'mon man. You comin'?"

She noticed the two men in the street. "You get a good look? Sonny? I'd offer you two a ride but you wouldn't know what to do after. When I got you home. Two dumb ass fags. What'd you start that for? Think you have to be fuckin' heroes! Two losers mama's boys if I never saw none."

Body Suit reiterated the boot stamping process: her ponderous physique had left her relatively unharmed. "Yeah, man. Leave us to go. You two queens better be careful about next time you might could go out together? Next time you was to try and to *protect* somebody. Pick on somebody who needs protectin'." She stumbled to the F-350, Bikini following resentfully. The massive V-8 roared, catapulting the truck forward crazily into the darkness, the driver tearing angrily through the gears.

Buck moved slightly. Besserian lay motionless.

"My mom always said to be helpful to ladies."

"She was right."

"You OK? Poufter?" He mimicked the DJ's drawl.

"Sure as hell not. No, I ain't: fag."

They laughed as much as weariness would allow. "We're sure a sorry bunch of fuckers."

"Yeah?"

"Yeah. Sitting in the street in the middle of the night. Our faces busted." Buck winced. "You get my bag?"

"It's over there. Back where we were."

They remained quiet, apprehensive that by moving they would discover new injuries. The aches began to intensify. For both of them: sharper with more intense throbbing. "If my leg's not broken, it sure feels like it. Hurts like hell. Teeth are all there." Besserian moved his jaw warily.

"See if we can make it out of here. Can't stay here all night. I got my reputation to think about. People be sayin' those girls were right. About us."

"Let's make it back to the car. I'll drive you. You can get your car in the morning. Or sometime."

Releasing each other, using each other, they crawled to their feet.

"Well, I guess I'm facing reality now."

"Shit, man. Don't go down on me. OK? So, sometimes I can be an asshole too. Give me a ride to my place? I can pick up my car in the morning. Or Arlene can."

"I guess I can drive."

"Sure, you can. I'll watch you."

---

## *A Conversation*

"Just keep driving, buddy. Relax. Quit worrying about shit. I'll show you. Stay cool. And you better wipe yourself. That cut over your eye! Damm! You'll drive us off the road. We don't need more problems. Here. Take this." Buck, grasped the wheel with one hand, and fumbling in his jacket with the other, extracted a grimy handkerchief. "And take the freeway to the 6th street exit. Then up to Adams and make a right. It's OK, I'll show you. Shit! Bastard got me in the ribs too. How about you? More than your eye?"

"Upper leg. Thigh. And this thing over my eye won't stop bleeding. I can drive OK. Stop grabbing the wheel."

Buck reaching over for a closer look was knocked into Besserian as the SUV swerved. He grabbed the other man for support. "Sure you can drive this? You almost got us killed before and now you want to do it again?"

"Right. It's me? That got us almost killed? I don't think so. Seems to me, you're the one who started it with those two bozos."

"Whatever. Last thing we need is to be picked up by some antsy cop. Think we're coming back from a bar! No! Keep on going. Not too far. Couple of miles. A ways yet. I'll tell you. Relax."

Besserian navigated the off-ramp, taking surface streets.

"Not here. What're you doing?"

"You said next light."

"Shit, buddy! I didn't mean this one! Keep going! Next one! Maybe the one after; I'll tell you. My eye's getting blurry now. Anyhow we make a left. Pretty close now. Somewhere. Don't get yourself distracted."

"Just give me the directions. No last minute calls. Damm, leg hurts! How far is it?"

"A mile, maybe. Not too far. Keep going. Couple of miles."

"You've been saying that for the last hour."

"It's right around here. Hasn't been an hour. You're a slow driver. Anyway, end of this street. It'll dead end. Quick right. Another right. Then a left."

"I don't see anything." Besserian, navigating through the instructions, slowed the vehicle: an apprehensive creeping. "These look like factories. Or warehouses. Sure you live here?"

"Hey! I know where I live. Keep going. Stay cool! I'll tell you. Trust me."

Still uneasy, Besserian funneled the vehicle through the murky maze of narrow streets. Still no traffic but the mist, on the verge of rain, together with the dimness and the sharp turns, all stymied his sense of direction. The wipers hammered a four-four rhythm that intruded an unwanted melody into his apprehension. "You're sure now?"

"OK. Here! Here! Stop! Now! Dammit!"

"Stop?" Besserian braked, peering through the opaque, watery mist. "There's nothing here. You live in that dumpster?"

The street was shadowy. What passed for lamps, possibly gas, were dim. And infrequent. The windowless industrial buildings, walling them in, brick and stone, were old: Besserian surmised 1920.

Buck was fumbling for a remote. "Shit. It's in my car. Wait." Jumping out, he punched in numbers on a wall keypad, motioning for Besserian to enter.

Besserian hadn't noticed the metal door. The crashing jolted him as it shuddered violently, a grand mal seizure, beating itself against massive tracks as it began its ascent, then shifting to a heavy rumbling, the discolored bulk grudgingly wound itself upwards into the darkness.

"OK. You can drive in." Buck was beside him, bawling above the noise. "Don't have to wait for it to go up all the way."

"You sure you live here? Looks like some kind of factory!" Besserian twisted, lowering his head, squinting upward, straining to decipher the surroundings.

"Keep your eyes straight. Keep going, pal. Pull up over there."

The sparse interior lights were even less effective because of the steel uprights and overhead girders. And far from dispelling the shadows, the interrupted glare of the exposed bulbs enlarged and deepened them, adding to the mystery. As his eyes adjusted, Besserian sensed the space was extensive. Definitely some kind of warehouse. In one area he could make out bulky metal drums: on pallets, each bearing yellow, block-printed letters with numbers stenciled in white.

"Watch it! I said over there. Beside the elevator."

Besserian didn't see an elevator. He did notice, however, another area: ponderous burlap covered containers, belted with metal straps.

The smell of oil and grease was strong. Mixed aromas of hemp, rubber, gasoline, rusted metal, and another smell, sweetish, that he couldn't identify, competed to confound the precise identification of the containers. Or the place itself.

"OK. Out." Buck shouted to make himself heard over the downward crashing of the entrance barrier. It struck the concrete floor with a reverberating, hostile thud.

"I'm not sure . . ."

"Keep your drawers on. Nothing to worry about."

The dirty, metal-laced glass skylights, permitted a refracted light: the perfunctory streetlights and the glow of the wet haze. The translucence eddied along the recesses of the brick walls, without dispelling the gloom. For sure, the building was near the river: the industrial east side.

They were in front of a wood barrier. Rumbling again: jerky and sporadic: descending. Elevator. Of some sort.

"Slow. But it works. There's a Fireman's Pole. Good if you're in a hurry. But, hard to go up. Anyway it only goes up to the fourth floor."

Pressing down on them, the conveyance darkened the space, as it trundled past, slamming to a stop at their feet. Grease and oil-saturated wood; the smells were pungent. Besserian could make out planks reinforced with steel bolts. The ends of the platform were open with planked sides and a ponderous grating above.

Buck heaved at the barrier that resisted obdurately, then flung itself up with a vengeful clatter.

"Watch your head, Under the gate."

"Got it."

He tugged again at the crosspiece. It resisted, then hurtled down and slammed itself furiously into place, A loud whine, almost a shriek, corroborative indignation, then a wail of steel cables as the irritated behemoth—Buck having felt for the panel of three oversized buttons—began its slow, halting rise into the upper recesses of the building.

The ascent was slow. Besserian could distinguish, by the eddying of dank air, the successive openings. In some the light was less dim. Once he thought he could make what could have been weight lifting equipment. The remaining floors were darker.

"This place is huge. How much higher we going?"

"To the top. Won't be long. Get you buttoned up. Five stories plus one on the top." Besserian continued counting the openings in silence.

"OK, Champ! End of the line! All out." The conveyance jolted them to a stop.

The night of the unexpected was just beginning. No blank, dark, opening here. They were facing a lighted metal door, cleanly painted. Buck punched the keypad and they emerged into a vestibule, spacious, decorated with thick, potted Ficus. There was a diffused glow, even with the mist, from the skylight that extended the length of the ceiling. The floor was a patterned tile and led to an oak door, easily eight feet in height, daunting and studded with antique nails. On the side wall was a fountain: a monstrous creature spewing a stream of water unabashedly into a copper basin. Buck, caressing the keypad beside the door, scowling, waited for the sound of the released bolts.

"Here we are. Home sweet home. Come on inside." He pushed easily against the barrier, entered, and held it for his guest.

If Besserian was surprised before, now he was dumbfounded. He was in a hallway, walls paneled in chestnut colored wood, mellow lighting from wall sconces indicating its length. The marble floor was a lustrous green, black and white with a Greek Key design border.

Half way along the passage, they were at a wide door, containing a stained glass panel, the massive oak frame indicating the weight. Besserian was struck by the quality of the glass, the workmanship, as well as the depiction itself.

A seated figure, a rugged herdsman, affectionate ewe licking his hand, was accepting from a young man, his face a study in trust and respect, a gift of a young lamb. The herdsman cradled the lamb, reluctant to give it up. To the side was a grotto that could provide shelter. In the background were cattle watching with their young. A pastoral scene. But not idyllic.

What struck Besserian were the expressions. Neither wore the insipid, maudlin, effete 'goodness' characteristic of Christian art. The robust young man offered his gift with appealing masculine confidence. His eyes were dark, even bold. The sinews of his forearms, biceps, back and calves were prominent; his jacket pulled open by broad shoulders. It was a figure dominated by the nascent surfeit of confidence, strength, and sexuality. Only experience was lacking. A deficiency that intensified the attraction.

Nor was the recipient less self-assured. Clad in a plain tunic, his shepherd's crook, ribbed with metal, on the ground beside. Dark shadow defined his face and recessed eyes. The relationship seemed recent: tentative but clearly portentous. With consummate skill, the artist depicted an intensity that invited the viewer to surmise their interchange. Nevertheless, a Gothic lettered scroll across the bottom stated: 'Be Not Afraid. I Will Show Unto You the Way'.

"Different, eh?"

Besserian had difficulty hiding his amazement. "Very."

"Got it from a church. Being demolished. I got connections in construction." Buck pressed a button to release the door. Although they entered a darkened room—the spotlights from behind, on the stained glass gave an indirect light—a huge window of French doors, at the extremity, brought into relief by the mauve of the skyline haze, projected the furnishings into bulky shadows. And suggested the dimensions.

"Hang on a minute! Get us some light."

Immediately, swathed in a soft, indirect glow, details replaced the shadows: an expansive and, to Besserian, magnificent space. Wide planked walnut floors displayed a variety of carpets: Turkish, Persian, Armenian, Indian; beautifully contrasting shades of burgundy, gold, blue, topaz inlaid in fields of cream, turquoise and alabaster. There were Tabriz, Qum,

Kerman, and others he couldn't identify. The furniture was appropriately large, upholstered in silk and tapestry, bolstered with fringed contrasting pillows. One side of the room, between two floor-to-ceiling windows was a marble Renaissance fireplace: large enough to stand in. And facing outward from a corner, a burnished grand, top raised, a score open on the music rack.

Partially covered by an expanse of striped awning visible through the French doors was a terrace, lights playing through potted ferns, spruce and jasmine.

They were standing under what Besserian surmised was a gallery. Four brown and white marble columns, deeply veined, fluted and twisted, Bernini-like, supported it.

"This is amazing. I guess I have to say I'm impressed."

"You don't have to say anything." Buck stood beside his guest. "But I guess I have to say, I never come into this room without, well, sort of savoring it. In a different way. With a new kind of, well, security. I need a refuge sometimes, too. And it grows on you. Like a lover. The right kind of lover." His grin was embracing. "Glad you like it."

Besserian was still absorbing the surroundings. "I do like it. It's beautiful." He imbibed more of the details: silver, crystal, porcelain, multiple framed photographs. He could make out a gallery, an extension of the balcony above them, extending the length of the adjacent wall, lined with books, each of the sections, labeled, subtly illuminated.

"Here. This way. Need to get you repaired. Quick." He looked over his shoulder. "Want some music?" Without waiting for a reply Buck moved to a bank of recessed components, displaying tiny amber and blue lights. The lush harmonics of a Beethoven cello sonata, delighting in the acoustics, spilled into the room.

"Sure. Some. I like that."

Buck snorted. "Figured you would. This way." He motioned with a nod, the extremity of a hallway, a bathroom: a 1930's gallery of glass, marble and chrome. "Get that cut fixed. Over your eye. Punk clipped you good."

The only window extended from floor to ceiling. The remainder of the outside wall was glass block, completing the Deco look and sending ripples of light over the gleaming purple, green, white and black tile; the bulbous porcelain fixtures. White towels and wash cloths, monogrammed in black, the three letters grouped into a diamond shape, were displayed on a polished nickel stand.

"Get you cleaned off. Grab one of those cloths over there, will you?"

"Here?" Besserian fumbled through the towels. His hand brushed against a black nozzle, the end of a rubber tube.

"Got it? Yeah! That'll do fine." He snorted. "Pull off those jeans. You can hop up on the counter. Stretch out your leg. OK. And just bring the cloth. That's all we'll be using. Don't worry."

Buck wet the cloth. "Not too bad. Not as bad as you made out. That hurt?" He wiped the cut, brushing on iodine, inhaling its aroma. "How's that? Bruise is what's hurting. Knife didn't get you too bad. You lucked out. Must have tossed him before he could get you all the way. But you banged the bone pretty hard. When you fell. It's going to show. Hurt? Now?"

"Yes. No. It's OK."

"Let me see that part over your eye. OK, champ?" He scrutinized it. "Looking better now. That's what comes of being in good shape. Heals fast." Appraising his work with an air of self-congratulation, he was satisfied. "Guess I'm a pretty good nurse. So! How about your Plan? Your Project? With your class? You said you had one. And don't tell me you're not going to follow through. Or the AP job."

Besserian pulled his head away and stood, pulling on his jeans, using the mirror to check his eye. "My idea? For the Project? For the kids? Get them involved. And some ideas for the AP job? If I get it?"

"Don't pull your jeans back on yet. Not finished. Sit back up there on the counter."

Besserian winced as Buck, his voice soothing, wiped the gash along the inside of his thigh with iodine. "OK. You're doin' OK. You sure came through, tonight.""

"Damm that hurts! Finished? I better check you."

His face pushed into the mirror, Buck was examining his own eye. He felt his ribs and winced. "Actually, isn't as bad as I thought. How's it look? No teeth lost. Jaw not broken. Nose OK. Probably ache all over in the morning. Basically OK. Now. I think."

Besserian observed critically, taking care not to touch the injured area. "You'll be OK." Noticing a larger discolored area on the neck, he lifted the torn shirt, holding it away from the wound. "You OK? On the back here? Looks like Leroy got you here too."

"Fuck, man. Go ahead! You can touch me! You probably don't have AIDS. Damm! Be spontaneous. Shit, buddy! We helped each other out. You're OK. You backed me up."

"Did I have a choice? Happened so fast."

"We'll be OK. Arlene'll be here. Later on. I'll call her. Let her finish me up. She likes playing nurse. Give her a thrill. Right now? I could eat anything. Let's find us something."

Besserian stood, pulling on his jeans. "This is a great place. I love it. All those books! You play? The piano?"

"A bit. Shit, well, don't laugh, but . . . I like to sing. I can accompany myself. Believe it or not. . ."

"What? Tell me."

"I'm my own best audience." Besserian nodded affirmation. "And it's a kind of therapy when I get screwed up at work. Or personally." The hint of diffidence was a revelation. "But, come on! Let's do it! See what we got in the fridge. Got to take care of my favorite student."

"Hey! This is nice. We haven't finished ours. Our kitchen. This is better. Than ours."

"I think it's called High Tech or something. Designer guy did it. He was OK. I helped him. That's why it's better."

He rummaged in the refrigerator, pulling out some cold meat. "Bread in that plastic thing behind you. Fresh today. You'll like this. Room temperature: Bel Paese, Camembert, Gorgonzola. And some Chianti. Already opened. And not refrigerated. Beer, if you want it?"

"Chianti's great. I'm surprised I'm here. You fixing my leg. Showing me your place."

"Shit man! Guys can't get more connected than we did. Tonight. You saved my ass. Fuck, you're a real tiger when you get going. You don't give yourself credit. Stronger than you think. And quicker. Aggressive. Damm! You sailed right in there! Like gangbusters! After those two jerks. You sure used that right hook! Bet that creep? Jamesey? Hurting now. Worse than us." He laughed enjoying the picture. "Those two creeps wondering what went wrong. Two shit-heads."

"You're pretty good yourself. Thought you were going to break his head. Guy could hardly crawl to the truck."

Buck relaxed against the counter. "I wanted to. He came at you from behind! The punk! And hey!" He laughed loudly, stood, banging his palm on the butcher-block table, moving his fists in a fighting stance, bouncing on the balls of his feet, weaving and ducking. "You see that little fucker run?" He shot a left hook. "And the way the other asshole tried to back over him when he was trying to get up in the truck? After you got him?" He slapped the counter delightedly. "Man, that was funny! Two dead-enders. I laughed my ass off." He discovered some more cold meat, additional mayonnaise and another brand of beer-flavored mustard. "Dig in. Help you get your strength back." He gulped the beer, a dark Belgian brew.

Neither was self-conscious. Besserian relaxed into easy laughter, tilted back his chair, holding the heavy crystal, watching the deep luminescence through the beveled edges. "Meat is good. And the bread. Tastes good. Goes with the cheese. And wine." He smiled easily. "But you know something? I don't think those girls liked us. Or me. I mean they didn't like me before. In the gym."

"Them?" Buck winced. "Screw them! They got their own hang ups. We came across as; what's the PC term? Traditionalist? 'Protecting'? And that's a crime: in case you didn't know it!"

"Thing is that spontaneous reactions are forbidden. Because PC is code. Covers up reality. Spontaneity breaks the code." Buck poured some beer into his glass. "Take more of the wine. Got plenty." He hesitated. "Don't usually make mistakes. About people. Guess I had you figured wrong. I was a sort of jerk in that restaurant."

"I can get my ass turned around too. I thought you were a kind of a creep. I mean in that restaurant."

Buck snorted. "Probably. Thing is you got lots of aggression. Good aggression. PC says you got to keep that bottled up. Wrong! Take the AP job. Use that aggression. Bring in some good reform. Nothing wrong with helping yourself too. While you're at it."

Buck loosened the cork with his teeth, took a swig from the bottle, and poured some of the liquid into Besserian's glass. "Take some more. Cheese. And this is good wine. Good for you. Put hair on your chest."

The rain now was heavy, loud, washing across the glass wall in swirls. The light was indirect: from under the cabinets and small ceiling spots, giving the room an ethereal air, as if suspended in the haze: isolated from the surrounding buildings.

"Feels good in here. Safe."

"So long as you don't nail me with that left hook of yours. Shit! Jamesey? That fucker. He's feeling you now, bronco. For sure."

"That's nice!" He waited. "The music."

"Music? Oh, sure!"

"The way it sort of drifts in here. From the other room. Restful."

"You know what?"

"Tell me."

Buck began to say something. Then hesitated. Thinking better of whatever it was, he looked at his watch, disjointedly, as if covering his thought.

"What? Tell me."

"Nothing. Really. Just thinking: beats the shit out of me: my watch isn't broken. Whatever. Anyway." He stood abruptly. "You get enough? To eat?"

"I'm OK."

"Penny'll be worried about you. I'll walk you down. To your car."

# *CHAPTER XXI*

## *A Plan*

"Z'appen', man?" We not goin' to do it? Reform Project?"

"We're going to do it. Start tomorrow. First, we need to clarify some points." Besserian resumed his pacing. "Unlike a regular History course, we'll be looking at some Primary Sources: original documents. In this case proposed policies pertaining to the Reform Plan: attendance, testing, curriculum, discipline. The original planning."

"So, Primary makes our Project a different kind of ball game!"

"Yes." He surveyed the room. "Everyone have a copy? Project Outline?"

"Of what?" There was a flurry of excitement. Papers flew between the desks.

"Hey! Over here, girl. You forgot me!"

"Just gave you one, 'Sandro. You can just look on with your homie, Mr. Big Mouth! Teacher's right! You not pay attention. So you not know nothin', boy!" Griselda sneered, "Trog!"

Allisandro squeezed his frame into the too-small seat. "Punked you on last test, girl!" He guffawed, jabbing Felipe in the ribs.

"Watch who you callin' girl! Boy! Your brain be stuck in first gear."

"Enough of that! Ladies and gentlemen! Let's understand some basics. The purpose of this Project is to get information. Correct information. So we can make correct judgments. Arrive at correct conclusions."

"You mean like James Bond? Undercover agents?"

"Similar."

"Sounds like a winner. Let's do it!"

"Not with verbal abuse. Insults. Not without mutual respect. We need each other. Everybody is important. Valid. There's a progression: respect. Then knowledge. Then leadership. They're interconnected. And interdependent. In this Project? We're going to follow that progression."

"Like us being teachers?"

"Yes. Good teachers."

"Cool."

"We'll need to be dependent on each other. More than in a regular class. We won't have the security of a text. The apparent security. Providing us with the answers."

"So, we need to respect each other! Go for it!"

"To reiterate: truth and knowledge are contingent on respect. Valid truth and knowledge."

"Teachers respect kids, Mr. B?"

"Where the goal is Truth. Knowledge. Yes."

"Then, not many respectful teachers in this school!"

Besserian reflected for a minute. "As I said, we have to discover the answers. They're not given to us. That's why it's exciting. But! We'll need to rely on each other more than in a regular class."

"So, we got to respect ourselves. Cool."

"Mr. B? My uncle said that when they was makin' landings? In 'Nam? If the guys in the landing crafts not hold the nets proper? Control them depending on how the water was going up and down? Its roughness? Then the guys comin' down the side on the nets? They'd be squashed between the landing craft and the side of the ship. Seems like this Project sort of like us holding the nets for others of us comin' down? So's they don't get crushed? Protectin' them. They need us. We need them? So all of us get to the shore?"

"Analogy makes sense to me, Jesus. With one difference."

"How's that, man?"

"In our Project, you not only hold the nets. You also make them."

"Mr. B? Seems like with all this knowledge about Reform Plan? Its Truth? And us working together? Like you said?" Felipe was reflective.

"Seems like maybe we might find out more stuff than we bargained for. About Reform? About ourselves?"

"There's the bell! See you all tomorrow! District Resource Room. First floor. To begin!"

"We be trippin', Mr. B."

# *CHAPTER XXII*

## *Same Thing 'cept Different*

"This story is some weird-ass shit."

"You're weird yourself, dude." Raquel rolled her eyes and continued the languid application of the pungent lotion to her hands, legs and arms, feigning indifference to the enthralled stares of Jose and Allisandro. Another of her Learning Center partners, Claudia, sniggered and pointed to a photograph in a frayed issue of *The Hill,* the Fillmore Year Book.

"You guys comin' out tonight?" Claudia whispered, her voice metallic and rasping.

"Where?"

"Dunno." She drawled the words carelessly. "*The King*?"

"He's cute. Sure looks like he knows what about. He got a brother who still in school. Was, anyhow." Raquel finished her ablutions, stuffing the dispenser into her purse.

"Brother might could be a college or somethin'? Dunno. Anyhows, he works somewheres? Chitose? She seen a picture of him? At the beach? In his Speedos? She say totally hu-u-ge! And plus with a butt to totally jest to die for! Could see his crack real good!" They doubled over, palms compressing their mouths, to suppress the giggles, jabbing the photo with iridescent fingernails.

"O sto-oo-oop i-i-i-t!" You ba-a-a-d, girl! You so-oo-o bad! Totally!" The girls pushed each other exaggeratedly, sniggering. Raquel slapped Claudia's arm with her fingers.

The male members of the Learning Group looked around uncomfortably, forced to reconsider the teacher.

"What's been going on here, young ladies? Boys? In our story? Of course, we don't know anything about their futures. That's not where they're at. It's all about the mistakes of what's been done *to* them. In the before. Put on them. From the past. That's what's totally important. Past hostilities towards them and their gender. That's what shows them the obstacles in their paths. Now. For them it's all about making sure the Past's not covered over."

"Like taking a walk using a rear-view mirror? Why don't they just do what they have to do now? Forget the past? Even if it's, like bad? Still can't be changed. It's like water over the dam? Sorta like they don't care about the 'right now'?"

"Why, Felipe? *Why*?" Consternation dripped from her voice. "Why do they look at the past?" The teacher's question was rhetorical. "Because they're owed! That's Why! *Owed!* For the bad things of the past. It's past oppression, past wrongnesses that keeps on going. It's Past. Past. Past."

"How's that, Miss? When it's not happening to them? Only was to their great grand-mothers and stuff?"

"Because they're *victims*! Victims of their fate. And they need to be compensated. And who said it isn't happening now, anyhow?" Roxanne Turner, Grade 10 English, tossed shimmering, straight, bleached hair and adjusted her position: ensconced on an empty student desk, feet planted on the seat. She looked around vacantly, blue eyes punctuating sharp features. Her accent had an 'English' affectation.

"An another reason? For looking at the Past? Because it needs to be looked at. Now. Otherwise it will be forgotten. That's what this story is about. They know that the stuff, the stuff of the Past is still on-going. Now! And don't let anyone try to say different! So, that's what this story's about. How the hero of this story, Fallon: she's a strong woman? How she won't knuckle under and say things is being corrected now. That's like them trying to make her sweep all the garbage under the rug. And she won't do it. She's too smart. Too much into her own selfhood. Too strong. For that."

Turner rolled her eyes. "Wrongness done to her grandmother? Same as done to her."

"Same thing 'cept different?" Felipe drew his fingers over his face making the rasping sound that Ms. Turner found so irritating. He shrugged. "Not what I was thinking. Maybe having bad stuff continue? Maybe that's what's good? For her? It can work for her?"

"Not what the story is about, Felipe. You're trying to twist it. No! It's obvious to anybody. Fallon is keeping on fighting the battle. That's her strength." She twisted her legs, crossing them. "Now! Is it clear what this story's about?"

"Sorta. But what I was thinking, Miss? I mean maybe this girl, Fallon . . ."

"Young lady?"

"Whatever. Maybe there's stuff going on around her to change the bad things that happened to her grandmother? And she can't see them 'cause she's so much looking into the past all the time. I mean, the bad things of the Past are what turns her on. Without those bad things? She wouldn't have something to cry about? Anymore? She'd have to do changes in herself?"

Turner turned sharply on another student. "And Jorge, stop shuffling and turn around in your Learning Center and look at your book. We always work with partners! And I think I have told you that before." Her long neck, bobbing like a rubber bathtub toy, emphasized the admonition.

"I am looking at it."

"Page one hundred and seventy-six?"

"He not be on that page, Miss!" Marlene, seated across from him smiled disdainfully. "He lookin' on at some other ones."

The young man slouched further into his seat, flipped the pages aggressively, tearing at them, found the hated page and glowered at it resentfully.

"So, we need to clarify. For Felipe: he's lost. So, let's back up. Reconsider. Now! This story's about what happened to Fallon and Teddy. Did they consider their spiritual overlay in their interconnectedness? Their togetherness journey? Their emerging Selfhoods?"

Jorge sprawled in his seat and shrugged. "I guess. Whatever?"

"What would you have done? If you had been them?"

"You know, Miss, I guess I have to say not really sure about that? Leastways, not right now. Still thinkin' about it? Probably'd just go with the flow? Seems like there's nothin' you can do. About stuff. I mean if it's already happened."

"Why not read the story to find out?" Rigo Gonzalez was in a teasing mood? "And Miss? Jorge got a IED.[25] Made it at his house? Says he don't like this school."

"That's right, man. I seen him in his bathroom? Makin' it? Got his underwear on backwards. Tryin' to find out which side is which." Aldo laughed with gusto, fanning the distraction.

The teacher tossed her hair, sending it spraying over her shoulder. "You know, Rigo, that is such a typical remark from you. Uncaring. Andocentric. And you *do* know what that is?"

"Know? Sure! Sure, I do." Inhaling deeply and slowly, lost in introspection, he rubbed the bald spot on the back of his head—it was still there.

"And Rigo. I did not yet experience your last assignment! But anyhow. We can't wait for you. For people who aren't interested. In learning."

"I'm interested."

"You don't seem to be. Let's move on to important things. We need to discourse about the story. Felipe needs clarification. So? Can we help him? To better understand? Young ladies? Boys? This story opens up to ourselves. Fallon, the hero, is trying to get in tune with the unerring compass within her. So, is she keeping her spiritual journey-life?" The teacher tilted her head interrogatively, smiling patiently. "And yes, Kassidie? Your thoughts? Perhaps you could help Felipe?"

"Miss, can't say that I really have much of a thought about stuff? Leastways, not as of yet." The girl looked indolently at the teacher, shifting in her seat so the inscription—*The Original Bubble Gum Surfing Wax*—on her T-shirt, bobbled loosely. "I guess she's OK. What's not there to like? You can't never know nothin' about stuff people say."

"Let me put it this way—and Rigo, you can keep your hands to yourself?" Turner compressed her lips, neck bobbing vigorously. "Off Sandra? That's why you can't follow the story. Either." Her eyes compressed. "Or else get yourself into just a whole lot of more trouble." She uncrossed her legs and glanced briefly at the text. "Fallon stays fluid. She's not hung-up in accepting present Structures. That distract from Past injustice. Past bigotries. She's telling us she doesn't want to pretend that everything's getting better now. Because when you look at the Past you realize it isn't.

25 IED Incendiary Explosive Device: Homemade bomb: used by insurgents against invading troops.

It couldn't be. She'll find her own way. Through the oneness of her self-hood."

"Miss Turner! Claudia be puttin' junk on me."

"Jesus! Just you to leave Claudia alone! Now, I've already told you that before." She inclined her long neck interrogatively. "And what do you think is the integrity of her persona? Fallon's? How does she find her interior oneness?"

"She's lost? I thought the story said she was in her house?"

"The point, for your information, Jorge, is that she is taking a centrist position about her relationship with Teddy. Moving to a new Chakra level. He is waiting for her guidance."

"I don't see why. I mean if she's so interested in past stuff that's so wrong all the time."

"Why? Why is Teddy waiting for her guidance? Because he recognizes her strength. Her interiority. And true. She guides him. But she can't let him be an anchor tied to her foot."

"How's that, Miss?"

"Why?" She was incredulous. "*Why*? Because she hasn't yet experienced all her life options. And that's what she needs to move forward to. She's tearing open the oppression of the Past. Shows how it's still in an aggression mode. And to do that she can't be caught up in 'teaching him how to swim', to evidence an expression."

"Gotcha, Miss."

"What?"

"Tryin' to teach anybody to swim that had a anchor tied around their foot? My uncle said that when the guys was swimming in Vietnam, it was like . . ."

"Let's move on, Jesus! Here, Fallon is the hero. Teddy is the boy in the story. That she has to instruct. As the story moves forward, Fallon realizes more and more that Teddy, even though *he* is unaware of it, is a symbol. Of the Past. The Traditionalist oppression out of the Past. Continued into the Present. The Structuralist power group. That he will drag her down like a anchor. She realizes that he has no right to obstruct the wholeness of her own self-hood. She doesn't have to permit that. No. Fallon's priority lies in her personal interiority. That's something Teddy has no right to intrude into. To obstruct. None whatsoever. People forcing bad things of the Past—injustices, oppressions, demands—on her. But through her relationship with Teddy, she comes to realize, to understand, as a woman, that oppression is still going on. And that her first priority is to Self-Realize."

"And another thing. She doesn't have to look outside, for different ideas, for answers. Her own self-hood is her womb, and it already contains what she needs to know. And Teddy has to learn to venerate that. The story deals with underneath motives, emotions, and feelings. How Fallon finds her nuclear self. Fallon is experiencing her personal wholeness by working through the past oppression as it tries to swirl around her. She's exploring her persona. But she doesn't use words to say it. She realizes it. Sensitizes it. For her individual oneness."

"So, Teddy's like what? Unaware?"

The teacher, distracted, adjusted the flexible wire frames of tinted aviator glasses. "And Candyce? Geronimo? This is *not* the place? *Nor* the time? I believe I told you that before?" She nodded aggressively, calling to the back of the room. "Now, you need to turn the TV down! And finish your compositions." The couple in question were huddled together separate from the other Learning Centers, sharing a bean-bag cushion. Watching, intermittently, *Long Day's Night*, they caressed one another's forearms, occasionally kissing, eyes roaming dreamily, from TV screen to each other.

At another table students were whispering, drawing, looking at magazines. A few were doing assignments from other classes.

Ms. Turner disengaged herself from her perch, her stretch white chinos revealing the outline of her bikini underwear. "OK. I said we were going to begin a new project? Sometime soon?" She smiled breezily and walked to the front of the room.

"A new project, Ms. Turner?"

"Yes. This is related to what is actually happening in the story. How Fallon experiences her Pastness. How we can do that. Too."

"We ain't finished the last Project, yet."

"You were supposed to be!" She looked at Robert archly.

"Not enough time."

"You had every bit as much time as everybody else did." She twisted her lips, lower jaw hanging, and peered through her glasses, eyes wide. "I think so."

"Don't knock it man." Jorge whispered loudly. "Beats doin' homework."

"It's an alternative to more structured work assignments, yes. Thank you for that input, Jorge. And you don't have to wait for corrections. Because you correct each others."

"Will we be able to work in groups again? Like last time?" The question came from Learning Center Number Four, 'The Aztecs', identified by a painted cardboard Priestess, brilliantly robed in ritualistic garments ornamented with feathers, wielding a ceremonial knife, the image dangling—protectively or threateningly, depending on one's viewpoint—over the group.

She continued. "That is our learning modality, yes."

"Great! Hey, cool, man. Real cool."

"What'll this Project be, Miss Turner?"

"I'm glad you like these Projects. They're designed to allow students to work at their own paces as well as develop kinesthetic, auditory, and spatial relationships skills. Not just structured, academic, left brain usages. As in Traditionalist courses. Enables students to experientiate different kinds of life styles—holistic and intuitive, different modalities of life choices."

"What's that?"

"Learning modalities? Non-structured learning."

"Just like the books we read?"

"It would be in the same learning modem, yes."

"Cool. Real cool." Felipe squirmed in his seat and beamed a huge smile to Sandra. "So, what's it goin' be, Miss?"

She began pacing the front of the room displaying a long, angular figure. Her jeans were low cut and her tank top revealed, contingent on the movement, her midsection. She wore sandals. On her shoulder was tattooed a small psychedelic symbol. When she stooped, a marijuana leaf was visible, inscribed in color, at the base of her spine, just above the pink line of her panties.

"You seem to have a need to focus on details, Antonio. That's perhaps to be expected: considering the learning curve of your age and gender experience. But literchur, good literchur, can help us to avoid that. Move beyond that to maturity. And then to shake off the oppressive culture. Define our own uniqueness. You remember what Stephyne Hellwig did in *The Purple Sonata*? And in a similar vein, how effective Bonnye Forsythe was with her *Probing Inward*. And in one of our films? That we looked at? *Golden Compass*? Acknowledge the unerring compass within us. I think we got a lot out of those stories. I *know* we did."

"Is this sort of like guessing? About stuff that we can't never see? Like being blindfolded? Like we's at the end of the food chain?"

"Kinda confusing?"

"Confusing, Aldo? If the story is confusing to you, I wonder if you really passed English literchur last year?"

"Yeah, I did. I'm confused because shouldn't it be that education is about finding out what's going on right around us? Maybe comparing it to the past. But not saying it is the past. You're sayin' education can't teach new stuff that's goin' on? Has to hang out in bygone years? Like being victims?"

"Felipe, the point is, and I'm not going to rehash this over and over just to benefit you! Fallon establishes her interiority by campaigning, by fighting, by struggling to make sure nobody—nobody—forgets about how bad Traditionalists were. And are. And, I said, *some* are gender victims."

"OK. So she doesn't want any change? That would be like somebody knocking her off her soap box? I mean how does she know the Traditionalists is still bad?"

"Felipe, I'm not going to go on . . ."

"Ms?" Sandra interrupted. "Seems to me that what Felipe's saying is that Fallon's 'interiority' sort of depends on continuing the campaign about bad things in the past. She's doing OK by it. I mean later on, in the story, doesn't she get a scholarship to college to study how bad things is still going on?"

"So? She gets a scholarship? How is that bad?"

"Not bad, exactly. But it's like she's got a good deal going for her by saying bad things is still happening: sexism, bigotry, gender domination, all the things you said?"

"So?"

"So, why not have her involve herself? Change the bad things? Seems like she's not doing that because she's got a good thing going by making the bad things to keep on."

"Melissa? You have a question?"

"Sorta. Fallon's like so caught up in proving the bad things still happening now, she not want any changes? Even better changes? And maybe there is some better changes. And she can't see them. She don't want to see them. 'Cause she's already made her play?"

Caught off guard by the interchange, the head bobbing recommenced, meditatively, eyes closed, nostrils flaring. "Well, Melissa, I'd say you're not experiencing this story. In its fullness. We're not here to force an interpretation on the story. What we're doing is: we're probing. For interconnectedness? How a woman reaches her pain? Gets in touch with it? It's more like interior questioning. That funnels into predicting."

"Pre what?"

"Predicting, geek." Myra called across the room."You know, when you try to figure out if somebody else's goin' do it? Go all the way? Or not?"

"You should know, girl!" Marco exploded in annoyance. "You got plenty of What For about experience!"

"Marco! I told you to watch gender-biased remarks! And your anger! And I told you: personal attitudes forms part of your grade in this class. I'll need to conference with you on that later. Let's stay on track here. Back to our reading. When we read works of literchur here, in this class, we need to not be worrying about what the author 'means'. That's like trying to think ahead of her? Beyond her, even. What we need to do is not to analyze other people's words. But to use the story to trigger our own interior valuehood."

"We could maybe read the telephone book and see if any thoughts come to us?" Allisandro shook his head supportively, straining to reinforce the teacher's insight.

"What if the story don't, well, sort of bring out any of our own self-values? Ones already inside us?"

"Charleze, good point." Turner ignored Allisandro. "Writers who point to other value systems, especially structured, gender-Traditionalist and out of touch with contemporary cultural value systems? Those are of no interest. To us. Here. In this class. That's what makes this class special."

"So, why is the writer writing? If she's not trying to tell us something?"

"She's like trying to wash her feet with her socks on?"

"Just keep it up, young man! That'll do Felipe. Obviously, this story is a challenge for you."

"Hey, man! You challenged!" Jesus guffawed.

"All of you! Listen! Unsolicited comments, remarks, do, and I repeat, *will*, affect your mark. For this class. The writer is going to il-licit the realization of our own values. Charleze, back to your valuable insight." The teacher imparted an admonitory glance at the male wrongdoers, before exploring the girl's observation.

"Writers who try to tell us what to think, to show us a kind of life different from what we are experiencing, in our own togetherness: are trying to spin our minds. Playing mind games with us. We're already where we are. Already know what to think. We need to reincarnate Past modalities. We don't need to be 'taught' anything. Except how we're oppressed."

"Ms. Turner. Why do kids come to school? If they already know what they have to know? I mean what are teachers for? Seems to me they be, well, sort of, well, not needed? If kids already know what to think?"

Turner moved her head slowly, "Laura, sophisticated readers look for signposts in writing that back up what they already know. Their own individual personalized? Values? You need to learn to look for those signposts—building blocks, steps, some people call it Fate—about the Past in your reading. Some, the bad Fate, . . .

"Like the bad cholesterol?"

". . . the bad steps, bad Karma, have to be changed. By us. Or for us. For example, the pattern of our culture, the way it's been organized: Traditionalist, andocentric, needs to be changed. Right brain stories, like we have in this class, help untie thinking knots about how things used to be. And if we don't, then we can't realize how many of us are continuing to be victimized. And might not even to know it. And just let me add again, for the benefit of those who are finding this difficult: that is Fallon's quest. To point out that gender oppression makes people still victims. Especially if they don't' know it."

"So these writers tell us how to act? What we're supposed to think? Control us? They're supposed to do that?"

"I wouldn't use the word 'control' exactly. Modification? Sensitizing? Adjustment? Try those, Robert. What our writers do, is, they reinforce what we already know. Knowledge is already in us. So a book, any book, can't really 'tell' us anything. Authors may give 'a' point of view, perhaps their own. Perhaps not. But does it matter?" Turner answered her own rhetorical question. "No. Not really. If what she says is 'in sync' with what you know already, what you believe, about yourself, what you have in your own interiority, then that proves the author is authentic. That's what this class is all about! That's what literchur is all about! That's what school's all about!"

# *CHAPTER XXIII*

## *Stay Focused*

"Watch it. Careful. Hey! Some tricky spots here! And, next one's sharp. More than it looks." He swiveled on the tiny seat and yelled to make sure the other man heard. "Keep your eyes focused. On the road!"

There was no one behind him.

"Hey. This is OK! Wow!" He turned the full force of his concentration back to the exuberance of the ride. "OK. Suck up this shit! Go for it!" Inhaling the blast of air which competed with the high-pitched whine of the tires and the hum of the perfectly honed bearings, he hugged the inside of the turn tightly, under a vertical wall of slate, then exploded into the open stretch. Here, the road leveled for perhaps two hundred yards, and Buck, seizing the challenge, crouched low, head close over the low-slung handlebars, his torso forming a forty-five degree angle with the center bar. He dug the balls of his feet into the pedals with the full force of his thighs and calves. "Damm! Might catch me at that!" He swung another glance over his shoulder.

Besserian's bike shot into relief behind him. Ignited by the pursuit, Buck increased his thrust into the next curve racing towards him, leaned far over to his left and plummeted into the descent.

Besserian, coming out of the flat stretch, drove his legs into the pedals, unleashing more power—more than he was comfortable with—from the *Benotto Mark VI.* That was a mistake. He overshot the approach. The curve, sharper and steeper than he had anticipated, caught him, too quickly, before he realized, too late, the greater danger.

A swathe of water, from the seepage on the granite wall, was wending its way carelessly, meandering across the sloping asphalt. Instead of using the speed to overshoot it, he jerked the front brakes. The miniscule patch of rubber lost its grip in the moisture. Demented, electrified, the twelve-speed whirled itself into a vortex, sucking him, almost horizontally, making a furious spiral, hurtling him into the sand and gravel on the opposite side of the road.

In former days an automobile rest area, its slight upward grade braked him: he was spun onto his left thigh, away from the precipice.

Stunned, he gradually accessed the damage. His loose shorts were ripped exposing multiple abrasions. And the entire left side of his body was throbbing furiously. Easing himself away from the bike, the extent of the danger he had, amazingly avoided, became clear. Miraculously too, the *Benotto*, although scratched, seemed intact. He spun the wheels, checked the gears and chain. "Can't believe it. Nothing broken! On me. Or the bike. Why was I so damm stupid? I shouldn't have tried this. Overreached myself! I shouldn't be doing this. Guy is a jerk!" He shook his head, furious with himself. "My lucky day? Or unlucky. Don't know which!" Gingerly, donning the helmet, he placed his right leg over the seat, protecting the left and eased onto the deserted road. Less speed. Much more caution.

Coasting most of the time, he had time to berate himself for his mistake: "Shit! How could I be so dumb!"

Buck was nowhere to be seen. Besserian was glad. The last thing he wanted was that supercilious 'I told you so' attitude. Incredibly, he had avoided a disaster. "Was a miracle I didn't go over the edge or break my back. Damm! OK! Give the guy some kind of credit. He did warn me. Earlier. That it was dangerous up here." Grudgingly, he smiled, "Say one thing! It's a roller coaster with that guy!" He reached down and brushed some of the gravel and sand from his thigh. "Competitive bastard! Seems always to come out on top. With no effort."

The park was extensive, over five hundred acres, someone had told him. The roads in these high hills, meandering in seclusion, at one time had been well maintained: a favorite place for scenic afternoon drives, to escape summer heat, the noise and traffic of the city. The peaceful lookouts, like the one that, almost certainly, had just saved his life, had been vistas, even picnic spots: a bygone era, a different family oriented culture. But in recent years, park rangers had closed the upper roads to cars: an effort to stop hit and runs, assault, robbery, murder, gay cruising.

In fact, since the prohibition, bicyclists, joggers and walkers were at greater risk. Safety measures had increased the  isolation and hence the danger. Mugging, murder, sexual assaults had increased. And Gay cruising was accomplished more effectively on foot or by bicycle.

And there were other problems. With the elimination of cars, bicyclists became more aggressive, using the roads as raceways: an increased threat to joggers, other riders, and themselves. And there were added hazards from lack of maintenance: loose gravel, cracks in the decaying asphalt, potholes, sand, and falling rocks. In recent years, they had worsened. Also, isolation had emboldened the roaming bands of coyotes, often rabid. There had been several attacks on early morning joggers and stranded bicyclists. Under the present prohibition, if a pedestrian or bicyclist did need assistance, the probability of help was remote. Besserian recalled the jargon from an Economics course: diminishing rate of elasticity? Limited freedom, rationalized by increased protection, ultimately erodes the freedom it was designed to safeguard.

He was rolling smoothly now, allowing the humming wheels, the confining freedom of the stretch T-shirt, even the boldness of the torn shorts, to compensate for his throbbing leg and arm. The soothing whine of the bearings reassured him, gradually lulling him out of the frustration, resentment and physical ache. "Hanging with him? One thing's for sure: the guy knows his stuff. Never changes his focus: Knows how to win. An independent SOB if I ever saw one."

Shifting gears, sometimes just for the pleasure of it: hearing the complex mechanism guide the chain precisely on the sprocket, confirming the precision of the engineering, imparted a reassuring logic.

Penny had encouraged him to get back into biking and he was glad he had decided to spend the money. That the bike was not only fast and smooth but also had the strength and the ability to respond to a split second command had just been confirmed. He could only guess the, probably, hundreds of pounds of stress in that furious spin. "God, was I lucky! And stupid! I make so many mistakes! Things distract me. He never seems distracted. From what he wants. He's always got his eye on his target."

The park exuded the power of uninhibited nature—a power accentuated by the isolation. He began to absorb the aroma of the scenery: the gnarled, scrub oaks, sparse evergreens, and everywhere the harsh, gritty soil, infrequently spotted with ground cover. The boulders. There was a distinctive sultry musk. Ravines and arroyos dropped precariously away from the road on one side and parapets towered over the other. He visualized the gullies below, swollen by torrents during rainfalls, spewing their surging, muddy contents, one level to the next, eventually into cement channels miles away.

It had been a brilliant early Spring day, but now, as he glided through the turns, continuing his descent, he detected a chill when he sailed under the shade of overhanging Oaks and Eucalyptus. When he moved into the open spaces, sprayed with the brilliant afternoon sun, it caressed his gleaming, tensed muscles. Moving effortlessly, with only the smooth whirring of the wheels to break the silence—the seclusion—he felt free, liberated. His senses primed, converged, awakening a heady eroticism.

On the lengthy ascent, their conversation had been sporadic, restricted to definitive comments about the road, the geometric evaluation of the last hill, the relative merits of the Shimano Deore XT, SRAM-7, SRAM X-Gen, and the respective maneuverability of the Vapor Pro versus the Vapor Vertical Pro.

He recalled three other riders shooting past, heads down, seats elevated exaggeratedly, encased in stretch fabric, brilliant in striking blacks, reds, greens and golds, emblazoned with lettering: *Giro, Izumi, Vittoria Zaffiro.* There were a handful of joggers, gliding effortlessly, sides of their notched running shorts flapping.

His reverie was interrupted as he deciphered the figure ahead of him, and he shook off his introspection. The road had turned a corner, ran straight for about a quarter of a mile, then approached a mound spotted with pines, where it wound around the base and continued out of sight. Coming closer, he could see tracks in the sand, a path, at one time perhaps a road, leading into the embankment and protected by an uneven row of low, massive, creosote pilings.

Buck was sitting on one of them, back wheel between his legs, extracting the tire from the rim. Frustrated, he was muttering peevishly, curses intermingled with whistling. Besserian glided into the sandy clearing and, easing himself gingerly off the seat, straddled his bike, leaning on the handlebars, foot on the right pedal.

Buck didn't look up. His expression shifted from glowering to a near smile, depending on the cooperation of the tire. "Hey, where you been? You get sidetracked? Something happen? Soon as I fixed this SOB, I was going back to see if you went over the side. Or ran into somebody."

"I'm OK. Looks like you're on top of that."

"This? Not a problem! Road's full of nails and shit. Flat tire. No big deal. You got to watch out for yourself. You got a spare?" He didn't wait for a reply. "Never want to get caught out here with your pants down. This is easy. Once you get the knack."

He looked up. "Hey! What the hell happened to you?" He shook his head incredulously, smiling. "You run into some of those joggers? You OK? Look scraped up. Pretty bad." His laugh was a kind of reproach. "Shorts ripped? Don't want you arrested. Indecent exposure! Like that bike club? Their initiation ride was up here. In jocks only. Guess they stopped that." He chuckled at the humor of his own joke.

"I'm OK. Now. Had a problem on that big curve."

"Got some antiseptic in my gear. Wait 'till I get this tire buttoned up?"

"Sure."

"Check in my pack over there, will you? There's a cloth. Scoot it over to me? Hands got greasy. And the pump, too?" He was sweating and Besserian noticed he had a bruise and cut on the left calf. "And that tire kit? Remember when these guys had tubes? Piece of cake now."

"Look like you're OK. Need me to do anything?"

"I'm OK. Got this zipped up now. Only take ten minutes from here to the cars. Got more antiseptic and shit there. Take care of you."

"And don't say it."

"I didn't say anything. Don't say what?"

"That you warned me. About those curves."

Buck rotated the tire slowly, scrutinizing the inside, spat several times, moistening suspicious sections with his middle finger. Locating the perforation, he applied the gum-like substance. Using the fingers of one hand, he peeled the backing off a patch, setting it deftly in place. "Good as new. Better!" His laugh was confident. "Just got to know how to go about it. Look out for yourself. Get this baby buttoned up, real snug, and we'll be ready to roll."

Repositioning the rim between his legs, his large hands manipulated the tire, turning the wheel slowly and checking the fit. "Skill wins out every time. Check this out for a good job, buddy." He spun the wheel through the gear mechanism, nodding with satisfaction as the chain clicked into place. "Ticking like a clock. Let me in there—yeah, that's it big guy, just like that—and we'll get this baby back on the road before you can say . . . jack shit. Pumped up, good as new."

He was wearing yellow and black bib shorts, deeply scooped in front, but had discarded the black shirt with two diagonal yellow and red stripes, red lettering across the back, *Castelli Sierra Nevada.* He bent over to pump the tire, the fabric glued to thighs and back. "So what happened to you? Watching the scenery?" He laughed loudly and worked without raising his head. "So, don't say what?"

"That you warned me."

Buck's teeth gleamed, framed in the russet shadow extending from high on his cheek bones and, late in the afternoon, almost masking his face. "You know this place has a reputation? I didn't warn you about that."

"It does?"

"Sure. But, shit, you've been up here before. That's why these roads are closed. Supposed to stop all the cruising. So now you got to walk up here or come on bikes."

"No cars?"

"Could easily get a car up here if you wanted to: cut one of the padlocks on the road barriers, you know, where we left ours? Anyway it makes a hell of a place to ride and jog. These roads go for miles. And it's peaceful. Without the cars. You never expect a car to come around a turn in front of you or get you from behind. If it did? Wouldn't stand a chance! Hell, did you see the way we came around those turns? Easily doing thirty. Thirty-five? You hit a car at that speed! Or it hits you! Sniffing daffodils in the Great Beyond. Anyway. What did happen?"

"Came around that big curve, Corkscrew? Just after that flat space. Skidded on some water and it flipped me over. I was lucky."

"Sure were." Buck held the bike between his legs, thumping it up and down as a test of his workmanship. "Perfect." He appeared to be absorbed making the final adjustments. "What did I tell you! Take it easy? I know these curves. You can get killed up here. Sure, it's looks nice and peaceful. But you got to be on the lookout."

Finishing the job he gathered up the remaining tools. "It looks like you handled yourself OK. OK, ready?" He unhooked a plastic water bottle from the bicycle frame, took a large gulp, and handed it to Besserian. "Here. Finish it. Let's go." He noticed Besserian's hesitation. "It's OK. I only got a few diseases." Besserian tilted the bottle and swallowed. Buck snorted and adjusted thin wrap-around-mirrored sunglasses. "That Corkscrew? As you're coming into the turn, you can't see anything until you're on top of it. Somebody up there could see you from the top, where the road drops down to cross this road, but you'd never see him. You'd come speeding around that turn! Car coming the other way? Be like hitting a brick wall. Anyway! Ready! Let's make it!"

It was a comfortable two-mile descent to the road barrier where they had left their cars. They spoke occasionally.

"So, big guy! Class Project still going OK? Find out anything special, yet?"

"Could be. Not sure. We found some information we couldn't figure out."

"Secrets?"

"Some folders with stuff that looked like code."

"Code? Weird!"

"We'll be looking at it closer tomorrow. And the guys are working on it this weekend." Besserian adjusted his helmet strap using both hands, then, following Buck's lead, shifted into a higher gear. "Want to ask you something."

"What?"

"Is your company, TriDelta, hooked up with Pritchard's Reform plan?"

Buck, startled momentarily, shook his head. And hesitated. "Not now. If it goes OK, and with you as AP it will: sure, it'll be better for us. Schools will need more management help. And that will help us. More investments. More money for us."

They were riding abreast. Momentarily, without raising their heads, their eyes searched each other: Buck over his right forearm into two deep furrows masking Besserian's eyes and Besserian over his left forearm, into his own reflection.

"OK. Relax. You got to make your work fulfill your dreams. You need to find yours. You have your drives. Your motivations. I got mine. I don't see Reform from the kid angle. The way you do. In the classroom. I want Reform. I want them to make good investments. Get themselves on track. Right now they pay me big bucks mostly to untangle them from their legal and financial screw-ups: that they never should have gotten into in the first place. Reform? Hopefully, School Board, administrators will make better decisions. So? In my way, I help kids too. So, sure TriDelta has a stake in Reform. Look at it this way. Right now administration's not accountable. For mismanagement. They're not hired for their competence. Me? There's not one of them I'd hire in my own company. Penny has far more on the ball than LaDorc?"

"Jones-LaPorte. Dr. Elayne Jones-LaPorte."

"Whatever. Actually, she's no worse than the others over there schlepping around in management stuff they don't have a clue about. I try to keep them from spending more than fifty percent of school money on management and personnel screw-ups."

They rolled on easily, effortlessly, keeping the same comfortable pace, changing gears together, instinctively, feet turning in unison: bodies arched over the low handlebars. The barrier at the beginning of the uphill road where they had left the cars was almost unwelcome.

"You'll be finding out stuff pretty soon. My guess is those kids are more resourceful than you realize. Give them a chance to go on their own. No telling what might happen."

# *CHAPTER XXIV*

## *Another Perspective*

Shoving open one of the five, iron-studded, oak doors, the sound enveloped him; a swirling cyclone, resonating against the marble and into the vaulted ceiling of the cavernous vestibule: the spiraling harmonics of the Lemmens *Fanfare in D.* The blast hit him—he shook his head to clear it—a musical sonic boom. Friday night at *Chico's*, very different harmonically, was less overwhelming. Making the turn at the top of the first landing, he hurdled the remaining steps, three at a time, and pressed his shoulder into the door which had been left unlocked.

At that moment, as if in acknowledgement, the Pedal re-asserted itself into the composition, jolting him with its reverberating power, articulating the melodic churning of the cascading notes, punctuating the martial beat.

This he liked. Satisfaction welled up in his face. The thundering of the 32-foot and 16-foot stops: *Bombarde, Soubasse, Bourdon.* The resonating 8-foot stops: *Diapason, Salicional, Trompette, Cor Anglais,* produced exhilarating sensations. He lingered, savoring his feelings, emotionally transported.

From the gallery the view was unobstructed: central aisle to the apse. Whereas the vestibule, the *narthex*—Besserian's designation—had been brilliant with sunlight, the interior, the nave, was shadowed, washed by shafts of luxuriant color—fuscia, amethyst, amber, saffron, cerulean—

streaking with laser precision from the clearstory, splashing over sections of pews, floor and walls, revealing the sensuality of the muted splendor—gold, mosaic, marble, damask, carved oak—forming puddles which oscillated, trying to catch the luscious sounds: inhale them, ride them, as they threw themselves against the walls and into the tracery, desperate to burst the confines of the building. The same exhilaration of the clubs: cascading lights; flashing, swirling to the throbbing music, enveloped him, surged in him.

And up here, so much closer to the double tiered bronze chandeliers, extending the length of the nave and aisles, he could appreciate what he had surmised from below. They swayed rhythmically, responding to the power of the instrument. He savored his private fantasy of the Phantom of the Opera.

The aroma of heavy, sweet, musk—incense from countless liturgies—permeated the interior and caressed the young man with its pungent sensuality. He inhaled deeply, relishing the eroticism, to be recalled later in private fantasy. The cloying perfume of innumerable beeswax candles, a succulent vanilla, over sixty-five years, had saturated the silk and wool Persian sanctuary carpet, the silver and gold embroidered tapestry, even the stone arches and the expanse of oak pews. Continually growing heavier, it offset the efforts of the antiquated air conditioning. Felipe could taste its languid, saccharine aroma. His tongue depressed his lower lip—he was mesmerized by the votive tapers flickering in the distant chapel of St. Bernard of Clairvaux—and he ached with need to extract the nectar, the surfeit of their succulence overflowing from his nostrils.

And up here, so near the source of the power, with the ranks of pipes soaring over him, under the cantilevered spray of the *trompette en chamade*, his emotional confusion surged, confounding him with frustration. Bathed in the pungent sensuality, he acquiesced to the delirium of the feeling.

Taking the right passageway, illuminated at intervals by frosted yellow apertures, protecting the leather case from the stucco walls, he emerged just behind and to the left of the enormous, gleaming, mahogany console.

Possibly he tripped on the frayed carpet, or the organist caught him in the mirror angled over the four rows of keyboards.

"You're late." Besserian turned, his left foot still depressing the D-pedal, after lifting his hands from the keys, causing a discordant growl.

"I barely got here. It's not that much late. What's up?"

Besserian shook his head in irritation, pushed an engraved button from a row under the *Positif* keyboard, and an array of Stops, from the walls of ivory which rose on either side, thumped back into place with military precision.

"You know, I'm irritated. With you."

"Oh, yeah?" The young man moved his head gravely and frowned in contemplation, noting some of the exotic Stop designations—*Unda Maris, Cor de Nuit, Nasard.* "Me?"

"Yes. If you're not interested, don't say you are." He raised his hands and shrugged his shoulders. "You're not obligated to be here. It should be something you want to do."

"Hey, Mr. B, I want to." Felipe was unruffled. "I'm here. Now. Not that late. Let's do it." He moved his head solemnly. "Hey, you got that Intro buttoned down pretty good. Now. Smooth. Great sounds. Cool. Real cool. I like it." He gave two 'thumbs up' and moving his head affirmatively, expelling a mass of air from his puffed cheeks, pulled a folding chair toward him with his foot, turned, and opened his case. "See? Got it right here. All set."

"So, we're amateurs! Doesn't mean we can't act like professionals."

Felipe extended his arms and frowned, in mock confusion. "You're no amateur, Mr. B. Anyway, I'm here, now: for you. Let's do it."

Besserian flicked his fingers across the music and swiveled his legs over the bench to face his associate. "Got a message from a Church administrator, Monsignor Albert, this morning, Albert Wojeck ..."

"Hey! Wow! I been hearing stuff about that guy! A real hard ass." Besserian scowled as his partner continued. "You know, I heard he's like—outa Jurassic Park? Prehistoric? Like in dinosaur times? Acts like he was higher up than everybody else and like he has all this, like, special kind of 'authority'? That only belongs to him. Like everybody else has to do what he says. Like a slave driver? Knows all the answers. And nobody else does." Felipe glanced over his shoulder. "Lots of people? Tune him out? Definitely not a cool camper."

"People say the same thing about teachers. Authority figures are not popular. If they exercise their authority."

"Hey, yeah! Know what you mean!" Felipe laughed easily, ratifying the observation. "I guess Sandra's girl friend, you know, Macrina? Says he's like some kind of, like, white male chauvinist? Fascist? Sexist? Control freak? From the Andromeda Galaxy, or some place. She's a science geek, that's how she knows about stuff like that."

"According to you and Macrina, this man may be a what? A pathological accretion."

"No, probably German? Like maybe from Transylvania?"

"It seems he's interested in the music for the wedding."

"Well, some's sayin' that this Father Albert guy heard about the wedding at the head office where he works? And the bride and groom: you know, Macrina's uncle Bordo, that's marrying his live-in, Shawndynne? They been dating now a couple of years? Well, she wanted some song like 'One, Two, Three a Woman'? And this Father Albert, whoever, well, he got ants up his . . ."

"Now they want singing? I didn't know that."

"Whole thing got itself twisted. Everybody bent out of shape. But, there probably won't be any. He killed it. This Father, who? Albert, ..."

"Monsignor."

"Bombed everything? Told them to screw theirselves." In the mirror, he saw Besserian wrinkle his face. "Not those words, maybe. But he's down on stuff that's not his culture: 'Rock', 'Punk', 'Rap'. Sh... stuff like that. It always has to be *his* way. Like the world belongs to *him*. You know what I mean. How *some* people are? Control freaks?" He rummaged in his case for a polishing cloth, shooting a glance up to the mirror. "Guy needs to marinate himself."

"I don't see your point. He objects to 'Punk'? Isn't a wedding, supposed to be religious? Isn't that why it's in a church? Macrina, Sandra, and Shawndynne, can't understand that?"

"He said music has to be 'spiritual'? I guess that means the kind of stuff *he* likes. Traditionalist? Not the spiritual that grabs everybody else. Of course, they're only the ones that's getting married!" Felipe sniggered. "They think it's really 'cause he's PO'd 'cause Shawndynne's pregnant. And he's getting back at them."

"Is it possible that he's concerned about their commitment? That secular music detracts from the spiritual aspect of marriage? That they may see the church merely as a traditional, neo-Gothic, stage prop? With no spiritual significance?"

"Maybe. But the priest at this church, Father Tim? Who's going to marry them? They said he laughed when he heard she's pregnant: 'So what else is new?' And that PO'd Monsignor Albert. Even more? And Father Tim? He told the girls! That Father Albert had disrespected him, too! Yelled at him! That's the real reason he had bagged on their music."

Felipe spread his hands. "Not taking sides. Just saying what I heard. No kidding. Anyhow, they think he's a nerd. Anyhow, Mr. B, I didn't think people got married in churches any more. Father Tim said it'd be the first one, here, in a while: called it a 'buyers market'. And Macrina said nobody was coming to church here, anyhow? Like, maybe twenty or thirty on Sunday? And in this big place. There's room for probably: thousands? At least hundreds. Probably 'cause of all those rules Father Albert wants to make them do here. Like he lives on another planet? Like somebody blowed out his pilot light?"

"Isn't he in charge?"

"Whatever. I still don't see why people can't just get married if they want to. And I mean what's the point making all those boulders and causing problems and all? Not when they're already doin' it." Moistening it with his tongue, he adjusted the mouthpiece precisely into the gleaming metal instrument. "Hey, Mr. B? You probably got married in a church? Right? In your day people still did it?" He scrutinized the saxophone. "I mean got married in churches?"

Besserian, now scanning the music, ignored the question and then reconsidered. "Yes, I did. We did."

"Bet you had cool sounds? Rich Anglo church like this one—in its day? Right? Stretch limo, buddy guard, bachelor parties, tuxes, dancing, lots of good food, plenty to drink, mariachis, cool sounds ... all that stuff? Say 'Goodbye to Freedom: Hello to Slavery'?" He laughed, relishing his own humor. "Forget all those telephone numbers? Right Mr. B? You like to dance? Me too. Me and Sandra, we have a good time when we hit Mindy's and Chico's and other clubs. You?"

"I guess our wedding was considered large. It seemed so to me."

"Mind if I ask you something? Personal?" Besserian's eyes flashed in the mirror but Felipe interrupted the reply. "You think it's a good idea to get married in a church? I mean a big wedding? And all? I mean was it a big deal for you? I mean why even get married at all? I mean if you're doing it anyway?"

Besserian looked around and squinted. Felipe cleared his throat. "Hey, I'm not sayin' you. I mean normal people. You know? Young people? In the today world? It wouldn't make their wedding any better after a couple of years anyway would it? Anyway, by that time maybe you'd forget all about it? So lots of money wasted? Beer, booze, parties, cakes, dancing, girls, music, light show? You know what I'm talkin' about. The works?"

"Leaving aside the wedding as spiritual, I suppose we do rethink a marriage later on: a few years later." Besserian ran his fingers over the double rows of ivory couplers under the music rack. "Yes. I think relationships do change. Deteriorate, unless there's honest communication. He watched his colleague in the mirror. "Felipe, what do you expect—want—in a marriage?"

"Want? You know! You're a guy! What do guys always want?" He laughed. "OK, Right! You mean else? Well, I guess, like I'm not really sure. *I'm* still a young man. I got my needs too. And it's like—complicated?" He followed Besserian's eyes in the mirror. "Like not know exactly. You know, I heard some Gays at school: in your Period Four? Talking about getting married? Some day they might have their own weddings. I guess you can't never tell. The way things are going, and all? But you probably don't dig that. But, least ways, they won't be married here in *this* church! For sure, not with Hitler's around like Father Albert! No way, José! I don't think so. It's like now it's not sensical to get married in a church if you don't think the Church should tell you stuff. Or doesn't know what to tell you. It's like people want a church wedding? But not the rules? And the Church needs them, more than they need the Church? So the Church doesn't talk about the rules. Pretend like there's no rules. Least ways not ones that can't be broken? Except for Father Albert. Anyhow: Sandra and me? We're pretty close."

"You about ready? We've lost some time."

Felipe selected the precisely folded cloth to caress the already gleaming metal. "Just about. For me, Mr. B, sometimes, I can't figure her out. Sandra? What she wants? Used to want a big wedding. And that's OK with me. Don't know who's going to pay for it, though. But now she says she's not too sure: about the wedding. And you know what?"

"What?"

"I won't lie to you. Sometimes, it's like—weird? And I didn't say this to the other guys? But sometimes I think maybe she might not want to get married. At all. Or with me? But then things be OK? So, I figure it will work out. I just like to be with her. Most of the time. I get P.O'd lots and we fight sometimes, but then I miss her and think about her. I just like to be real close to her. So? I say I'm sorry. Even though I don't know what for. What else is new?" He held up his hands and shrugged.

"Sometimes it's hard to figure out stuff. I mean if guys not supposed to be in control, and that's OK with me, but why's it cool for chicks to control guys? Right now? Like she's playing with my head? Doing a mind .... like I can't never figure out what she wants?"

Besserian ran a finger across his notations on the music, pulling out Stops with his other hand, confirming Pre-set buttons, scowling. "Have you asked her what she wants? Said what you want? What's important to you? The way I see it, now? Marriage, friendship, any worthwhile relationship, has to be based on honest communication. No assumptions. No judgments. Acceptance. Respect for the other person as he, she, is. Make up your own mind about those things. Say what you want. Listen. Discuss the issues. Not pretend they're not there. By saying you're sorry."

Frowning, he made additional notations. "So, if you're not sure what Sandra wants? Then: ask her. Tell her what you want. If you can't do that? You have your answer. Relationship where you can't make differences work for you both? Not a relationship. An association."

He continued. "Have you discussed your careers? Right now, that's essential. Isn't she thinking about graduate school after college? She wants to go into politics? Into corporate management?"

"Me? Right now? Not sure of stuff. She's not cool with me having a career. In music." He was giving attention to a possible blemish on the shimmering instrument. "I figure, just let things happen?"

"I don't agree. Things might happen that you don't like. Don't want. As I see it now, if you want to get straight answers, you have to ask straight questions. A relationship isn't a time for empty, sweet smiles. Take your sax. It's shiny, attractive, impressive. But it's appearance is secondary. What's essential are the sounds that you produce with it. How those sounds express what's important to you. What's important to other people." He grimaced. "The relationship isn't with the sax as a metal instrument. But with how you use it. Express what's important to you. And to other people."

"Same thing for you, then?"

Besserian hesitated. "Probably. Sure. People do tell us what's wrong. One way or another. Classroom is an example. Problem is when we don't want to hear. What they want changed. Takes courage to hear: the reality. So, we have to ask ourselves. Me? You? Do we want reality? Or a perpetual soap opera of 'assumptions'; 'implications'; 'Oh, you know'; or the 'I don't know what love is', cop out? Continual guessing? That isn't a relationship. Isn't love. It's manipulation. Disguised incompatibility. It's dependency. The relationship isn't there. So it makes no sense to talk about love: which is a relationship. Anyway, if a person can't face himself, herself, how can the two people face each other? Add to the problem: over time, people change. Their values. So, can two individuals communicate the change? If not? Relationship shrivels. Becomes a cover up. Communication is encoded."

"Mr. B, she says guys over-analyze too much: 'cause they're immature? Self-centered. Over-sensitive. Control freaks. That I should just roll with it. Don't try to figure out stuff. Because women are too complicated: for guys. Superior. She didn't used to talk like that. We just used to have fun. Laughed and stuff. I guess the thing is now chicks get to call all the plays. And they don't think guys have feelings. I know I got feelings. And you know what?"

"No."

"Sometimes, I don't know what to do with them. They're so, like, well, so *different* all the time. I feel one way. Then another way. Like twisting me around all the time. Like playing jingle-jangle with me."

"How much have you discussed her career? Sandra's?"

"Not that much." He scrutinized the brass for a non-existent blemish. "I like kids. And I want to be a musician too. She's not cool with that. Too insecure, she says. Not steady money. And she says kids get in the way of a woman's career."

"A relationship? With somebody? With your work? Without love? Doesn't exist. And even with love it can drive you crazy. Want it. Hate it. At the same time. Love doesn't make the craziness go away. But it's the only way you can deal with the craziness."

"Drive you crazy? You sure got me pegged! I'm like doing mind flip-flops all the time. Don't know whether I'm standing on my head. Or my feet."

"Right now, we need to assert our own strength." He placed the score on the music rack and flipped out the *Tuba Mirabilis,* alternating with the *Röhr Schalmey* and depressed single notes and chords. Piercing metallic sounds ricocheted the length of the nave and those not absorbed by the gold, marble, and colored glass, eddied back with a sweet, caressing, velvet fondness. "Reeds are better. So? The Telemann? The *Adagio*?"

"Yeah. Like it was, could be, a prayer?

Besserian nodded agreement in the mirror.

Adjusting the mouthpiece, Felipe's eyes absorbed the pleasure of what he was about to do, smiled excitedly, self-confidently, scrutinizing his partner, alert to the possibility of misunderstanding. "I'm not that late so often? I mean like this morning?" He ran a square palm over his scalp—an already receding hairline—reached through his legs and adjusted the chair, drawing the stand closer. He was expectant, stroking his cheek bones, quizzically and approvingly with thumb and fingers, savoring the coarseness, aware of the shadow which defined the sculpted profile. His eyes smoldered; responding to a challenge, bearing down on a physical restraint, already savoring the duet—easing strongly into it—the euphoria of simultaneous taking and receiving.

"Good. They'll call up from downstairs when they're ready. So we have to be waiting."

"Got it. Whatever. Sir."

"Watch each other in the mirror. Where you have your chair now is fine. This is yours. You're the star. My part is easy. I'm your back-up. The receiver."

Felipe pursed his lips, nodding rhythmically, his concentration absolute.

Besserian pushed two of the Pre-Set buttons and pneumatic pressure flung out the *Viole de Gambe, Voix Céleste, Hautbois,* Stops. He raised the fingers of his left hand and counted: two-and-three-and-four-and, nodded at the mirror, depressed the keys with his right hand and feet, and the muted sensuality of the organ, cradled the aggressive response of the saxophone.

The melody flowed into the recesses of the building. Panels of glass, walls of stone, marble pillars and burnished wood pews caught the sounds, quivered, and held them lovingly. Felipe poured out his surging, undulating feelings. At the points of melodic transition their eyes met, communicating the phrasing, the rhythm, the emphasis: the solemn tempo reaffirmed the haunting melody. It became a mutual entreaty, a supplication, eddying around the colored shafts of light, moving across the floor, soaking the tapestries, finally coming to rest at the agony of the Crucified Christ: the final chords, resonant in the brass and warm in the organ.

Two sets of eyes, dark brown and brilliant green, were reflected in the console mirror, savoring the beauty of what they had created: reluctant to let it go.

****************************

"Splendid. Magnificent. Perfect choice." The visitor broke the loud silence—the drone of rushing air. "But, I'm interrupting. Excuse me." Tall, sinewy, dark eyes recessed, he was in black levis, braided leather suspenders, turtle neck sweater and Wolverine work boots. "Beautiful and spiritual." Placing his '30's tweed driving cap on a chair, he smiled and squeezed Felipe on the shoulder and moved toward Besserian who, following him in the mirror, swung around on the bench.

"Albert Wojeck. Diocesan chancellor. Director of parochial schools. I think we met? At a Civitans Award meeting? You received an award? I recall you also requested clarification about education reform."

He watched Besserian quizzically. "I wasn't aware you were a musician. As well as a distinguished teacher. You brought out the spirituality of the composition. Beautifully. Both of you. I, myself, am partial to the Baroque." He pronounced the 'o' as a broad 'a'. "And the Voluntary before? Rousing. And this." He indicated the nave with a sweep of his arm, "The perfect recital hall."

Besserian slid off the bench and shook his hand, smiling. "And not only the building. This instrument. A particularly fine *Cassavant.* Wonderful for the Romantics, too. Not that I do them justice. I'm an amateur. But yes, that meeting? I do remember. What? Ten months ago?" He indicated Felipe. "Monsignor, this is Felipe Estrada. A very good student. And talented musician."

The priest grasped the young man's hand solidly. "To be sure. An extraordinary sound: commanding, yet, at the same time, a plaintive *timbre.* Sensual. Haunting. I concur with Mr. Besserian. You're talented, indeed."

"It's kind of a specialty saxophone, sir. Called a *sopranino?* Pitched high. Rolls all over the place. Like it's looking behind the columns, and up into the highest part of the ceiling? Under the pews? Behind the drapes? Checking all the hidden places? Wants to make sure it shows off how beautiful it is. To everyone. Super cool. Love it."

The priest, relaxing, nodded assent. "Exactly. Piercing yet caressing. A mellowness? Sweetness? Amazing! And, you're quite right. The acoustics *are* excellent: a magnificent concert hall." He took off his jacket. "It's worthy of your artistry. Both of you." A self-confident smile illuminated his face. "Can we sit for a minute? I always enjoy it when I can get over here. To this parish. And up here. It's a refuge. Secluded. A respite from clerical in-fighting. And competition. My private retreat—I like to think of it that way. We can talk now that they don't keep the Sacrament in the church."

"Break-ins? Robberies?

"Not especially. Our staff say it's the homeless people. They're let in, occasionally, to use the kitchens. Sometimes allowed to sit in the church. To socialize. With some degree of dignity. But robberies? By them? I don't think so. Theft, yes. Unfortunately. But 'inside' theft: carpets, silver, ivory. A gold chalice set with emeralds. A gift from one of the founding parishioners. Very, very expensive! And beautiful! Will never be replaced. Even several of the old Latin Missals which, apparently, are sought after now by antique dealers. This isn't for public consumption but staff, clergy, are implicated. The Sacrament? Now? Many of our clergy consider it representational. Another example. Of eroding dogma."

"But enough of that. I recall your remarks about educational reform. Civitans awards meeting?" He motioned for Besserian and Felipe to take the chairs across from the bench he had selected for himself. "Your views impressed me. If you have a few minutes?"

"Sure, Father. Mr. B doesn't need much practice. And I got it down pretty good. I mean with him."

"I was taken by your thoughts on Reform. It occurred to me then, that there might be a similarity between Reform in my Church and Reform in public education."

"Similarity? Your Church and schools? They're totally different."

"The similarity of Reform."

"But . . ."

"It occurred to me that what we have in common—Reform—is that Reform is: code."

"Code!"

"Code! That's sorta . . ."

"Hear me out. Please. Let me hypothesize that Reform for both our institutions is code: all the changes for us: vernacular Mass, hand-held Eucharist, reversed altars to mention a few. For you? Bi-lingual programs, Diversity, No Child Left Behind, Special Education's least restrictive environment, Standards Based Instruction *et alii*."

"Et alii? Never heard of that one, Father."

"And other things. Now. My hypothesis. If, again I say, *if*, Reform for both of us is code?"

"Got it!"

"Then, it has to be decoded? Deciphered? To get the truth. The reality? Correct?"

"Sure. Give you that one. But how?"

"Precisely. You're ahead of me Felipe. There has to be a key. A word, symbol, number, whatever, to plug into the code so you can get the true meaning. Of the code."

"Cool."

"Obviously then, the key has to be correct. Or else the decoder will get the wrong, incorrect, message. Right?"

"Beats the . . ."

"Makes sense, Monsignor. Then, what is the key?" Besserian interrupted.

"There you have the problem! We, Church and Education have been using the wrong key. So the decoding of Reform has given us the incorrect message. Has not given reality."

"What is this incorrect key?"

"*Learning.*"

"Learning? Holy . . ."

"Felipe, both our institutions say the key to Reform is Learning. For you; academics and maybe technical training and job skills. Whatever you say students need to become productive adults."

"And for you? Your Learning?"

"Increased learning about our Dogma and Morality. Dogma—teaching and belief system—supposed to be strengthened. Our moral tenets supposed to be believed and *practiced* by Clergy. Also by non clerics: the Faithful, we call them."

"May I ask this, Monsignor? How do you know Learning is the incorrect key to Reform? For you? For us?"

"Because Learning—Dogma and Morality—isn't happening. Our Dogma, Moral Teachings are neither taught; nor practiced. Neither imposed nor, even, believed. Not the *sine qua non* of membership. And your academics: reading, writing, mathematics, science: similar: not imposed. Intellectual level is eroding."

"But we're trying to . . ."

"Precisely. No, *you* aren't! And no, *we* aren't! No! After fifty years! Of 'Reform'? Still *not* accomplished! More confused, muddled than ever! No, we are not 'trying'. And No! You are not 'trying'. Unless, we acknowledge total incompetence! And that would be to prove my point."

"OK! Got it! So, if the key isn't Learning. What is it?"

"*Politics.*"

"Politics? That's the key to Reform?"

"Politics, the key, unlocks, deciphers, decodes the reality. Of the Reform messages. And gives the correct message."

"What's the correct message then? That Politics unlocks?"

"Preserve the institution, yours and mine: those who control it. Preserve their personal power. And wealth. Institution at the *expense* of members: sacrifice dogma, spirituality. Sacrifice learning—the very thing we, you, espouse!"

"That's what Reform is? Keep things the same? More power and money for the leaders? So, Reform is a farce? Ours and yours?"

"Precisely. We, like you, have betrayed our beliefs for relativism. Result? Phony education at the expense of your students. Phony morality, dogma at the expense of our members. Both our institutions are moribund. Reform, for us? St. Martin Luther."

"Our leaders, yours, aren't leading?"

"They're leading all right. The question is: where? And why?" Monsignor Albert stood and picked up his jacket and cap. For the first time he lost his composure. "And what's happened to Truth? Absolute Truth? 'Reform' has erased it in favor of convenience. Political convenience. Distracting people! From the internal corruption of the institution by keeping people 'happy'. You're musicians*!*" He spat out the words: "*Orrenda, orrenda pace! La pace è dei sepolcri!*"[26] Breathing heavily, he recovered himself. "Enough talk. Let's walk down. And thank you again for such beautiful music. A pleasure meeting you. Thanks for listening. For helping me. To clarify my thoughts."

"Father? Monsignor?" Felipe was thoughtful. "Suppose what you say, your hypothesis? Is true? Maybe the ones—leaders—writing about Reform in code? Maybe they don't know how's they're on the wrong track? Talking in code?"

The priest punched him playfully. "Felipe, I recall an adage: 'Is the pope Catholic'?"

---

26 Verdi, G. *Don Carlo;* Act II, Scene 2: "You gave peace, yes! But what kind of peace! A horrible, dreadful peace! Peace gained by slaughter: the peace of the tomb!"

# *CHAPTER XXV*

## *Unexpected Documents*

"Ladies and gentlemen. Just to tell you how impressed I am. The way you've been working on the documents"

"We're only looking at the regular files."

"But there's some stuff that's different. Need to know something, Mr. B."

"What, Jesus?"

"Well, you tell him, Macrina. You seen it first."

"Mr. B. It's files that's what we thought might be maybe a foreign language?"

"Not Spanish. For sure."

"We're due to go back to the District Records Room tomorrow. We can look at them together. Could be important."

"It was sort of jammed behind some other files? You sure we supposed to look at it? Maybe somebody wanted to hide it? Like a secret?"

"We gotta be careful, Mr. B. Might get brain damaged: at an early age? I mean like happens when people get to be over forty! Like old and sh... stuff?"

"Mr. B, maybe it could be better for us? If we was to sorta stay inside the box? Chill? Not get ourselves too motivated?"

"Miguel, the brain is a living organ. It grows with use."

"Aldo says he knows what else grows with use." Jorge punched his friend on the shoulder, knocking him backwards.

"Hey man, you're the one who knows. For sure. You been practicin' enough!" They convulsed in laughter.

"Let's stay on target here."

"Put out our best foot forward? And hey, Mr. B. don't pay some attention to those cholos. I'll help you. That's what I'm here for."

"Thank you Marco. Appreciate it."

"No problem! I'm here for you." Marco gave the thumbs up sign.

"Seems to me, Mr. B? Need to check this hidden stuff out. Concentrate on it."

"I disconcur, Miguel." Gloria was perplexed. "School's about doing the right thing. Learn what you're told to learn. We not supposed to learn to be Terrorists. Or something. I mean some other teachers been sayin' just to read about Reform in the classroom if we want to. Not to go poking around in other peoples' business. That's not what school's about."

"We sure don't do much of analyzing of stuff in our regular courses, Mr. B. Even stuff that's in the book."

"So far, we haven't hit on anything extraordinary yet. But we've just begun our analysis."

"Analysis? That's like the answer? How about if we was to just to get the answer book? And look it up?" Rosalba rummaged in her backpack.

"You baggin' on the Project, girl? It's a dork? You not respecting other people that way! Mr. B might to have some good stuff going here." Jesse was indignant.

"Rosalba, I'm sure you'll make your contribution just like everyone else. But back to the immediate issues. First, absolutely, it's important to review together those special files you found the other day. Second, review our strategy. We have a hypothesis: that the Reform Plan will benefit Cathedral Heights schools: public education. We investigate. Gather the facts from the documents. Test our hypothesis. Put the Plan under a microscope. Right now, as you said, we don't know very much about it. We only have a smidgen of information ..."

"A what? A pigeon?" The young man laughed with gusto.

"A small amount, Roger. Right now we know only what we've been told: in the news and by people proposing it. Are they biased? Need to find that out. No, the Project, our Project will get the facts. For ourselves. That leads us to the next step."

"What's that, Mr. B? My teacher, Miss Weatherby? She say that Reform's not gonna be good for us? And when somebody told her say so? To my other teachers, Miss Cort-ayer, and Ms. Turner? And some such? They said Miss Weatherby's some kind of nut bar? A terrorist? A socialist? And so did Mr. Warfles. He started yelling like always when he gets mad and such. He said teachers that talk dirt like that be the ones that not join the teachers Union. The ones not wantin' to save the environment: for global warming? Not want minority rights. The ones that screw up everything for the other teachers? The dedicated ones?"

"Does she know why, Marlene? Ms. Weatherby? Why she has doubts about the Plan?"

"Maybe. Dunno. Might have been only a kind of feeling that she had?"

"The point is that with our Project, we'll be able to analyze her 'feeling'. Find out if it's correct. Right now, how about if we review the Project Outline. Make sure we're on the right track? Daniel why don't you read, if you would, please? You can sit here at my desk."

"OK, Mr. B. On my way." Besserian walked to the back of the room. The young man assumed an exaggeratedly officious tone and demeanor. "Listen up, folks. And anybody who's not giving attention's gonna have real regrets. With me." He grasped the paper with both hands.

"One. Identify the Area of Investigation: Cathedral Heights.

Two. Hypothesis: Reform Plan will benefit local education.

Three. Facts: Research the information, the documents that pertain to Reform Plan.

Four. Conclusions: What do the facts show?

Five. Recommendations to the Principal. Or the Superintendent: Accept or reject Reform Plan. And that's it: what you guys got to do."

"Thanks Daniel. To reiterate: we'll continue to read the documents, get the facts, draw our conclusions and report on them.

"Mr. B, can I say something?"

"Of course. Go ahead, Shaunisha."

"Well, don't we already know about it?"

"What do you mean?"

"I mean look at stuff. I mean when you think about it. I mean Mr. Baques he say he want Reform Plan. Been talking to kids? And teachers? And Mr. Warfles he says same thing. And I heard the Superintendent, Miss, whatever is her name: like LaFork or somesuch? And then some of teachers sayin' they think it's the best thing since sliced bread. So, lots say it's a good idea. Already. And that man? Mr. Dickard ..."

"Mr. Dickhard! Hey girl, you watch yourself! Some talk! I tell your mama! She wash your mouth out with some soap."

"Mr. Pritchard, Shaunisha. Ignore those comments. Rigo, that's inappropriate." The boy was sitting with his head on his arm, hand over his mouth, pointing, as if horrified.

"Project is a microcosm of what Education should be. Discovering new information. Amplifying what's taught. Drawing your own conclusions. Based on the facts you've uncovered. And know to be correct. True we may not find anything spectacular. The point is we're using all the available information. To find out for ourselves. Reality. Something else, Shaunisha?"

"Mr. B, we know this school's got lots of problems. Seems like your Project is really different? From what kids usually do? Maybe it could like start some really big changes? In the school? But we start with ourselves?" She turned to the others. "Guys, let's keep on with this. Have some faith in our coach. We're winners if we make up our own minds by what we find out. How often do we get to make up our own minds about stuff we have to learn? About anything?"

"Don't forget change involves risk."

"Could be like a drive-by, Mr. B?"

"Could show us things we don't want to see. But, that's the point of education: looking at new things. And old things in a new way. And fear? Only have to be afraid of what you don't know. Not what you do know. The idea is to keep looking. For facts. Reality. Be open to change."

"There could be something to be afraid of if the people who wants Reform Plan don't like our opinion? Of what's going on?"

"Is this what we should be doing? I mean we're kids. Isn't school supposed to make us safe? Keep us protected?"

"That's the bottom line for this Project, girl." Allisandro, regarding Macrina indolently, was flipping a pencil in his hand. "Seems like Mr. B. not want us to take somebody else's word, like in a school book, but to find out for ourselves. What's going on. So, no, not as safe as being in a classroom. We can't be safe all our lives. Gotta grow up. Stretch our wings. Not stay in our nestes the rest of our lives. If school not teach us how to take care of ourselves, then what's it for?"

"I agree. Jesus?"

"My uncle say the only thing you got to fear is secret stuff inside you that concerns yourself. That you want to pretend's not there? That you not want to think about."

Besserian came back to the teacher's desk. "Obviously he's a thoughtful man, Jesus. To get back to the Outline. The subject of our inquiry is the school Reform plan: our tentative assumption, hypothesis, is that it will be beneficial. The facts will confirm or negate our hypothesis."

"This could be like one of them three-dimensional puzzles? I saw on TV? Where they can find out how smart are monkeys that goes out into space on rocket ships? And you know what? They found out that some was smarter: than people!"

"Smarter than you, for sure, Mr. Big Mouth. Somebody needs to send you up in a rocket. To the moon. One way!"

"Yeah! One of them kinds which gets lost, and falls into a Black Hole." Allisandro slapped his fist on the desk to emphasize his point."

"You watch yourself, boy! So, what you know? About anything? Diddly. I throw you down outside, dork." Rigo was beginning to seethe with rage.

"Yeah? I know more than . . ."

"Let's move on. Remember what we agreed on about Respect. Education is hearing opposing views. Right now, let's get back to analysis of the documents."

"Yeah! Cool! Let's hit it."

"Will it save money? Give people who live here more benefits for their tax dollars? Especially will it enable Cathedral Heights to raise its standard of education: better education for more people? Find out how the Reform Plan defines 'better'."

"So far what bothers me, Mr. B?"

"What Shaunisha?"

"So far stuff we've been looking at just give general stuff. That Reform Plan is a good idea. Will be good for everybody. But not say how."

"The purpose of our Project is to answer that question. If the information isn't there? Doesn't that alert us? To a possible problem? Your point is well taken."

"Yeah, 'cause if Reform Plan means our own school district and our own city, I mean, maybe that'll cost us. Somebody got to pay. Could mean higher taxes?"

"Exactly, Rigo. If we find the Reform Plan hasn't answered these questions, we'll have doubts about recommending it. Good point. You guys are on target."

"They got to tell us exactly how our schools will be better." Sandra nodded agreement.

Griselda pulled scrawny legs onto her seat. "I have to disconcur. This stuff is weird. Doesn't make sense. We never do anything like this before. And we not supposed to get work that makes us to have to go outside of the school. Or do stuff that's not in the book. No. This is no good. Our parents won't like it. They don't want us taking on all this kind of stuff. They say teachers already giving too much homework. Right now."

"You don't even know all that we'll find out yet, Twiggy. Let the teacher explain, like he's trying to. Looks like something we could learn from. Could help us." Hector Estrada pulled his desk closer to Theresa Hedges and jabbed at the Outline with his fist. "Let's toss it around. See if it makes salad! What's not to like? Mr. B, we going to be graded on this? Project? So's we can explain it to our parents and such?" The young man nodded affirmatively. "Looks like we going to get some special experience. We don't get that in other classes." He flicked the paper with his thumb and middle finger.

"As I said, it will be an extra credit Project. Completely voluntary. You can use this as a Community Service Project. On your college applications. I'll point out your Project participation in letters of recommendation. Osbaldo?"

"I think when a teacher asks us for our opinion he's showing us respect. How many teachers do that? Sure never seen any. Not at this school."

"And you never will," interjected Monica Alvarez.

"For me, I still don't think it's a good idea." It's just not the Way of the Hill. Don't do it that way here." Guadalupe shook her head disapprovingly. "I guess you want to be a good teacher, and all, Mr. Besserian, and everybody appreciates that, but, well, and what if we can't get into college anyhow? And JC's don't ask us for Community Work."

"Yeah, girl. This Plan ain't gonna help us." Veronica Valdez ran a comb through long tinted russet hair and picked at the tines thoughtfully. "Teachers know that they can get away with doin' nothin'. Most of them don't teach. No point in the kids sayin' something because the Principal don't care. And teachers know it." She took out a bandanna and blew loudly. "They always sayin' there's no money. But they's always asking for higher pay. And my auntie? She work for the state and she say that teachers to not be askin' for more money and should do their work. And what if this don't work out for us? What we goin' tell our parents? And I don't think we should be lettin' other kids to do our work for us. I mean in these groups? And I sure don't want somebody else copying my work when they don't want to do it theirselves. But other than that, I guess it's OK. Might could work."

"OK. Concerns about group work? Why not help the people in your group? Motivate them? Be a teacher yourself? Help them learn from you. So they can do it on their own. In a regular class are you worried about copying from the teacher?"

"But what if we can't decide what we supposed to learn to remember? About what we find out?"

"You'll be able to do it, Gloria. Trust me. You'll discuss your decisions among yourselves. With mutual respect."

"What if we don't see stuff the same way? Mr. B, I mean this is totally overpowering for us. I mean what if we never do find out? Anything? I mean we could be goin' on and on. Forever. Sort of scary."

"We have three months, the end of April, to finish. At that time we'll write our conclusions and recommendations, Gloria. Scary? Of course. This is a radical change. We're moving into a place we've never been before. I understand your concern."

"Mr. B? This Project's sort of like us writing the text book? Cool."

"I think so, Daniel. We're risking change. Change in the way we learn. That's a big risk. It's worth it. I think we'll learn a lot. We'll see democracy, Reform, at work."

"Yeah, Mr. B. What if we find out stuff that we not supposed to? Maybe they try to blast us? Highjack us. Do a drive-by?"

"Hey, man! Do a Extraordinary Rendition on us? To Gitmo?" Allisandro laughed heartily.

"As I said, we'll deal with that later. At least it won't be boring. This puts us on the 'cutting edge' as the expression goes. School work becomes exciting."

"Project is different. I mean just to look at this school. Now." Robert was cynical. "I mean how many parents come to Parent Night? Or ask why information about the school, especially why the school budget, not given out to the Parent Reps or the School Community Committee? Like it's supposed to be? Never happens! And they wouldn't find out if they did ask. Everybody knows the Principal not want to tell about it. Anyhow, asking about stuff's not what people think they can do. Because they don't learn to do that in school. So they got no experience in asking about stuff. So, with this Project, we're learning something that most people don't' know about. But can't do for themselves: glued to their boob tubes. So, it really is community service. Great!"

"Yes, Theresa?"

"Mr. B., our Project's going to be different from the Project Mr. Broomfield has: after school Bible Study? Now there's people to say he should have it during regular day class? So, maybe our Project can be during a regular class, too?"

"We'll have some Project discussion in our regular classes."

"Mr. B. They should let you take over the school district. And we could be your advisors? We're gonna know all about how to run schools. Cutting edge? More than anybody else."

"Coach, this Project's not us pretending to be students. Not playing at being students like most times here at school. In most classes. This be like us headed in a totally different direction from other classes here? Learning for ourselves. Finding out stuff for ourselves. Not just reading it in a book: learn stuff because we have to? Project lets us find out what's really happening. Sort of becoming leaders? Be pro-active? Like somebody said earlier: like writing our own text book. By ourselves."

"I think so, Hector. That's the issue for us. Getting the knowledge and then taking it to the next step."

"We gonna research with our regular classwork, too, Mr. B?"

"Good point, Felipe. Let's check our course Outlines. With the Standards. We moved into the Age of Reaction: failure of the 18th century revolutions. Subsequent developments: liberalism, nationalism, colonialism, industrialism, Socialism, Communism. We'll see where revolutions were crushed. By economic power groups: but under the guise of extending democracy: just enough to keep people quiet. We won't have primary sources. But we can use the inquiry techniques of our Project to comment on the text information. But now? Need to check those special files you guys found."

"You mean the secret ones?

"Yes."

"Go for it. We're on a roll, coach."

# *CHAPTER XXVI*

## *An Offer You Can't Refuse*

"Well go-o-ly! Ya'll, I just do believe this was *my* house? In a former life? I mean, ho-o-o-ly! I swanee! I really do! And I wish I hadda bought my daater. But you guys know *teenagers*! When they're in those advance college prep courses! For Gifted! Why, they are just so *sm-a-a-rt*! Private schools! And don't ask me the cost!" Rayella Brauphman hunched flabby shoulders and twittered, grimacing and biting her lower lip, as she plucked three chocolate truffles from one of the silver trays on the inlaid Louis XVI table behind her. "You know, I really shouldn't. But on, well, special occasions?"

"Go for it, girl!" Lydia Hastings-Bruce, Art and Ceramics, smiled benignly.

The group were standing, ill-at ease, opposite the French doors opening onto the flagstone terrace. Framed by a gardenia hedge were potted Orange trees, and brilliant purple Bougainvillea towered up the stone wall to the third story—lush, striking. Beyond, the lawn sloped toward a pool in the far distance, the entire expanse illuminated by soft lighting.

"This is just awesome. And I do mean awe-some! And would you grab ahold of the size of that pool! Wow! Imagine skinny-dipping in that! And would you just to look beyond it?" Lydia squeezed Rayella's arm, directing her attention to a secluded grotto of olive trees, boxwood and jasmine: a fountain. Three female figures, life-size, gleaming black marble, supported a bronze urn on their shoulders, from which water trickled over their shimmering nude forms into the pool below.

"Go ahead, sweetie. Eat your heart out! This place cries out to spoil yourself in. Reminds me of Forest Lawn." Rikki Bacon-Gaither chuckled amiably. "If this is an 'inside view' of what Reform is all about, I'm sure for it. And, don't somebody take a look now but did you happen to hunker down on that dress?"

"Whose?" Rayella, eyes like saucers, was slurping traces of chocolate from the tips of pudgy fingers.

"Old lady Pritchard, of course. My Gawd! Might even could be a Sally Thompson! For sure not out of Meryn's. Hate to even *think* the price tag. But that color! And neckline! Twenty years too young for her! Who does she think she's kidding? And that phony French name!"

Lydia, in a flamboyant gypsy skirt with uneven hem, multiple bracelets, *décolleté* blouse and paisley scarf braided into her hair, was nonchalant. "And would you catch the emerald broach! And the matching bracelet? Wow! Talk about size! There goes twenty plus years of my salary." Her voice was a dark contralto.

"Gottcha." Brian McCauley was comfortable in white bucks and polyester pin stripe suit, shirt open at the neck, "So long as Reform is good for sports, football, I got no problem with it." He turned to Cyril Jacobs. "Guess that's not too important to you, eh?"

"I wouldn't say it was unimportant. *Chacun son goût.* [27] However I was noticing an interesting group over there. Standing by that settee—the red damask that looks like it came from Blenheim Palace?"

"Who? Where?"

"Try not to look too obvious, but only just the great Mr. Besserian. And the lady with him? His ever-so-successful executive wife? Penelope? I think that's her ever-so-affected name? And with *the* Mrs. Peter Pritchard. And another man. Could be a pro football player. Looks like *he* sure knows what for!"

"Well, can you just imagine that! She's actually not all that bad! On the plain side, of course. But, you know how hunks go for plain women. As wives. Props up their ego."

"From the looks of *that* guy, nothing needs propping up. Ho-o-ly!"

"She probably makes quadruple the salary of her husband. And Huguette told me, the one that looks like a NFL hockey player? Was her

27 *Each to his own taste.*

boss! Gawd! I'd sure be willing to work for him. And I do mean W-O-R-K!"

Rikki Bacon-Gaither was breathless. "I see what you're looking at. You heard what he's doing? Besserian?"

"Sure, it's going around."

"Settin' himself up for the AP job. Getting his kids to study about Reform. Buttin' in. Make like he's better than? Get in like gangbusters with Pritchard. And Baques. Makes me sick. Using kids that way. To get the AP! Ugh!"

Cyril was gushing, "To die for, folks! Crystal! Silver! These forks! Can hardly lift mine."

Overcome by the surroundings, Rikki hugged Rayella as if unexpectedly reunited after decades. "Can you guesstimate what they shelled out for this place?"

Rikki, fluttered her hand to Dr. Allsbury who was surveying the buffet table.

"Magnificent. A showplace of Los Altos. Do notice the Gobeleins in the dining room. And there?" Allsbury pointed, with elaborate eye movement, to the three sprawling bronze and crystal chandeliers glittering overhead.

"Well, I guess you should know, Ms. Allsbury." Immediately Bacon-Gaither realized her error. Aghast, she sucked in a vortex of air, eyes rounded, then doubled over in shrill laughter. "Have I lost it?" She slapped her hip in irritation. "Why can't I *never* remember? It's *doctor*! Of course! Why am I so stu-pid?"

Allsbury draped an elongated hand over the other lady's arm, smiling hugely, and pecked her on the cheek. "I understand perfectly, darling. Remember! It's because I didn't have a doctorate when you first came to Fillmore. In fact, barely out of school myself! And you had been a teacher for how long? But look over there, dear!"

"Where?"

"At the end of the room. Between the two *Kiang-xi* urns. I think we're about to receive some important information."

Peter Pritchard was smiling. Impeccable in Savile Row suit, he exuded the benevolence of the aristocratic host. "May I interrupt: for a moment?" He smiled slightly. "Ladies and gentlemen? My wife and I take great pleasure in welcoming you to our home. Many thanks to you all for coming. We hope that our Reform partnership of school and municipality will generate many more social opportunities."

He turned to Eugénie who, speaking in a cultivated voice, exuded gracious hospitality. "Indeed. My husband and I are *thrilled* to welcome you!"

Peter resumed center stage."School Reform! Essential to maintain our democracy. And, to provide trained minds to succeed us in the corporate world. At the executive levels. But, to achieve that, Reform must champion you, the teachers."

He was magnanimous. "My friends! The Reform Plan is the crucible in which we, you, will mold our youth. Advance them intellectually, culturally, morally: give them the training and experience they need, to assume leadership. In our community. In our state. In our country. If we do not want that success for them, then we should reject the Reform Plan. Because that is its goal."

"To repeat, our Reform, unlike those mandated by other state and federal 'so-called' reform plans—I won't mention 'No Child Left Behind'—does not mean punishing teachers. Or administrators. Or students. Setting impossible Traditionalist-culture standards which our students cannot achieve. It means championing our *teachers*—each one a highly trained and dedicated professional—encouraging them, giving them the tools they have long been denied, through no fault of their own, to achieve what they want most: the academic excellence of our children. The opportunity to bring our youngsters to the top of the academic scale, enabling them to compete against those with more advantages. A few names come to mind: Ms. Cortère, newly arrived but already an icon at Fillmore. Ms. Brauphman. Ms. Turner. Mr. Warfles. Mr. McCauley."

"And working with them, sharing their goals for student achievement are our administrators. First, Dr. Elayne Jones-Laporte our distinguished Superintendent with her determination to abolish the 'at risk' student."

He interrupted the scattered applause. "Supporting Dr. Jones, as Assistant Superintendents are Ms. Rikki Bacon-Gaither, Dr. Joycelin Spellman-Landyce, and Dr. Claudia Obesso who, as director of Secondary Education, leads that vital division of Bi-Lingual Education. Let me not fail to mention Ms. Cerise Fuentes-Mullion ably assisted by Ms. Graciela Melendez-Sanchez; Assistant Superintendents of Student Affairs and Human Resources respectively: both student guardians."

"And at the Fillmore helm, is that tireless supporter of teacher and student achievement, our Principal: Mr. José Baques. And assisted so ably by Assistant Principles: Mr. Brampton Falange, Mr. Marion Johansson, and our gracious Dr. Patricia Allsbury."

He cut short the shavings of applause. "No speeches tonight. This evening, let us mingle: get to know one another better, as we set our course on the revitalization of school and community—always in service to our youth."

Mrs. Pritchard brushed against him, leaning up to whisper. He exuded a gracious smile. "Fine, my dear. I'm being urged to hurry, by *my* supervisor: the person who guides my life: Eugénie: my mentor, my strength. My bride." He bent and kissed her hand. There were the appropriate clucking of tongues: "Oooh!", "So swe-e-e-et!", and "Isn't that just adorr-able?"

"Enough about politics. A male weakness." There was additional tittering and the perennial wistful expressions, clinched smiles, lips downturned, eyes locked, heads tilted benevolently.

Eugénie Pritchard, dignified and refined, stepped forward, palm across her breast, fingers toying with the flashing green. "Peter has been my inspiration. My guide." She spoke slowly; poise and enunciation perfect.

"At the moment, however, I have a special surprise. And a confession!" She savored the reaction: the arch expressions. "We did have entertainment planned for you, a student group. Apparently, they were detained. And, what Peter was saying about helping one another? Making new friends? Throughout the evening it has been my privilege to meet so many fascinating people associated with our schools and community. As I was talking with two gentlemen, Mr. Henderson, President of the TriDelta Corporation and Mr. Besserian one of our distinguished teachers and their delightful companions, my mind racing all the while, trying desperately to appear calm despite the entertainment crisis. . . what do you suppose I found out? To my utter surprise? And relief? About Mr. Henderson and Mr. Besserian?" She waited for the wrinkle of interest to spread.

"They had both switched to GEICO?"

"They had thought it was real butter?"

The hostess laughed cautiously, self-consciously, distrusting the enthusiasm of the responses. "Charming! Let me reveal their secret." She lowered her voice. "While chatting, I discovered that Mr. Besserian is an accomplished pianist and Mr. Henderson, an equally accomplished vocalist!"

"Hey, go for it."

"Far out, guys."

"So, ladies and gentlemen, when I mentioned my plight! No entertainment . . ."

"They said they had to leave on the next train to Dubuque?"

"Indeed!" She attempted to grasp the humor of the audience. "I begged them to, as it were, step into the breach! Of course, they were reluctant. But Peter, as usual, saved the situation. He made an offer they simply-could-not-refuse!"

"A year's supply of pencils!"

She smiled and allowed the tension to mount. "Peter, always the problem-solver, offered a college scholarship to a Fillmore student if, indeed, these two gentlemen would volunteer their talents for us. Tonight!" She stepped to Peter's side, clasping his hand. "So? What could they say?"

Bracelet flashing shafts of green, palms upward, she continued. "Gentlemen? The piano is at the other end of the room so could we all group ourselves there? I believe attendants are placing chairs now?"

There was a great deal of chatter, uuu-ing and ah-ing, as some assisted servants by taking chairs and shuffling them over the parquet.

"This better be good."

"I didn't know this was Amateur Night."

"I coudda' brought my electronic mouth organ." Brian McCauley whispered to Henry Morton, Remedial Math.

Eugénie took each of the performers by the hand and walked them the length of the room, beaming encouragement. "It will be fine. I know it. Not to worry. Just think about that scholarship. How appreciative some student will be. And everyone is dripping with jealousy."

Reaching the arena, Buck and Besserian looked at each other warily. Buck clenched his jaw rigidly and scowled. Besserian ran the back of his hand over the dark shadow on his face, took the score, seating himself at the piano, the ebony reflecting the glitter of the chandelier. He studied the music intently, moving his index finger across the page.

Buck appeared relaxed. "Before we start, I want to say I hope whoever gets this scholarship appreciates us." There was some encouraging laughter. "Also, have to tell you." He waited. "We've never done this before. But we'll give it a try."

Again the polite chuckles and smattering of applause. "You'll do great."

"Show em, Warr-ieers!"

"Go Knights!"

Allsbury and Jones-Laporte stared icily at Bruce Warfles and his group.

The two performers, seemed as enthusiastic as Polar Bear Club inductees at their first January plunge.

Buck paced slowly and Besserian adjusted the tufted leather bench as Mrs. Pritchard smoothed the music on the rack and gestured for the top of the piano to be lowered.

"If my partner doesn't know this better than I do, you're in trouble." Buck's explanation was as much to delay as inform. "Anyway, it's called The Crusader: *Der Kreuzzug.* A Schubert song, a favorite composer of Mrs. Pritchard's, that's why she has the music. And thanks for making a copy. So I don't have to read over Mr. B's shoulder."

He moved to the side of the instrument. "Song's theme is that it's nice to be recognized but what really matters is living up to your own ideals." He looked at Besserian. "Also, the ordinary life can be the most heroic. The most difficult. To accept the reality of your own situation in life."

Besserian nodded, intent on smoothing the crease in the paper. The men made momentary eye contact, Buck turned to the audience, and Besserian riveted his attention on the score.

The splendid sound of the *Böesendorfer* spread through the room. The opening chords, resonant, haunting, plaintive, even solemn, established the mood of introspection. The vocal line entered almost as a hymn: typically lyrical but atypically lacking in technical complexity. Accompanist and soloist articulated in turn the shifting harmonics, especially the verse where the accompanist took the melodic line and the soloist the descant. Buck revealed a resonant baritone, made more appealing by a hint of diffidence. Immediately they were absorbed in the subtlety of dialogue.

| | |
|---|---|
| Ein Münich steht in seiner Zell<br>Am Fenstergitter grau,<br>Viel Rittersleut in Waffen hell<br>Die reiten durch die Au. | A monk stands in his cell<br>At the grey window-grating.<br>A band of knights in shining armor<br>Come across the meadow |
| Sie singen Lieder frommer Art<br>Im schönen ernsten Chor.<br>Inmitten flieght, von Seide zart<br>Die Kreuzesfahn empor. | They sing holy songs<br>In fine, solemn chorus;<br>In their midst the banner of the Cross<br>Made of delicate silk, flies aloft. |
| Sie steigen an dem Seegestad<br>Das hohe Schiff hinan,<br>Es läuft hinweg auf grünem Pfad,<br>Is bald nur wie ein Schwan. | At the shore they climb<br>Aboard the tall ship.<br>It sails away over the green waters,<br>And soon seems but a swan. |
| Der Münich steht am Fenster noch,<br>Schaut ihnen nach hinaus:<br>Ich bin, wie ihr, ein Pilger doch,<br>Und bleib ich gleich zu Haus. | The monk still stands at the window<br>Gazing out after them:<br>'I am, after all, a pilgrim like you<br>Although I remain at home. |
| Des Lebens Fahrt durch Wellentrug<br>Und heissen Wüstensand,<br>Es ist ja auch ein Kreuzeszug<br>In das gelobte Land. | Life's journey through the treacherous waves<br>And the burning desert sands,<br>Is also a crusade<br>Into the Promised Land |

The final notes brought the silence of the room into relief. There was a glint of moisture in Buck's eye and he closed his mouth firmly. The performers exchanged resolute nods. Then, as Besserian stood, Buck planted one palm heavily on his back and, impulsively, flung an arm over his shoulder.

The size of the room echoed the polite applause.

"Hey! Great! Right on."

"Batting a thousand, guys." Brian McCauley slapped Besserian on the back.

"I think that moved my inner personhood," Rikki Bacon-Gaither whispered to Claudia Obesso. Baques's cell phone rang, and nudged by Allsbury, he fidgeted to turn it off.

Mrs. Pritchard was gushing, "Magnificent. Absolutely *thrilling.* Thank you so very much, gentlemen." She stepped back to appraise them, then kissed each one on the cheek. "Another? Please?"

Buck shrugged. Besserian spread his palms, "Better not push our luck."

Peter joined them and clasped each in turn by the shoulder. "Thank you gentlemen. You earned some fortunate student a very generous scholarship. We'll discuss the details later."

"Now. Time for some men-only talk." Pritchard motioned to Besserian, Buck and Baques.

"Well, I don't think that's very politically correct. When we're jest getting acquainted!" An indignant Rikki Bacon-Gaither, who had positioned herself at Buck's side, was distracted by Mrs. Pritchard taking her arm, motioning to other ladies. "Ladies? Please join me. Permit me to tell you some details about our home."

"Oh! Do! It's not haunted, is it?"

The chatelaine laughed generously at Cherry Hamilton's inquiry. "Heavens, no! Nothing as exciting as that? But this room, this house has some remarkable architectural features."

"I'm sure everyone would be interested in hearing about them, Mrs. Pritchard ..."

"Eugénie. Please. And I'll call you Huguette? If I may?"

"Peter's the expert on architecture. The house is inspired by the Villa La Gamberaia outside Florence: home of the Capponi family. Peter even had their crest incorporated over the main portico."

"Amazing! You've been to Italy?"

"Every year. Peter speaks Italian. In fact, five languages. His hobby is Byzantine history."

"Really!"

"He was an army cryptologist during the war."

"Wow!"

"In fact, there is a photo of him in the library. Receiving the Medal of Merit at a White House ceremony. Instrumental in breaking several German codes. Worked with British cryptologists. He received an OBE.[28] Undoubtedly saved hundreds of allied lives."

Warfles laughed heartily. "Reminds me of Dodger Stadium. And over there, Mrs! That looks like the door to nowhere? Weird? Like might be a door painted on the wall so it looks like there's another room but there, maybe, really isn't? Cool! Real cool!" He nodded vigorously, sucked his

28 OBE: Order of the British Empire: awarded for significant contribution to a political or military enterprise.

teeth, tilted back his head and quaffed a long drink from the fluted *St. Louis* beaker.

Mrs. Pritchard smiled. "You're aware of the 17th century fashion. It deceives us; but not really. *Trompe d'oeil,* trick of the eye: a deceit. Architectural code. The device fascinated Peter."

"Truly fab! I've never seen anything like this. Sure beats being a school secretary." Marvella Lorenghar, who had joined the group accompanied by her boyfriend, was overawed.

"You are most welcome to come again. I do hope you will. There's nothing Peter will not do to help young people succeed."

"Like the scholarship!"

"Precisely. And there will be others."

Pritchard and his three associates had maneuvered themselves near the French doors.

"Gentlemen, drinks?" The negative nods were expected. "Mr. Baques, you were telling me about Mr. Besserian's Project? It seems quite interesting."

"Very creative. I gave Mr. Besserian permission for an extra credit class, after school ...."

"Good. I'm impressed. I understand Mr. Henderson may be assisting him. Also, Mr. Besserian and the Assistant Principal position? I presume the interview will go as expected?"

Baques basked in his proximity to the great man. "As you know, we have to comply with Equal Opportunity, Diversity, Title IX, gender and racial quotas, and all the rest. However, I feel confident about Mr. Besserian's chances. Would like to have him aboard."

"Good. Dr. Jones will be speaking with the other members of the Board. To ensure the correct result." Peter smiled. "Indeed, I believe my wife has invited those ladies to luncheon next week. Well, Mr. Besserian your class Project appears most appropriate: students learn the details of the Reform Plan. Discuss it in the school, the community. Excellent."

He faced Besserian directly, smiling engagingly. "Let me ask you, sir, if I may? What are your observations about Reform? The Plan?"

"I'm in favor of raising the academic levels of our students. To where they should be." Relaxed, he savored the purring caress of the lustrous Burmese that intruded itself into the group. Pritchard beamed approval, as Besserian instinctively lifted the magnificent feline, obviously a champion, caressing the soft sable, rubbing it against his cheek, noting the engraved gold name tag on its collar: *Photius.*

"Of course. And as Assistant you should be the catalyst for Reform at Fillmore. I understand you will have the managerial expertise of Mr. Henderson? Should you wish it. Perfect! None better! You will be the key to ensuring faculty support for Reform. I am aware of your Civitans award. So, your Project could not have been better timed. Also. I understand your wife is associated with TriDelta."

He studied Besserian closely. "Excellent. Mr. Besserian I believe you will make a strong contribution to school administration. And the Reform Plan. You can unite our faculty and staff behind it. Fillmore needs your loyalty, sir. Loyalty is critical in any administrator. In any organization. Absolutely."

He smiled effusively. "Good. Things seem to be moving along quite well. Mr. Henderson, if you two work together as well as you perform, I see nothing but success: for us all. You will recall our Costa Rica project? The benefits to the CEO." Buck returned an enigmatic smile.

"As Principal, I feel that Mr. Besserian's Project makes him the leading contender for the AP position."

Peter was ebullient. "Quite so, Mr. Baques. I know you will do everything necessary. For the benefit of Reform." The agreement was ratified by shaking of hands all around.

# *CHAPTER XXVII*

## *My Country*

In honor of the Cinco de Mayo festivities, Administration had decreed that the assemblies would be held in the morning. Auditorium capacity was nine hundred and fifty-one, so there would be three performances, starting at 8:30, in order to accommodate seniors and those lower classes chosen by ASB lottery.[29] Selected students would miss one and one half of the four morning class periods, not including any classroom parties before or after the Assembly—food, drinks, games—held at the teacher's discretion.

The last two periods of the day were cancelled. Instead of academic instruction, students would participate in the culminating event of the celebration—the outdoor Carnival—to begin at one o'clock. For this, approximately twenty-five booths were set up at the juncture of the Administration and 'B' buildings. Food sales—burritos, enchiladas, nachos, menudo, various *carne assada*, 'soul food', gelatin, cakes, pastries, corn dogs,, hot dogs—comprised the basic edibles. Candy, popcorn, ice cream, and green, orange, red, blue and yellow iced *refresco* were especially popular. Also, *Ladies* and *Machote* [*Tough Guys*: remote controlled car club] each had a booth offering perennial favorites: coconut-milk: *leche frío,* or the succulent rice-cinnamon drink, *horchado.* Most of the edibles were homemade, brought to school and stored: classroom, lounge, Science lab,

29 ASB: Association of Student Bodies: organization regulating student groups

locker room, office, X-rox area, teachers' lounge: wherever refrigeration or storage space could be commandeered.

Besserian was a faculty advisor both to the Student Activities Committee and the ASB. As such he had been involved in adjudicating which student organization could sell what product and at what cost. Carnival was more than a 'fun event'. It was the financial mainstay for organizations excluded from the school budget. Athletic teams, the Band, and other 'official' organizations, however, used Carnival to augment budgeted funds.

For example, the *Adorables*, the previous Monday, already had set up the profitable, 'Love Grams' booth, where, for one dollar, a magnificently decorated heart-shaped envelope, containing—and this was their solemn pledge—a 'One Hundred Percent Secret' message, would be delivered to the lucky recipient. Classroom delivery of the enormous three-feet by two-feet cerise envelopes was guaranteed to catapult students into paroxysms of emotion: joy, anticipation, triumph, despair, or revenge.

> "You are the one, You are the one;
> If only I could have you,
> Our life would be one." -A Tormented Admirer

> "You are my everything,
> Without you, I am nothing.
> Please help me. Please assist me.
> My body is aching
> To release my filled-up needs." –Your Suffering Slave.

*Grupo Folklorico* again would have the 'Flower Gram' booth. These young ladies, attired in full skirted costumes—green, red, and white with blue, yellow or black trim—made a similar guarantee of delivery, except that in this case, the recipient, student or teacher, would receive a red rose and a photograph, face blacked out, with the card. Usually anonymous, the messages were emotionally intense.

> "From out of the shadows of my heart I watch you,
> Even though you'll never know I exist and of my pain.
> Thinking, wishing, to feel your muscular body.
> I need you so much, so desperately.
> Help me to release for you my life-juice of love.

And to receive the explosion of your desire.
Allow me to worship at the altar of your manhood."
--A Friend

And this year, the 'Kissing Booth', fund-raiser of *Hot Pans for Teens*—the cooking club—had generated more excitement than usual: males as well as females would be featured. Student and staff titillation exploded when rumors circulated that a number of male football, baseball, weightlifting and other jocks were taking twenty-dollar bets, dares really, that they would kiss a male booth attendant. Accordingly, AP Johansson, directed that faculty could supervise but, "under no circumstances either receive nor dispense 'favors'". In this he aroused the ire of the FTA, Female Teachers Association, who alleged "another example of administration sexism".

The *Martial Arts Club* secured the perennial favorite: the Pie-Throwing Concession. A red and black banner over their booth proclaimed: "Get'em Hard. Get'em Good." Although all activities were required under Title IX to be 'gender co-equal', the faculty moderator, Ms. Sylvie Barannoci, Geography, claimed there was a 'situational protection' clause in the law. Males only, therefore, would be the 'targets': those who thrust their heads through the cardboard cutouts. And the cutouts themselves were redesigned: male cartoon figures depicted in various stages of undress—bikinis, jock straps, and clinging wet boxer shorts. Female club members would supervise and collect tickets. With the gusto of traditional side-show barkers, clad in bikinis and low-rise jeans with bare midsections, they would entice participants by offering the opportunity to 'Get Back at 'em', 'Show 'em Who's Boss', and enjoy a 'Fun Example of Girl Power'.

In a display of entrepreneurial genius, the Paintball Club's 'Cyber-Man Destruction Booth', was a foregone sensation. For two dollars a student would be provided a sledge hammer and permitted to inflict as much damage as possible on a car: three swing maximum.

When first proposed, AP for Student Affairs, Brampton Falange, rejected the project as, "fostering violence when we already have more than we need of that around here now as it is". The Student Counseling Office, however, had overruled him declaring the activity "instructional"—essentially an "aggression management restorative".

A club member's uncle, manager of a wrecking company, donated the car, taken from the police impound. Hauled in late at night, it was placed under a canvas cover at the periphery of the Carnival where club members mounted a twenty-four hour guard. The shrouded vehicle and its sentries generated intense excitement and speculation. Before 'Carnival Friday' and in violation of Carnival policy that prohibited pre-event ticket sales, the club had already recovered more than twice its costs.

Female members of the ASB, began decoration of the *Jovenas Muchadas* booth [candy, cakes] on Thursday morning, their exuberant shrieks continuing past eleven that night. Other clubs started early on Friday morning. Although Carnival policy required students to be in class all morning, it was 'a given' that teachers would count as present any student involved in booth preparation: few were willing to risk faculty ostracism or student retaliation.

Early on Friday morning, it was clear that the great day had arrived. First, a Mexican flag, thirty feet by fifteen, was draped from the top railing of the 'B' building. It rippled in the breeze, dominating the Carnival area.

The second indicator was the arrival of the remaining decorators. Hauling sundry paraphernalia, they began appearing by six a.m. Although Mr. Baques had stipulated that this year's Carnival would be 'International', most of the booths soon sported green, white and red bunting with Mexican flags capping the uprights. Students set up portable gas camp stoves, and convulsed in delirious laughter as they lugged enormous metal pots and plastic containers of edibles from the parking lot. They pushed and tugged, oblivious to the trails of sauce and food particles left in their wake or splashed on their clothes: the containers slopping and sloshing their red, green and brownish contents. Others strained with cumbersome plastic storage boxes filled with crushed ice. These provided ammunition for impromptu 'snowball' fights. The ensuing epithets, cursing, and threats of, "My home-boy get you, girl", "You watch your white ass, you mother", "Up you, black boy", "Screw off, wet-back", accompanied by finger gesticulations, intentionally obscene, were dismissed with scoffing laughter as routine interpersonal communication.

These diversions delayed the preparations. When the first bell rang, therefore, it was ignored, not only by the student workers but also by a number of other students who took advantage of an unrecorded absence. They raced up and down the stairs, along hallways, banging on classroom doors, yanking open those that were unlocked, and yelling, 'Viva la raza', derisory epithets about 'Carnival', a particular teacher, student or administrator.

The marauders hindered instruction. In one instance, Ms. Allen, Grade Twelve Economics-Government, peeking around her cautiously opened door in response to a barrage of kicks, was hit with a wad of soft-drink soaked paper. In other classrooms, where the instructor had less control—old Mr. Perry's Driver Education Class, for example, and where students were even more aggressive—the interlopers flung open doors, and groups of students darted out in response to invectives to, "Hey guys, dump this shit", or "Let's kick ass outa here". Hurdling overturned desks, students dismissed the scant teacher objections: "Screw you old man" or "Catch you later, Miss"!

The main gate, at which most of the two female and sixteen male Security officers had stationed themselves, was also the scene of contentious interaction. Indiscriminate groups: parents, students, and visitors—many carried infants or were accompanied by small children—protested their exclusion, hurling invectives at the guards.

Eventually they began to vent their spleen on each other. The issues were cultural and national. Placards proclaimed "*Hoy está el día de nuestra revolución*", "*Viva la raza*", "No Border Hoppers", or stated that Fillmore High was a "Community Service Paid For and Owned by Us!"

Differences notwithstanding, the visitors were united in their objection to and disregard of the administration's decision that school rules *would* be enforced on Carnival Day. The activists demanded admittance—to assist with preparations or participate in the festivities. Excitement teetered on the precipice of pandemonium. And chaos.

Under the pressure of the crowd, school police abandoned ID checks even though the School Safety Plan stipulated that all 'Unauthorized Visitors' must be searched. The danger was increased because some agitators, also in disregard of administration edicts, were in costume.

Masks were endemic. Grotesque ghouls, blood dripping from rubber fangs, were prevalent. Deluxe models had liquid reservoirs controlled by pressure bulbs that could shoot a jet of sticky red fluid from the protruding incisors. One security officer, 'Steroids', so-called because of his Herculean size and bulging biceps and thighs, blind with fury, exploded in rage and lunged at a masked demonstrator, who had smeared his immaculate, skin tight trousers with the iridescent and gooey substance. 'Widgit'—scarcely five feet in height, a female security officer—restrained and soothed him by wiping his trousers and face with a tissue, reassuring him, "that girl, she don't mean nothin'. She jest a no-account piece of pork, so don't you take it personal. Nohow."

In addition to masks of prehistoric monsters, skeletons, and the wrinkled deformities of green-skinned witches, there were also costumes.

These included cow 'persons' and animals. Those in Bunny suits were jostled by Streetwalkers in mini-skirts, stiletto heels, lace stockings held by garter straps submerged in sponge-like thighs, males and females heavily massacred with gleaming purple, brown or crimson lips. Finally, there were those who simply sported an interesting headdress: oversized fringed, black or silver sombreros; red, black and green turbans; knitted dreadlock caps.

As always there were the ornate 'boom boxes' and 'ghetto blasters'—in violation of a standing administration prohibition—blaring their earsplitting and thumping reverberations: Rap, Power Rock, Hip-Hop, Metal, *Salsa Merengue,* Retro, and Kidz. The cascading competition of the raucous sounds intensified the overall apprehension, excitement, and frenzy.

The cynosure of activity was the decaying auditorium. Renovation had been forestalled in anticipation of the proposed new high school. Many of the molded pressboard seats were broken. Above a type of linoleum wainscoting, were perforated acoustical tiles. Not a few had been partially picked from the wall, leaving ragged edges and holes. Others were wadded with pink and brownish gum. The ornate, Art Deco ceiling fixtures, originally quite handsome, gave a muted illumination. Bulbs were protruding, twisted fluorescents.

Today the lighting was augmented dramatically. Brilliant spotlights played on the faded and frayed crimson curtain, still tightly closed to mask the frenzied activity behind.

What was most striking, however, were hundreds of helium-filled balloons: red, white, and green, straining to reach the ceiling, each trailing multiple colored streamers. They dangled, just beyond reach of the manic audience, clamoring, laughing, to snatch them, standing on the backs of the creaking seats. Hysteria increased markedly when females scrambled up on male shoulders, using ears and hair as handles, legs and feet anchored through armpits and around biceps. They bobbed and weaved, flailing their arms, clutching, snatching at the trailing appendages. Some scrambled to sit on the boy's head, squeezing with their thighs, their bare feet on his shoulders. "You drop me and it'll be your ass, boy!" Hilarity was endemic and seemingly uncontrollable.

Band members, required to assume their places by seven-thirty, were excused from all morning classes and the three center rows had been removed to accommodate them. They bustled around, arranging their small chairs and music stands. White pompons on their glittering shakos bobbed like nervous rabbits. Except for one of the clarinet players—her locker had jammed—they were all resplendent in their famous silver and blue uniforms, white suede shoes, multiple strands of silver cord over the left shoulder, large sequined 'F' emblazoned on the chest. Dr. Reginald Bannister motioned them to their places, lifted his baton listlessly and they meandered into sometimes recognizable tunes: Arizona *Tejano* medleys; selections from *1000 Dalmatians, Swan Lake, and The Bohemian Girl.*

By 8:15 students were pouring in, yelling, shouting, and running. Student guards were posted at the side doors to ensure that only the assigned classes participated and that strays didn't sneak in under cover of another class.

"Hey, there, boy! Where you think you're goin'? Where your teacher be?"

"I be in *his* class", was the petulant reply, pointing to the nearest teacher.

"He's not in my class. I've not seen him." Mr. Thompson, Physics, already exasperated, explained, trying to manage his students as they squeezed through one of the two double doors.

"Teacher! Your class not supposed to be here. Look at this here schedule."

Thompson waved another seating chart in the guard's face. "Have mine right here. This is the last revision. You must have an earlier one. So just let us in."

The guard shrugged and directed his irritation to the obdurate student.

"Boy! You get youself outa' here! Fast! You find your teacher or you don't come in here nohow."

"It's OK. He's with me. Come on, Lyle, honey. You can sit with *my* class." Mrs. Park Chuoy, Science, pushed her way into the mass, wrapping an arm around the young man to mask her lie. She was the perennial mother: protector of 'abused' students. Lyle Childers beamed smugly, and once inside flipped a finger to the guard, raced to the far side of the room, "Catch you later, Miss Park," to join his misplaced and unattended peers.

The excitement of anticipation was infectious and a renegade group of about twenty students darted through the restricted entrance, at the rear of the auditorium, scurrying frantically to occupy the back rows.

They were not immune from detection. "No, you will *not* sit there, Jesus Pendejo! And don't you try your crap with me today!" The teacher's scream pierced the general clamor. "I'm fed up with you! You get yourself right back over here and sit down with your-own-class! I'm not gonna put up with any more of your male nonsense today. Or any other day." Mrs. Simpson's mou-mou clung to her corpulent and perspiring body as, desperate to apprehend the culprit, she squeezed through a row of students. Several turned their heads exaggeratedly to one side, holding their noses and gagging in disgust or giggling unpleasantly as her posterior brushed close to their faces.

She was determined and Jesus stood up. "Aw, Miss. Gimmie a break! Brenda wants to sit beside a man!" He laughed loudly, gave a high-five to several of his buddies, leapt over the back of a seat, into the designated area where he slumped down, slamming his knees into the back of the seat in front.

Cyndie Paz, buttressed by her two neighbors, swirled around, teeth bared, and fists raised. "Screw you, idiot! You do that again and I'll clobber your boy ass."

"Hey, boy. You was punked! Punked by a girl!" Jesus' buddies slapped him on the shoulders and the back of the head, doubling over in spasms of jeering laughter.

Other teachers, Ms. Stevenson, Grade 10, History, for example, were having problems with colleagues. "Ms. Jefferson! If you would? I believe it's *my* class that's been assigned row fifteen through seventeen? Stage left! Now-will-you-kindly-move-your-class-so-*my*-kids-can-sit-theirselves-down! And! In-their-right-places!" She enunciated carefully and slowly as if speaking to a mentally challenged person. "Thank-you! Very-much!" She nodded extravagantly.

"My teacher ain't no retard." Darnell Ernshaw, from Ms. Jefferson's class objected. Students shouted encouragement, "Go for it!" "Say it, bro."

Stevenson snarled viciously to cover the insult. "Where-they're-supposed! In their proper rows! God almighty! Ho-o-ly, wo-man!" Miss Stevenson's students were bunched at the contested rows pushing against the occupants who either glared at them balefully or snickered conspiratorially. Then seizing an opportunity, Robert and Orlando jumped up. "They take our seats, Miss. We don't need 'em! Here you go, Miss."

"Si'down you two! FAST!" Ms. Stevenson's face contorted in frenzy. "The both of you!" Her shrill tone cascaded over the noise of the hall. "Now!" She turned back to her nemesis, struggling to control herself, her voice oozing contempt. "Ms. Jefferson: you-really-*do*-need-to-check-the-seating-plan! It was given out to each and every teacher. *Left*-is-on-the-*other*-side-of-the-room! Over *there*! Next to Mr. Mugwabe! Turn your paper backside!" She swirled her long braids aggressively, and gesticulated with a loosely rolled sheaf of test papers.

Several of her students continued intense private conversations heads lowered against their knees, indifferent to her consternation, while others sniggered, bumping each other with shoulders and thighs, guffawing at her plight, hands over their mouths, in excruciating delight. Still others, seeking to attract the attention of a friend in another class, waved their arms erratically.

Darnell Ernshaw, untangled his lanky frame from the seat, gently taking the offending seating chart, turning it so the heading was at the top, and pointed to the correct area. "We's supposed to be there, Miss. Want me to take 'em?"

Ms. Jefferson touched his forearm lightly. "Oh, thanks, Darnel, honey. You're a blessing. Yes, you do it, would you?" Trying to compose herself, she turned to her class. "OK class, we're moving. The seating chart was revised after it was sent to me. All of you'ns follow Darnell."

Peevishly, Stevenson motioned her students into the vacated places. Her face rigid, she ignored a student, Tammie Feliz, "These is good seats, Miss." Still smoldering, she noticed Mr. Thompson observing her. His Physics class was relatively quiet. Several had their heads together, checking notes to complete a Hydraulics project. She moved closer, nudged him with her shoulder, speaking conspiratorially, mouth covered by the back of her hand, eyes roving the ceiling. "And this is *not* the first time, don't you know! She's done it before! Can't even read a simple diagram? Makes-me-sick! And she calls herself a profayshonal? Hardy-ha-ha!"

Although the curtains were still closed, there was excitement on the stage. Pushed to the left, was a diminutive podium, caught occasionally by the roving spotlights. The PA system was 'finding itself', progressing through stages of humming, thumping, and whistling.

The young lady at the podium was ebullient. "This is our glorious day, everybody! This is the day of our ancestors. The day we've been waiting for. Let us remember the heroes of our forefathers in defending our homeland against this savage invai-ders." Her screech—impeded by barely intelligible barrio accent, mismanaged sound system, and the frantic consternation among the students—tumbled out of her mouth.

Her male companion, less frantic, confined himself to repeated requests for order, ". . . so's we can begin as soon as possible". He was ignored.

Clusters of students continued to wander erratically, aimlessly, half-heartedly looking for seats. Many, replicating those ensconced in their seats, waved plastic Mexican flags in response to unintelligible but frantic tirades from the sides of the hall: "Viva! Viva Mexico! Viva! Viva! Viva Mex-i-co! Mex-i-co! Mex-i-co! Mex-i-co!"

Disregarding their patriotism, a student announcer, attired in a low-cut, skin-tight, black, cocktail dress, draped at the hips in sateen, paraded in front of the curtain, portable microphone tilted to the ceiling, exhorting students to "Take your seats quick so's the program could begin?"

To corroborate the aggression in her voice, a spotlight snapped on revealing a huge graphic in brilliant oils: the product of Mr. Geronimo Lone Eagle's art class. Over the picture, letters four feet high proclaimed: "*Viva La Mujer. El Año de la Mujer*", the *leitmotiv* for the event.

The painting itself was a twenty foot depiction of a cowperson beauty: thick, heavy lips drooping, enormous eyes oozing mascara, Stetson dangling on her back, and mostly unbuttoned gingham blouse—metal tipped collar points—straining to contain aggressively bulging breasts. She was poured into leather jeans, gleaming black, which emphasized a crotch, that would have been the envy of a male gunfighter, whose confrontational stance, hands on holsters, legs spread wide, ornate boots firmly planted, she, manfully, had adopted.

With threatening and cajoling from the podium, the lights dimmed erratically, and after several hesitant jerks, whether through back stage mismanagement or as a spontaneous effort to bait audience attention, the curtains suddenly flung themselves open.

Immediately a paean of frenzied cheering rose from the audience. The chant: Viva! Viva! Viva! Viva! Viva Mex-i-co! Viva Mex-i-co! Mex-i-co! resounded in unison emphasized by thunderous stomping of feet. The noise was deafening and resounded from back to front, floor to ceiling, causing the massed balloons to bob and swerve in agreement, themselves caught up, unwittingly, in the frenzy. To corroborate the hysteria, colored spotlights twirled over the ceiling, stage, and into the audience, where exploding emotions perpetuated mindless flag waving and shouting.

Pacing indignantly in a side aisle, brows furrowed, Dr. Allsbury, struggled with a massive bullhorn. She motioned to Brad Damien, Security Officer, who broke off his conversation with senior Letty Jackson, and jogged over. "Yes, sir. Miss?"

"Does this contrivance work? Check it, please." She handed it to him, eyes swiveling fiercely, surveying the seething mass of the audience. "Mr. Warfles! If you would! Now." The din, escalating as the hall reached capacity, drowned her call.

"This here is OK, Miss. Switch on the bottom. See?"

"Mr. Damien, check outside and close the doors as soon as Meldonian's class is in. And make sure students and teachers milling around outside get sent back to their classrooms. And give me a list of those teachers who brought their kids over at the wrong time. They'll be getting letters! See that they and their kids go back to their classes."

She took the horn and would have dropped it had not Damien supported her arm. "Want me to use it for you, Miss? It's kinda' heavy."

Momentarily, she considered the offer. "No. It's more important that we don't have a disturbance from those kids outside who shouldn't have been sent over in the first place." She struggled with the horn, hoisting it with matchstick arms, still disdainful of Damien's help.

"Teachers! Young ladies! Young gentlemen! I need you to be in your seats. Now-ow!" A few students toward the front, looked at her vacantly. Several teachers threw up their hands in dismay, shrugged their shoulders, faces registering confusion and frustration as they tried half-heartedly to comply by redirecting students somewhere, anywhere, else. Ms. Roberts called shrilly to a colleague to organize his class, "Gimme a break, fella! Just-follow-the-damm-seating-chart? Would-you-please!" Ms. Cortère, conferring with Mr. Simms, slapped her copy of the seating chart with the backs of her fingers, her bouffant threatening to unravel itself. "Dis crock of who know what! Dey give out may-be tree see-ting cart dis mor-níng!" She was explosive. "Tout dif-fer-awnt! Sacrément! What happ-níng?" She crumpled the paper, threw it on the floor, and stomped it, the remainder of her barrage of explicatives lost in the din.

Allsbury struggling with the volume of the bullhorn, motioned to Dr. Bannister to quiet his restive musicians: tuning their instruments, crouching in conversation beside the chair of a fellow band member, or shouting to friends in the audience. "And Mr. Simms! Your class is *late*! And we *are* waiting! And Mr. Warfles. If you *please*! I-need-you! Here!" The student Warfles was talking to took him by the shoulders and turned him around to face the administrator. He was puzzled. Allsbury motioned vigorously with her index finger. Looking at his students, he shrugged resignedly, and shuffled over, shaking his head slowly in consternation and disbelief.

"Mr. Warfles. This is getting out of control! You need to help those teachers who don't know what to do. Also, check outside. Make sure all performers are ready to come in. We can't start until they're in place."

"But I . . . "

"Ms. Sylvester, Mr. Korngold. Look at them! And there are others. You can see teachers whose students aren't in their assigned places."

"But they don't know where to . . .."

"THEY NEED TO BE IN THEIR SEATS! PERIOD! NOW! We're late already. It's past 8:30! And-you-are-needed-OUTSIDE, Mr. Warfles! Take the security officer at the back to help you, if need be."

She motioned vigorously to Dr. Bannister. "Get ready to begin, Dr! We're starting." Bowing elaborately in acquiescence, the maestro made a sweeping gesture with both palms. "Musicians! Places!" He rapped the podium sharply. "And that means you, Rodney." Then, with brows arched, head tilted back, chin lifted and showing two yellowed teeth protruding over his lower lip, he scrutinized the band, arms extended, baton twitching. "Get ready, folks!"

Allsbury, face rigid, picked her way to the back. Teachers still in the aisles stepped aside as she made her way furiously up the incline, ribbons and chiffon fluttering.

"Mr. Simms, see me in my office before you leave today."

"But I . . ."

"Before-you-leave, Mr. Simms . . ." Her eyes darted menacingly. "And where are the other administrators? Mentor teachers were assigned supervision today. So just exactly where are *they*?"

Without warning, there was a discordant blast from the horn section of the band. The main doors swung open.

Four cadets in brown fatigues, high-topped boots, and green scarves, entered, flagstaffs tilted until they cleared the doors. Capt. Melody Rasmussen, color guard commander, held the national ensign and Sgt. Nancy Ramirez clasped the state flag. Each girl sported red lacing on the left shoulder. Flanking them were two male cadets: privates, each overweight. One, trouser cuffs trailing, strained against the weight of the weapon he held with both hands against his right shoulder, head tilted left, face contorted.

"Port . . . ARMS! Ma-arrr-ch!" Rasmussen spat her falsetto. The two underlings, obviously dreading the command, heaved their weapons clumsily to the left shoulder, heads now canted far to the right. The quartet began its trek to the stage. Ramirez hissed, "Get in step, you two clowns!"

The drone of muttering escalated, especially among those who did not stand as the color guard advanced. Dr. Bannister gesticulated and the flutes, oboes and piccolos, began the 'Star-Spangled Banner'. They played hurriedly, in 2/4 time—hushed *sotto voce*—without brass or drums. The color guard shuffled to the front, executed an about face, and stood self-consciously at attention.

"Right sho-uuul-deeerrr. . . . ARMS!" The privates heaved their weapons unsteadily.

"Or-derrr-r-rrr . . . ARMS!" Rasmussen squeaked. They dropped the rifles to their sides, banging the floor loudly.

On stage, a spotlight shifted to stage right and an announcement was made in a garbled, hesitant voice with a slightly suppressed giggle. "You will now placed your hands to your hearts and repeated after me Pledge o'legiance? To 'merica?" There was a semblance of silence and muffled comments spread through the audience. Then, reading from a three by five card, she chanted uncertainly. "I pledge 'legiance to U-n't States o''Merrrica. . . ." She droned on in a singsong, fluttering tone, haltingly, most of the words incomprehensible, and intermixed with restrained giggles as if deciphering a humorous coded message at a private party.

The few students who chose to stand, looked around indifferently, aimlessly. Of those who remained seated, some chatted quietly, or examined packets of photos, oblivious to the proceedings. Others adjusted make-up, looking intently into mirrored compacts, rubbing lower lip over upper and then reversing the elaborate process, all the while grimacing exaggeratedly. Others polished front teeth with their tongues, or adjusted teeth whitener strips. Females touched up hair with jets of spray, tweeked eyelashes with frightening, hydraulic-like scissors, and checked mascara lines with tiny, wickedly spined brushes.

Ms. Rawlings, General Science, in response to her cell phone—a whining *Für Elise*—bolted away from her class, and speaking hoarsely and intently into the instrument, trotted to the back, head down, left palm over her left ear, oblivious to her surroundings.

"At-tenn-en-shun! Ri-i-ite FACE! Fo-o-o-eerd . . .MARCH!" Rasmussen squawked and the foursome, in single file, headed toward the side entrance.

The spotlight careened around the stage, finally resting on a podium, stage left. "ASB wants to thank the Fillmore color guard for the hard work. Please give them your big hands." Perfunctory applause meandered through the assembly.

The lights went off and the stage was a black void. Unexpectedly, there was a thunderous drum-roll followed by a brilliant brass fanfare. The stage streamed with light revealing a Mexican flag, encompassing the full width and height of the stage backdrop: thirty feet by fifteen. It was lowered precipitously, edge bouncing as it hit the floor. Someone had placed fans to the sides and it rippled dramatically, undulating gracefully, emphasizing the red, white and green panels with the emblazoned golden eagle. Strategically placed lights accentuated the billows.

The band stood at attention and burst furiously into the stirring staccato of the *Marcha Zacatecas,* followed immediately by the *Himno Nacional Mexicano.* Now, the entire audience stood, turning, and straining to see the cause of the commotion at the entrance, where, just inside the main door, the entourage for yet another Mexican flag, was forming. There were twelve honor guard members: three males in ornate boots, white shirts and black trousers with the females similarly attired except for trim, ankle-length black skirts. All wore white sombreros. They held their right forearms rigidly across their chests, fists clenched, in salute. The color bearer raised the large silken tricolor, waving it to reveal its three panels, and proceeded solemnly, slowly, down the central aisle, taking one step to every fourth beat of the music.

Solemnly, the honor guard wound itself to the front, mounted the steps and did a smart left-face at center stage. The music stopped: cymbals resounding. The cavernous room was hushed. The tricolor was lowered and the ASB President, already waiting, kissed its hem and stepped back as it was displayed to the student body, the Honor Guard immobile in salute.

The audio system thundered the Spanish.

¡Mexicanos, al grito de Guerra
El acero, aprestad y el bridón,
Y retiemble en sus centros la tierra.
Al sonoro rugir de cañón.

¡Cina! Oh patria tus sienes de olive
De la paz el arcángel divino
Que en el cielo tu eterno destino
Por el dedo de Dios escribió.
Mas si osare un extraño enemigo
Profanar con su planta tu suelo
Piensa. ¡Oh patria querida! Que el cielo
Un soldado en cada hijo te dio.

¡Guerra, guerra! sin tregua al que intente
De la patria manchar los blasones!
¡Guerra, guerra! Los patrios pendones.
En las olas de sangre empapad.
¡Guerra, guerra! En el monte , en el valle
Los cañones horrisonos truenen,
Y los ecos sonoros resuenen
Con las voces de¡ ¡Union! ¡Libertad

Mexicans! Hear the battle cry!
Take up your swords!
Mount the cavalry charge!
Guard every town and village
With blasts from your roaring canon.

Remember! Your motherland holds out
The olive branch of peace!
A gift from the divine archangel!
Which the gods have decreed
As your eternal gift and destiny. But lest the enemy dare to grind
Your fields under his heel;
Remember also, O beloved motherland!
That heaven has given you
A soldier in each of your sons.

War! War without truce against those
Who dare to stain our shields with blood!
War! War! To those who drench our battle standards In waves of blood.
War! War! From every mountain and valley
Our canon shall thunder
And from every corner of our country
Shall resound the cries of
Union! Liberty!

At the completion of the final verse, applause still ringing, the honor guard carried the flag to the stage apron where it was deposited ceremoniously, highlighted by a spotlight.

The ASB President, Monica Munoz, took the microphone, speaking in a monotone. "We will now have the beginning of the program of today. And should you all have to pay attention!" Most of the noise had subsided. The enormous flag behind her, still fluttering, slid upward silently, leaving a completely black backdrop. Her voice chirped stridently, "There's, first of all, a dance which is from Michoacán and the Grupo Folklórico is going to have you with it." She rolled her accent familiarly over the Spanish words.

In response, colored lights splashed the darkness revealing twelve male and female dancers. Motionless, the males were kneeling on one knee, hands behind their backs, gazing upward, adoringly, at their partners. Each female stood poised, head thrown back, long hair trailing below the waist, right arm raised, grasping an open fan, left hand resting on left hip. The dramatic effect was punctuated by the placement of the feet: right foot extended and sharply turned, left toe firmly planted with high heel raised.

The recorded *Yumba,* sparked the first notes of the strong, pulsing rhythm, and the six couples leapt into the wide, sweeping turns and intricate steps. Graceful, agile, self-confident, all of them, even the two corpulent females who dwarfed their partners, propelled themselves into the dance. The women twirled their enormous, multi-colored skirts, laughing loudly and gutturally, pulling them high on the thigh as they executed the final swirling turn of each sequence, legs arched. Their partners cantered around them, hands behind their backs, stamping their boots—a staccato clatter—provoked by the overtly sexual movements of the females. The overall effect was flawless: furious movement inciting a mass of color, punctuated by the pulsing rhythms of the music.

Then, in a burst of intricate steps, the women pounded the floor, toes and heels, and churned themselves back into their original statuesque poses, as each of the males slid across the floor on both knees, sombrero extended in salute.

There was mild applause, the stage darkened and the performers scurried into the wings. The narrow spotlight wavered as it tried to find the podium. Behind it, Maruetsu Leavens, the new MC, five feet three inches tall, strained to make herself seen. Her barrio accent further obscured a voice, naturally hesitant and self-conscious.

"That was the Folkloric Group and the director is Mr. Geronimo Lone Eagle, arts and crafts teacher. I think we all to give them a big round of applause because they worked so hard." She interrupted the over-enthusiastic applause and continued.

Her voice was an adolescent singsong, intentionally cute. "Next we has the "Discotheques" and that's a dancing group ready to perform for us here on staige todie."

The "staige" submerged into darkness and nothing happened. Occasionally, there were loud thuds—heavy objects dragged and dropped. Long minutes passed but no entertainment. Resentful murmurs spread through the audience.

Several minutes passed, then, an iridescent glow began to dissipate the void. First a deep green, shifting to purple, then blue, then red, gradually blending into an opaque yellow patina—a multicolored haze. The colors evolved from the floor and spread slowly up the sides and back of the stage. They washed through the plaster detail of the proscenium arch, throwing it into relief. Finally—a visual surfeit—swirls of fog billowed from the floor, enveloping the lighting into a multi-colored mist which having filled the space, rolled into the theatre over the heads of the enthralled audience.

Cheers welled up from the spectators and the lights brightened: four couples locked in varied positions of close embrace. The females were especially striking: buxom and athletic, in black vinyl, low-rise, mini-skirts, riding high on the thigh, with white blouses cinched close under their low-cut bras, so that the fleshy undulations of their midsections were revealed from the breasts to below the navel. They wore glossy black high-heeled boots and mesh stockings.

Males were in gleaming, silver-grey, nylon parachute pants, billowing in the legs, but stretched tight across the haunches and in the crotch. The heels of their boots were capped in metal, and their buccaneer shirts were open to the waist. With sleek hair pressed against the scalp in tiny waves, each was a Ramon Navarro: the epitome of *art deco.*

Electrified by the dissonant opening chords, the dancers leapt into movement, responding aggressively to the sensuously guttural sounds of the recorded guitar: Luis Soria's *Tango.* The music was classical but the choreography was not. The couples seldom interacted directly. Each presented an individual interpretation of free-form modern dance.

As the women moved, they caressed themselves with elaborate sensuality: breasts, arms, and thighs. The choreography included various provocative postures: squatting, strutting, leaning into the audience to expose their breasts, and then turning, flaunting their posteriors.

The males stomped their boots sharply, hands clapping: a loud staccato, responding vigorously to each shift in the musical cadence. As the intricate steps brought them closer to their partners, their self-absorption intensified. They executed the movements flawlessly and, with impressively confident ease—weaving, shifting, and turning—torsos luxuriating in themselves, occasionally pleading with their partners, but never touching.

The men, clinching their small waists, set off by tight cummerbunds embroidered in silver, held their bodies rigid. At the finale of each section, they spun into an athletic leap, dropped nimbly to the floor: immobile—poised to continue.

In the next sequence, the females, with pulsing gyrations, responded to the rhythmical triads of the chords, leaning forward, poised on one shoe, thighs bulging. Kicking back strongly, accentuating legs and flashing spiked heels, they circled their quarry, predators whose goal was never in doubt, confident in the self-absorption of their prey, who, enthralled by the intricacies of their own steps, nevertheless appeared oblivious to the assault.

The *Tango,* however, was a prelude to an even more exotic work set to the music of José Viñas: his *Vals*. Again, sensuous, aggressive opening chords set the erotic mood. This time, however, the couples flowed into the rhythm, male clasping female at the conclusion of each section, in response to the strident demands of the strong rhythmic music.

The precipitous, almost erratic, changes of movement gripped the audience. But in this dance, it was something far more interesting than choreography that detonated the pent-up audience frenzy.

In the finale, the performers came to a complete stop, assumed a statuesque pose and—waited. Then, without warning, the women—releasing strategically placed clasps—tore off their blouses , hurling them disdainfully behind them. Relishing their triumph, the four couples leapt into the next sequence.

There was a ripple through the audience. Would they take off the tiny bulging bras? It was too much to hope for. Audience rapture increased boundlessly—'exponentially' as Mr. Melvin, Economics, described it later. They burst into ecstasies of delirium, stamping their feet and screaming epithets in barrio Spanish. Their emotions were intensified by the eroticism of the music: whining lisps and gliding runs in a minor key, brought to an end, finally, by furious plucking of the strings.

The audience waited breathlessly for the second finale. Again the classic pose, the pause and . . . this time the male dancers ripped off their shirts, flinging them high in the air, revealing their own muscular, gleaming torsos.

Pandemonium swept the audience. Deafening shouts and stamping of feet. A riot was only averted by audience ecstasy at the stupefying possibility of even greater revelations—'paroxysms of delight'—was the description later offered by Mr. Watkins, Government.

And it did happen. At the final loud, harsh, resonance of the guitar—a musical ejaculation—the performance ceased: the couples stood, one arm extended, the other holding their partner. The men had tossed off their trousers and the women their miniskirts. The men, gleaming as if polished, held the women who had thrown back their heads allowing their hair to trail on the floor. The lights dropped almost immediately but not before the audience could revel in the dancers attire: males in black jock straps and women in bra and thong.

The sound was deafening. Pedestrians beyond the wall of the football field later said they thought there was "maybe cuda been a fire or a earthquake . . . or something?" Inside, one thousand, nine hundred and two feet pounded the floor mercilessly. Sylvie Blackstone, Grade 11, her face contorted deliriously, thumped alternatively the front and rear wheels of her wheelchair. The hoots, yells, screams, and shouts reverberated up and down, left, right . . . everywhere. Mrs. Simpson, Grade 11, Reading, observed later in the faculty lounge that the emotional outpouring of the audience, "coudda been a good thing 'cause it was their version of poetry."

Mr. Falange, eyes dilated in combined horror, terror, and consternation, rapped Dr. Bannister sharply on the shoulder. "Start some music! Now!"

"What? What do you want me to play? I can't control these kids. That's your job, buddy."

"Anything! Play anything! Play Jingle Bells. Do it! Now! This has to stop!" His voice was a painful shriek: "This-shall-be-stopped! Forthwith!"

Bannister waved his arms: eliciting a discordant rendition: *The Wedding of the Painted Doll.* Some musicians, overcome with excitement, had left their seats to join friends in the audience. Several of those remaining sat motionless, mesmerized.

Teachers exchanged excited looks. Mrs. Smythe-Goode ran over to Mr. Phillips and threw her arms over his shoulder. "Did you see those boys! God, almighty! Those pecs! Those abs! Those butts! To die for! I thought I hadda died and went to heaven! God, almighty, almighty. Save me! Help!"

"Turn up the lights!" Dr. Allsbury marched furiously backstage. "Get those lights ON, I said!"

"Which lights, Miss? Which ones you want?" The lighting crew, usually overly self-confident, were frazzled.

"Switch broke, Miss!"

"Alberto! That switch is NOT broken! And where is Mr. Samuelson? Mr. Simms! They're supposed to be responsible for the backstage crew. Tell them to get the lights on. NOW! Somebody! Call Security!"

Alberto, Brad and Dwayne, remnants of the stage crew, jostled each other, struggling with a single flashlight, fighting to decipher the panel box.

Then it happened. In a flash of intensity, all the lights in the auditorium exploded into full brilliance. The result, however unintentional, was sudden quiet. The audience, completely disconcerted, subsided into a strange, ominous hum.

Cynthia Rowland, Government/Economics moved the podium to front center stage and motioned to Narda Teklebrahan, senior class Moderator who was standing mute.

"Young ladies! Young gentlemen! We do need to move on." She spoke tensely, ignoring the catcalls and whistles, aware that the eruption might flare up again.

"Our final presentation . . . ." There were harassing jeers: "Outa' here, man!" "Get this shit on the road!" "We need to get back to our class." "We want to do our work!"

Aggressive laughter and piercing whistles punctuated the comments. High-pitched female squeals predominated.

"Mellissa Sommers," Rowland was losing her patience, "who is in Mr. Morton's Math class, will now give us a history of the Mexican Revolution and why important for us to know about." She turned to stage left. "Mellissa, sweetie, over here. That's it, honey. Don't pay some attention to them. Be quick, now."

The girl slunk shyly half way across the stage, then summoning the courage of a drowning person, lurched toward the podium and clutched it desperately.

"Fellow students?" Her tiny voice, combined with slurred speech, was that of an elementary student. She read from a script through compressed lips, terrified by her own voice.

"We gotta remember that we gotta free ourselves from the past just like in Mexico where the people attacked the French that had captured them and was treating them bad. And they shouldna' been there 'cause it wasn't their country and belonged to the Mexicans and they killed them. And Padre Hidalgo, he was a Cadolic priest, told all the people about the Mexican flag: red is for the blood of our martyrs, green for the greeness of our pastures and white for the purity of our holy religion. He told them they should fight against the French in-vai-ders and get rid of them because they was bad and . . .." The monotone continued and audience restlessness increased. " . . . 'till finally, the Mexicans, 'cause they not want them there anymore, they killed the French king and then the people had lots of democracy and freedom for theirselves. . . . And this is the why the Aztec, he's holding up the snake? On our flag?" She concluded her monosyllabic reading, in no way assisted by the hum and screech of the audio system, and scurried off the stage as the band blared a medley from *Cats.*

Mr. Falange, greeted by the audience with extensive booing, waved his arms for attention. "Students! Ladies and Gentlemen! You are now dismissed! Return-to-your-classes! Be apprised! Students: get to classes instantaneously! And teachers! It is TEACHER RESPONSIBILITY to make sure all, ALL, students DO return to their classes. No students . . . repeat . . NO-students-are-to-go-to-other-classrooms-for-any-*repeat any*-reason! Teachers, you are to mark *each and every* student absent who is not there for *any* reason. No expectations! Repeat! No students are to be caught in areas other than their own classrooms! And if they are, they will *not* be allowed to attend Carnival and counselors *shall* be notified. I will summons any expectations."

As he was speaking students and teachers were jamming the exits and his closing words reverberated over predominately empty seats. Security guards barked commands and students swelled outside—running, jumping and pushing. A few teachers walked with students but many held back, forming their own groups, to delay the return.

"So, what did you think, Cyril? Good performance?" Sandy Weatherby came alongside her colleague.

> Oh, mia patria si bella e perduta!
> Oh, membranza si care e fatal!
> Le memorie nel petto raccendi,
> Ci favella del tempo che fu!"

"I know that must be from something. Some opera?"

"My country, so lovely: yet lost! Remembrance so dear and ill-fated! Re-kindle in our breasts, from these ashes, the memory of our former greatness. Verdi. *Nabucco.*"

"Prisoners in our own country. Lost ideals. Interesting thoughts. Well, maybe kids got something out of it. The Assembly?"

"Indubitably. The question is 'what'?"

She laughed and slapped his back. "Cheer up! After all, this afternoon is Carnival!"

"Carnival? Just this afternoon?" He snorted.

She smiled.

# *CHAPTER XXVIII*

## *A Meeting*

"We're on a white water trip, folks. It'll take us where it'll take us."

"Maybe, Bruce. But as for me, I think we're here, correct me if I'm wrong, Mr. Baques, so's to iron out the glitches. Now!" She spread her hands, palms up. "So, I'll give you: maybe we *don't* know all that much about it, the Reform Plan: what it will do. Exactly here. So. Maybe we should toss the ball around some more. Make a Plan B." Arvetis Jamgotchian, Algebra I for Seniors, nodded approval of her own words. "Because, OK, let's just say there's the outside chance—I'm not saying it will, mind you—but the off-chance, that Reform won't be all that great for us."

"Where's the community rep?"

"Hang on!" Baques shifted in his seat and smiled his rabbit grin. "Ms. If we're going to run over the edge, let's do it on the cautious side. And I'm with you on that, Arvetis. All of us here has put in too much—given too much—to this school, our school, to have it flushed down the drain. And that's a positive. And, by the way! Thank all of you for coming. Quite a outpouring. Show the Team we got here. And this is a community meeting. Because we're a community based school. We want to let our parents and community members have their say. In their school. Be a part of it."

He held up his hand for caution. "But let me say at the top. For starters! That this is informational. An informational meeting. This would not, repeat *not*, be the time to bring up issues like budget and programs. Classroom problems. Selection of faculty. Building repairs. Assessment. Salaries. Discipline. Drop-outs. Teacher extra duty assignments. Academics."

"Isn't that all part of Reform?"

"That's substantive. And this is informational. So, let's all of us stay on the informational super highway, here today? Anything else is a not required."

"A nugatory?"

"Well, maybe at least we might talk about how teachers 'ull get finally some Due Process? For a change. That sure'd be informational! More like miracle-ational!"

"Allys could be a first time for everything. Go for it Seraphina. You know what I think? ...."

"No, what? Tell us."

"Probably should just tread water and wait and see what happens. Hope that we're well enough protected. Careful is the name of the game. Remember, back when? Oodles of years ago, that geeky guy, what was his name ..."?

The group moved restlessly in the student chairs arranged in three irregular non-concentric circles. "Hey, Agnes, you wouldn't be thinking of ole; now what was his name? O yeah! It'll come to me. Hang on. Give me a New York minute."

"Roscoe Pennington? Guy who used to be Principal?"

"You made my day, sweetie! Bingoed! And that was back donkey's years. I guess you forget the things you don't want to remember. Right! He was the guy who tried to reform by his own self? It was a bomb: lesson plans, discipline plans, always snooping around in classrooms, wrote up teachers who didn't have stuff. Or came late! No, I'm not ragging you. Teachers *he* said wasn't teaching good. Said they wasn't—now what was that stuff he used to say? Hey! It's coming back to me—'not putting students first'! Godfry; the dork even said teachers couldn't wear shorts into their classrooms: 'cause it was lacking in, 'professionality'! He toggled index fingers. "I kid you not! And as hot as everybody knows it gets here! Gimme a break, dude! Well, teachers got rid of him. He left in a trail of dust."

"Right! Teacher accountability he called it. Or some such! What was that stuff he used to say: 'every class every day takes two steps toward the goal'? Help! His goal. Not ours."

"We sure don't need a repeat of that. We don't want to step into water that's up over our heads."

"Sure. Let's stay in the Garden of Eden." Baques smirked and nodded sourly to Sandra Weatherby. "You wanted to say something, Ms?"

"Do we want Change? Or do we want Reform?

"They're the same. What you talking about, Ms?"

"Not the same. One is a band-aid. Can mean anything. Other is surgery. Corrects specific problem."

"Things are pretty good now. Need to have Reform that's not changing what's good now. What you talkin' about?"

"Reform. To achieve it I think we need to back up. Decide what education, here in this school, is supposed to do. For whom? How? By whom? Until we answer those questions, we're spinning our wheels."

"Sounds Traditionalist to me. What you're sayin'!"

"Call it what you will. The proposed Pritchard Reform plan? I have yet to find out what it will do to address our reality: drop-outs, physical and verbal violence, low academic achievement, Math and English illiteracy, lack of preparation for college, turned-off teachers, drugs, other addictions, discipline infractions, physical and verbal violence ..."

"Speak for yourself, lady."

"... Standards Based Instruction? Assessment? Accountability: students, teachers and administration. Low academics?" She pulled a chocolate bar out of her purse. "Will the Reform plan take the stand that we're here for the kids? Or the kids are here for us?"

"Get real, Sandy! Anybody who thinks we're not here for kids shouldn't be here theirselves."

"A concurrence on that. Frankly, Miss, I don't think there's any question about why we're here." The speaker's tone dripped sarcasm. "That's not something that needs to be reformed. Not hardly. What with low teacher pay, hard over-work, and putting up with kids!" Dr. Rosalba Sanchez-Mullen twisted her lips unattractively. "Frankly, I don't know why anyone would even ask a question like that. I mean what color is the American flag? Bla-bla-bla! It's clear as frosting on the cake that we're here for kids: help them overcome minoratyism, uneven playing field, gender bias—the whole nine yards, help them to get off the downward learning curve."

"Fine. In that case we need to evaluate why they've been on the downward learning curve for the past fifty plus years."

"That's racism all over again. Get real, Miss."

"Hang on! Let me put another spin on that thought, Sandy, if you would. Main point is not to have us open the floodgates to bureaucrats to come in and tell us how to teach. Interfering in the privacy of our classrooms. Too much of that already."

"First off, we need to have a head's up if Teachers' Union will still be there for us. Only protection we ever had. That's top priority." Brian McCauley looked up from a copy of *Gridiron*.

Someone else interjected. "Sure thing! Will we have to keep roll books exactly the same with every letter dotted and crossed? Help! If we don't watch it; first thing you know, they'll have us giving special help after school: on our own time! For free! Yikes! And don't think it hasn't been tried. In other districts!"

Weatherby was irked. "Let's cut to the core. Let me repeat. The issues are two: very simple, very clear. First, what kind of reform do we want? Fundamental or cosmetic? Second: will the proposed Reform Plan provide it?"

"You know, I've been hearing some weird rumors about some things? One class in particular?"

"Who's that, Lydia? Sweetie?"

"Well, of course I couldn't say for sure. But!"

"But what? Who? We need to know." Laura Yi, PE, was bursting with interest. "Now, c'mon, girl! Let's have it."

"OK. But with the tape recorders off! OK? And remember, you didn't hear it from me!" Lydia Arlekian, Reading IV, surveyed the ceiling, rolling her eyes upward, as if for inspiration from an other-worldly source. "Well, my kids been talking. Now, normally I don't listen. To kids. What they say. You all know my Kids Tolerance policy..."

"Sure, sweetie."

"Well, my kids were talking to kids from another teacher's class, and who, I positively will not say, who ..."

"C'mon, girl. We need to know."

"Yeah. Could affect any or all of us."

"Nope! Finality on that." She scrunched up her lips pensively. "Well, I will let on that's it's a male. Traditionalist. I shine you not!"

"OK. Now moving up on the interest scale."

"Folks. And thank you Rikki. We need to memorize that we can't be discussing other teachers. Who aren't present."

"Exactly, Mr. Baques. As I said, that's why my lips are sealed. But! In the interest of greater good, kids be saying, and again, what do they know? Kids be saying that one class is meeting, on its own, with their teacher, and at District headquarters doing some kind of research project. Snooping about this Reform Plan. Messin' around! Maybe finding out stuff he shouldn't. Gettin' his kids to stick their noses where they don't belong."

"Mr. Baques, don't you think ..."

"Just a minute, Mr. Falange. I'll handle this. Yes, I am aware of an 'outside' project conducted by one of our teachers. It's after school and under adult supervision. District administration is in a concur mode. It's not an 'investigation'. Yes, it is teacher-driven. Done by students. But it is directly under control. Students can, will, *only*—repeat *only*—be looking at whatever documents and official policies and procedures are *already* in the public domain. Project is strictly informational."

"Stuff has a way of getting out of control."

"It will remain strictly under administration control, Mr. Warfles. Trust me."

Falange interjected. "As I understood it, it was to be a community service project, that kids could use on their college applications. No glitches, so far. So far as anybody can see. Won't find out about any private arrangements. Can't; 'cause it's locked."

"Hang on Mr. Falange! Folks. I understand your concern. I'll be making a report to you on this. It's a pilot program, really. Involvement of students with the community. Better yet, the teacher in charge will be making a report at a faculty meeting. Not to worry, folks. Everything's shipshape. His Project gives proof that we are a community based school."

"Why can't they ask that teacher himself, Mr. Baques. Directly?"

"He's not here. He's with his students at the District now." Baques arched his eyebrows at Dr. Allsbury's observation.

"That guy needs to watch himself. He's an outsider."

Roger Mulhausen interrupted, munching on an apple. "Let's talk turkey, folks. I don't know about you but there can't be any reform without first giving teacher salary increases. That's primo. Let the chips fall into place after that. And number two? Teacher rights. Has to be primo."

"Good boy, Roge, ole buddy. You got a base hit on that one, guy!"

"And let me pop-corn that thought."

"Ms. Meldonian? Seraphina?

"Student rights all fine and good. But! Not at the cost of teacher rights." Several nodded vigorously in agreement.

"And not have salaries tied to student test scores. No way, Jose! It would be fine if we were in a white Traditionalist district where the kids do the work? Yeah! That'd be great! We'd probably all be millionaires! But with minorities? Like we have? Do that: tie teachers to test scores? And this is one teacher who's gonna be like 'outta here'! Rapido!"

"Go for it, girl."

"A bummer, for sure. I mean who's supposed to evaluate us? Who knows what we're doing?"

Baques broke in. "Let's hear from our community rep." He beamed a huge smile, angling his head energetically. Marvella whispered in his ear that neither Board President elect Señora Arcáña nor Señora Dolorosa Sanchez, community rep, had been notified of the meeting time change.

"Seems we'll be hearing from those ladies at some later time."

"Won't Reform, Pritchard's, give special, sort of money perks to teachers to go out into the community?"

"Obviously, Mr. Pritchard is a community oriented person. He'll be detailing for us if that item surfaces on his list. In the meantime there may be conversations privately with our Team Players. So, let's keep that on a back-burner for now, Cynthia. Simmer it. But, sure, they'll be a way for selected teachers to augment their salaries. In the community. Do an end run around the state legislature that's so cheap about teacher salaries."

Baques smiled earnestly. "Before I forget: let me say how much we appreciate our community rep. Whenever she can make it. I know she has family obligations. She'll be here. At a substantive meeting. But no! We can't discuss salaries and the complete budget. Any special private arrangements. That's classified. Privileged. Sensitive. To protect confidentiality."

"Mr. Baques? Sir?" Wilfrid Phillips, Gr. 12 Health, was inquisitive. "We sure don't want Reform to be like, that guy, Roscoe Pennington, somebody just said: tried to make teachers do 'extra duty assignments', not get paid for after school programs. Wrote up teachers for fighting. For no lesson plans. For too many class parties. Showing unauthorized videos? Wouldn't allow field trips to Disneyland! Or the Petting Farm! Wow! If that's Reform. No way, Jose! Didn't work before. Teachers got rid of him."

"First thing you know, they could be investigating us when we call in sick! Or for not returning homework! Or not even assigning it. Whew! Land o'Goshen!"

"Scheduling."

"Scheduling, Mr. Johansson? Not sure I follow that thought."

"I mean scheduling. That's the operative word. Need to have teachers scheduling—deciding—the work the kids do. They're the ones who knows kids needs. And what they want. Not outsiders. Hundreds and thousands of miles away."

"Right. O-o-o-k-a-a-a-y? Thank you for that heads up, Marion."

*"Ah! Non sai che i miei legami come sacri, orrendi sono, che con me s'asside in trono, il sospetto ed il terror!"* [30]

"Go for it Milton, buddy boy! Whatever turns you on!"

"Point is, we got to protect our you-know-what's! Or nobody's gonna do it for us. For sure, *amigos*."

"Chief moment here is that teachers' rights stays protected. That's the way it's been up till now. Union policy." Bruce Warfles thumped a heavy fist on the desk to vent his determination.

"If reform means ranking one class against another one: one teacher who's doin' as best as they can against another one with all 'A' students? Well, count me out. On that! For sure!"

"Perhaps reform can investigate the success of Bi-Lingual programs at the expense of English learning."

"Wow! Get a load of that! Mr. Mugwabe, that's a racism remark if I never heard of one. Bigotry rides again!"

"Really? Bigotry? I think you could make an argument that preventing kids from acquiring English and Math, is the real bigotry: the real racism. Also, exactly how much is this proposed Reform Plan going to cost? Taxpayers? I don't think cost of Reform has been discussed."

Mr. Mugwabe, Algebra II, scratched his head pensively. "Why don't we form a committee: isolate the problems we want to solve; make a plan to solve them, and do it? Ourselves? Most of us here, in this room, know what the problems are. And how to solve them. We don't need reform from outside. I've heard people refer to 'our' school today. I like that. If it is, truly, 'our' school, then it should be 'our' reform. Planned by us. Carried out by us. And teachers should be active in the community because they want to be. Not because they're paid extra for community involvement."

"I think we're spinning our wheels, here, folks. Why not find out what Pritchard's Reform Plan will do? Then make our decision based on that? He could be throwing us a life saver? Be stupid to not catch it. I thought

30 Donizetti, G. *Anna Bolena*: Act I, Scene 3, "Don't you know my obligations are as sacred as they are hideous: that seated beside me on the throne are suspicion and terror?"

we were going to find out the details here today. As usual, we're having a discussion without even knowing what the topic is."

"OK. Folks. I know tempers can get pretty hot. Thank you for that input, Arvetis. Most of you are Team Fillmore. Else you wouldn't be here. We just got different slants on things. Some of us. Gotta keep in mind that we're all of us in the same boat."

"Sink or swim time, folks."

"We're all paddlin' in the same direction? Great!" Brian McCauley snorted energetically. "Let's just make sure we know if it's away from the falls? Or towards them?"

"Mr. Mugwabe nudged Sandra Weatherby. "Team Fillmore or Team Baques?"

"And, Oh! I'll need to be conferencing with you tomorrow, Mr. Mugwabe? At your conference period?"

# *CHAPTER XXIX*

## *Puzzling Information*

"Hey, Mr. B. Over here! Weird ass shit, man."

"Jesus. Not in the classroom! Not around ladies."

"This isn't a classroom. That? Oh, they don't care." He shook his head as a self-reminder. "Forgot. You're right! Need to remember: respect."

"Good man, Jesus. So, what do we need to look at now? You guys found something?"

The Record Room of the Cathedral Heights School District was cramped with the fifteen Project members.

"Sir, this stuff we told you about yesterday? Like we thought was foreign language? Sorta weird. We got more of it." Marvella Littler draped an arm around Jesus as he redirected his interest to the file.

"OK. Let's take a look."

"See here! Watch!"

"Yeah. Check these out, coach." Jesus pointed exuberantly to the page. "It was Sandy that clued us to think different. About it. Bad stuff."

Besserian scrutinized several pages from bulging accordion files: typewritten with handwritten notations at the top of each. "I don't understand it."

"That's what we thought, Mr. B. Us neither."

"Odd. Unusual way to keep records. You say there are several files like this?"

Sandra interjected. "Yeah. In this like, box? That we found in the back of that file drawer over there. See? Drawer was marked "O-P" but this stuff not have to do with other stuff in the drawer. Leastways nothing that we could make out."

"What was in there apart from this? The other files in the drawer?"

"Regular stuff you'd expect to find in a "O-P" drawer. You know: Organization. Personnel. Policies. Procurement. Lots of stuff about that: procedures, government regs, forms, dates for Projects. Just about what you'd expect. Some statements from teachers: that they don't think Reform Plan will work. Want more information. List of teachers and administrators with some names checked. Others with a question mark."

Felipe interjected, interrupting Besserian's perusal of the mystery folder. "Right. Operating Procedures: Emergency, Security . . . all that stuff. Boring. Just what anybody'd suspect. In a school."

Jesus placed his hand on Besserian's forearm. "But this other stuff, the stuff we found, here in this file? Well, it's different! From the regular. Not seem to belong there. Like wrong place? But something says it isn't. Wrong place."

"Curious. Puzzling."

"Could be a terrorist plot, Mr. B?"

"You're a terrorist, Marco. I seen you making homemade incendiaries."

"This is serious guys."

"I'm curious about the designations on the folders. They're numbered one through thirty. Let's check out this first one."

"Already did, Mr. B!"

"So? What do you make of it?"

"Wanted to ask the brain."

He mused. "What sort of information would be here, in this file drawer and look like this? And why?"

"And who put it there!" Sandra handed him the file. "Right. Here you go, sir. Sure is weird. This writing."

"Let's consider what we've got. What seems to stands out most clearly? At this point?"

"Way ahead of you, Mr. B. We already figured that out. The letters are all in groups of six."

"Except when they aren't," Sandra sighed.

"They only don't be six sometimes in the last grouping. Sometimes the last group of letters has only two or three. Letters."

"They're all capitals?"

"And written in ink. Red ink. Not typed."

"And real careful lettering. Like calligraphy. Like my sister learned how to do? With a special pen? And these letters are the kind like you could see on blueprints? We did that kind of writing in my wood shop class. Mr. Lone Eagle showed us."

"So there won't be any mistaking the letters."

"Right." Jesus was leaning on the table around which they were grouped. "Allisandro, why don't you write down these letter groupings. We can analyze it later."

"Right, coach."

"You think we can figure it out, Mr. B?"

"We can try. Let's do the first step. Ready guy? Groups of six. Make a notation that this is File One, please. First group: DSFFLS. Next: ZDNOPF. Next: UBIRAB. And that's it. For this section. The're others. In other sections."

"Could be Latin numbers?"

"Ummmm. No. I don't think so. Not with 'y', 'w', 'r', 'h'.

"And I saw 'z's in some others."

"Check out the next folder Mr. B? Maybe somethin'll turn up? An implosion?"

"OK. Ready, 'Sandro?"

"Right here."

"These are also groups of six."

"OK. Here goes! And make a notation that this is Group Two. I'll read the groups. NFAUQX; EHCNLS; ZSTSAB."

"What do you think, Robert?"

"I think it's code."

"He's a code freak! Mr. B. I already checked the other info on these pages. Want to look at it?"

"Of course. But explain it to me."

"Well, first off, there's lists of numbers and then what might be their explanation. Check this one for example: Net Operating Capital: $250,000. Initial return per dollar invested: $5.8324. Projected Net Annual Profit; $86,000. Number of full time employees; 7. Inventory: $420,000. Operations; $63,000. Expenses: $32,000. Franchising Revenue: $71,000. Consultants: 3. Marketing $12,000. Advertising: $16,000. Initial costs: $80,000. And there's more. You can see. You make anything out of this?"

Aldo pushed the paper toward Besserian and pointed to the numbers. "Looks to me like it could be a financial statement analysis. I figured out how to do that in my Computer Accounting class. To see if a company is OK financially. What kind of profits it can have. This is the kind of stuff you look at."

Sandra was thoughtful. "Makes sense. Somebody deciding whether it's a good investment or not. Projecting? Maybe startup costs for a company? Could be? I don't know." She paged through some of the other folders. "Look at these, you guys. These folders are all organized the same. Same two or three pages, same red circled number on the file cover. Same groups of six letters."

"Yeah! And same stuff about profits and expenses written out in English. Except for different numbers." Rigo skimmed through the other files as Sandra put them down. "You know what I think, Mr. B?"

"No. What?"

"Some kind of financial analysis. Maybe for some company?"

"Could be a product. Or a person. Or even a place." Lupe seemed dubious.

"Robert, tell us about code." Besserian was inquisitive.

"I got some books on code. At home? Yeah. Sort of a hobby with me. There's different kinds of code. Lots of different kinds. But am pretty sure I recognize this one."

"You do? Man, you're somethin' else." Jesus was incredulous.

"Go for it, guy!" Allisandro slapped him on the back.

"This here looks to me like it's something could be hooked to what's called a *Vigenère Tableau*."

"What the. . . ?"

"A code system. I read about it. Kinda' hard to explain. Let me show you a little bit of some things. Can you let me take that piece of paper you got there, Mr. B? Thanks. OK. Now." He wrote the alphabet across the top of the page—a horizontal row of letters, "A" through "Z". "I'll make these in red so's you can see better." Down the left margin he repeated the process: again "A" through "Z". "I'll use red again. OK. You saw what I did. Now, I'm going to fill in between the horizontal row at the top and the vertical column on the left with all the letters of the alphabet again. Like this. I'll use black."

"Again?"

"Right. Again. Watch. Starting at column 'A' row 'A' I'll fill in that first row writing 'A' through 'Z'. So, what I'm doing, as you can see, is I'm writing the alphabet from left to right, using, of course the twenty-six spaces. Robert drew a lettered box.

| **A** | **B** | **C** | **D** | **E** | **F** | **G** | **H** | **I** | **J** | **K** | **L** | **M** | **N** | **O** | **P** | **Q** | **R** | **S** | **T** | **U** | **V** | **W** | **X** | **Y** | **Z** |
|---|---|---|---|---|---|---|---|---|---|---|---|---|---|---|---|---|---|---|---|---|---|---|---|---|---|
| **B** | C | D | E | F | G | H | I | J | K | L | M | N | O | P | Q | R | S | T | U | V | W | X | Y | Z | A |
| **C** | D | E | F | G | H | I | J | K | L | M | N | O | P | Q | R | S | T | U | V | W | X | Y | Z | A | B |
| **D** | E | F | G | H | I | J | K | L | M | N | O | P | Q | R | S | T | U | V | W | X | Y | Z | A | B | C |
| **E** | F | G | H | I | J | K | L | M | N | O | P | Q | R | S | T | U | V | W | X | Y | Z | A | B | C | D |
| **F** | G | H | I | J | K | L | M | N | O | P | Q | R | S | T | U | V | W | X | Y | Z | A | B | C | D | E |
| **G** | H | I | J | K | L | M | N | O | P | Q | R | S | T | U | V | W | X | Y | Z | A | B | C | D | E | F |
| **H** | I | J | K | L | M | N | O | P | Q | R | S | T | U | V | W | X | Y | Z | A | B | C | D | E | F | G |
| **I** | J | K | L | M | N | O | P | Q | R | S | T | U | V | W | X | Y | Z | A | B | C | D | E | F | G | H |
| **J** | K | L | M | N | O | P | Q | R | S | T | U | V | W | X | Y | Z | A | B | C | D | E | F | G | H | I |
| **K** | L | M | N | O | P | Q | R | S | T | U | V | W | X | Y | Z | A | B | C | D | E | F | G | H | I | J |
| **L** | M | N | O | P | Q | R | S | T | U | V | W | X | Y | Z | A | B | C | D | E | F | G | H | I | J | K |
| **M** | N | O | P | Q | R | S | T | U | V | W | X | Y | Z | A | B | C | D | E | F | G | H | I | J | K | L |
| **N** | O | P | Q | R | S | T | U | V | W | X | Y | Z | A | B | C | D | E | F | G | H | I | J | K | L | M |
| **O** | P | Q | R | S | T | U | V | W | X | Y | Z | A | B | C | D | E | F | G | H | I | J | K | L | M | N |
| **P** | Q | R | S | T | U | V | W | X | Y | Z | A | B | C | D | E | F | G | H | I | J | K | L | M | N | O |
| **Q** | R | S | T | U | V | W | X | Y | Z | A | B | C | D | E | F | G | H | I | J | K | L | M | N | O | P |
| **R** | S | T | U | V | W | X | Y | Z | A | B | C | D | E | F | G | H | I | J | K | L | M | N | O | P | Q |
| **S** | T | U | V | W | X | Y | Z | A | B | C | D | E | F | G | H | I | J | K | L | M | N | O | P | Q | R |
| **T** | U | V | W | X | Y | Z | A | B | C | D | E | F | G | H | I | J | K | L | M | N | O | P | Q | R | S |
| **U** | V | W | X | Y | Z | A | B | C | D | E | F | G | H | I | J | K | L | M | N | O | P | Q | R | S | T |
| **V** | W | X | Y | Z | A | B | C | D | E | F | G | H | I | J | K | L | M | N | O | P | Q | R | S | T | U |
| **W** | X | Y | Z | A | B | C | D | E | F | G | H | I | J | K | L | M | N | O | P | Q | R | S | T | U | V |
| **X** | Y | Z | A | B | C | D | E | F | G | H | I | J | K | L | M | N | O | P | Q | R | S | T | U | V | W |
| **Y** | Z | A | B | C | D | E | F | G | H | I | J | K | L | M | N | O | P | Q | R | S | T | U | V | W | X |
| **Z** | A | B | C | D | E | F | G | H | I | J | K | L | M | N | O | P | Q | R | S | T | U | V | W | X | Y |

"OK. That does it." He surveyed his handiwork proudly. "Now! You see a *Vigenère*: the Tableau. Completed."

"But how we supposed to use it?"

"Yeah! To crack the code."

"Sure. That's the next step."

"Now, we're hot on the trail."

"Not exactly. There's a problem. Because you can't plug the six-letter code directly into *Vigenère*. Whoever did this knows that. It's tricky."

"Thought you said you could do it?"

"I can do it. If. If. *If* I got the *Key*. Problem with *Vigenère?* You got to have a Key. Here? Key will be some six letter word to plug into it. To make it work. Like a car key."

"How?"

"Relate each letter in the six-letter boxes to each letter in the key. Then relate each of those into the *Tableau*. And you get your message."

"If you got the six-letter key."

"And if it is a *Vigenère* code."

"Sure. Of course."

"So we need to find a six letter Key?"

"Exactly."

"So, what's the key word, buddy-boy?"

"The million dollar question!"

"So we need to find a six letter English word. Great! Only a couple million of them. Only take us eighty years to try them."

"Who said it had to be in English?"

"Who said it couldn't be a proper noun like, SANDRA?"

"Or FREDIE? Or a plural like SPORTS?"

"Or we have to take every five-letter word in the world and see if it can be made plural with a "S"? That's easy. They'd only be a couple hundred thousand of those."

"Or every four-letter word and see if it could be made plural by adding "ES". Or a three-letter word and see if the plural is "IES"."

"I hear you." Robert was sympathetic. "And to make it more complicated, I've read about cases where that key word is itself encoded. Can be real complex."

"Hoo-oo-ly. This guy, whoever he is, has got us tied up. There'd be maybe millions of possible six-letter words or some such to try. We can't do that."

"Could this be tested by using a computer program of some sort?"

"Right on Shaunisha. I just was wondering that, too." Hector Munoz leaned back, impressed with his own powers of induction.

Robert ran his hand along the top of his T-shirt stroking the thick russet hair pushing over the neckline. "Right now, this is all I can help with. But I'll give it some more thinking. But you guys do the same. We need that six-letter Key. Can't get to first base without it. Somehow! Got to find it. Otherwise we get nothing."

"OK. We're making progress. We're on the right track. I'm sure of it." Besserian began rearranging the files. "That's enough for now. On a hunch, let's copy out the rest of these six-letter codes in the rest of the files."

"So nobody will come back and take the file away?"

"Mr. B, we're due to come back here tomorrow."

"Mr. B. You think this drawer could be a sort of relay station for somebody to pick up stuff?"

"Could be, Amarantha. Makes sense."

"And you know if this is so important, and is about lots of money and somebody wants to keep it so secret? They might not like for somebody to find out what it was. I mean if we was to break the code . . .

". . .looks too complicated for us to do that, guy."

"But if we was, then it could be dangerous for us."

"Right Macrina. Let's put back everything as we found it. In case whoever put it there comes back. And we can start again tomorrow. And Robert, can you help us with this? Be the leader here? We need you. You're the brain about code."

"Don't know as how I'm a brain. But, I'll do my best. Check my resource books at home tonight."

"Sounds like a plan."

"And you know what, Mr. B?"

"What's that, Jesus?"

"I think we're on to something. Big time."

# *CHAPTER XXX*

## *Unpredictable*

"Keep your focus! Don't let up! One! Two! One! Two! Breathe deep!

Besserian leapt back as Buck flicked a padded mitt into his face.

"Now, come at me! Keep your fighting stance."

Besserian, pivoted hard and there was a shower of moisture from his soaked shirt and shorts.

"Jab! Double jab! Come on, boy! Don't let up! One more minute! Jab three times. Then a left."

The fighter followed the command and threw a hard left. Culling up energy he didn't know he had, his next punch exploded into the mitt with a resounding crack.

"There you go! Good work! One! Two! Now Hook! Right! Sit on it!"

His right missed the center of the mitt. "Shit."

"Don't beat yourself up! See what I've been telling you. Keep that chin down. Get it down! And pivot! Let's go! Don't arch like that. Loosin' power! C'mon! Double Hook. Follow me."

Buck moved back with the speed and grace of a gazelle. "Move with me. That's it." He shifted to the side and flicked the back of the padded mitt into Besserian's face as he came too close. "Judge your distance! Go! Go!"

Besserian summoned all his strength and placed the punches harder and from the shoulder.

"Chin down! Keep that chin down!" Buck stepped easily to the side drawing Besserian toward him. "Double jab! Triple!" Besserian's eye caught the white light of the timer indicating the last thirty seconds. "Forget that! Focus!" Besserian gulped huge mouthfuls of air.

"One! Two! Get under! Hook! Right! Under again! Com'on!" Buck pushed closer, forcing Besserian back. He recovered his stance, shooting out the punches: resounding cracks as he connected. He ducked, and felt the swish of air that creased his glistening hair as Buck's mitt passed over his head.

"Keep your eyes open. Watch! Focus! Snap 'em. Burn 'em in."

The bell rang. Buck ignored it. "One more. Hard right! Hard!" Besserian crouched, chin down and delivered the punches cleanly but with decreased impact.

"C'mon guy. You got more than that. You scared?"

The challenge caught Besserian more than the stinging blow that followed. He pivoted, shot out with a left hook that caught his overconfident assailant hard in the mid section. His right streaked out from his shoulder catching Buck on the underside of the jaw, partially on the neck. Buck scrambled, dazed, eyes swimming, catapulting into the ropes, where he swung, trying to balance himself.

Besserian stood awkwardly. Confused. Seeing the other man reel, holding the sweaty head, fumbling because of the gloves, a trickle of blood partially hidden by the red leather.

"I'm OK. You got me. Let me get my wind back." He looped his arms over the ropes for support. "You put weights in those gloves?"

"Didn't think . . ."

"Shit! Forget it. Had it coming."

Both of them were heaving, giving way to their exhaustion, and exhilleration, heedless of the room.

"Damm near stopped me, Champ."

Besserian patted the top of Buck's head with his glove. "Let's get out of here."

The changing room seemed smaller than usual. Wherever they turned, they collided. Clothing, equipment, all conspired to impede their progress. They bumped each other repeatedly.

"Gimme your towel. Forgot mine." He caught it in midair. "Sounds like you might be on to something big. What you started to tell me? Before? Code?"

"It may stonewall us. Couple of the guys may have recognized a code. But it seems that we need to figure out a key word. To decipher the message."

"How you going to do that?"

"Beats the shit out of me. We know it has to be six letters."

"Piece of cake. Couple hundred million tries should do it." Buck gave up struggling with his shorts, "Forget these", tossed them into the bag and pulled on his jeans. "Say it is code. Even if you don't decode it, and especially if you do? Could be dangerous."

"Worries me."

"You're scared?"

Seated on the bench Besserian moved as Buck scrambled for the rest of his gear, brushing a thigh against his face. "Sorry. You got me good. I'm still stumbling. Anyway, you got reason to be apprehensive. Obviously something important. To an important and pretty clever person."

"Maybe."

"Nothing wrong with that. You got me scared to get in the ring with you." He laughed.

"I wanted this thing, the Project to be successful. Now it looks like it'll be a failure. For me. For the kids?"

"OK, champ. Finished." Buck zipped the outsized bag shut, flicking the towel back to Besserian. "Nothing to feel bad about. Being scared. Means progress. Not sitting on your ass. Means you're doing something. Shit, I'm scared lots of times at work. Don't know what the shit I'm doing. Make a guess. Hope for the best. You owe me for knocking me on my ass. Luigi's? Couple of cold ones?"

Buck stood, placing himself beside his opponent, his face inches away. "Good manager never tries to read too far down the line, around the bend in the river. See what you did today? Never know what might happen. He brushed his palm over Besserian's sweating scalp.

---

# *CHAPTER XXXI*

## *Secret Information*

"We're on a roll, Mr. B."

"Yeah, man. Pull up a chair. See what Robert got!"

"What *we* got. You guys are all in on this."

"Right again! That's us! José punched Antonio's shoulder playfully.

"Hey, guy. Cut that out." Both of them hooted with laughter. "Mr. B. I ain't gay. Like this guy 'Tonio here. He's a prevert!" José dodged a punch and grasping the desk top with one hand and the seat back with the other, twisting his body, swung his legs underneath. They were convulsed by the hilarity of the situation.

"Don't forget me. I was in on this, too." Sandra was not to be outdone.

Robert was bending over the *Vigenère* Chart, totally absorbed, moving a right-angled triangle across and down the columns.

"I don't see how you figured out . . ."

"Let me just cut to the How! It works. The result. I'll explain the background later." He motioned to the chart.

"But you needed the Key."

"Precisely. OK. Let me explain that first. Because it comes first. Knew the Key had to be six letters?"

"Right."

"I, lots of us, tried six letter words that had to do with the school? We guessed that connection. Otherwise we'd never be able to get it."

"Makes sense."

"Actually the real word, the Key, was sort of about school stuff. But using school words gave us the clue. Anyhow, we plugged the code—what we found in the documents—into our guesses for the Key. To see if it could make any sense."

"We did educated guesses like's OK to do in Math? Solving quadratics? We learned that in Algebra II: Mr. Mugwabe."

"You want to hear what they were, Mr. B? Our educated guesses? That we tried?"

"Of course, Jesus."

"Sports; school; knight; Baques, lesson, even tried cholos, and apples . ."

"Mr. B? They gave you apples. And you made applesauce!"

"I'm not doing it. You are."

Jesus nodded. "We was stumped. Until Shaunisha had a brainstorm. Let her tell you."

"Just was thinking about all these words. And us getting nowhere? Going to take forever? So, in Mr. Bathersea's Geography Class? It just hits me. 'Cause he's always talking about *Babble* a lot? Backwards Scrabble? So? Try them backwards. What I guessed for the six letter key. What's to lose? So I goes home and plugged them into my computer program. But backwards. And ran a search. I just had to try a couple of the codes, you know the ones we found here, to see if I was on the right track. If I was making sense."

"Absolutely. Makes a lot of sense. Then?"

"Then was on the phone with Griselda and Lupe and Gloria and Marco? They all came over. To my house? And we kept trying the same words backwards. Then, it was Guadalupe who had a brainstorm. Big time!"

"She thought outside the box, Mr. B."

"She thought not 'school' exactly but school 'related'."

"You want to tell us, Lupe?"

"I'm cool. Let her keep on. Shaunisha's the brain."

"So we got stuff like Reform; and Mr. Pritchard? And that made Lupe and Griselda think of his company? EduCom? So? we plugged that in. But backwards: MOCUDE. And guess what? It worked! We got it! The Key!"

"Go for it Lupe. You're a brain, girl!"

The girl basked in the approbation, caught up in the excitement. Griselda squeezed her hand. "You shouda seen us yelling and hollering! We was so happy! But let Robert show you. What he did."

"All I did was carry out what Shaunisha did. Mr. B. Here's some diagrams. So's you can see. For yourself?"

Robert drew a six-letter box. "I just used Griselda and Lupe's idea. Put Substitution Cipher, her educated guess, the Key, MOCUDE, in the top row and, in the next row, in red, just to keep from getting mixed up, I put in the six-letter code that we found in the files." He held up the template in which he had made his entries for the remaining codes for that page.

| | | | | | |
|---|---|---|---|---|---|
| M | O | C | U | D | E |
| D | S | F | F | L | S |
| | | | | | |

| | | | | | |
|---|---|---|---|---|---|
| M | O | C | U | D | E |
| Z | D | N | O | P | F |
| | | | | | |

| | | | | | |
|---|---|---|---|---|---|
| M | O | C | U | D | E |
| U | B | I | R | A | B |
| | | | | | |

"Fascinating."

"OK. Now! Look at the Chart, the Tableau. Everybody watch your copies. Work with me."

| | | | | | | | | | | | | | | | | | | | | | | | | | |
|---|---|---|---|---|---|---|---|---|---|---|---|---|---|---|---|---|---|---|---|---|---|---|---|---|---|
| A | B | C | D | E | F | G | H | I | J | K | L | M | N | O | P | Q | R | S | T | U | V | W | X | Y | Z |
| B | C | D | E | F | G | H | I | J | K | L | M | N | O | P | Q | R | S | T | U | V | W | X | Y | Z | A |
| C | D | E | F | G | H | I | J | K | L | M | N | O | P | Q | R | S | T | U | V | W | X | Y | Z | A | B |
| D | E | F | G | H | I | J | K | L | M | N | O | P | Q | R | S | T | U | V | W | X | Y | Z | A | B | C |
| E | F | G | H | I | J | K | L | M | N | O | P | Q | R | S | T | U | V | W | X | Y | Z | A | B | C | D |
| F | G | H | I | J | K | L | M | N | O | P | Q | R | S | T | U | V | W | X | Y | Z | A | B | C | D | E |
| G | H | I | J | K | L | M | N | O | P | Q | R | S | T | U | V | W | X | Y | Z | A | B | C | D | E | F |
| H | I | J | K | L | M | N | O | P | Q | R | S | T | U | V | W | X | Y | Z | A | B | C | D | E | F | G |
| I | J | K | L | M | N | O | P | Q | R | S | T | U | V | W | X | Y | Z | A | B | C | D | E | F | G | H |
| J | K | L | M | N | O | P | Q | R | S | T | U | V | W | X | Y | Z | A | B | C | D | E | F | G | H | I |
| K | L | M | N | O | P | Q | R | S | T | U | V | W | X | Y | Z | A | B | C | D | E | F | G | H | I | J |
| L | M | N | O | P | Q | R | S | T | U | V | W | X | Y | Z | A | B | C | D | E | F | G | H | I | J | K |
| M | N | O | P | Q | R | S | T | U | V | W | X | Y | Z | A | B | C | D | E | F | G | H | I | J | K | L |
| N | O | P | Q | R | S | T | U | V | W | X | Y | Z | A | B | C | D | E | F | G | H | I | J | K | L | M |
| O | P | Q | R | S | T | U | V | W | X | Y | Z | A | B | C | D | E | F | G | H | I | J | K | L | M | N |
| P | Q | R | S | T | U | V | W | X | Y | Z | A | B | C | D | E | F | G | H | I | J | K | L | M | N | O |
| Q | R | S | T | U | V | W | X | Y | Z | A | B | C | D | E | F | G | H | I | J | K | L | M | N | O | P |
| R | S | T | U | V | W | X | Y | Z | A | B | C | D | E | F | G | H | I | J | K | L | M | N | O | P | Q |
| S | T | U | V | W | X | Y | Z | A | B | C | D | E | F | G | H | I | J | K | L | M | N | O | P | Q | R |
| T | U | V | W | X | Y | Z | A | B | C | D | E | F | G | H | I | J | K | L | M | N | O | P | Q | R | S |
| U | V | W | X | Y | Z | A | B | C | D | E | F | G | H | I | J | K | L | M | N | O | P | Q | R | S | T |
| V | W | X | Y | Z | A | B | C | D | E | F | G | H | I | J | K | L | M | N | O | P | Q | R | S | T | U |
| W | X | Y | Z | A | B | C | D | E | F | G | H | I | J | K | L | M | N | O | P | Q | R | S | T | U | V |
| X | Y | Z | A | B | C | D | E | F | G | H | I | J | K | L | M | N | O | P | Q | R | S | T | U | V | W |
| Y | Z | A | B | C | D | E | F | G | H | I | J | K | L | M | N | O | P | Q | R | S | T | U | V | W | X |
| Z | A | B | C | D | E | F | G | H | I | J | K | L | M | N | O | P | Q | R | S | T | U | V | W | X | Y |

"This is the decoding process. The deciphering. In the top line of the Tableau: find 'M'. Read down the column, directly beneath it until you find 'D'. Then read to the left, and locate the corresponding letter in the left vertical column. Use the key: MOCUDE for each box."

"R'". Allisandro yelled triumphantly.

"Exactly. So I'll place the letter 'R' in the box under the 'D'. The code. OK. Let's complete the boxes and see what we get. Remember. Accuracy is super important. No prizes for being fast but sloppy. Let's try these groups starting with: DSFFLS."

Robert showed them his diagrams and they compared their own.

| M | O | C | U | D | E |
|---|---|---|---|---|---|
| D | S | F | F | L | S |
| R | E | D | L | I | O |

| M | O | C | U | D | E |
|---|---|---|---|---|---|
| Z | D | N | O | P | F |
| N | P | L | U | M | B |

| | | | | | |
|---|---|---|---|---|---|
| M | O | C | U | D | E |
| U | B | I | R | A | B |
| I | N | G | X | X | X |

Jesus held up his paper to show his results. "Red Lion Plumbing."

"What'd we tell you, Mr. B! Griselda! Shaunisha! Robert! Gloria! We're all brains!" Jesus was ecstatic.

So was Besserian. "I get it! And they added the 'x's' at the end, so it wouldn't be obvious that the last word had fewer letters. And prevent the decoder from getting a 'foot up' with the letters U, D, and E. Cleaver. Very cleaver. And you guys are even more cleaver. Because you figured it out."

"And we got some others. When we decoded more of what we found in the documents. Look here."

"Let's fill in the rest. Use your templates."

They quickly produced the following sets for the next message.

| | | | | | |
|---|---|---|---|---|---|
| M | O | C | U | D | E |
| N | F | A | U | Q | X |
| B | R | Y | A | N | T |

| | | | | | |
|---|---|---|---|---|---|
| M | O | C | U | D | E |
| E | H | C | N | L | S |
| S | T | A | T | I | O |

| | | | | | |
|---|---|---|---|---|---|
| M | O | C | U | D | E |
| Z | S | T | S | A | B |
| N | E | R | Y | X | X |

"Bryant Stationery. And the 'x's to make it legit. I know them, you guys. Bryant Stationery just started up. On Pacific Street. Wow! Hot stuff."

"Yeah, Mr. B. Used to be over there by the freeway. Mr. Baques wanted them to do the Senior Grad Night couple of years back. But the other guys, Seniority Printing, came in with a price that was half theirs. And Seniority's closed down last couple of weeks."

"Guys, let's get this next one to see what's going on."

Sandra grabbed her blank template. "Let's do this one on our own." She emitted a sharp laugh. "OK. Top row is the key: MOCUDE." I fill that in on the top. See? Next, below that I write the code we found in the files: EWOGVN. The first set of six. For that file."

"In red. That's the way we're doing it." Robert handed her the red pen.

"Whatever. And guys think they're the only ones that's structured! Watch this! Anyhow, I was just going to do that, Robert. Then we use the Table to translate.

"Get the Clear." Allisandro chided.

"OK. Let's handle the first one. Let's see. Now, don't tell me, you guys. M to E to ah! Q. Then O to W is K. Then C to O is R. Then U to G is, ah, A?

Jesus shook his head, smiling. "Let me help you. Show you again. You'll get it."

"Sort of confusing at first, Mr. B. For everybody."

"Robert, why don't you steer this one through. Until we get the hang of it."

"Sure, Mr. B. Here you go, Sandra. Everybody. You were reading down the left side of the Tableau. You got to read down the column *under* the key letter and then, *after you did that*, over to your left to the corresponding letter in the vertical alphabetical column. So we got, M to E is S and O to W is I and . . .

"Simms Janitorial," Jesus and Sandra yelled in unison. "Got it! This is great. Look. They held up his completed templates.

And Felipe held up his paper. "Got it, too. Look at me!"

They passed their completed templates to the others.

| | | | | | |
|---|---|---|---|---|---|
| M | O | C | U | D | E |
| E | W | O | G | V | N |
| S | I | M | M | S | J |

| | | | | | |
|---|---|---|---|---|---|
| M | O | C | U | D | E |
| M | B | K | N | R | V |
| A | N | I | T | O | R |

| | | | | | |
|---|---|---|---|---|---|
| M | O | C | U | D | E |
| U | O | N | R | A | B |
| I | A | L | X | X | X |

Besserian was thoughtful. "We're obviously on to something. We've got the names of businesses. Lots of them."

"What do they mean, Mr. B?"

Robert interjected. "Hang on, guys! Big time problem! Look! Another group! Of *Seven*! Seven letters!"

"You mean we need another key word? Seven letter? This is too much for us! Never gonna find that one! Impossible!" Rigo slammed his fist on the desk.

"Need to do some heavy thinking, Mr. B. Sir. "

Besserian moved his head. "Hope we can."

"We'll do it. Somehow! Brain power! All the way!"

"On a roll, Mr. B! Need to make some more applesauce!"

# *CHAPTER XXXII*

## *Different Kinds of Danger*

"Something's bothering you.

"Could be dangerous. Probably is. For you."

"How's that?" Besserian, frowning, tugged irritably at the white lycra bike shorts.

"You should be able to figure that out, sonny boy. It's obvious." They were riding in tandem and Buck had moved ahead. He called over his shoulder without turning. "You got names of companies. With their financial specs."

"So?"

"Number one rule in Management: you uncover somebody's secret? Somebody's secret tied to lots of dollar signs? You got to find the message. Or it'll hurt you. And now there's more to the secret? The code? A seven-letter Key? OK. Somebody wants to keep you from figuring out the whole puzzle. Because that's what you're going to get when you figure out that seven-letter key."

"If. We do. Kids might not be able to get it."

"They will. They've got a mountain lion up a tree. Not going to give up. Not a chance. And they're smart."

"Might not have anything to do with the Reform Plan."

"Dream on, buddy."

"You're right. No stopping them. They're after blood."

"So are you. You'll take the risk. You've come this far. You'll get the AP job. Heard rumors. At the school district."

Spring was turning to summer. It was hot. Besserian enjoyed the sweat running down his chest and back. He sat back, guiding the bicycle with his legs, and wiped his face. He pulled abreast of Buck.

"Talk about danger. These turns! Anything were to come barrel assing around one of these? They'd be no way to get out of the way. Even if you saw them, road's too narrow in most places. To move."

For all practical purposes the upper roads of the park, winding steeply for miles, were abandoned. During the week ponderous, grunting, gravel and sand trucks made their way down the hilly stretches, brakes squealing, gears grinding; battered, steel container beds resenting the top-heavy loads, spewing clouds of dust and loose gravel. The city continued to pillage the old quarries for gravel, stone and dirt: a self-defeating project to maintain the infrastructure.

"For sure. Like getting run over by a steamroller." Buck smiled over at his companion. "But statistically improbable. Next to impossible. Unless somebody had an 'in' with municipal government and was able to get a key to unlock the car barrier."

"Or bolt cutters."

"Not going to happen. So, relax. Enjoy the ride. Get the AP job. Accept the Reform Plan until you find out it's no good. And who knows? You might like it. Might work."

"I should be like you? Try anything?"

"Sure. Like with people. Doesn't work? OK! Then you know."

"Sure is deserted up here. Now."

"That's what's we're here for. Escape time, buddy! Don't have to worry about cars and shit." He spread his arms twisting his torso on the tiny seat; holding his bandaged fist like a trophy. "Like flying. Free as a bird. Forget about stuff. Like that exhausted feeling just after you do it? The best! Light as air. Floating. Like you escaped from the world. And people say there's no heaven! It's right here. If you want it. If you're smart enough to take it."

They rode without speaking. Each lost in his private reverie. "Guess you're right." Buck was muttering mostly to himself. "I'll give you that. It's possible. Something could come around one of the turns! Might think there was no one else on the road. Just like we do. And be tear-assing along. Not expecting to see two guys on bikes. Not be able to stop. Shit, we do twenty on the flat stretches and thirty or more on the hills. Ever hit somebody coming the other way? Be all over. For us."

"Riding up here can be dangerous. Project might be dangerous."

"So is going to the gym. Look at my hand! Anyway, wasn't my fault. Bear said the hook on the bottom—you saw it: the double end bag? Wasn't fixed right. That's why it caught me. Fucker flipped up at me. Hurts like hell, too! But, up here? Dangerous? Not unless some idiot unlocked the gate. Where we left the cars. Park rangers? They're not going to do that. Most of them got their heads screwed on. Not like some crazy ass gang-banger."

Buck leaned deep over the under-slung handlebars, gripping with one hand, balancing with the other. "Let's get up some speed. Just because I've got a bum hand's no reason to think you can take me." The bicycle cantilevered from side to side as he raised off the miniscule seat and dug the clips of his shoes into the pedals.

They shot down the straight stretch, evenly matched. Then the road wound through the turns, the incline increasing gradually for a mile, to the base of the final twisting hill. "Called Cardio Summit. Better take this one easier."

"Could be risky. If somebody has a hidden agenda."

"Will you forget code! Anyway, depends on who that somebody is. And what his agenda is."

"Chances are it's somebody important. Powerful. Somebody wants to keep something quiet? Money involved for sure. Lots of it. He's got a reason to cover up what he's doing."

They were both breathing heavily, occasionally choking on the words. Still close, in tandem, to lessen the assent, they took the hill at forty-five degree angles. Besserian was reminded of his college Junior year in Europe: his bicycle trip over the Alps: the criss-cross windings through the Splügen Pass.

Buck was uncharacteristically pensive. "You wouldn't expect to find coded information hidden in office files. Coded messages? It's out of the Hardy Boys."

"You read them? Hey! That's funny! Me too! Don't know if I read all twenty-seven. But pretty close. How many were there?

"Thirty-three."

"*The Old Mill; The Secret Tower; The Deserted Boathouse.* Great!" He laughed unselfconsciously. "They never seemed much interested in girls?"

"Why should they be? Written for guys about twelve."

"I'll be twelve all my life. In some ways."

The hundreds of acres of the park isolated the riders. Liberation from the noise of civilization, it was, normally, a respite. Calming. On previous rides Besserian hadn't been as aware of the isolation. Or the danger. Or associated the two.

They sprinted the remaining distance to the top and started the descent. The only sounds were the hum of the tires and the occasional clean, reassuring, clink of chain moving through gear train.

The effortless drone of the spinning wheels enveloped Besserian in a temporary security. The glint of the sun caught, in a metallic blur, the spokes of the bike ahead. He watched the chain skip, precisely and cleanly: the game of controlling speed without hand brakes. As usual Buck's style was flamboyant, drawing himself upright, hands free of the bars, twisting his torso, moving his arms, sometimes backpedaling, oblivious to risk.

Now the hill plummeted. They raced through the turns, bodies angled. Then a long level stretch. Buck held up his left hand pointing over his head to a park-like area to the right, sloping smoothly up from the road. There were scrub oaks and a grassy area near a few pines; a few weathered tables with benches and several neglected stone fireplaces. It was deserted, quiet, except for the breeze moving lightly through the trees. The sky was getting dark. It was an April afternoon and, unusual for the season, there was a smell of rain.

The bicycles glided into the isolation of the place, coasting up the rise, stopping smoothly.

"Something wrong. Flat, maybe? And we can use a rest. Still have some time. Not that late. If the rain holds off." Buck straddled the frame and threw off his helmet. "Ready to explode." He stood the gleaming yellow and black twelve-speed against a tree and walked to the periphery, pulling down the stretch fabric of his shorts. At ease, he talked back over his shoulder, surveying the scenery, enjoying the relief. "So what are you hoping will come out of all this? What do you want me to do?"

Besserian, intent on checking his own tires, stiffened, without looking back. "I don't want you to do anything."

"Hey. You OK?"

"Yes. Of course. What do you mean OK?"

"Just asking. Need to chill, guy! Nothing wrong with asking." He ambled back, still adjusting the shorts. "Twenty pounds lighter! Great! You're wondering how this Project will work out. What will happen. Been meaning to ask you something."

"Yeah! What?"

"Did you ever think about me and Penny? We were talking about danger before. So maybe her working for TriDelt could be dangerous. Do you trust me? Us?"

Besserian looked at him incredulously. "Dangerous? What're you asking that for?" He stopped rummaging in the small canvas bag slung between the handlebars. "That's a weird ass question."

"No. It's logical. Do you?"

Besserian found the water bottle and unscrewed it slowly. "OK. Yes. I trust you. Her. I don't think you're having an affair. If that's what you mean. Should I? You trying to tell me something?"

"No. Nothing. You know how good she is. Damm good. Come a long way. Fast. Now? She's pretty much on her own. Could probably take over the whole thing. Herself. Of course she had a good teacher." He spun the tire of the bike. "And you encouraged her to go back to work."

"Yes. So?"

"So, you're a generous guy."

"Not really. She's talented. She should use it."

"You told me awhile back? Remember? Kids coming to school in costumes? On Halloween?"

"Don't see your point."

"The politically correct word for you, as an all-American husband, is what? Generous? Supportive? Caring?"

"And?"

"Code? That's hiding what you are. The reality. Costume? That's advertising what you'd like to be. But aren't."

"And?"

"I don't know whether your 'generosity' with Penny is code or costume."

"What the hell you up to? Cut the double talk."

"You tell me. Costume? Or code?"

"You got something on your mind, buddy? Say so!"

"I mean it seems to me—as an outside observer, of course—that you sort of go your own way. She goes hers. 'Generous' could be a cover up? Code. For something you don't want to what? Say? Admit?"

Besserian stared at him. Speechless.

"Don't get your ass in a tailspin. I don't see it. And I wonder why. That's all."

"Don't see what?"

"You panting after her. The jealousy. The unreasonable protection. What women call male illogic. You're not playing the usual game. Husband game. Shit, man. She works all the time. It's great for TriDelt. But, it, well, sort of surprises me."

"That's what she wants. I should stop her? She's good at it. I couldn't stop her. Wouldn't if I could."

"Maybe you really haven't leveled with her. Or with yourself. Haven't been quite as 'generous' as you like to think. Maybe 'generous' is code. Not costume."

"What gives you the right .. ."

"No right. No right, at all. Look! I like you! It sorta seems that you're almost too generous about her success. I don't see you making demands, being unreasonable, angry, even violent, pouting, sulking. About her spending so much time working. Being so involved with TriDelt. And it's not like you don't have strong emotions. I've seen them. OK. Sure. Maybe you need to decode yourself? To me 'generous' isn't in sync with desire; passion, sex."

"Get to your point. If there is one."

"You're an emotional guy. But you try to hide it. With her. Shit! She has a right to that. Maybe that's why she's working so much."

"You're getting ahead of yourself, buddy. You making some personal observations. I don't get into your personal life."

"So? Maybe you should." Buck shook his head slowly. "Why not be 'generous' with yourself? As 'generous' as you are with her?"

"Generous? What . . .?"

"Code hides stuff. The essence. The reality. Costume reveals it."

Besserian could feel the moisture on his chest and back. He got up and walked over to Buck who, satisfied with the tire, was crouching, testing the gear train.

"Get up!" Besserian spat out the words, pulsing with anger. He stood over the other man, legs braced wide.

Buck stared at him as if uncomprehending then shrugged. "So, what you going to do. Hit me? OK. I'll stand up." Carefully, bracing himself on his good hand, he eased himself up. Backing slightly, his stance wide, he looked at his hand. And back to Besserian, heaving with pent-up tension. "You going to hit a guy who can't hit back?"

"Shit!" Besserian, furious, kicked the ground, stubbing his toe on a protruding root. "God damm it!" His body was gleaming with sweat. "Damm you! I was right about you from the start! At that restaurant! A conceited ass hole." He turned and made for his own bike. "Fuck! God damm it! God damm you! Shit head!"

Buck began putting the tools back into the roll-up canvas bag. "Let's get going. Getting dark."

Besserian swirled, fists clenched. "I get it. All along you had some kind of weird ass ulterior motive! Thinking that because I respect my wife! That makes me what? Weird? Why don't you say it? Is that what you've been hinting at all along? Gay? Is that what you're trying to say? I'm supposed to be like you? Use everybody. Anybody? You're supposed to be so 'open'? Shit, you're the biggest closet case I ever saw. . .

"Not a closet case."

". . . and if you want to think something? Or prove how fucking superior you are? Then say so, dude. At least have some guts. Not tip-toe around like a little fucking girl! Trying to be so fuckin' cute. But I forgot! That's your style. Fucking closet case yourself. Damm fag!"

"Gay? I don't remember . . ."

"Get fucked!"

". . . don't remember saying that. Must have missed something. You made your point. Let's pack up and move out. You have to get home. So do I. There're a lot of different codes need to be broken. Soon as my hand heals up, we can settle this any way you want. Just . . .

"God-damm right we will!"

"Just don't get me from behind. On the way down. Ram me with your bike. I mean you're a pretty emotional guy!"

"Shit! If I wanted to check you out, fucker? Listen, shit ass. I don't need to get you in the back. I'm not like you. A buddy fucker." He was still heaving. He wiped his eyes.

"C'mon. Let's do it. It's all downhill from here. May as well enjoy the ride. You're so good at deciphering shit! Figure out our *own* code."

# *CHAPTER XXXIII*

## *A Discussion*

"So? Right now? Everything hinges on cracking the code. Can you?"

"We found out about businesses. With the six letter code. Now, we need to find out what they mean. With the seven letter. Need the seven letter key."

Besserian continued stabbing at the logs. Poking. They shifted on the andirons causing one brass lion's head to move; to look at him, reiterating Penny's inquiry. The fire flared.

"This oak is great. Good idea you had about having them trimmed. Get rid of the dead stuff. Supports ecology. And lots of free firewood! We got something free from this place, anyway."

"Call me skeptical. Whatever. But it seems that what started out as a good idea? Your Project? Might turn into a monster. From what you're telling me. Something that could hurt you. Professionally. The AP job. Or even personally."

"A monster? Like this house! Just joking! But not get the AP job? You know how Pritchard said he wanted me. Remember at that party? Seemed to think the Project was a good idea. Baques too."

"That was before the code." She held up the cut crystal to the fire, examining the facets, turning it carefully, teasing the refractions of light.

"You're assuming a lot: something wrong about those businesses. The six digit. That . . ."

"Somebody went to a lot of trouble to keep something secret. Must have a good reason." She was reflective.

"Somebody? Pritchard?"

"Reform Plan is his, after all."

"It's possible we find out something Pritchard didn't know."

"And he'll embrace you like the Prodigal Son?" She shrugged. "Possibly. My female intuition tells me that isn't the case."

"And?"

"No Assistant Principal job. Maybe no job at all. Maybe personal danger. Pritchard doesn't have enemies. Gets rid of them."

She waited while Besserian poured himself another drink.

The library was still their favorite room: perhaps the warmth of the mahogany paneling, the soft light. Penny watched the beads of water on the beveled glass of the five French doors. Two were partially open and the sound of the rain was soothing; condensed from the thick haze it had been earlier. Now, it was dripping onto the shiny leaves of the potted gardenias; splashing noisily, making puddles on the irregularities of the flagstone. The air seemed cleaner than usual. It's refreshing coolness was tempered by the warmth of the fire.

He was standing at the bar—a burled mahogany armoire acquired through one of Buck's Central American associates. Perhaps the dimming light, the already cloying dampness of Spring? Something made her uncomfortable. About him. Different? Distant? Self-confidence? That she hadn't seen before?

"I don't want you to get hurt. I'm afraid. I don't think we should have gotten into this."

"We? The Project? You didn't know anything about it! I'm the one who did it; maybe with a certain amount of pushing from Buck. But, no. You didn't do anything. To get me into it. In any case, I never expected to find code: secret information. About the Plan. And for sure, you didn't. No. Get rid of that idea."

He was unaware that the confidence in his smile elicited apprehension. "Think positively, as they say. We probably won't break the seven digit cipher so what do we have? A list of companies. No big deal. And if Robert and the others do break it? Who knows? Could turn out to put the Reform Plan, and Pritchard, in a good light. Then I'd score a run. As McCauley would say."

She shook her hair, pulling her sweater around her shoulders. "This Scotch is awfully good. He said single malt was the best."

"Who?"

"The owner of that new liquor store. They've been a number of new businesses in the area."

"What's the name?"

"Mega Liquor, I think. Something like that."

He looked back from the fire. "You know! I think that was one of the businesses we found out. With the six digit code."

"Like Mega Liquor associated with Reform plan? School reform? Road is taking some interesting turns. Extraordinary!"

"More like amazing! Why would Mega Liquor Store have anything to do with the School Reform Plan?"

They were both silent, listening to the crackle of the huge logs, the smattering of the rain, savoring the snugness of the room as if it might be taken from them.

"I've watched you change."

He came over and sat beside her in the leather couch. "You have? How?"

"This Project. Your friendship with Buck. I think he's worn off on you."

"Bad? Or good?"

"Good. Probably. But I don't know." Now it was her turn to go to the bar although she didn't pour a drink. "I need to tell you something."

"OK. Shoot."

"You're the one who really gave me the job with TriDelt. With Buck. And . . ."

"Come on! You're the one who made it . . ."

"You encouraged me. Supported me. And I wanted to support you. Give something back to you. In return. I mean, let's face it. Our personal life isn't exactly what? Passionate? I wanted that to change too. I thought the AP job would do for you what TriDelta did for me. If you got the AP job, you could go up in administration. And now, it seems, it could be your undoing or worse. I'm scared. You might get . . ."

"Look. Let me tell you something. Return? Watching you succeed in Tri Delt? With Buck? Is what? Unbelievable 'return' on my investment. I'm so proud of you. Damm! You've got so many talents and skills. I'm so impressed by you. The way you can . . . Hey, what's the matter?"

She was sobbing.

"C'mon! Tell me. What's wrong!"

He held her and she collapsed in his arms. She gave way to tears, emptying months of confusion and doubt.

"Did Buck do anything? He try something?"

She recovered immediately. "No. Nothing. Quite the opposite. I know him. He's not interested in me. Not that way."

"Because, if he did, . . ."

"Nothing. He's OK." She recovered. "OK. All this talk about code? Maybe . . ."

"What?"

"Maybe we're sort of coded. Us? Our relationship? What we want. What we need. Maybe we haven't found the, what's that thing that Robert talks about?"

"The Key? To unlock the message. To get the Clear?"

"Something like that. Look. Buck has been a Key for me. Maybe he is for you, too? To decode our reality."

He looked away, irritated. "He can be a pain. I don't need him."

"Maybe you do, sweetie. Maybe you do."

They were silent together, feeling the warmth, the silence. The security of the fire was dimming.

"Want me to put another log on?"

"Wait a minute. You remember that woman in your teacher training class. It was years ago? I think her name was Cynthia? A math teacher. And you talked about her 'Cynthia Experience'?

"Maybe. Think so." He scowled.

"She told how once she was explaining something to her Math class and she turned around from the board and she experienced a kind of what? Sensation? That at that moment, for some reason, she 'knew' the material completely. In some sort of deeper way than before. Even though she knew it, had explained it many times and the kids had learned it."

"Now that you mention it, yes."

"That's how I feel. Like I know you in some way that's more complete. Who you are. What you are. I knew before. But now I know you, what? Better? More?" She smiled resignedly. "Maybe I broke the code. Our code."

"I put clean sheets on my bed. This morning."

"OK. She felt for his hand and held it in both of hers. Both of them could feel the moisture, the wetness, on their hands.

"The problem isn't that people can't decode relationships. The problem is they can. But they don't. Because then they'd have to risk finding the reality."

"Our code?" They were both silent, listening to the rain, now pouring onto the terrace. "We could try? To break ours? Get our own Clear?"

# *CHAPTER XXXIV*

## *Reality*

"A bummer, Mr. B! Nada!"

"Yeah! We didn't get nothin'" Jesus laughed, "Like Rigo gets when he goes on a date!"

"Even Robert's stumped. Big time, man."

Besserian turned to him, surprised. "What do you think, Robert? No luck? Nothing?"

"Not really. Zero. I tried every seven-letter word I could think of that might of made any sense. WARFLES; POPCORN; COURSES; HISTORY Used a computer program that gives you words in different categories: hundreds of them. And you can sort by the number of letters. Tried words about education and business and . . .

"And students: SCHOOLS; HISTORY, PHYSICS. He even tried words about animals and . . ."

"Why would animals have something to do with schools and reform and kids and stuff?" Sandra was exasperated. She pulled away from Felipe's encircling arm.

"Oh! Kitty got claws. Meow!"

Besserian turned back to the table around which they were all clustered. "Guys, how about words related to finance, investing, banking?"

"Zero on that too, Mr. B. Got us nowheres."

Macrina Lopez was pensive. "Mr. B? How about if we tried names. Like peoples' names? I mean it might work."

"Of course, it's a possibility."

Allisandro shrugged. "Me and Felipe we did some names. About a hundred. Could do some more, I guess if you want, Mr. B. But I'll clue you: this could take a long time. We only got what? Three more weeks?"

"Like Rigo said: even tried animals. We're desperate!"

"Animals! Hold it! Everybody! Wait! WAIT!"

"You look like you seen a ghost, Mr. B."

"I think I did!" His eyes were almost dilated. "Robert, let me use one of your seven-letter templates, will you?"

"Sure. Here you go, sir. You got a idea?"

"Yes. Just came to me. From what you guys just said."

"Go for it, man!"

Using his finger as if spelling a word, Besserian then filled in the seven spaces: SUITOHP.

"What's that you're doing? Some other language?"

"May be nothing. But we'll soon know. Let's fill in the first several seven-letter codes. From the documents." They worked quickly.

| | | | | | | |
|---|---|---|---|---|---|---|
| S | U | I | T | O | H | P |
| T | U | Y | N | S | Z | Y |

| | | | | | | |
|---|---|---|---|---|---|---|
| S | U | I | T | O | H | P |
| T | L | I | N | D | O | B |

| | | | | | | |
|---|---|---|---|---|---|---|
| S | U | I | T | O | H | P |
| O | U | Z | Y | Z | L | H |

| | | | | | | |
|---|---|---|---|---|---|---|
| S | U | I | T | O | H | P |
| S | H | Z | T | M | L | A |

| | | | | | | |
|---|---|---|---|---|---|---|
| S | U | I | T | O | H | P |
| E | S | Z | H | B | S | O |

| | | | | | | |
|---|---|---|---|---|---|---|
| S | U | I | T | O | H | P |
| T | U | K | H | B | N | P |

"Now, all that's left to do is plug these into the Tableau: the *Vigenère* chart? Just like we did before with the six-letter key word."

"OK. So what you're sayin' that now we use your word: SUITOHP? As the new key? Same thing but different?"

"Now let's add the third row—the Clear—using the *Tableau*, like we did before with the 'six' . . ."

"But using the seven!"

"Bingo! To get the new answer, the . . ."
"Clear. Right on, man. Makes sense."
"Go for it, Teach. Crazy!"
"So? Let's see what falls out."."

| | | | | | | |
|---|---|---|---|---|---|---|
| S | U | I | T | O | H | P |
| T | U | Y | N | S | Z | Y |
| B | A | Q | U | E | S | J |

| | | | | | | |
|---|---|---|---|---|---|---|
| S | U | I | T | O | H | P |
| O | U | Z | Y | Z | L | H |
| W | A | R | F | L | E | S |

| | | | | | | |
|---|---|---|---|---|---|---|
| S | U | I | T | O | H | P |
| E | S | Z | H | B | S | O |
| M | Y | R | O | N | L | Z |

"Well, ho-ly! Hell's splittin' apart. At the seams. Man. Would you believe it. Look at those names!"

"Weird ass stuff!"

"Say it, guy! Felipe! There's J. Baques, Warfles. And Myron? Z? Who's that?"

"Isn't the 'Z', possibly what you called a 'null' before, Robert?"

"For sure! A letter added to fill up the space. Right. A null. Because the meaning is obvious without that letter. And it throws the Decipherer off the scent. We seen that with the sixes. And Myron? L? Hey! The Social Studies teacher? Mr. Lancaster? His first name is Myron. So, it's gotta be him."

"Guys, what we've done is broken the cipher."

"Hallelujah, I died and gone to heaven." Felipe, Allisandro, and Robert slapped 'Big Fives' loudly, hugging one another. Jose danced with Antonio. Besserian, Sandra, Gloria, Jesus and the others did the same, with huge smiles and shouts. Felipe kissed Sandra and Shaunisha, dancing with them exuberantly.

"What about the rest. Make it, man! Do it!"

"Robert poured over the ciphers, filling in the spaces:

| | | | | | | |
|---|---|---|---|---|---|---|
| S | U | I | T | O | H | P |
| T | L | I | N | D | O | B |
| B | R | A | U | P | H | M |

| | | | | | | |
|---|---|---|---|---|---|---|
| S | U | I | T | O | H | P |
| S | H | Z | T | M | L | A |
| A | N | R | A | Y | E | L |

"This is it, guys. Rayella Brauphman. For sure. And look! That other one? That Allisandro's got? Marion Johansson! The AP!"

"So, what does it mean? They're involved in all this Reform stuff? But in some special way? Must be."

Gloria was agitated. "Look, you guys! These are all teachers or administrators. Obviously, we can see that each name is hooked up with one of the businesses: the sixes? So? There must be a connection between the names of the companies and the names of the people—the school people."

Besserian nodded thoughtfully. "Excellent thought. What do you make of this, Robert?"

"Good call, Mr. B. Let's look where we found them. Need to back track with the six-letter ciphers and see how they're associated with the 'sevens'."

Allisandro stumbled over himself in his eagerness to check the folders. "Cool, man. Look, guys." He rubbed the incipient bald spot highlighted by closely cropped hair. "Each of the 'sixes' groups has one, no, in some cases, two or three, 'seven's hooked to it. Get a load of this, guys."

They poured over the documents, comparing the newly discovered Clear to the ciphers. Robert guided the process. "Mr. B and Felipe! Maybe you two could begin taking some notes? So, with *Bryant Stationery* we got the 'seven' of TUYNSZY: that's Baques. J."

"Yeah! And with *Red Lion Plumbing* we got OUZYZLH: Warfles! Holy sh. . . I mean wow, man!"

"And look at this: Mr. Falange with Simms Janitorial! Wow!"

"And the next has three sets of 'six' with another two sets of 'seven' hooked on. Looks like: *Boot Camp Fitness*: TLINDOB SHZTMLA. Makes it 'Rayel[la]' Brauphman. We got a teacher Ray somebody?"

"That's Ms. Brauphman!. Rayella's a girl's name. But some stuff, man!"

"We already did all the 'sixes' Mr. B. So, let's just make a list of them and decode the 'sevens' that go with them. So, with *Paxton Stereo Video*:

there's BIPTBZH and GHUTFPD. That's 'Johanss' for the first one. And 'onmario' for the next. I think we already got that?"

| | | | | | | |
|---|---|---|---|---|---|---|
| S | U | I | T | O | H | P |
| B | I | P | T | B | Z | H |
| J | O | H | A | N | S | S |

| | | | | | | |
|---|---|---|---|---|---|---|
| S | U | I | T | O | H | P |
| G | H | U | T | F | P | D |
| O | N | M | A | R | I | O |

The energy was contagious: an exuberance whipping all over the room, out of control, like a cut power cable. "Exactly. What was that you said about 'nulls', Robert? They add letters to complete a block? Of seven? So, the 'onmario' could mean 'Marion' to complete Johansson. Hey, that's what his first name is: Marion? Dorky name! But? A teacher. Gotta expect weird stuff."

"Very logical. You got it. Sure does, Destiny. Smart girl!" Destiny LaDestina smiled smugly. "Got to be. Fits the context. Of what we're finding. And the other one? Must be that Bacon-Gaither lady? At District?"

| | | | | | | |
|---|---|---|---|---|---|---|
| S | U | I | T | O | H | P |
| T | U | K | H | B | N | P |
| B | A | C | O | N | G | A |

Besserian shook his head in agreement. "Absolutely. In some cases they don't write the entire name. Didn't notice that before."

"That's OK, Mr. B. Don't take it too hard. We all make mistakes sometimes." Allisandro and Jesus laughed loudly, slapping each other on the back, jabbing with their elbows. Jesus got his friend in a choke hold, and making a fist, raked the top of his skull.

Sandra discounted their antics disdainfully. "Can we get back to the work?" She was petulant. "Next one is BIVXGSP and HIZMSGO. Look here, Mr. B. I think I've found your nulls. Look! It's JONESLA and PORTEZZ. Jones-Laporte with nulls at the end. Obvious. With *Premier Testing Consultants.*"

"Right on, girl. What else we got?" Felipe slapped his palms together, ready for the next offensive.

"OK. For *Paris Secrets Lingerie*, what we found in the 'sixes', there's two 'sevens': UIZMSYT and ZOONSAI. Crank up your decoders, guys!" Felipe produced a remarkably accurate rendition, although perhaps overloud, of a race car motor revving up at the starting line.

Sandra spoke loudly: "*Paris Secrets* is Cortere, Huguette, missing the final 'e' which is obvious: understood."

"Next! Hop too, you guys. What 'sevens' with next groups of 'sixes'?"

"It's VUDXBWD and JNZACUS. That gives us DAVENPO and RTRHOND. And these go with the 'sixes': *Johnson Collection Agency.*"

"That's Ms. Davenport! GATE! Hey, this guy's got everybody in his harem. I mean you could tell he was turned on by code."

"For the next 'sixes': *Reliable Electrical Service*, there's GVMLGVR. That's Obesso, C. Hey, guys. Who's that? Never heard of him."

"Some kind of muckety-muck over there at District? I heard about her one time: Claudia Obesso. It fits. District administration. What else?"

"For PDQ Firing Range: HBQEZPE, KQQETYX. OK. Let's see. That makes it PHILLIP, SWILFRI: Hey, who' that? Sounds real weird."

"I got it! Mr. Phillips? The Health teacher? He's got some dork name I heard: like Wilfrid? Help!"

"Yeah, man. Got identity repressions. Big time!"

Sandra interrupted. "Look. We all know how to do this now. We got all the sixes done already ..."

"Robert did them."

"I did some of them, too, just for your information. Anyhow. It's time for us to get in groups and see what we can come up with in the next thirty minutes. Finish all these 'sevens'." Monica Alvarez' excitement approached frenzy. "Group-up you guys! See what crawls out."

"On a roll, man!"

++++++++++++++++++++++++++++++++++++++++

"Busy?"

"Of course. Always. You know that."

"Shouldn't have asked. Look at this. You know your contact in EduCom; in Peter's office? Jackie Stevens? We've become lunch buddies."

"Tell me."

She pushed a button and spoke into the phone. "Jeffrey? No calls, Sweetie. OK? Let you know when."

Buck eased himself into one of the three dark blue leather wing chairs across from her desk.

"Sounds interesting."

"Seems that Phase Two is the essence of the Reform Plan: what happens outside the school. In the community. Not in the school. School reform, if it happens at all is a cover up."

"How?"

"Real purpose—Phase Two—is to make Cathedral Heights a separate city. Why? To bring in new businesses. And, here's where it gets interesting: Reform Plan will control them: plumbing, stereo equipment, janitorial and cleaning, electronics, office equipment, security, roofing, contracting, landscaping—you name it—even a firing range, ..."

"Firing range? Odd."

Penny luxuriated in his attention. "That's what I thought. Pritchard training his body guards? Oh. And there's also a retail gun store. And it seems that he's acquired options on several apartment houses. Commercial and residential real estate brokerages. Jackie has her ear to the wall, and her hand in my purse: she suspects that more acquisitions are in the works: caterers, trash collection, insurance, health care: dieting, massage parlors, porno shops, chiropractors, gyms. For sure at least one bank; First Citizens Bank will become the First Women's Credit Union of Cathedral Heights. And be a subsidiary of EduCom."

"And all this activity means?"

"It means, Pritchard, through EduCom and its subsidiaries will own more than the schools. He'll own the entire municipality. The profits of these businesses will be funneled to him. Through an elaborate network of subsidiaries."

"So school reform isn't important?"

"It's important all right. But not to help the school: kids."

"Got it! But the details?"

"Don't have them. Who's involved. How? Why?" She continued. "Guess B's told you about the code? Information his Project group found? The part he's deciphered gives names of businesses. But there's more information. That he hasn't decoded yet. Maybe that's what we need to know. Why the businesses? What they mean?"

"For sure. Look. As soon as he tells you? I mean we need to know this."

Penny was concentrating on the small print of a document. "Better if you asked him."

"Maybe. Not sure."

"The important thing is that we're on to the tip of an iceberg. A big one." Buck was curiously reticent.

"The connection between these businesses and Reform Plan? Damm! Got to get the rest of his information decoded. Maybe he can do it? Look how far he's gotten so far!" Buck shifted in his chair. "Why don't I have chairs as comfortable as this in my office?"

"You do. But you're always behind your desk."

"So? It's this Phase Two that's the real thrust of Mr. Peter's plan."

"Boss, let's look at what we know. Peter said publically there would be new businesses. Right? And they'd be owned by minorities? Maybe that's what's happening?"

"Now! You're making sense. Go on!"

"You remember how Pritchard said he'd fund the start-up costs: every minority person can own his, or her, business?"

"His original speech at the school. OK."

"Well, according to Miss Jackie, that's only part of the plan. Seems that yes: he'll provide the start-up costs. But: what's not clear is the pay back of these loans."

"You got more out of her than I ever did. How?"

"She likes expensive lunches. *Prego's.* Scarfs up that *zabaglione* like it was going out of style. We're pinky close now. Girl friends!"

"I don't get it." He was confused.

"Exactly. It seems pay back would be based on the earnings of the business. So, if they're having a slow time, they can pay back less. Touted as his 'concern' for minority people. Helping them."

"Go on."

"The reality? It seems that our Ms. Stevens has been listening at more keyholes: if the business *doesn't* generate sufficient profit—as determined by Peter's bank—the owners will be replaced. And they'll be in debt for the start up loans. Business resold to someone else. And if the business *is* successful, payback will be based on a percentage of the profits: a percentage that increases *exponentially* as the profits go up."

"Owners will be owners on paper. Employees, really."

"Right. Win-win for Mr. Peter!" Penny adjusted her chair to avoid the glare. "Reality check! Minority people will have purchased a franchise, not a business. And they'll be in long term debt to Peter's bank. And even *after* the loans are repaid, his bank will get a percentage of the profits. And, of course, he has his own law firm. In case somebody objects."

His attention was complete. "You started to say something about code?"

"B told me that they, his Project, found more coded information. "

"More?" Buck was enthralled. "Can they figure it out? Could be the evidence we need." He stared at her. "Amazing."

"Kids are amazing. Seems they're the ones who are figuring it out. So far. The businesses."

"So he doesn't know. Yet. For sure? The new information?"

"They're working on it now. The code is extremely complex. He seems to think it may be impossible."

"Never know. At this point, I wouldn't put anything past that guy. Let me know. When he finds out?"

++++++++++++++++++++++++++++++++++++++++++

"OK, guys! I think we're about finished. Let's pool our information. You've all been working hard ..."

"Like Trojans, Mr. B?"

"How would you know, Marco? You have any place to use some? Even if you needed 'em, boy?" Sylvia sniggered and laughed unpleasantly.

"Sylvia, we agreed on respect."

"He can't help the way he is." She tossed waist-length hair. "You're right, Mr. B. He's basically OK. For a guy. No. Seriously. I like him. Sorry, Marco."

"Back to work, team. Felipe and Marco, why don't you give us a synopsis of what everybody has found. Decoded. You have the compilations. The ciphers and the Clears."

"Good, Mr. B. Real good. I'll read the Clears, the decoding of the 'sixes'. And my assistant, Mr. Marco here will read the 'sevens'. Let's go, buddy boy. Hop to!"

"Don't forget: some of these names has more than one company: like ones we read before. Here's a few names we got. Money amounts weren't coded. Here goes."

| | | |
|---|---|---|
| Simms Janitorial | Falange, B. | $25,000. |
| Custom Electric. | Lopez-Workman, R. | $15,000. |
| Reliable Office Supply | Turner, R. | $20,000. |
| Mille Pene Restaurant. | Hamilton, C. | $15,000. |
| Designer Optical | Arcáña, A. | $15,000. |
| Rialto Car Rental. | Allsbury, P. | $20,000. |
| Lennox Bakery. | Donner, B. | $15,000. |
| Johnson Building Mgt. | Bacon-G. R. | $15,000. |
| Text Book Clearing House | Jones-Laporte, E. | $70,000. |

| | | |
|---|---|---|
| Top Notch Roofing | Lohengrar, M. | $20,000. |
| Desconso Landscape | Smedley, F. | $15,000. |
| Pilot Security Systems. | Martyn-West, B. | $15,000. |
| First Women's Bank | Hollyfield, A. | $15,000. |
| Economy Moving/Storage. | Hamilton, C. | $15,000. |
| Remodeling Suppliers. | Pimmentade, M. | $15,000. |
| Mega Liquors | Baques, Jose. | $40,000. |
| Premier Testing Service | Jones-Laporte, E. | $50,000. |
| Pacific Exterminators. | Johansson, Marion. | $25,000. |
| United Security | McCauley, B. | $12,000. |
| AmeriMex Check Cashing | Warfles, B. | $15,000. |
| Triple A Construction | Turner, R. | $20,000. |

There's others too. Obvious: some people hooked up with a couple of companies. Big bucks total. But look: teachers, Board members, administrators. Everybody."

No one spoke, as if waiting for him to give the official interpretation. "Let's back up for a minute, guys. See what we've got. Before we do the rest of them. There're quite a few more."

"What we've got are businesses associated with people. School people."

"So, lots of school people. Getting paid?"

"Right. Lots of money. But why?"

"So, what does it mean? I mean do these people know, right now, they're on what? A payroll? And what are they supposed to be doing? To get their pay?"

Besserian was reflective. "Not sure. What do you guys think?"

Felipe was pensive. "Let's put together the pieces. It's businesses with school people. And something else. Somebody wants to keep it secret. This stuff. So what would have to be kept secret? About businesses associated with teachers, board members. And administration?"

"We could always ask them?"

Destiny laDestina's eyes were shining. "Hang on, everybody! Maybe something: only supposed to be a secret *for awhile*? Until the vote? The vote to accept the Reform Plan? I mean after that, it wouldn't matter. Not if extra pay was to get them to vote for Reform Plan. And another thing! That guy, Pritchard? Didn't he say about 'advisory fees' or 'consultant fees' for teachers who would be working with local businesses? On how they could provide services to school reform plan? And maybe to the city government too? So? Why not these sums of money be what they'll be getting paid. Probably every year is my guess."

"If! If! Reform plan is approved. Otherwise they'll get diddly. Up s… the creek."

"I get it. If it's told out in public? Now? Then people might think it was like paying teachers, or them's that's on this list to vote for it."

"Good point. These people, the names we found, have good reason to make sure Reform Plan passes. And to hide the money they'll be paid. The dollar amounts we got here are what they'll be paid for their vote: *now*. And for being consultants: *later*. Every year."

"Not bad. Twenty-five percent increase in annual salary? For smoothing the way for their companies to get contracts with the school district. For repairs and services."

"Yeah. That kind of bucks? Shows these people got a very good reason to support the Reform Plan. And it's a very good reason *not* to advertise that now: before the vote! I mean Jones laDork getting 100 K plus! Warfles! The others! Not too bad!"

"Mr. B? Do these people, names we found out, know? That they've been sort of preselected?"

"We'll have to find that out. My guess is they've been informed verbally: to ensure their vote. Why this stuff is in code: recorded but kept secret at the same time. Nobody to know. Officially. Until *after* Reform is passed. Always the possibility it might not pass? Peter and Baques got to protect themselves. And if not pass? Use this to incriminate, punish, those who didn't vote for Reform. Lid blows off everything."

"And Pritchard said that teachers could be owners of businesses too. That's like having two jobs? Might not be a good idea to advertise that."

"Or to advertise that the Superintendent and Board Members will be paid big, big, bucks in addition to their salaries—which will be increased also. They got every reason to vote for Reform Plan."

"So, what do we make of this, guys?" Besserian was thoughtful. "Ladies and gentlemen, this was coded, excuse me, put in cipher, for an important reason: to keep it secret. And done by an extremely competent person. With a very analytical mind."

"We know Jesus not do it then, Mr. B!" Rigo smirked at his friend's discomfort.

"Jesus is exceptionally competent. The point is that we've uncovered something obviously very important. And? Very sensitive. Robert?"

"Seems to me we got to decide if we're going to say anything about what we found out before they vote."

"Could be dangerous. If we do?"

"Yeah. For us. Or Mr. B."

Robert, the obvious leader, was reflective. "I think we need to finish. Finish all these 'sevens'. Make sure we don't miss anything. Mr. B. I think it's your call. What to say? When to say it?"

"Seems to me that we owe it to Mr. Pritchard to tell him what we've found. It's possible—possible but improbable—he doesn't know anything about this. We owe him the courtesy, the professionalism of alerting him privately prior to saying anything publically. Speak to him before the vote."

"Can you do that, sir? We think you should."

"I can arrange a meeting with him. Certainly."

"But what if some people here starts talking? He could find out anyway."

"You guys use your own discretion about what you say. I won't tell you not to. I do request—ask—that you wait until I've spoken to Pritchard. Had the chance to find out his reaction."

"Go for it! We can do that. If Rigo can keep quiet, I guess anybody can." Destiny smiled. "Just fooling!"

"I'll talk to Pritchard. After that, how about if we plan to meet within a few days? Make our final plan? And don't forget your groups. You're supposed to draw conclusions about this yourselves. And once again. Great work. All of you."

"You did pretty good yourself, sir."

"On a roll, now, Mr. B."

They began to gather up their paraphernalia, milling about and talking.

"Later, coach."

"Hasta la bye-bye, Mr. B!"

"Wait! Hold on, everybody" The room was quiet. "Mr. B. You didn't tell us how you figured out the key? SUITOHP?"

"Yeah! You psychic?"

"You guys put me on to it, talking about animals, and proper names. *Photius* is the name of Pritchard's cat."

---

# *CHAPTER XXXV*

## *A Strategy*

"Look, sweetie. You know I *love* you." She squeezed the girl's hand. "It's all about your *future*, honey bun. That's all that matters. So, I'm just sayin' that *if—ahf*, mind you—you should just *happen* to found out something on that, well, you know, that—*Project*? It, well, might could help us out ...?"

"I don't know. For sure, yet. And I already told you stuff. And jesterday he said we should . . .well, you know. . . sorta keep it, well, *private*? Like to ourselves? For now? 'Till we decode all the stuff about it. And totally make our plans? And all?"

"He did?" She stifled her first reaction. "And OK! O-o-o-K! Let's to switch over real quick to a side track here. Play your cards right and this Project could be your big break-through. Because it's sink or swim time, baby girl. Your future."

There was a tapping on the frosted glass pane of the door. "Hang on!" The distraction irritated her. "They always come at the wrong time. Listen, sweetie pie. I've been thinking about what you told me? Those six and seven-letter names? Word's been leaking. People been talkin'."

"Everybody agreed not to talk about it until Mr. B was to tell that Mr. Pritchard guy about it."

"What? Him tell Pritchard! Him? Land o'Goshen, girl! You got to bail! Fast. Show Pritchard you're on his side of the fence. First. Before Besserian gets to him. It's your chance!"

"I said I wouldn't say . . ."

"Just you listen *up*, girl! And listen up *good*. Your future is in front of you. It's grow up time! No more cutesy little girl stuff. Now, what you going to do about it?"

The knocking was repeated. "I said, HOLD IT! I got but two legs!"

A timid face was peering in warily—the door was slightly ajar. Raven Lopez-Workman thrust the chair back four inches, banging the pockmarked baseboard with two of the chipped wheels, and squeezed past her visitor. The interloper, confused, apprehensively was retreating behind the glass panel, covered by photos of Lopez socializing with female counselees.

"But, M-i-i-s—s-s, you tole m-e-e-e ..."

"Not *now*, sweetheart. So-o-r-r-y! Give me a interlude? A New York minute! Maybe tomorrow? O-o-o-k-ay-ay? Try me: tomorrow afternoon? Late?" The Cheshire smile, punctuated by affirmative head vibrations, did not invite discussion.

Lips zippered, eyes like CD's, she squeezed herself back, between Sandra and the desk, re-packing herself into the abused chair. "Now, let's gyrate back to our own needs." Mouth gaping, tapping a thumb nail on lower front teeth, she squinted, shook her head briskly, and grimaced, as if just forced to swallow a tablespoon of alum.

"No." She waved the glossy sable nail of an index finger negatively; following it wide-eyed: a self-administered optometrist's exam in double-time. "Skate around the rink one more time with me, honey, on this! Looks like Project gonna show up stuff about teachers. And other whoevers. So? We got to get you out. First. Fast!"

"Miss, they got names like Baques, Jones LaDorc. Cortair. Coach McCauley. Warfles. Lots of others. And you."

"Me? Baques tole me it to be secret! Ho-o-o-ly!"

"Seems it's teachers that's mostly been talking about how good Reform Plan will be. And this separation city deal."

"OK. Let's change our horses right here. In the middle of the lake. You got to know there's some politics going on here."

"In schools? In education. I thought . . ."

"Never you mind what it was you *thought*. Just think this: you got to get used to politics in education. It's the way it is. So you got to make it work for you. Hop back up on the turnip truck." She picked at loose strands of russet hair, arranged in an insecure bun. "Project? Devil's underpants! Something's gonna bust. For me! For you! Unless we get off our butts. And to do something."

"What?"

"Teachers could lose their dollar 'benefits'. As community advisors. If Reform doesn't pass. And you lose the scholarship. Neither I or you needs somebody like that fascist Besserian to waltz over and yank the carpet out from underneath us?"

"Project could get you in trouble, Miss?"

"Ab-so-*lut*-tul-ly! Now, hunker down time! Two things. First you need to come down on the right side of Pritchard? You gotta have this scholarship. Your mom sure not sending you to some college! Second. You don't have other offers. Third. This scholarship pays big bucks. Could take you all the way to the doctor's degree: if, just *ahf*, you play your cards right. And, sweetie, you might just be holdin' a winnin' hand. And not even knowin' it."

"So?"

"So, let it get out that you *didn't* like the Project? From the git-go? Was *pushed* into it? And because you found out that Besserian was using the Project with all his talk about codes just to say lies about Pritchard? Lies about Reform Plan? That he was the one who *made up* the code! And that's the reason why they was able to decode it. Because he *made it up* to begin with! So's he could get the AP job! Him arousing everybody about how Reform Plan was really pay-offs to Baques 'team players'! That it's business profits first and school reform second. You scrunch Besserian Project and My Godfry, girl: Pritchard'll return the favor. Big time."

"I gu-e-ess. Sure. Yeah!"

"No guess, girl. I'll make sure he gets told about it. I got a 'in' with some Evergreen Board members. Who want to be team players too, with these new businesses? Girl, you got to do turn-about on this Project."

"You don't want to get yourself busted. 'Cause of me."

"That is a true statement. We're here. To help each other. I love you, sweetie. And you already found out my association to be set up with Custom Electric. And maybe get some more tie-ins with other companies. Big dollar signs on the horizon. For the ones Pritchard likes. Both you and me gets a piece of the pie."

*******************************

"Holy shit! Guy's incredible! You said they found the seven!"

"Right. He's proud of the kids."

"OK." Buck was exuberant. "Now we know! How it's going to work. How EduCom will control Reform. Hell, I recognize some of the companies as EduCom subsidiaries. See if Ms. Jackie can check the rest of them."

"Just happens, we're going shopping. Saks! I'll pick up the bill."

"That'll work?"

"She's a woman, isn't she?"

"This is a gold mine! Big bucks!"

"Exactly. You let the Project go ahead? Find out what Peter's really up to! How he's using Reform Plan to benefit himself. And the teacher-administrator 'team players' who support him."

"Bingo! Project has to spill the beans. With their information. Expose Peter. How the new companies become a hose to siphon the school district and then municipal budgets right into his manicured claws."

"OK. What's your strategy? To replace him?"

"Good point. I'll represent all those "concerned and indignant" citizens who, of course, none the less, feel indebted for all Pritchard and his family have 'done' for the community: over the last decades: all that crap. So, they'll let him bow out gracefully. And be replaced by somebody close to him. Who knows his organization. Put a new lid on the same pot. That still keeps boiling."

He won't roll over like that. Never."

Buck snorted. "He won't have a choice. So? We pay him some big bucks. He's got ties with other school districts. Can do it with them." Buck laughed unpleasantly. "He made the one fatal mistake: decoded Political Correctness. That it's designed to screw minorities. By saying, pretending, to help them. Covert screwing of minorities is one thing. Not overt. Reveal that? And your games' over! The Achilles heel of the ruling class. So? Don't ever take off your shoes. And he did. With the code."

"Kids pulled off his shoes. So, what will happen, is that it will be same thing but not different. Reform Plan under your control?"

"OK. I, Tri-Delt gives teachers, board members, administrators the same perks. The payouts. To keep them quiet. And everybody's happy. Put Reform in costume. Plus encode it. And that's fine. They get to keep their extra money. And everybody can dump on Peter and say how terrible he was, the personification of corporate greed, and all that bull. Dumping on Peter is the cover-up for them keeping the financial perks *he gave them.*

And they can still blame him for any reform snafus that happen to be made public later on."

"You: in Peter's shoes."

"Us! In his costume. Exactly. And everybody wants the Reform plan. Because they're too many people getting a piece of the pie. So, remove Peter. And it looks like the nasty part's been eliminated. Everybody can feel good. About themselves."

"And B? What about him?"

"He'll be great! He gets the AP job. And starts moving up in administration. Soon as we can, we dump that jerk Baques. Then put B in as Principal. Then, easy to get La Bork shoved out and up to State somewhere, anywhere. And he replaces her as Superintendent. Here."

"He's your protégé? He trusts you."

"He should. He's got a lot to thank me for. And he'll have more reason to. Great! I'll be advising him. Helping. With managerial strategies. Advancing him. I'm not abusing him." He walked closer to her. "Hey! This doesn't bother you does it? You've known all along. Just because he doesn't know all the details, the behind the scenes stuff, doesn't mean it will hurt him! Hell! It will help him. He'll be an executive. Just like you. Like us. And with the most aggressive reform package in the state behind him: the sacred aura of 'education reform'? He can't lose. At the same time, we'll be building up our control of TV. Newspapers. He'll have that behind him too. Hell, we'll put him into the State Superintendent of Education slot. Especially when we're able to 'adjust' student test scores up to at least mid range, probably higher. *Hell, we'll own the Assessment company!* He'll be the wonder kid of reform! Nobody can argue with that kind of school progress! He doesn't have to be in on all the *details* of what our testing consultants do. To 'up' the scores." He looked quizzical. "That's bad?"

"I'm not sure. That depends on him. You know what he's like?"

"Idealism? For education? Hell! He'll get over that. When he tastes the power! The prestige! The money! He understands that it's better to accomplish *some* reform than be outside and not accomplish any. Some's better than none! True of anything."

She was quiet.

"You're acting like you betrayed him! Not true." Buck looked pleased. "You're helping him! He's not better off now? Than he was: wasting away? Doing nothing? Closeted? You're sending him to the top! I don't call that betrayal."

"I think I know him better. Better than I did. See something else in him. That's different. Now."

"Damm! Be practical. Achieve what we want. For us. For him. We need to have him dump all this code stuff out in public. First step is to get rid of Pritchard. Then we can tidy up any sore spots with Besserian. He'll come around. You haven't done anything that wasn't supportive of him. And loyal. He understands that. And you know what?"

"What?"

"All this will pull you two together. As I said. He'll come around. He needs you. To push him up the ladder. I mean it's not like he didn't want to get power too. For reform. It's just that we don't agree entirely on the details of how to get it. We're all in this together. Me running Reform Plan. You making big bucks as VP of TriDelt. B moves up the administrative and financial ladder: Principal, Superintendent, then State Superintendent of Education. And *some* reform *is* done. Shit! The guy can't lose. And with the "unprecedented" increase in student scores that we can get from our Testing, excuse me, 'Assessment' consultants, he'll be the guru of education reform. He's in line for a Cabinet Post. In DC. Hell, he and I are the same. And it's the three musketeers! All over again. "

**********************************************

"And sweetie, then there's that other tiny little eensy-winsy problem? That we got to take care of? Smooth out any of the wrinkles? That could block you from getting the Evergreen?"

"Wh-a-a-t? You talking about?"

"Thank again, sweetheart. Thank again. Real hard. Real, *real* hard. What I'm talking about you know very well. And you should have figured out by now that we have to swing away from that, well," she nodded understandingly, "shall we say kinda mucky uh, little *occurrence*?" Her jaw dropped, tongue extended and clasped between upper and lower incisors. "That happened in that Alley. About last October?"

"How's that?

"You're not being too smart. Look. You told me Besserian saw you. If he should mouth off about that, you don't stand a chance of getting that scholarship. We need to keep that as quiet as a mouse pissing on cotton. If you was to spill the beans about the Project? Say how Besserian was able to crack the code because he made it up? Hisself? And then he was to say you was in the Alley with Felipe? Hell's bells, girl! Obvious! He's out for revenge! But! You holding cards you not know you had. Nobody'll believe him. Especially when teacher perks, with those companies, are hooked into giving Reform a green light?"

Lopez canted her head to the side, looking over the tops of Benjamin Franklin glasses. "We just can't be sure. That Alley incident has been barned? He could say something. Or, there's always the option that he wasn't the only one to see you two. You think that closet case Williams won't start singing if he saw you? To keep you from gettin' the scholarship?" Neck arched, glasses lowered, dilated eyes simmering, she personified the logician. "You get my drift? We need to ensure that if anybody, *anybody*, starts a rehappening about the Alley? That they fall into their own slop."

"Let's have a suppose that somehow, somewhere, somebody *was* to talk! A suppose that there's a somebody, in addition to Besserian, who was watching you and Felipe? And kept quiet up till now? Suppose Evergreen committee was to hear about it? From that somebody? And, trust your little butt, they will! As God is my witness! Not sayin' whether it's right, wrong, or anything else. But am sayin' we got to have a *strategy* to hush it up. To make sure any spouting off of somebody's big mouth, not matter whose it is, won't hurt your scholarship chances. Need to put a plug in that pausability *before* it happens! Muzzle it. To the scholarship committee."

She brightened and smiled effusively, smugly. "So-o-o", she drawled her words as if waiting for assent, and not finding it, resumed cautiously. "Anything we can strategize on to put you in a win-win position for that Scholarship is, well, dead on for what we need to do." This time her nodding was fussy, impatient, without a smile, tongue tucked in behind upper molars, lower jaw skewed.

"And the counselor of whoever's selected gets about fifteen K? Interview lady from Evergreen told me."

"Is that the figure? OK. Bettern' nothing. For all my work."

"Besserian'll never say nothin'. Neither would Felipe."

"Listen, sweetie. I mean you're seventeen and all. But you still got some things to learn." She spoke slowly, emphasizing the gravity of the subject. "Felipe-may-be-seventeen! But he's a man! And that means Male! Besserian, whatever his inclines, is one too. Now, even putting aside any special sexual inclines, what is the one thing, the one single most important thing, that all of *them* like to do? Most?"

Sandra stared blankly, then rummaged in her backpack.

"Shoot off. Their mouths. To each other. About how often they 'scored'!"

"Felipe wouldn't do that. Even if I was to rat on their sacred Project. He got respect for me. Besserian too."

"Exactly what I'm talking about." She leaned closer for emphasis. "Wrong! Respect has got its own special meaning in the male dictionary. And-yes-they-would-talk! Get back at you!" She enunciated slowly and carefully. "They're-all-the-same! Scout's honor. May *look* different! May *act* different! Don't get yourself fooled. Point is: they're *not* different! You remember that song of Dottie Barnett? Gawd, how I love the way she swings her hips so the leather fringe just flops all over the place. Number Something on the Country Hit Parade number o' years back: '*I Got Tooken', By A Good, Good Lookin' Guy*'? So here, in this case scenario, girl, here's my take: we never know. Never can let 'them', to get the upper hand. Point is *he could, they could. Somebody could.*"

"What?"

"T-A-L-K! Talk! Yakety-Yakety! Blabber mouth! Listen! Let's say Felipe was to get mad. Because you don't want to do it with him anymore! Or not want to get married, if that's his bag. Begins to get wise that you 'led him on'! And after you gave permission to go to the next level! When all he wanted was to 'sacrifice his life' for you." She did a theatrical imitation of a whining child. "All that kind of their squallerin' bull? Or Besserian if he was to think you weren't 'committed'," she toggled her fingers, "to his Gawd-almighty 'Project'? Or 'betrayed' it! Help!"

Lopez permitted the gravity of her words to sink in. "Sweetie, you got to know that guys got 'loyalty' up the ying-yang. But! *But*! Only to each other! Never to us. And They think we should be the same way to Them. Makes them mad as hornets if it's 'violated'. Big time! They're all the same! Blabbering about 'commitment' and 'loyalty'. Help! Right! Only to what it is *They* want!" She spat out the words. "Don't let him get away with that crap! And you better keep on remembering that They write Their own rule book! About 'honor' and such. And about us."

"Besserian! Felipe! They're not like that."

"See! The Little Miss Sunshine reaction! Just standin' there waitin' to get 'tooken'. Sweet dreams, honey! Bye-bye land! Thing you don't see, don't want to see, is the M-I-G-H-T! The C-O-U-D! Just what if Mr. God-almighty Superior Besserian *was* to say somethin? And *ahf*—just sayin' *ahf* now, don't get yourself in a tailspin—*ahf either* him or Felipe was to talk, shoot off their mouths, because you wasn't 'loyal'?"

She was vehement. "No, Buttercup. Our strategy is to protect Evergreen from having to come right out and admit their secret guidelines is more important than their published ones. Or even worse, that they gave preference to a girl who 'sleeps around'? They'd have to switch the shoe to the other foot! Sure it's the same shoe but it's still discomfortable. And looks nerdy. And they don't want to do that. Never. So, for them to get out of doing that, they might just dump little Sandra. And little Sandra just might find herself on the trail to nowheres land. Scholarship out the window! We don't need that! We need to make sure little Sandra looks like the victim. Of the Project."

"So you don't trust Felipe? Besserian or others?"

"Trust? Male? Those two words mix together like chocolate and oysters. Not a matter of trust, sweetie." She munched on the remainder of her chocolate bar. "Have some? I learned years ago not to trust: *any* of them. *Any* time. *Any* place. I tole you, they're-*all*-the-same! And you got to learn that too. *All* of them has only one thing on their minds. Theirselves! Who? Why? Isn't factors. For them. To jump back to my point again: Evergreen don't want to select someone who's going to cause their policies to have to be hung out to dry in public!"

She exhaled heavily, exasperated. "Try this one on for size, hon. Something else. Could've been a complete stranger. Who saw you guys. In the alley. I mean if Besserian could, why not others? So, there's another possible song bird."

"And finally look at this. Felipe, he's been braggin' how he's gonna *marry* you! Everybody knows he's hot for you. And you for him. When you tell him 'no', you can bet your you-know-what he'll start blabbering. It's called revenge! And ain't he real close to Besserian, too? Some sort of musical compatibility? Yeah! Right!" She rolled her eyes sarcastically. "No. Not at all. Here's another take. You could be being his cover up: his alibi? His screen? Protect his sacred manhood! If he's like involved? With Besserian? That makes you even more necessary for him. And something else: Felipe might could start thinkin' you put your career needs before him: more important to you than he is."

"He respects my career values."

"Sure! Sure, he does!" Her eyes were in motion. "You dealing with the male animal, here, girl! Wise up! See how much he respects your career when you tell him No! Starts hollering. Pounds his fist into the wall. Remember like that time after the Prom? 'Cause his male pride was hurt!" Leavering extended her confidentiality. "Honey, have to tell you they're none, not one, of them that can stand up to that. They're as sensitive in their heads as between their legs. Some, maybe even more so. No tellin' what he, any of 'em, could do. Something crazy. For sure! You don't never, *ever,* want to lose your control. Over their feeling responses. Not never."

"See, angel, Evergreen Foundation that awards the scholarship? Most people don't know it, but this is Pritchard's foundation. They can't choose without his approval. And if you've already shown him you're on his side of the fence? By sayin' how Project trumped up bad things about his Reform Plan? Sweetie? You're a shoe in."

Sandra rummaged in her pink back pack and drew out a large plastic comb.

"And too. If you're a part of the Project and the Project's accusing Pritchard? I guarantee, you won't get the scholarship! For sure."

"So I need to dump the Project?"

"For sure. Something else, too." She paused. "Need to dump Felipe."

"How's that?"

"Two reasons, baby-girl. Shows you're completely separated from the Project. Number two? Scholarship has unwritten guidelines. The unwritten ones is the ones that count."

"Yeah. What are they?"

"See sweetie, Evergreen is made up of Board members who has cracked the glass ceiling. That's why Pritchard supports it. Makes him look politically correct. Hides what he really is."

"So?"

"So, don't anybody hold their breath about it being awarded to a boy. And another thing. They want somebody to get it who's not going to get married real quick." Guarantee that will surface on their list of concerns. Yes. Sure could. Twist their heads around. About Felipe."

"Why they care about that?"

"Because they want somebody—and they'll support her with big bucks—all the way up to the doctor's level. Or professional level if she wants to go into law or accounting. Medicine. They know they're the token females. Now. But give 'em some more time and they plan to pull the carpet out from under the male power brokers. Back-fire 'em. Double-cross!"

"So?'

"Girls who get married usually lose interest in their school work. They can get tied down with babies and such. And let's face it sweetie-pie, guys can get pretty darn persuasive when They want. When it suits Them. And possessive. Wantin' to be 'protective' and all. Say how 'Gonna die if you don't love me'. Bla-bla-bla."

"They can mean it."

"Sure. Then! But that was ten minutes ago!" Lopez stroked Sandra's hand. "Sweetie, follow the Evergreen lead: that it's you that's gonna do it to Them. Never let Them, male animal, to know: that you're gonna do it to Them. That you know."

"Know what?"

"That you're the logical one. Not Them. That you're gonna pull an end run. *You* know They're totally controlled by Their feelings. But *They* don't. They think They're the ones that's totally logic. That They know: everything."

"So?"

"So, keep it that way. Follow Evergreen's lead. Don't tell 'em." She paused for emphasis. "What They don't know? Won't hurt you! Name of the game, sugar."

"We're not married."

"Not right now. But Felipe's sure been talking. How he wants to. And you two been pretty close for over a year now. Everybody knows you two are a Item."

"Evergreen's only, maybe ten, years old. Why should they care about feminism issues?"

"We all got to work to correct the past. Even if we weren't in it directly. So as to make the future different. And it's the future that concerns us." She inhaled painfully.

"That what you think?"

"That's what I know, baby doll. Felipe and Project and Alley: for sure anchors around your neck: keep you away from Evergreen. And your career. It's up to you. Not you or me wants any sticky stuff happening. Dicey." Her upper lip flared slightly. "So? You see the road ahead of you, girl! Now? So? Make tracks!"

# *CHAPTER XXXVI*

## *Discussion*

"Hey man! I wish I had one as big as that. Hot dude!"

They appeared fascinated, watching AP Brampton Falange manipulate the massive gold nugget ring with his left thumb; at the same time, with his right forefinger and thumb, self-consciously, massage a turquoise and silver bolo.

"And check out that Rolex! Looks totally important! Musta had a sale at Rite-Aid?" Guffaws and horse laughs, somewhat muted, punctuated the back slapping, general camaraderie, and dragging of chairs into position.

Brampton's voice rose self-consciously, "I think all of us should be about ready? To begin? Time is of the essence, my friends. With that in mind, we'll be doing a mind share about how Reform Plan will help us here at Fillmore High School."

"Is this covered in the Ed Code?"

"Right on! Yeah! Section 6969?" A group of stragglers convulsed at their own humor, enjoying the approbation of two ladies flanking them.

"Thank you everyone for your insights." Falange continued, ignoring the comments. "I know our Reform Plan will put us on the cutting edge of school reform. I know it's been on everybody's mind since we were challenged by that super spectacular elucidation by Mr. Peter Pritchard way back, now, when was it? Last September? As I recall? And I know all of us can remember that? And how we all did a mind connect about it? At that time! And since? Mr. Pritchard, plus our esteemed Dr. Jones-Laporte, is one of our distinguished guests here with us today? No! Reform Plan, and I know Mr. Pritchard will correct me if I'm not one hundred percent precise on this topic, since he's the obvious expert; no, Reform Plan is about our *future*." He smiled smugly. "But, *but*, and here's the bottom line: how new is this future going to be? The sixty-four dollar question! We don't want to be walking the plank into the future. Not to make us forget what our achievements has been so far. You guys done pretty darn good so far." His smile resembled a sneer: "Needless to say we're still a *darn* good school! I don't care what you say! We're the best. And anybody who doesn't think that, well, maybe they'd better take out membership in the Bogon club!" [31]

"Reform not need to reinvent the wheel."

"Thank you Mr. Warfles: the heroism of what our teachers been doing for donkey's years." Falange continued. "Now folks, first off! I know you can all say how you're birded out by end of the year extra work—exams, grading them, general clean up, and even from thinking so much about Reform Plan!" He alone, laughed at his own joke. "OK! But! And I know we don't want to bunny hop the separate city idea. No! Not at all. I encourage you to bear with me just through this—hopefully last—meeting, so's we can all figure out the benefits of Reform Plan and so's we'll know how to vote at the final Board meeting. In three weeks time! So's we can come to finalization. Finally! So, folks. Now's the time to say what you gotta say. About Reform."

"Go for it, Brampton!"

"O-o-o-K! We're in a fact-finding mode. Let's to start off our mind share? Quay-sh-t-ion? Vangie? Ms. Stillcart?" He bobbed his head mechanically, tongue depressed against upper teeth, jaw rigid, eyes roaming the ceiling.

"No more havin' plug and play dorks outsiders tryin' to come in an tell us how to teach. Focus Walks? Hocus pocus?"

"Say it girl!" Feet stomped the floor in approbation.

"You're on a arrow course there, Vange. Go for it! Stay on top, girl!"

There was a muffled groan as Sandra Weatherby waved her hand. "May I say something?" Falange shrugged his shoulders skeptically and lifted a pointed chin toward her, the corners of his mouth turned down.

31 Bogon: slang: a person who is bogus or who says bogus things.

She spoke quietly and rapidly. "What I've seen is a brochure, some generalized TV interviews, and Mr. Pritchard's generalized overview. But I haven't heard details: the precise nature of the reforms. Who will do what? Nothing about plans: costs: goal setting, accountability, projected results, time tables. Let me ask this! Is there anyone in this room who knows the specific issues? What will be 'reformed'? And how?"

"What specifics, Miss?"

"Will Reform reevaluate Dropouts? Academic curriculum? Level of teaching? Assessment tools? Discipline? Teacher selection? Teacher evaluation? Open discussion about the school budget? Role of parents? Accountability of administrators? Of teachers? Of students? Consequences? Community, parent participation? Dropout prevention. Safety? Academics? Job training? A Nursery? These are a few. Seems to me Reform Plan should have made clear how it will address these problems."

Millicent Pimmentade interrupted stridently. "Problems is your definition! We all have the same information, Miss! The problems will be corrected on a 'need to know' basis. As we sift our way through the maze. What's not to understand? About that?"

Sandra smiled at her interlocutor. "Thanks, sweetie. But that's not quite enough. Let me restate on a second grade level what I just said. Reform Plan says it wants Change. Teachers say they want Change. But nobody says what kind of Change. Wanting Change but not saying what kind of Change, the specifics, is gobbledy-gook. Non-Speak. 'Change' *per se* means progress? Absurd!"

"I agree, Ms. Weatherby." Mr. Mugwabe was grouped with Sandra, Huerta, Gibbs, Bourda, Besserian.

"It will look at what it needs to look at." Roxanne Turner moved uncomfortably in her chair."

"Frankly, I'm confused. Do we know or don't we? *Quamquam nonnuli sunt in hoc ordine, qui aut ea quae imminent non videant, aut ea quae vident, dissimulent.*"[32] Perplexed, Cyril Jacobs threw threw out his arms, palms up, in consternation. "Vote? On what?"

"Good boy, Milton. Tell it, guy! You know, folks, There's rumors that Reform Plan somehow—don't know the details—might be going to give special benefits—like money—to some teachers? They're the ones that's going to be taken care of. The rest of us? That's a different story." Roger Mulhausen, Computers I, was skeptical.

32 Cicero: *Oration against Catiline*. Book XII. "*Are there not some in this council who, either do not see what is imminent, or who do see it, but deny it?*"

"Say it, Roge, boy! Scuttlebutt flying all over the place about secret codes? And special funds of money? This stuff about teachers involved in businesses? How about the one who started it. Him tell us! He on 'ah-fence' or 'de-fence'? Or maybe it's that he's tryin' to snag an end run on Reform? On helpin' kids? For himself? To get a AP?"

The room was silent. Besserian looked straight ahead. Then at his accuser. He sat back in his seat. "Mr. Mulhausen, I'm not surprised that this issue has come up. Naturally, you're concerned. Yes, you're owed an explanation."

"May I interrupt here? As a visitor?" Pritchard, nodding to Jones-Laporte, assumed his regal height. "Ladies and gentlemen. Let me say that it was generous of Mr. Besserian to give much of his own time to this Project. An interesting harbinger of the kind of future the Reform Plan will effect in our school—and which we all want."

"Now, it seems there may be a possibility, albeit remote, that out-of-the-ordinary information may, let me emphasize, *may,* have been what? Discovered? If so, certainly, it does need to be reviewed. If I might suggest, as an outsider? That Mr. Besserian make known, privately, to the appropriate persons, whatever information he may have: uncovered? In that way we can protect student confidentiality—always our paramount concern. Later, and I am sure his information will be routine, not inflammatory, it will be disseminated to our faculty. Would that be acceptable to you, sir? Private discussion? In the interest of safeguarding the confidentiality of students?"

Sandra Weatherby, reached over and touched Besserian's hand. He spoke cautiously. "Sure. I'll accept your word that after a private discussion, there will be public disclosure. Of the facts."

"This stuff has got our kids confused and scared! Teachers too! And parents! Secret codes? Money amounts. Sounds like 007 stuff."

"Right! Fillmore-gate!"

Dr. Jones-Laporte broke her customary disdainful silence. "Once again, it seems we have Mr. Pritchard to thank for assisting us with a solution." She smiled hugely at the guest. "Sir, we are most appreciative. Indebted."

Narda Teklebrahan, Spanish II, raised her hand tentatively. "I was thinking. Something? In order for Reform to be successful, doesn't it have to be placed in the framework of the overall culture?"

"Better explain that, sweetie. Or else you're going to lose us."

"I'll try. Somebody was talking about code? Our education system should lead the world? Hasn't happened. In fifty years. So, maybe we need to look deeper? If that's what we really want?"

Arvetis Jamgotchian interrupted. "Whatever happens, we sure don't want it to hook our pay to what kids don't know on tests. That idea sucks! If that's what you mean, sweetie, forget you!"

"Yeah, that would be like letting kids write our paychecks. Or do the hiring and firing! For the birds, man!" Dolores Lomerdosi, Grade 10 Counselor, reiterated the thought.

"Education should be independent thinking. But it really means conformity. Code for sameness. I mean does this government really want people who disagree with the ones in power? Be critical of them? People who say it's not the best of all possible worlds but let's make some changes? So it could be?"

"Your point, miss?" Falange was peeved.

"I agree, one hundred percent, Narda: Ms. Teklebrahan." Mr. Mugwabe interrupted. "Our Reform Plan needs to do just that: cut down the cultural weathervane. Run up our own flag—our Standards—on our own flagpole."

"Specifics? OK." Narda seemed irritated with Falange. "One example. Gender equality. The reality? Boys don't get equal SAT training: if any. Don't get special help with college applications. Hardly get any scholarships. Literature that stresses not the equality of the sexes but male inferiority."

She continued. "Decode public education: diversity means low-level sameness. Kids won't drop out if they're successful. If they're not successful, maybe it's not their fault. Maybe our fault. We need to provide other programs: technical; job training; art; auto repair and body work; cosmetology, construction: allow kids to utilize personal skills and talents. Education needs to validate learning modalities in addition to reading."

"Folks, time running out! Seems there's a group that not want to jump on the bandwagon! For reform! And we'll be conferencing with them."

Narda ignored him. "Our Reform Plan needs to provide alternative programs for differences: differences in intellect, psychology, talent, skills, personal background. Reform needs to place students where they can be, want to be, successful. Not pretend they're all exactly the same. This is done, not by lowering standards for everyone, but by providing appropriate programs allowing for differences. This culture equates 'difference' with 'inferior'. Not true! Result? Perpetuates the inferiority it claims to disavow.

Obviously we're doing something wrong with a fifty percent drop-out rate and turning out graduates who are marginally literate."

"So, you sayn' all kids shouldn't go to college?"

"Good point. Excellent. What is college? Its reality! A lifetime of debt? Political conditioning and values conformity. A four year play pen? Where an "A" means average? No marketable skills? Not courses in Mathematics, Engineering? Physics? Literature? History? Accounting? Instead? Courses like 'Finding Your Sexual Identity'."

"Damm, man. You want to reinvent the wheel: set up a new kind of public education system? Might just as well to say our democracy's no good! Not the best in the whole world. What kind of Commie terrorist are you, anyway?"

"Everybody's getting kind of philosophical here. Let's cut to the quick guys! There's just no use in us talking about any kind of reform without first—now lemme just drop a rock in the bucket here and let it splash—talkin' turkey. Salary increases! That's what the union is for." Bruce Warfles was indignant.

Peter Czerney was restive. He brushed the top of his moist skull with a sweaty forearm. "We got to do what we got to do. We sure don't want to put our shorts in the washer and find out that we don't have any more in the drawer? I mean, to wear? I mean; we're the ones down in the trenches. Day by day! Reform has to look after us. So we can look after kids."

The door banged open. Jesus Gutierrez stood looking intently, searching the faces. Sighting his objective he pushed past the clustered desks, knocking several of the occupants.

"Hey! Watch it there, boy. You kids not running the school yet."

He whispered desperately. "Mr. Besserian. You gotta come! Something terrible's happened. It's Felipe. Real bad." Jesus bent close to his ear.

Besserian started from his seat. "I need to leave Mr. Falange. An emergency. Mr. Pritchard, I'll call your secretary!"

**************************************************

"Something about Sandra. His girl!"

"Good job, partner. Thanks for getting me." Sprinting through the hospital entrance, ignoring the guard, he thumped Jesus on the shoulder.

They barged out of the elevator. "Just down there, Mr. B. On the left! Number Seven-Twenty-One. I'll wait here."

The semidarkness of the room didn't hide the patient's ashen pallor. Felipe opened his eyes slightly wider in greeting, attempting a smile. "Hey, coach." He tried to lift his head. "Glad you could make it. Thanks."

"What happened?"

"Not that much. You could say I got my arm caught in a meat grinder. Nothing serious."

Besserian pulled a chair from the wall and sat beside him. He touched his shoulder. "But you're OK? Now?"

"Yeah. Sure. I couldn't let you have to carry off that wedding. Not by yourself. Without your favorite saxophone player. And you can't wind up the Project all by yourself, either."

Besserian could only move his head in acknowledgement.

Felipe turned away and then back. His eyes were red. "I made a mistake, Mr. B. Big time. Did it to myself."

"You're not the first guy who's made a mistake, buddy."

Felipe exhaled. "Like this? Mine? I guess you got it figured out. Already. You always got things figured out. Like you can see inside other people's brains."

"Not really."

Felipe waited, as if unsure of his emotions. "She told me I was like, blocking her career? That she wanted that scholarship and there was no way she was gonna marry me. Ever."

He struggled for the words. "I was in the way. Of her career." He choked. "Mr. B. I told her I'd wait. However long. That could give us time to get to know each other better. Figure out how to help her career."

"That was the wrong thing to say?" His eyes motioned to Besserian who handed him the water glass from the side table, bracing his neck, placing the straw in his mouth. "It was a bummer? To say? Because she got real nasty, like I was some sort of creep. And said she was tired of me always pestering her. When anybody else would have figured out that she wanted to get away from me. Figured it out long time ago."

He fell back on the pillows. "That she had wanted to for a long time. And she knew I was a guy and guys are always so 'dependant' and 'emotional'. 'Cause of male ego being so fragile. She said I fell out of her plan book." He motioned again for the glass and lifted his hand slowly to brush a fleck of dust from his eyes.

"I wanted us to be married; like in secret. She said too risky. 'Cause if they found out they could get their money back. Anyway, I was too immature. Self-centered. And hard for musicians to get a steady job."

"Rest. For a minute. Maybe easier to tell me later. If you want?"

His eyes welled and he looked away. "It hurts. Mr. B. It hurts so bad. My wrist, arm, hurts like hell, too. But not so much as I do. Inside. Wish I coudda been better. Stronger?" His eyes found Besserian. "Like you are." He wiped his eyes. "Guess I was stupid but I thought I mattered. Like she did to me. That I was good enough. But I'm not."

"You're good enough." Besserian gripped his hand, then placed it on the sheet. Neither man spoke. He watched Felipe's suffering, wanting to take it from him. "You're good enough, buddy. More than good enough."

"Anyhow, it's done. But I feel so empty. Like there's nothing inside me. Like I'm nothing. I mean Mr. B I been lying here and I haven't even got a . . . you know the stuff guys think about? Thoughts? And usually they're all over me. You know what I mean. It's like I'm . . . hollow. Or something. Changed into a different person. But I don't know what kind. I guess I was more, well, close to her, Mr. B than I ..." His voice faltered and he turned away. "What about all the good times we had? Supposed to forget them?"

Besserian took the glass and placed it on the table.

"Now, I see this was a really stupid thing to do."

"I'm glad you screwed it up, buddy."

"I piss you off? Sometimes? Being late. Being a wise-ass? Sometimes in class? I guess me and some of the guys like to see you get angry. I guess I really am immature? Not ready for marriage?"

Besserian said nothing. He watched him and shook his head, slowly, negatively.

"I guess I like to screw around sometimes. But basically? Mr. B, I don't think I'm that immature. Maybe a little. Not all the time?" He looked directly at his teacher. "Mr. B, she told me her career had to come first. And her scholarship, well, put me out of the running."

"I was so tore up inside. Like she was ramming my stomach through the shredding machine? It was like she pushed the button and turned it on and, well, there was like, nothing I could do. It was like she grabbed me and was pushing me in. And it hurt. God! It sure did! Being cut up into pieces: shredded. I got dumped. Shit-canned. Like scrap paper."

"You love her."

He winced. "Yeah. But the worse thing! Mr. B you know what the worse thing about it was? She said I brought it on myself. That I didn't have love for her. Didn't know what love was. What I called love was really my own ego. Needed somebody to protect. Somebody to be smaller and weaker than me. And she said she wasn't like that. That she was stronger and more powerful, and more intelligent than I could ever be."

It was pointless to conceal the tears and Felipe let them roll down his face. Besserian fumbled for the handkerchief in his back pocket. It was rumpled but he found a clean section, to trace the watery tracks back to their source.

"Guys are weak as water's what she said. All guys."

Besserian found a confusion of thoughts coming to mind. He didn't say anything.

Felipe turned his face away, wincing at the pain and then looked back at his visitor. "Somebody put those ideas in her head. She didn't used to be like that. I felt like she was a stranger. Guess she'd laugh to see me now. The mess I got myself into." He convulsed in a huge sob that he tried to hold back. "She got me on the ropes, Mr. B. Kicked my ass." He turned to the other man. "I don't understand. Why? What did I do?"

Besserian spoke slowly. "You have feelings. You're not afraid to show them. That's not being immature. Being vulnerable *is* maturity. Taking the risk. That's courage. Strength." Besserian pulled his chair closer. "You're still in the ring. You're not down yet, buddy. And you're not going to go down. Let the ropes hold you for a minute. Brace yourself on them. Use them to pull yourself up. You're not going down, Champ. Nobody can hurt you. Not anymore, they can't." He leaned still closer. "Listen to me. Nobody can hurt you like that. Ever again. Never. Because you're going to survive this. You're a fighter. You're strong."

He shifted in his chair. The room was quiet and the thoughts rushed at him. The light was subdued with a constant low hum of traffic from below. He saw that his friend was dozing. And he touched, for a second, the fingers below the bandaged wrist.

He was running, terrified, scrambling on the soft earth of a bridle path in a large city park. He thought he was alone. But then he saw, as he looked around terrified. They were pursuing him. Thundering down on him. He tried to run faster but his feet were being pulled down by the weight of the deep, soft earth. Two mounted riders, in tank tops and jocks, were bearing down on him. At full gallop. He couldn't go faster: the earth was too soft. It kept pulling down his feet, ensnaring him. They were gaining on him. He could feel the thunder in the earth. He knew it was inevitable. What had he done? Why him? Who were they? And then he saw a female figure, standing among the trees framing the path. He reached out his hand. To have her pull him off the path. He couldn't see who it was. He called to her for help. Her eyes were sad as if she wanted to help. But she remained motionless, moving her head as if to say, 'I can't'.

Maybe it was the aftermath of the stress. He had dozed; how long he didn't know.

Probably only a few minutes because Felipe was speaking in a monotone, watching the ceiling. "Sometimes in class Mr. B? I used to watch you. I think some of the other kids did too. Guys *and* girls. It was like you had a struggle with something. Kids wanted to help you. Knew it was important to you. Like you were trying to give us something that was important to you. A part of yourself. Even before the Project. And we wanted to give back some parts of ourselves. But we didn't know how."

"You did. You gave me a lot. More than I have a right to."

"I just keep seeing her, all huddled up on that bench, spitting at me like a alley cat, where I pushed her? And she screamed at me how she'd told about the code. So'd she could get the scholarship. And didn't care what happened to you. Or the Project. Or me. I think she wanted me to hit her. But you know? Then? I didn't want to. I saw her different. Like a stranger. That I didn't know? And there was no reason to hit somebody I didn't know."

They waited in silence. Besserian clasped Felipe's hand firmly. He was thinking of what he had to do. "I'm going now, buddy. Be back tomorrow." He clasped him on the shoulder. "You'll make it. I need you for the wedding. And when they vote on the Reform plan. Need you there, too. For me."

"Mr. B. Come here would you? For a minute?" Besserian moved to lower the shade and mask the late afternoon sun. "It's OK. Not bothering me. You know I was thinking. And I don't want you to take this the wrong way. Sometimes, you get real uptight about sh . . .stuff?"

"I do?"

"Yeah. Really. Me, and a couple of the guys, we felt sometimes like, well, almost like wanting to see if we could deck you. Take you? But it was like, only guy talk. We didn't mean it. Really. I mean not all that much."

Besserian exhaled, nodding slowly, self-confidently, lower lip imperceptively extended. "You'll get your chance. Once you get up out of that bed. We'll go to *Deuce is Wild*." He smiled. "That is if you think you're man enough."

"Don't have to worry about that." He smiled his old grin. For the first time.

---

# CHAPTER XXXVII

## *Reälpolitik*

"Delighted we bumped into him: Dr. Barclay? If only briefly. Possibly you are unaware? He is one of our newer members. Alas, I have not seen him for. . .", Peter shrugged, palms upward, ". . . perhaps six months?" He tapped the other man's arm. "I sponsored him for membership. Here. He is doing quite well. For himself." Nudging his guest's elbow, Pritchard indicated the stairway: unusual red marble, veined with white. "Yes, quite well. It seems he retired as Assistant Superintendent of the Santa Rosales School District: is now their financial consultant. Investments. I believe his retirement income is something over four hundred and eighty annually. Thousand, that is. It seems his regular retirement is not reduced because the County considers him a Specialist. And there are a few added benefits: car, expenses, travel, health insurance, entertaining. That sort of thing."

He was relaxed. "I am so glad you were available. You left the meeting quickly. Last week? You had an emergency? I hope everything goes well? At home? With your work?"

"Everything's fine. At home."

"Excuse me, but, if you will permit me, you seem to be looking a mite, what, puzzled? Dr. Barclay, perhaps?" He was affable. "Most people are unaware how lucrative education can be. For school administrators: those willing to play the game astutely. Ally themselves with the right people: powerful people who can help them up the ladder; as it were. And negotiate the politics: especially the gender and race games. On their behalf. Open the right doors." He smiled. "You know, Mr. Besserian, in the business world, only those very near the top rung of the ladder will be as comfortable in their retirement as Barclay." He watched his guest attentively. "So, yes indeed, it is possible. To do well for oneself."

He motioned with his arm. "In any case, to your right, at the top of the landing. More comfortable than the Drawing Rooms. Or library. More private." Peter almost grinned. "A drawback, of management, is that people are forever clawing at one for decisions: asking for help for things they cannot do for themselves. Or will not do. And that can be tiresome. It takes away from planning: professional strategies, personal strategies. We won't be interrupted here."

The broad stairs, carpeted in rose, had brought them to the colonnaded gallery. "This will be very private." The gallery quadrangle, a vaulted cloister framing the cavernous atrium, had recesses that projected into the expanse below. The bays were sequestered between the upper quadrants of the pink granite Corinthian columns. The intricate design of the bronze gilt balustrades obscured the view from below.

"Will you take a drink?"

"Perhaps. Later. Thank you."

He nodded his guest into the alcove at the far side of the landing. They settled into the soft lighting, seclusion, and winged-back chairs, each with mahogany side table.

"Good evening, Mr. Pritchard."

"Oh! Good evening, Hampton." Obviously pleased to see the uniformed attendant who had appeared from nowhere, he spoke graciously. "My Reserve? Please." He nodded to Besserian, "This is my special mark."

Besserian shrugged, "How can I refuse?"

The servant inclined his head. "Very good, sir. Will the gentleman have ice?"

Peter nodded inquisitively to Besserian. "Yes, please. Thank you." Hampton bowed and retired solemnly. "A rare specimen. A disappearing breed. Like so much in our culture." Peter unbuttoned the jacket of his impeccable, brown pin-stripe. "I keep special vintages and malts here. For particular guests. Who appreciate the finer things."

"It is always a pleasure to meet a teacher. In person. Make the acquaintance of someone who chooses to stay with children. Sidestep the unpleasantly competitive business world. Or, its rewards. But, I suppose, we are all students. Continually acquiring new information. In one form or another? About different areas?"

"Maybe." Besserian stiffened. "As for sidestepping unpleasantness? This club seems quite an effective shelter from, as you call it, 'the world'? With its unpleasantness?" He adjusted into the chair. "Mr. Pritchard, when I called your secretary, I expected to invite you."

"Nonsense. When we can come here? Private. No interruptions. What is a club for? If not for genteel conversation? Among friends? I thank you for your thoughtfulness, nevertheless. In any case, this is where I am comfortable. Restaurants, bars, are no longer permitted to be private. Not the way they once were. All too often, one is expected to endure the cackling, raucous laughter of, well, let us say, *other* kinds of people? In any case, you strike me as someone who would appreciate this environment. Mr. Besserian, if I may make a somewhat personal observation, I believe this is the proper *milieu*. For you." Exuding congeniality, he settled back in his chair. "Now, down to work! Mr. Besserian, I know what you want to say."

"You do?"

"Um-m-m. Surely, you knew that."

"No."

Now the smile was enigmatic. "Oh! Hampton! Wonderfully speedy you are! Just leave it. If you would. We will make do by ourselves. With the ice. For Mr. Besserian." He inclined an index finger, "Thank you. So much."

He raised the heavy crystal tumbler, eyes sparkling. "Your health, Mr. Besserian. And long life. And success. Professional. And personal." He touched his lips to the crystal waiting for the cautious, then surprised, nod of assent. "Splendid. I knew you would appreciate it. Aged, I believe, twenty years? Well! To you! So? You wish to discuss the coded information you found. Dash interesting, this business. Imagine! Code!"

Besserian almost stammered, "By accident we came upon . . ."

"Please! Allow me, if you would, sir." He leaned forward. "You found names: of businesses and individuals—teachers, administrators, board members—associated with those businesses. These are the business 'advisors'. The monetary amounts are their yearly stipends: for placing the reform projects—equipment, services, whatever is needed—with these businesses."

Besserian was astonished, "Yes. That's what we found."

"Jones-Laporte? She already has an additional one hundred and fifty thousand annually from book publishers. Why stop there! Rank has its privileges? Make sure she stays in the right camp? Mine. But you! To have recognized the *Vigenère Tableau* and then to have reconstructed the six and then seven letter Keys! Deucedly cleaver of you, I must say. I take my hat off to you, sir. I do indeed. Uncovered my recommendations to Baques for the faculty Senate and the Business Advisory positions."

Besserian stared incredulously. "This information suggests that you'll control the school Reform Plan. It's a money making plan for you. Lots of money. Don't you own these businesses?"

"For all practical purposes."

"The education budget is siphoned through the businesses: to you!"

"And with separate incorporation of Cathedral Heights, much of the municipal budget as well. Siphoned?" He smiled. "The businesses provide the services. The equipment. At a profit. Of course."

"So reform means what? No reform?"

"The *extent* of the Reform, sir? There well may be *some*! Reform. Controlled. I am not averse to that. For example, I can foresee a significant contract with *Red Lion Plumbing*—one of Mr. Warfles' bailiwicks, I believe—to repair the school restrooms. I believe they are unusable now? That is not reform?"

"No. Reform must address why students destroy their own environment. *Red Lion* will be needed almost full time. Thousands of dollars. Per month. You have a vested interest in perpetuating restroom destruction." Besserian was incredulous.

Peter shrugged and dismissed the reaction with a wave of his hand.

"And these businesses? You claim they will be minority owned? From what I've . . ."

"You have an amazing fount of inside information. With EduCom, it appears? But leave that aside. For the nonce. Let me be candid. Minority businesses do not have to bid competitively. Also, as far as the public is concerned, Reform, as the staunch upholder of Diversity, minority rights, naturally will prefer our local businesses. Minority businesses." He shrugged. "Point made?"

"And I've found out that you finance the start-up costs. Interest bearing loans. And, thereafter you take a share of the profits, determined exponentially by the profits. So, the businesses aren't really minority owned. They're franchises. You get most of the profits for the next thirty years. And you're paid: for the franchises."

"How else are these people going to be able to get out of the menial jobs lack of education has forced them into?"

"Amazing. Publication of this so called Reform Plan? People will reject it for the opportunistic scheme it is."

Pritchard savored the drink. "A tad more? One can almost taste the heather of the highlands. Very fine, indeed. No. Mr. Besserian, they will not reject it. Or me. They will reject you."

"Me?"

"Quite. You want to take away from teachers: what? A *de facto* salary increase of twenty percent? Perhaps more? Free of state budgets? Of the caprice of the state legislature? Not dependent on student test results. And: free of accountability? For student achievement?"

Besserian stared at him, speechless.

"A compliant administration: LaPorte, Baques? Those incompetents? Can muddle through because the Teachers Union will be effectively, what? Disengaged? Any *soi-disant* 'critics' of our Reform Plan will be denied the 'advisors' stipend. Administrators gain not only financially. They garner a *de facto* absolute authority: that of the purse. Recalcitrant teachers? Obdurate? Quarrelsome? Otiose from the standpoint of Reform? That will cease. Why? Dissidents are excluded from the stipends."

"They'll be a government inquiry."

"Only to laud me. And the Advisor appointees. Criticize me? Reform? When taxes are reduced! At the same time teachers are paid more!" He permitted himself a wry smile. "Admittedly *selected* teachers! The local school district pulls itself up by its bootstraps, does not ask for more taxes: and pays our long-suffering, dedicated teachers *more*! Is that not reform? Also, our Reform creates *more* jobs for minorities. I elevate them to 'management'. No. I will be applauded as the savior of education. If I am not careful I could be selected as Secretary of Education." He smiled hugely. "Just joking. The greatest political power is wielded by the puppeteer. Never the puppet."

"So, you think teachers will accept your Reform Plan?"

Pritchard squinted incredulously. "I know so. And, I have the culture behind me."

"Your Reform will destroy public education."

"How naïve you are, sir. Typical academic. Liberal. You are unaware that educational values always—since the inception of this culture based on capitalism—have been disguised—encoded. Look at the facts: the enduring current of anti-intellectualism. The distrust of academics. Of academicians? Tolerated, yes. But! Only so long as they do not cause too much mischief. So long as they do not upset the financial cauldrons of Wall Street. Me, for example. So long as 'educators' stay, carping, mindlessly, behind the ivy covered walls of their wood paneled, oriental carpeted prisons. Obscenely overpaid: so long as they do the bidding—under the guise of being critical—of the corporate, industrial class. Again, me."

Pritchard held the tumbler to the light allowing the facets to gleam. "Academics with their tiresome quarrels about the inconsistency of freedom and democracy with slavery, Native people, limited or no health care, no retirement plans, minority rights: all that? Schools? Universities? They serve as a fatuous Hyde Park Corner. Let them rant. It appears to be 'healthy' disagreement." He paused. "Actually now, with six figure salaries for academics, the bait of White House luncheons, lucrative government appointments, research grants? Wrangling by 'intellectuals' about the Wall Street ethic, has all but disappeared."

Peter was garrulous. "You, sir, do not understand the *reality* of Education. It, like Democracy, is encoded. What it says and what it means: the *reality*, are quite different."

"People won't . . ."

"Hear me. Please, sir! Education! It is presented as a portal leading to intellectual and material enrichment. Predominately, now, the latter, to be sure. A portal through which anyone can enter?" He shook his head. "Not exactly. True! It is a portal. But only for the *selecti quidem.*[33] My class. For the majority, including the naïve middle class, to which you belong, and certainly for the *hoi poloi*[34], 'minorities', it is a revolving door. Spinning around in a blur to hide how it only propels people back from whence they came. To perpetual debt—the cost of the insipid college non academic, politically correct courses like 'Reaching One's Own Persona' or 'Fanny Mendelssohn and Clara Schumann: Obscured by Gender'. Pseudo education which enfeebles. Makes the word 'student' a misnomer: code for intellectually sedated. Result? They're happy with what they don't know. But not as happy as I am."

"Some students study Physics, Literature, Mathematics, . ."

"Some. *Some.* Precisely my point. Of course! Members of my class. Or those we select. Not everyone. There are colleges within colleges. There are students and students. Student Alphas and student Gammas. Diplomas *look* the same. But are not."

---

33 *Selecti quidem*: select few.

34 *Hoi poli*: the common people.

He continued. "And underlying that? Greed. The *hoi poloi* have been taught, through the media—owned by my class—and have accepted: what? My philosophy, the philosophy of my class, the industrial moneyed class: Self-interest and Pleasure. It has been ingrained into this culture. Permeates it? Saturates it? People, the 'little' people, *menu peuple*, have accepted the Greed Culture because they seek to mimic their betters—as I say, the *selecti quidem*—like me. They think it, greed, will give them a life of ease, pleasure. Even power. They think, so far as they think at all, that because greed gives *me* power and wealth, luxury and pleasure, it will give it to them as well. And, to some extent, only to the extent that my class permit, they are correct. *And*, so long as they are cooperative with my plans. I, we, allow them superficial perks: like the Advisory posts you decoded. And the 'things' they are allowed to purchase at the ubiquitous malls, owned by my class: enormous television sets, technological gadgets, pornography, sex aids, food, alcohol. And drugs. The ubiquitous 'appliances'. They give up their freedom to think, their humanity, in exchange for these toys. In summary, their dependency on these toys makes them dependent on me."

"People are not so . . ."

"Mr. Besserian: yes! They are! Please allow me to continue. Having given up the freedom to think independently—and by now, with our depleted education system, also having given up the ability to think critically—to struggle, to expand their intellectual horizons, to challenge the cultural values imposed on them—to analyze, understand, the reality around them—having given all that up, education, as *you* wish to 'reform' it, is . . . Irrelevant. 'Education' has conditioned the masses to prefer the revolving door. Number One it is hidden, masked, encoded. Number Two: it is less risk, easier... than thinking, certainly achieving, by themselves. Result: an 'A' in a college course is, in reality, what? Average! Everyone passes? Think again. The reality: no one passes. But they don't know it."

"My Reform will give them the type of education they want. Really want. Coded, of course. Because they cannot face the reality of their dependency. On my class. And they will reject your offer to 'save' them from me. My class. Why? Because it—your type of education—requires people to acknowledge values they have now repudiated. Values about which, by now, they are largely ignorant and which are, therefore, useless to them: specifically hard work and possible failure, commitment, consequences, the inequality of talent and motivation. Most especially, Risk: of failure.

Accountability. Struggle. Responsibility for themselves. For their own actions."

"In short, people don't want your type of education. They don't want education 'reformed' or its values changed back to what they once were. No, your type of idealized reform will require them to give up the hollow, politically correct, vapid, type of 'easy' education that flatters them: perpetuates their ignorance. That has made the school into a nursery, a play-pen, filled with toys. The toys of Diversity, gender equality—in fact gender superiority—Victimhood, rejection of the western culture in favor of minority non-cultures, minority rights and many others, that my class have assiduously strewn in their playpens. Toys which now they are carrying into the post secondary educational institutions, the so-called institutions of 'higher' learning as they 'deconstruct', read destroy, the original values and content of 'Traditionalist'—sound familiar—education? But they are too self-serving to know that. To care."

"Mr. Besserian, let us speak candidly. I have carried the liberalism of the '70's to its logical conclusion. So, the reform you want, and expect, is *not* attractive to them. To you, perhaps! But not to them! Your reform model is incompatible with the philosophies of greed. Of Pleasure. Of Safety. Here is the critical point which the masses cannot, do not, understand: yes, my class practice those philosophies. But! We, not the *hoi poloi*, *control* them. For our advantage. Also: your reform is incompatible with *hoi poloi* toys: again those my class have given them precisely to hide the reality that we, my class, control the culture, a control which, by the way, we will never give up. Token concessions? Of course. To retain our power."

"Won't give up?"

"Absolutely. Because the real 'code': Minorities as Victims, Minority Rights, Gender Equality, Feminism, Ecology, Save the Whales, Global Warming: *ad infinitum?* We *give* them these toys—in fact inconsequential—not to raise them up as they imagine, but to keep them down. People—single parents *et al*—actually believe their lot is being improved! Of course, we give *token* executive jobs: some jobs. Outrageously over paid, to which we point with pride. And why? Code. Because our message of repression—Metternichian, return to the *status quo ante bellum*—of keeping power for ourselves is encoded? In Political Correctness toys. What could be better? On goes the dance! So to speak."

"They have accepted the philosophy and the toys. Therefore they will repudiate your 'exposé'. Of me. They need *me*. Not you, Mr. Besserian!" He shrugged. "Rather than admit their own complicity? Rather than repudiate me, the source of their creature comforts, they will repudiate *you*. And why? Because ultimately, in effect, to reiterate, you are requiring them to take responsibility for their own success. Or failure. And that, my friend, is the last thing they want. Indeed, the present system of education has already indoctrinated them with, as I said, the twin philosophies of greed and pleasure. With Entitlement. With Victimhood. And by way of drugs, which we also control, of confusing pleasure with happiness."

"And behind that, Mr. Besserian? Power, the real power, as I said, continues to be held by the ruling class. My class. Nothing changes. The system *appears* to change. Of course. *In order to ensure that it does not change*. Hence, the codes of Political Correctness. The reality remains. And what is that? As the masses capitulate to the ethos of greed they are sucked into my orbit. Snagged to do my bidding in the Pleasure nets thrown out by my class—the ruling class—that small group of power mongers: political, Wall Street moguls—Churches too, by the way—like me. Whom they have been conditioned to deny exist. Which, of course, is fine. They cannot criticize, excoriate, *decode*, what does not exist. What is invisible."

"You think people are essentially craven? Self-serving?"

"Recall, if you will, that increased salaries and benefits are the loudest chant at any Reform meeting?" He shrugged. "Put it this way. Tell them Reform will *not* include salary increases, will *not* include financial perks. But *will* demand accountability. For the academic performance of their students. And see how they respond! If they will accept that kind, your kind, of Reform Plan! Let me assure you, sir, they will not."

"*Reälpolitik!*"

"Precisely. A culture built on code does not need, does not want, cannot tolerate—decoding. It does not want substantive criticism. Analysis of reality. So? Why should it educate, train people to be critics? To decode? No, let them wave their flags. Support wars which make me rich and shatter their hands and legs. And ruin them financially. Destroy their savings. They pay the taxes used to expand my wealth." He shrugged. "No. Give them their huge television sets. Drugs. Pornography. Sexual license. Their distractions: professional athletics. *Reälpolitik* allows me to be the stalwart champion of Gay Rights and AIDS research. Same sex marriages. Choice!" He appeared wistful. "People ask to be imprisoned. So? I provide the prisons. And? Everybody's happy! Except you. Who want to give them something they don't want. Freedom. Because it demands accountability. For their own choices."

Peter looked up, pleased. “Oh, Hampton. So attentive you are. We shan’t need more. Thank you so very much.”

Besserian was silent.

“People like Baques, LaPorte, Turner, Cortère, Brauphman, and the rest? They ‘all have their part to play’ as the poem goes. People like Weatherby, Mugwabe, Huerta, Teklebrahan—and there are quite a few—either won’t stay or will be relegated to teaching remedial courses: have the same impact of those who rant on Hyde Park corner. None.”

“And now, Mr. Besserian. I think we have concluded our business. One question I have for you, if I may?”

“Yes.”

“Mr. Buck Henderson. I understand he has been your what? Mentor? Advising you? Informing you?”

“No. Not really. Were I to get the AP job, perhaps.”

“That, now, may be a moot point.” Pritchard, momentarily, was lost in reflection. “Of no consequence. Anyway. You, sir, have risked a great deal. By coming here. By offering to give me your information. And by hearing mine. I do admire you for that. Confronting me. Brash as it was. Impetuous as it was. You lead me to believe that someone within my organization may be disloyal. To me!”

“Students checked the directories. Records. The owners of the businesses. They stumbled onto the code. Decoded it themselves. No one gave it to us.”

“Indeed. Quite true. But, as you know, the seed of distrust produces a perfidious weed.” He smiled. “In fact, I do find your information disquieting. But not for the reasons you surmised. But come. Let us not degenerate into unpleasantness. This has been delightful. Allow me to escort you down.” He smiled warmly, and placed his arm affably over the other man’s shoulder, nodding behind Besserian’s back to his body-guard, Raoul, looking up from the foot of the stairs.

# *CHAPTER XXXVIII*

## *A Ride Together*

"Not all the way. Today. Got to get back early. Somebody may have told them about the Project. They seemed interested."

"Where?"

"Private school. Indiana. Strong academics. Good faculty." He was calling back over his shoulder. "Great ride. Glad we came out. Beautiful day. You OK?" Besserian turned his head quickly to check his companion.

"Can't hear you. What'd you say? Hang on a minute! What about the AP?" The chain snapped cleanly on the sprocket, and Buck leaned into the handlebars, raising himself high off the seat, driving the pedals hard—angrily, as if punishing them. The gleaming yellow and black racer shuddered: leapt forward.

"Trying to get away from me? Think again, buddy. Take your ass."

"Go for it! Just up ahead. Trees where the road winds around below the hill? Up ahead. Just before Corkscrew. See?"

"You're on!"

Both chains bit into the lowest gear. The yellow and black darted into the lead. "See? Get you, Teach!"

"Shit!" The silver and green overcame the momentum and shot forward. Besserian brutalized the machine. It rocked fifteen degrees, right and left off the central axis as he manipulated his mid section, riding the central bar as if infusing his own physical power.

Gradually, he gained on his rival. The full impact of his effort was exhilarating. He felt unstoppable: shoulder, back, abdominals, arms, all distended, generating power. His brain was supercharged with the physical energy washing back on itself. He was convulsed: with power. Thigh muscles bulging under the stretch fabric, he brought the silver and green abreast of its rival.

Both competitors, arched high off miniscule seats, were straining. There was no need to look: to evaluate the distance. They could feel. The unleashed physical explosion was delirious.

The skin-tight suits melded onto their bodies. Sweat dripped from the gold stubble onto the yellow frame, and from the black stubble onto the silver frame.

Each was isolated, a catalyst apart, yet bound to the other. Imperceptibly, the silver and green pulled abreast; then ahead of its opponent: six inches, eight.

Both combatants were bent low, consumed with determination, squinting to deflect particles flung up from the road; the stinging salt flooding their eyes. The goal, the patch of trees, at the turn, was hurtling toward them. Already Besserian could feel the exhilaration of the win—the climax—the inevitability.

Then he realized. "Holy Mary! Help us!" Not even time to shout a warning. It made no difference in any case. Seconds, fractions of seconds, remained before the impact.

A car: small, powerful, tearing directly toward them. Appearing from nowhere, skidding insanely out of the turn, ripping through its gears. In the middle of the narrow road. Besserian prepared himself. For what? Leap to the side? Impossible. A wall of rock loomed on his right. Dare to cross the left lane? No time! The hurtling projectile, exhaust spewing, reeking the smell of burning rubber, overhead cam roaring, adjusted its sights on the rider.

He braced for the worst. The screaming two-seater was upon him. He clutched the bars, hands frozen. But his thighs had never stopped churning insanely, disassociated from his body, driving into the pedals. He was in some sort of seizure: his limbs disassociated from his brain. And his brain was too terrified to make the hundredth of a second decision to throw himself from the bike with the absurd hope that the inevitable wouldn't happen. The projectile must have been doing ninety.

Incredibly, the inevitable didn't happen! The roaring bullet flashed past: Besserian could feel the speed. He turned immediately as the impact occurred: spattering the yellow and black into the slate wall: ripping, tearing, crumpling.

Terror? Relief? Besserian shook off the seizure, gripping the brakes like a drowning man, tore into a stop, swirling the bike, in a furious vortex of dust, sand and gravel, two hundred degrees. Disbelieving, he struggled to comprehend.

The driver had found his target, made his kill. For a fraction of a second, he paused. Silence. Then, roaring, the machine spun backwards, halted for a five second eternity. In that eternity, Besserian recognized the driver: Raoul, the Pritchard bodyguard. He tore into the clutch, catapulting the machine forward, spitting a fury of gravel. The air reeked of the stench of rubber and exhaust, enveloping the vehicle. The tumult disappeared. Interminably, the cloud of debris cleared. The road was empty.

And silence; total, eerily prolonged. An eternity? Crows, disgruntled by the intrusion into their Sunday morning, cawed their resentment.

Awakened from a nightmare? From some kind of secret place where he shouldn't be? From where he shouldn't look? Couldn't look?

But he had to. Because it wasn't a dream. He had to look at the reality. At first there was the tangle of wreckage. The  strips of yellow and black fabric, and shards of yellow and black metal, rolled, twisted, tangled. The crazily bent rim, still gleaming, where it wasn't crumpled: intermingled with the mangled gear train strewn along the ground.

"Mother of Christ! Help us!"

Straddling his bike, he walked it, awkwardly on the bike shoes, and too slowly, warding off what he did not want to find. A sandy, pebbled apron formed that side of the road. He lay the bike down and edged toward the contorted mass.

He had to look. At what he feared. The mass of his friend, entwined in the metal knot. And he saw from under the mass, the feared stream of dark liquid, a narrow but sinister line, eddying at the toes of his shoes, then moving on, finding its way through the thin layer of sand. He fumbled, not knowing where to start, as if looking for a key to untangle the mass of cloth, skin, bone. His reactions were slow, not wanting to do, not knowing how to do, what he must.

He was able to adjust the arm that was bent at a right angle, pushed up grotesquely under the back. The beautiful body: mangled, as if picked up, bicycle and all, by some enormous creature, lashed against the granite wall, and left. Discarded. Broken.

The familiar sound of the voice revived him. "Yeah! You got it, buddy. Thanks. You got me almost free. But hang on for a minute. Feels like the tire pump or crosspiece or something got rammed up my ass. Into my gut." He winced, contorting his face in pain. "Some shit, eh, buddy!" He waited. "Hey, man! Mr. B?"

"What?"

Buck winced, gulping some air. "Give me a few minutes. Get my breath. Be OK then. Been in worse places. You mind waiting for a couple of minutes?" He looked up confidently. "Till I get up on my feet?"

For answer Besserian eased off the helmet, maneuvering himself into a sitting position, propping his back against the still-intact but careening handlebars, now grotesquely counter-twisted, and placed Buck's head on his thigh. Picking up the helmet, he flung it toward the wall of rock. It bounced, reverberating into the pock-marked asphalt, rolling noisily and stupidly into the ditch.

"My water bottle there? I feel funny. Probably OK. I don't think there's anything broken. But I'm thirsty. See anything? Broken?"

"Broken? Uh! No-o! Not now. Don't think so. But this might hurt you. A little." Besserian positioned his friend's head on the ground, scrambled to his own bike and brought the water. "Here you go, champ. Want me to hold it for you?" He repositioned the other man's head. As he did so, he saw it. The open space, the bloody entanglement of internal organs, scarcely camouflaged by the shirt and shorts—where the stomach and groin should have been.

"Check me out, buddy. Think I'm OK but, well, you never know. Might be worse than we think. Give me a couple of minutes. Then I can beat your ass back down."

"Sure. Right." Besserian leaned over Buck's upper body, tilting his own head exaggeratedly, a pretense of examination, as much to avoid the eyes of his friend—staring upward, riveted on him, burning with trust—as to direct Buck's eyes away from the wound. "Everything checks out. Looking good. Maybe a few cuts. Nothing that can't be taken care of. You'll be back in the gym in no time."

Buck settled back. "Hand's OK. Now. Can settle our disagreement. Whenever you want." He winced. "You know it sort of feels like a dream. Hurts: like comes and goes? Probably means it's not serious. It's good, really. Lying here. Resting my head like this. You don't mind, do you? I mean just for a minute? I'll be up in a minute."

"It's OK. Don't mind."

"Wouldn't want you to get any ideas." He didn't wait for a response. "Hell. Remember when you had to patch up my shorts in the racquetball court? I guess it must have seemed funny. To you? But I was pissed."

"I know you were."

"But you got me something. A towel? Like now! And remember that fight? That was a pisser! When we took those creeps on. With those girls? And you know something?"

"What, buddy."

"I think that one, the butch one? I think she was hot for your ass."

He waited to reply. "Right."

Buck winced and smiled knowingly. "Holy shit. You're as stuck on yourself as, well, . . . Can't believe you, sometimes. Every time I think you can't do something, one way or another, you seem to, well, do it? Guess it comes from hanging with dudes who're stuck on themselves." He gulped some air and swallowed. Then winced: the pain momentarily excruciating. His grip on Besserian's hand was a vice. Besserian had felt the weight before—a playful slap on the back for some achievement; handshake after sparring—but never so intense. So desperate.

"More water?'

"In a minute. Right now, actually I'm kind of comfortable. Here. Pain's slowing down. A bit. Shows what happens when you get mixed up with the wrong kind of guys. You? You need somebody to look after you." He smiled. "You know as often as we've been up here? Biking? I was thinking before, how nice that was. Together."

His eyes surveyed the trees, the noisy birds, a few scampering squirrels, the floating clouds. "I didn't tell you something. Funny? Pritchard called me. Last night. Wanted me to go to Central America. Manage some stuff. And in Europe too. Give up TriDelt. Money was good. Too good. I told him Penny and I had things under control. We'd see what would happen after all this Reform stuff. Bastard may have been suspicious. That I was planning to ease him out. That I had a mole in EduCom. I mean, you didn't know that either."

Besserian adjusted Buck's head on his thigh, moving so it didn't cramp his own legs. "No need to talk now. Until I figure out what to do."

"Hang on! With that. What you doin'?"

"Doing? I'm figuring out what to do."

"Well, don't take too long about it. The way you usually do. About stuff. You don't have to analyze the composition of the tar on the road. Or the angle of elevation between here and the next turn in the road or whatever."

"I don't do that."

"Yeah, you do. Always! Right now, you can just take it easy here. With me. For a minute." Intermittently he dozed. "Funny how different we are. But seem to get along. Most of the time. Unless you get pissed off. At nothing! At least it's never boring. With you. We get into some weird ass scrapes? You and me? Sometimes you make me think of stuff."

"We need to get you some help."

"Hold on. Couple of minutes. I can tell it's goin' to hurt like hell more. If I move. Let's rest. For a minute. I don't think we ever did that?"

"What?"

"Rest. Take a rest together. We were always doing something. We can be together now? And not be doing something?" He tried to inhale but was caught by the searing pain. "I wonder why we didn't. Anyway, then I'll be OK. I can fix my bike and I'll race your ass back to the cars."

They were silent and everything around them was silent. Until the birds started again. And the breeze through the trees.

"You know, big guy? When you brought me home? Back to my pad? After that fight? Remember? I guess this is sort of like bringing me home again." He lapsed into a wearied daze. As if retrieving thoughts stored away, kept, but never expected to be looked at again.

Besserian leaned over, ostensibly to wipe his mouth, "What?"

"Why not? You remember that time? In the restaurant? First time we met? I was a sorta pain in the ass. The usual me. I'll give you that! Shit! Guess we didn't exactly hit it off. Thought you were a real candy ass. You got so pissed at me! Thought you were going to take a swing at me. In fact, wanted you to. Wanted to see you get pissed. Wanted to tangle asses with you. Then, later on? Maybe you, you know, weren't the creep I had thought you were."

"Water?"

"Thanks. And there was the fight. And I guess, sounds weird, but you sort of began to be, well, *my* teacher. Guess we helped each other. Nobody had ever helped me before. Not really. We had to kick each other's asses a few times but that was only to keep things even. Like getting adjusted?"

"And I learned stuff I didn't know. About how, well, what? Teaching. And I began to think maybe teaching was showing people they had power:

they didn't know they had. And *that* was power. Shit, I don't mean I stopped doing all my shit. But I could see you were different. That teaching, good teaching, wasn't a cop out. And maybe I was sort of a teacher, too: with Penny? With the other people at work?" He closed his eyes briefly. "Maybe with you? Even?"

His eyes closed again and he stopped trying to speak. Besserian watched keenly, prepared for the inevitable, but knowing that preparation was impossible. Besserian had never realized the blueness of Buck's eyes: translucent, shimmering. Buck squinted in pain and, opening them slightly, extended his arm, grasping Besserian's calf. "Got some muscle there, guy!" They both waited. "This may sound, well, weird and I don't want you to take it the wrong way."

"I won't. What?"

"I got to like you. The way you do things. Even when you know you could get your ass kicked. Because there's something outside of you that you believe in. Was inside you all along. Just had to come out." He grimaced in pain. "It's like now? Maybe I'm teacher's pet? Never had a teacher who liked me before. All my teachers, I mean up to now? Were dorks."

"I got to get some help."

"No. No, you're not. Hold on." He looked up: through Besserian's eyes. "I didn't tell you everything. About stuff."

"You made me get off my ass and do something."

"I don't mean that. AP job? I wanted you in it so I'd have an ally. I wanted to take Reform Plan away from Pritchard. Get it for myself. All along I wanted you to help me do that. I didn't tell you that." There was the silence of a few soaring birds that Besserian could see as he looked up. "I was using you. I was the biggest phony of all."

Besserian didn't turn away. "Maybe I was the one using you. And Reform might have worked. Been different from what Pritchard would have done."

"No. Not different. I may look different from that schnook. But, I'm just like him. I told you: money. Power. I was ready to fuck over the reform just like he is. Him out. Me in. Same thing. But different. You know the drill."

"It might have been different."

"Maybe. Because you came out of yourself. Me? I'm a user. Say it. A prick. A buddy-fucker. I'll never change."

Besserian muttered, "Honesty? In a relationship? In a friendship? It takes awhile. It's risky. But it's worth waiting for. Anyway, I was the one who took. From you. You're a good teacher. My coach. Teaching is a relationship. It's about honesty."

The pain abated and Buck relaxed. "Both of us teachers? You know? That's sort of nice? To be a teacher. And to tell the truth about yourself. Maybe it means there's trust?" And he smiled: the same guileless smile, always so disarming, but now, so different.

Besserian reached down to adjust the fabric near the bloody mass. He saturated his towel with water from the canteen and spread it as additional cover, over what both of them wanted to pretend wasn't there.

"I was supposed to be helping you. But as it worked out, I think you were the one helping me. To see shit. I hadn't seen before. And something else? You'll laugh but I was thinking, sometimes, how I wished I had you as my teacher. When I was in school being such a screw up. I think you'd have squared me away. I thought one time, if I had been a guy in your school? I'd need my ass whipped by you. I would have been bad. Just to piss you off. Like to watch you when you get pissed off. Like you think you shouldn't. But then do it anyway. Tickles my ass! And remember when we came home from the fight? And we were sort of bandaging each other? I think I wanted you to take care of me. If I said something I thought you'd deck me. I mean you're Mr. Super Macho. Maybe there was stuff neither one of us was saying? Maybe we were talking in code?"

Besserian adjusted the torso just off the center of his own body. "No code. Not anymore."

"Yeah, I'm glad about that. And I learned something else. Something you never thought I learned. That good relationships don't happen very often. Like a good friendship? A good teacher? Somebody you can trust. Completely? If you get one, you're lucky. You have to be smart enough to recognize it. When you get it. Even if it pisses you off sometimes. And you want to punch out the other guy?"

"Tell me."

"I was thinking. Before today, even. That's what teaching's all about. Like I said, help a guy do something he didn't think he could do?"

"You showed me."

"If a guy gets a good teacher? Somebody he respects? Sort of looks after him? Makes him see stuff different? That he never thought of before. Well, he's real lucky."

They were silent. Different? Completely together.

"You remember that girl in the bar? My friend?"

"Arlene?"

"She thought you were hot. Sexy."

Buck moved his head relaxing into a comfortable position. . He raised his eyes to the other man. "Sorta nice being here. Just the two of us. Seems right."

Besserian kept staring ahead, savoring the weight across his midsection. But he didn't see. He, too, was doing something he had wanted to do, for a long time. In fact, ever since—now it seemed so remote, so uselessly far in the past—that first meeting. In the restaurant. When he had wanted to lash out with his fists. Now the impulse gripped him again. But it wasn't to strike.

The blue eyes opened in a smile. "I'm not sayin' you're not a pain sometimes. You are. Always thinking about stuff. Tryin' to figure things out. Stuff that doesn't matter."

Besserian tried to think of something to say but was interrupted. "And you know something? You love those kids. Don't you?"

Buck didn't need a reply. "You know why? Because they accept you for what you are. The good parts. And the pain in the ass parts. That's what love is. You taught me that."

A hawk soared over them dipping, turning, floating gracefully. Besserian squinted, afraid to close his eyes, "Me too. I found that out. From you."

Buck looked up as if to reply. The intensity of the blue eyes had never been so intense. He smiled that wonderful self-confident show-off smile as if to say, "We're OK. Don't worry." He looked up at his friend. And they saw each other. Completely. Then, his eyes closed. The head dropped heavily. Into Besserian's lap.

Never again. It wasn't going to happen: the four-letter words, the exasperated gestures of pointless rage at trivia, the desperate competition, the frustration when Besserian hadn't read his mind completely, the guileless complements, masquerading in their sexuality.

But there was something else. Now. Some kind of completion. They were boys together. Enjoying being together. The rest of the world closed out. Dreaming together. Living the dream. The enjoyment of each other. Total companionship. That Besserian had never had. And Besserian ached with the same intensity of Buck's injury. He choked. Now he did want to lash out at him, hurt him. For leaving. For going away. For taking himself away. After having given so much. For being his teacher. And then leaving.

Him. Because it would never, could never, happen again. It had ended. Before it had happened.

In any case one teacher was having trouble seeing. He could feel that wonderful weight. Smell that pungent aroma. He could feel but barely see the matted hair pushing over the scooped stretch shirt. Because everything, sight, smell, feel, taste, even the sound of absolute quiet was an increasing blur.

The first time: the last time: Besserian could cradle the magnificent head, and he savored the weight, the aroma, the rough mask already by noon beginning to cover the face. It was a relief. An oddly exhilarating freedom. That had come. Finally. With impunity. Completely. His palms were smoothing the mutilated fabric: thighs, shoulders. No one else would know. Ever. It didn't concern anyone else. Once, his friend even seemed to move slightly, as if dozing. Savoring the intimacy.

Besserian rested his own chin on the cropped, thinning hair, inhaling the pungent musk, appreciating for the first time the peace, in doing, finally, something he had almost convinced himself, he didn't want to do. It was a unique feeling of harmony. Of completion. A Rightness achieved, in possessing something he never imagined possible: that he never imagined existed. To be possessed.

Heaven was peace. An incredible peace. Unutterable. That's why nobody could describe it. Now, intensified, racked to a painful degree because he knew he was experiencing it both for the first time—and the last: unbearably painful, as involuntarily the words came from him: 'If only . . .' Now, too late, he saw that Buck had been holding the door open. And then, finally, he allowed his body to convulse, gripping, seizing his friend, with bands of iron. Together. One.

Buck's words kept repeating themselves. And each time Besserian heard them for the first time. Eyes flooded, muting his reply, he whispered, so very quietly, touching his lips to that splendid head, so no one, absolutely no one in the entire world, except his friend, could ever hear, would ever know: "Maybe. Maybe. Bucky, boy. I wish. I wish. I wish."

They continued to sit there together. Beside the road. Their road. Travelled so often. Together. Even after he realized there would be no more tears. For either of them. Ever.

# *CHAPTER XXXIX*

## *Choice*

Felipe pushed his way through the rows of chairs, jammed uncomfortably close together. "Started yet? Mr. B here? He coming? To tell about it?"

"Not yet. He will. Hasn't started." Allisandro, Jesus, Robert, Marco, Shaunisha, Gloria clustered around the chair they had saved for their teacher. Rosalba and Veronica were grouped nearby with the rest of the Project members.

"Hey, you hear about Sandra? Heard she's outa the Project."

"We're shit-canned if we got to tell the Code. Ourselves."

"Falange says he got the right to hold diplomas. I know the way he is. When he don't like kids." Robert was not optimistic.

Destiny inched through the mass. "Could be bad."

Allisandro pushed himself over to Penny. "Mrs. Penny? You think he'll tell? What we found? 'Cause if not, kids be busted."

"I'm sure he will. Was on the phone when I left. He'll be here."

"Now, ladies and gentlemen!" Allsbury was unrelenting "I know we're anxious! To get started! But, it won't help if we can't constrain ourselves! Keep writhing about. I do realize it's somewhat cramped down here."

"You got that right, lady! We're all over each other!"

A strident Arnida Hollyfield shouted across the room. "Ho-o-ly! I can't hardly even turn around to see what's goin' on behind me."

The assemblage comprised teachers, students, administrators, parents. Community 'activists' waved placards:

- 'REFORM PLAN: Take Back Control: of OUR School'

- 'Our Own City: Our Own Schools. Pay Teachers What They Deserve.' The appeal was in 'kids' writing—backwards 'S's' and 'R's'.

- 'Standards, Standards, Go Away! Come on Back Some Other Day. All the way: School Reform means Minority Rights and Jobs.'

- 'It's all about KIDS! We Love You, Mr. Pritchard! God Bless!'

The noise in the cramped room with its shifting shadows, grew more raucous. "Arnida, sweetie! Hope you gonna stand and be counted up for teachers' rights! Pass this Reform thing?" Lydia Hastings-Bruce screeched.

"You got it, girl!"

"Ladies Night at El Toro Rojo! After? Two for one, Special?"

"Base hit! Catch you later, Honey-bun."

Sandra Weatherby touched Penny's sleeve. "How's it feel to be married to a celebrity?"

"Hi Sandy. Good to see one friendly face." Penny, jostled from behind, recovered her balance. "He was on the phone when I left the house."

"Word's out that Project is sabotaging Reform. Against teachers. Scarcely escaped from the Teachers' Lounge yesterday."

Penny shrugged agreement and mouthed an inaudible response.

Allsbury was persistent. "Now! I am-sure-I-will *not*-have-to–ask-you-again!" And skeptical. "Now, please! Students! Teachers! Ladies! Gentlemen! We-do-need-to-have-moving-stopped!" Her words took effect grudgingly. The noise was a viscous fluid gurgling down a clogged drain: leaving behind a thick, stagnant film.

"Ladies and gentlemen? If I might? I believe our honored guests *are* ready. To take their places?"

"Why get on *our* case, Pat? Them usin' candles? Look like shadows movin' round back there."

The flimsy black curtain, billowing aggressively, was pushed from behind by the 'shadows'. The dignitaries burgeoned through, faces masked in too-large smiles.

Baques held up his arms in a victory gesture. Dr. Jones-Laporte talked earnestly to Mr. Warfles, mouth too close to his ear, while AP Johansson contorted his mid-section, jabbed in the side by Cindye Jacobson, Special Ed: a private joke. Claudia Obesso and Dr. Cyndye Hernandez nuzzled up to a disoriented Brampton Falange, caressing his tiny shoulders, attempting to mask their discomfort at audience hostility.

"Let me introduce our ...."

"Let's get this puppet show on the road! Pat, we know who they are!"

Baques interjected, waving beneficently. "Good news, folks, is that voters approved Cathedral Heights as a separate city yesterday. So? Tonight, my friends we need to put the icing on the cake. Not obstruct each other. Tangled up in conflicting viewpoints. Go to the next level: School Reform Plan."

"Go for it, Joe."

"Folks! It's all about the Future! And we need to have everybody jump on the same bandwagon. Team Fillmore! All the way!"

"Go Knights! Go War-rrrs! Scrunch 'em!"

"Now, and just a super big Thank You to Ms. er.... Signora, Arce, for her assist? As translator? Always in there: pitching for us!" Baques smirked, making an exaggerated contortion of arms, shoulders and body, head canted to the side: as if swinging . . . what? A baseball bat? A golf club?

"Hey Joe! Can we break to the issue! We got a pretty good thing with this Reform Plan. Take charge of our own school."

"Let the ones who don't want Reform to go somewheres else."

Baques was wreathed in smiles. "Now! Want to hear both sides of the coin. Dr. Allsbury, as per usual, will be doing her us'l awes'm [awful?] job of fielding questions." Eyebrows puckered, he seated himself beside the Superintendent.

"And thank you so very much, Mr. Baques. I believe I see a hand?" Allsbury pointed with raised chin, then with an embellished wrist and arm movement, emphasizing sapphire ring and bracelet. "Sir? Er Miss? Yes?"

"Ex-cu-u-se me, everybody. But I just had to butt myself right in? First?" Rikki Bacon-Gaither smiled at Allsbury's glare, seating herself at the end of the dignitaries table. "Folks? Now, I know that all of us wants to fix up any of the eency-weency, teeny, little, cracks that mighta happened in the walls of our Fillmore dam? If you take my meaning! And yeah!

OK!" Her voice swelled. "Sure! There's some cracks!" She hunched her shoulders and grimaced, head bobbing. "So?" Her right arm fanned the air in a hammering motion. "Sure there is! OK! I won't lie to you! Right? S-o-o-o? You mighta heard already about some people accusing others of turning Reform into Not Reform? OK? Well?" Her voice increased several decibels. "Forget Them!"

Gripping the floor with her high heels, widening the spread of her legs, lower jaw extended, mouth open, arms bent upward—enactment of a fighting stance—she spewed her indignation. "Sure! Is anyone expecting it to be perfect? No way! We're still in start-up mode! We'll iron out the glitches as time marches on! Where's that city that's not built in a day?"

"How long'd it take, Rikki?"

Rikki stood and slapped the microphone cord against her thigh. Intended as a smile, she twisted her lips into a sneer. "Now, don't get me wrong! Not to be sayin' everthang is supposed to be 'letter perfect'! From the git-go? No! No! Not at all!" She shook her head vigorously, squinting painfully. "Now: Listen Up! Listen to me!" Her gaze roamed from dignitaries to audience. "Lots of stuff's not perfect! And we do it! Anyhow? Ever hear somebody try to sing the *Star Spangle Banner* at a ball game? There's some sour notes. Sure! Who cares?" She paused for effect."But we still sing *it?* Don't we? Sing it as best as we can! And proud of it! Don't throw it out for *Jingle Bells*! Better believe! And *why*?" Her voice leapt several notes. "*Why*?"

"Say it, girl!"

The hum of the sound system, offset by its mercurial hissing, further challenged her response.

"For *kids*! That's why! Reform's the tune we gonna march to."

Allsbury smiled plastically, left arm aloft, wrist contorted, hair ribbons fluttering, analyzing her jeweled watch. Palm inward, she flourished index and middle fingers at Bacon-Gaither, nodding vigorously. The noise of four individuals vying for a single vacant chair obscured somewhat a vulgar interpretation of her gesture.

"And we do thank you so very, *very* much, Ms. Bacon!" Allsbury was pained. "Now! Moving on! I believe Ms. Brauphman, always a strong student rights advocate, has some words? Ms. Brauphman, if you would?"

Brauphman giggled and shook the profusion of blond ringlets half concealing the bobbing, jello-like skin of her face and neck, and began moving toward the stage.

A disturbance, at the side door, interrupted her progress. A heavy groan gained momentum, rippling through the room, reiterated by the frowns of several dignitaries. Brauphman halted on the stage steps, alarmed that she might be the subject of the hostility.

"Well! If that jest don't beat all!"

"The nerve of some people!

"Traditionalists 'ull get you ever-time. Hey man! Find yourself some school that appreciates Fascists! KKK! That tries to blind our thoughts!"

Besserian adjusted his eyes to the shadowy room, and stood in the doorway, sillouetted by the light from the floor above.

Felipe pushed his way to him. "Over here, sir. Waitin' for you."

Rosalba elbowed herself through the crowd. "Glad you're here, sir! Don't mind them!" People stepped back as the two students, Besserian between them, rejoined the Project members.

"They offered you the job, didn't they? In Indiana?"

Besserian took her hand. "Yes. Sounds like they have a strong academic program. Could be an AP job, too."

Brauphman, emboldened by the criticism of Besserian, was confident. "Somebody's Pet Project? Sayin' Reform's bad! Jest would you please, jest to give me a: B-R-A-K-E?" She spelled the word, drawing large letters in the air with her index finger, calling out each letter for emphasis. "This is what democracy means. And I *ain't* just a-whistlin' Dixie! No sir-ree-*bob*!"

"I believe Mr. McCauley's hand is up?"

"For sure! Why not just 'Do It'? There's nobody here who's against it. At least nobody that matters. Reform and to control our schools. Winner both ways. Just Do It! And outta here. Soak up some suds!"

Yells of approval were punctuated by the screeching of the sound system, desperate to reach decibels an octave higher than the human ear could endure.

Allsbury called to the three students scurrying over the floor, checking connections, tracing wires, beckoning instructions to one another. "Boys! It's still no better!" In defiance, she was interrupted by a violent squealing: an ear-splitting, electronic whistle from the enormous stage speakers. She jumped, as if tasered. Several of the more squeamish, on stage and in the audience, threw hands over their own ears or those of an acquaintance, gritting their teeth in agony. And hilarity. The amplifier's cry of vengeance simulated hundreds of terrified rodents—captives—scratching desperately, futilely, the slate walls of their snake pit prison.

"It seems we have some audio system problems!"

"You got that one right, Pat!"

Grimacing, Allsbury, ankle bone digging into the floor, was not to be thwarted. "Yes, and it's still a bit shadowy. I was told the generator—and please, ladies and gentlemen, untoward remarks are *not* helpful—will be repaired as quickly as possible. And we can resume upstairs as originally designated."

"Hey McCauley! Keep your hands to yourself, guy! Just 'cause it's dark don't mean you have to act like yourself!"

"Yeah! You're not at home now, stud!"

A sing-song voice intoned, "Somebody's gro-o-o-ping me! And I think I know who it is-s-s! Be ni-i-i-ce, now!"

"Who's doing the hiring for District electricians now, Pat? The Three Stooges?" Inexplicably, the audio system decided to cooperate: it relayed the observation.

"I believe I see Ms. Lopez-Workman? Raven? Please!

"Folks, one thing I *do* know. For sure! We'll go all the way, tonight. The Right Way! "Why? 'Cause we're *Knights!"*

"But right now," Lopez spoke excitedly, "on the brighter side, want to present you with something jest adorably special? It's my supreme honor to give you the "Littlest Angels" from Pico Elementary! And their Principal, Ms. Lucille," she pronounced it Lu-sill, "Alvarez-Sampson? So: jest let's put our hands together for Ms. Alvarez and all her hard work! And I see they just about ready to come up? O-o-o-h! So swe-e-e-et! They're jest the cutest? Little tykes? I'd like to just hug 'em to death! U-u-u-mph!" She writhed in delirious expectation, arms embracing herself, body rotating, mouth clenched, eyes closed, face illuminated with a frightening smile.

"Now, y'all jest listen up? Thanks ever. The 'Angels' [Ayn-ge-els] are alamentary kids, and you won't believe it, but! Now hear this! Not one of them: Not *one*! Is-*over-ten*-years-old! Now! As if any of *us* could ever even *remembe*r back *that* far!" She smirked coyly. "Anyhow, they're gonna make us jest *real* proud of what we're doing here in education? And they're gonna do a song that, believe it or not, they even wrote theirselves?" She was arch, "With just a teency weency bit o' help? From Ms. Alvarez?" She chuckled, lower lip drooping.

The Ayn-ge-els shuffled coyly across the stage: in pink skorts, blue blouses, white rayon scarves trailing down their backs. All wore shiny black Mary Jane's; white ankle socks trimmed with pink pompons. Six of the seraphs displayed a hand-lettered square of cardboard which, if correctly arranged, would have spelled REFORM.

"Aren't they just dar-ling? Swe-ee-et!" Lopez reminded the audience who chuckled, then hushed as Alvarez, an oldish forty-something, pivoted abruptly, calf-length, accordion pleated skirt billowing, and fell on her knees in front of the choristers, arms extended beseechingly, fingers pointing inward, for the downbeat; face tilted, a study in benevolent severity. Her arms fell and eighteen tiny voices intoned haltingly, to the tune of *Three Blind Mice:*

"Re-e-form! Re-e-form!
See how it works! See what it does!
All of us can be as best as we are!
Nothing they can't do to us 'nymo-o-rr!
Mr. Pritchard helps what's best for u-u-s!
Re-e-form!

Artistry completed, the youngsters giggled shyly. Several ladies, teary-eyed, embraced them and with profuse, consoling hugs, pecked the corners of their own eyes with the perennial 'tissues', all the while, shaking their heads wistfully. "Ab-so-lu-te-ly *dar*-r-r-ling!"

Allsbury resumed as Master of Ceremonies. "And now, we have, if I'm not mistaken, our Board President-elect, currently ..."

"There she is. Give her a hand, guys!".

"... *currently* our Fillmore Community rep but soon to assume her new leadership? Chairman of the Board? Responsibilities?" Allsbury reasserted herself. "Our just wonderful: trustee, parent, community activist, classroom Teacher Assistant, and, most of all: friend? Please welcome: Señora Alma Arcáña!"

The applause was muted by the lady's progress. She stumbled through the labyrinth of chairs, whose occupants, not without difficulty, propelled her to the stage, unsure whether they were following the adage 'two forward, one back' or 'one forward, two back'.

Hindrances overcome, but not forgotten, she needed several hugs from Allsbury and Dr. Jones-Laporte, who, patting her back, mouthing words of empathy, were able to prevail upon the luminary to accept the microphone. Her voice faltered in response to 'o-o-o-h-ing' and 'a-a-a-h-ing' from commiserative pockets in the audience.

"What I tell my kids ever day when they try to study all them books they has to lug around with them all the day long?"

"Hey! Listen to her, you guys!"

"Jess. An we don't need more testes that kids can't do."

"Yeah, Señora! It's what happens when other races gets in our face. Take over our school. Put their value systems onto us."

"Still some bigotry against minorities in here, folks!"

"That's the still-there unlevel playing field, Miss."

"Teachers from outside that don't want our culture!"

KC Shore, recently promoted Girls' Wrestling and Assistant Varsity Football Coach, in stretch, thigh-length, PE shorts and form-fitting T-shirt, knocked her way through the crowd, bounded up the steps and wrenched the microphone from the confused speaker, giving her a peck on the forehead. "You said, it! There's still some Un-Caring! Gender-biased! Reform Plan'll squash 'em."

Allsbury spread her hands for quiet, nodding Shore and the President-elect off the stage. "Mr. Besserian, I believe your hand is up?"

He stood slowly. For the first time there was silence. He mounted the stage steps, taking a chair at the table.

"We remind you, sir, that we *do* have a three minute—no, hold that, correction—two minute, a two minute *maximum* on pre-sentations." Baques exuded benevolence.

"I'll be brief. My purpose is to alert you to a possible problem. With the Reform Plan. One I'm sure you want to know about."

Two of the stage personages nodded reflectively, lips clenched, eye-balls pirouetting. Claudia Obesso, head down, scribbled furiously. The remainder, with doleful expressions scoured the ceiling. Guidance? Inspiration?

"Several months ago, my students and I started an out-of-class Project. Our purpose was to research the Reform Plan. Study how it would benefit our school. We examined relevant data."

"Did you find information?"

"We found more than we expected. You need to know what it is."

"So, what you're sayin' is that the already published information is a lie? We're liars?"

Baques glared at his Assistant. "Not now, Mr. Falange!"

"I didn't say that. And you know it, Falange. We discovered information which suggests that Reform projects, *perhaps*, may be influenced by personal financial gain."

"Board is unaware of any such information." Laporte interrupted icily.

"Our information suggests that teacher-advisors to businesses might have a vested interest in reform projects that . . ."

"You tryn' to tell us Reform is not Reform?"

"I'm alerting you to the possibility of a reform distorted . . ."

"We don't need this."

"Guy's a kook."

"Where's your proof, buddy?"

"Encoded messages, so . . ." Besserian tried to speak.

"Code? Give me a f-ing break, man."

"You got your head up your behind, boy."

"So, what you're sayin' is that Reform Plan won't benefit our kids! Want to toss out any help for kids? Tonight?"

"I think you'll want to consider acceptance of this Plan in light of this new information." Besserian was calm.

"So long as it's true! We only got your word for it." Bruce Warfles called indignantly. "You decoded it? Sure! *'Cause you made it up!"*

Indignation spread through the room. "You're talking through your rear end, buddy!"

"How's all this supposed to help kids?"

"Get a life! And somewheres else! At some Traditionalist school. Get with your KKK, Fascistic buddies."

Allsbury was flustered.

Baques entered the discussion. "Let's cut to the issue, Mr. Besserian. If, indeed, you have 'secret', he toggled index fingers, "information, we need to hear it. Of course! I'm going to make an administrative decision that we review it. In private. To protect student confidentiality. Assure Due Process. . . "

"I think people need to know *before* they vote what . . ."

"Thank-you-sir-r-r! *We-appreciate-your-concern!*"

Felipe called loudly, "Why not ask the kids that's in the Project? If you don't believe what Mr. B's sayin'?"

"Of course! Thank you students! Of course you count: most of all. Always".

Marvin Johansson shouted an interruption. "Besserian? You say you 'uncovered' stuff, like the tomb of the ancient Egyptian fay-rows! Hidden in the school district files? Sure! 'Cause you mean you put it there! Yourself."

"Guy's a Traditionalist nut-bar! Mad 'cause they not in charge anymore."

"Same old story: Angry White Male!"

"Mr. Baques, I have some concerns."

"Ms. Meldonian?

"I'm Computer Graphics? Seems we need to hear *before* we vote. Not after."

"I'll ditto that, Seraphina. And, I'm Mrs. Jefferson, Grade Nine, Science? I don't like to say something but seems that, maybe, Mr. Besserian's information shouldn't be swept under the carpet. OK! Sure! Might turn out to be that it doesn't mean anything. But then, again, it just might! Besserian lying? I have to ask, why? Never did before."

"Mr. Baques, may I have the floor?" Lyndon Pemberton, Health, Driver Ed., was on his feet, eyes wide with indignation. "Mr. Warfles, word is out that you—and others—are designated paid Liaison officers with local businesses. Won't that compromise your vote?"

"Gentlemen! Ladies! Let's not forget professionalism." Allsbury gripped the microphone.

Pemberton continued. "Mr. Besserian notwithstanding, some of us have thought all along that Reform Plan is unclear about Drop-out Prevention, discipline, academics, teacher evaluations, . . ."

"We can't know that stuff until *after* we get started. Need to chill, buddy!"

Mr. Mugwabe resonated across the room: "We have the right, the need, to know NOW! If Reform will be determined by personal financial interests! And not by student interests!"

Baques stood and spread his arms, palms down. "Professionalism, people! Now, obviously some of us has pretty serious concerns. Shows we're here for kids! But we don't want to be accusing anybody whose family's been supporting our schools for three generations! So, I suggest we move on. And several of you," he nodded to Mugwabe, Pemberton, and Meldonian, "will need to conference with me. All of us needs to be reading from the same page. Oh, yes! Mr. Pritchard? Please?"

Pritchard accepted the microphone. "Of course there are concerns. That shows our democracy. But! You decide. Specifics? They will be discussed democratically. As we move down the Reform superhighway."

He passed the microphone to Jones-LaPorte, whispering, "Call for the vote."

The Superintendent spoke quickly. "Let's compromise. Accept the Plan. Iron out any little wrinkles later." She was Solomon. "Later, we can give any commentaries due attention."

"On a roll, lady."

At her signal Baques, looking around the dimly lit room, solemnly intoned: "School personnel only may vote. So? All in favor?"

Stamping feet, yelling, shouts signaled affirmation.

"All opposed?" The Project members looked at each other, hesitated and Felipe raised his bandaged wrist. Jesus, Robert, Allisandro, Shaunisha followed suit. Then all of them. Besserian did the same and was followed by Sandra Weatherby, Marcus Mugwabe, Meldonian, Pemberton, Huerta, Jefferson, and ten or twelve others.

Baques, Johansson and Falange pumped hands, smiling effusively.

Baques took the microphone. "You won! You did it yourselves! You got what you asked for! Teacher power! Student power! You made the decision: take back control of *your* school. *Your* school district. *Your* community."

The din resounded thunderously: delirious shouts of approval.

Baques resumed the microphone, arms raised, and the noise intensified then gradually abated. "Just a couple of totally important announcements. That I know all of you've been waiting to hear about."

"We're outta here! Don't keep suspencing us!"

"First off! Now, there's been just a diligent search for our new AP?" He waved his three by five cards. "Now, finally, our Selection Committee, *your* committee, with great dedication, *has* come to a decision mode. Folks, our new Assistant Principal for Student Affairs is:" he paused theatrically, "none other than ......hang on to your seats folks......Roxanne Turner! Ms. Roxanne Turner!"

"E-e-e-k! Oh, my Gawd! I can't believe it! Wow! Oh! Yes, there *is* a God in heaven!" The winner doubled over in amazement, wincing, shutting her eyes tightly, shoulders hunched, thrusting a hand above her head. "Oh, m'Gawd! Whoever coudda imagined ...?" She was swamped with hugs from females crowding around. "Bless you, sweetie!" "Another step in blasting the Glass Ceiling!"

"We'll be meeting together tomorrow, Ms. Turner?" Baques nodded. "Let me add my voice of condolence to you. Welcome to 'Team Fillmore Administration'!"

"Some of you may have heard? The tragedy that beset our District consultant, Mr. Buck Henderson. Truly, a sorrow. For us all. But! The good news! He will be succeeded by his able second in command: Mrs. Penny Besserian. And that definitely shows that there's absolutely *no* hard feelings about people doing what they think is best. None at all!"

"Go for it, Miss!"

"Another. Our proposed faculty Senate is in a go-ahead mode. And to get things going, initially, senate will comprise our community business liaison advisors."

"How they going to be selected?"

"One more item of note. With Reform we'll be cancelling any further teacher Projects. Teachers Rule! In their classrooms. Only!"

Jones-LaPorte joined him. "Mr. Pritchard has asked me to announce the recipient of the Evergreen Foundation scholarship." Waving an oversized envelope, she tore it open. "Miss Sandra Guzman!" There were screams of delight as Sandra, attired in backless evening dress, orchids on her wrist, gushed from the wings, receiving the envelope and profuse hugs from LaPorte. She was sobbing. "I just don't know what to say! It's so—heavenly! I jest died and went to heaven!" Choked, overcome with emotion, "Oh, God! Am I totally scared!", shaking her hair violently. Hand to her forehead as if swooning, she received accolades and kisses from the female stage dignitaries.

Face grave, Jones-LaPorte continued. "Some of us tonight have indicated they're not happy here? Not want to join us on the Reform Super Highway! And that's fine! Our new Senate will be empowered to recommend the transfer of stressed teachers."

Crash! A thunderous, flashing streak! Upraised hands protected eyes. Confused, they stumbled, crawling over each other.

Allsbury lurched to the microphone, left hand arched over her forehead, little finger extended. Squinting, ribbons cascading, she tried to make sense of the seething commotion. "Ladies and gentlemen! Obviously, the lights have been repaired." She raised her voice, unheard, in the swell of complaints, anger, hissing, sardonic laughter. Dignitaries were slithering ahead of the *mêlée* toward the doors. "We can now move upstairs? To the annual End-of-Year Talent Show?"

Ineffective words. The entire assemblage, entwined with each other, was moving to the stairs: the auditorium above.

Someone yelled derisively, "It's lifeboats on the Titanic time, guys!"

Allsbury's voice was stridently ineffective. "The Talent Show theme this year is 'Seize the Future: It's Yours for the Asking!'"

---

# *CHAPTER XL*

## *Fantasy*

The stage curtains had minds of their own. Cautiously, slyly, they peeked open. Then snapped shut. Parting again—eight, twelve, fifteen inches: they reconsidered and, archly, scampered closed. Impulsively, relishing their own cuteness, throwing caution to the winds, they leapt apart fully, revealing a mass of milling people in various stages of undress and unpreparedness. But, spooked by the indignant performers, and desperate to appease, the two halves reconsidered, and hurtled toward each other, billowing crazily, competing mindlessly to reach Center. And shroud the presentation.

The audience, gyrating, shouting, yelling, were consumed with themselves. "Over here, bitch! Sit here with your man, baby girl!"

"Catch you outside."

"Shit! Give it here! It's mine! Take your f-ing paws off of that."

"Later, dude!"

"Ho-o-o-ly! He hot for you, girl! You can make him!"

The female Master of Ceremonies stood in front of the heaving curtains, ineptly trying to synchronize gleaming, copper-colored lips, with the erratic hand microphone. "How many party people we got here?" In fairness to her artless attempts, the sound system perversely countered her efforts, emitting intermittent whistles, screeches, sonic booms.

Nevertheless, those who happened to be looking toward the stage, howled their acknowledgement, as behind her, the curtains, once again broadcasting signals of restlessness, opened slightly, closed, then, at a funereal pace, drifted apart to reveal *The Neon Babes*, denoted by an erratic spotlight and red lettering on their white, sequined, spike-heeled boots.

At center was Larri Mong, attired like her four associates, in a sheer, black, harem-like garment with baggy, draped, ankle-length trousers, over a white nylon thong. A miniscule gauze vest, over a white bra, revealed her mid-section. Gazing upward deliriously, tongue protruding, each *artiste*, holding a microphone loosely between thumb and middle finger, palm upward—highly lacquered nail of the little finger poised perilously close to the eye, a target ringed with gleaming mascara—hummed the lyrics mouthed by Larri.

> "I give up – nothin's good enough for any-b-o-o-di e-else!
> When I'm by mysa-al-al-alf, nobody else can say goodbi-i-i-i;
> Ever-thang is temp-o-o-r-ar-ar-y. That means you and me is quit.
> I quit. I give up. Nothin's good enough for anyb-o-di e-else.
> When I'm by mysa-aal—aal-alf, it's the best way to b-e—e-e-e.
> I qu-it! I qu-i-i-i-t!"

The audience gave a protracted hiss, presumably of approval. They squirmed ceaselessly, vying both to occupy and vacate seats. The few faculty and administrators, obligated to supervise, were apprehensive at the extent to which students were shedding articles of clothing. Experience told them that any end-of-the-year event could easily boomerang out of control.

"OK. Folks! Looks like we got us another sure time winner! And this time it's gonna' be, u-m-m-m-m, lemme jest to get this: Pedro Gallatin, Grade Twelve! Who'll bring you to joy." MC Gloria Wong, amended the statement: for comic relief? "He won't! A negativity on that! He'll be with Rudy Imue! Again this year. On piano!"

Pedro sauntered slowly toward the distressed grand. The audience cheered sporadically at the new distraction, but he ignored them, apparently lost in reflection. In any case, his musings were private, far beyond audience comprehension.

His accompanist was equally enigmatic. Rudy seated himself, and tinkered, morosely, with the keys. The piano had a curiously hollow sound, despite its size, as one might have expected from Schroeder's miniscule instrument. Pedro hung beside it, toying absently with the endless cord. Rudy tinkled an introduction, not assisted by the antics of the sound system and the mounting impatience of the audience. Unperturbed, the musicians maintained their expressions of total disinterest, until, unexpectedly, Pedro broke into Rudy's meanderings:

> "When I'm feelin' blu-uu, all I have to do, is take a look
> at yo-u-u-u;
> Then I'm not so blu-u-uu.
> When you close to me, I can feel your heart be-e-e-et;
> I can feel you breathing in my e-e-a-ar.
> Don't you know I start to shi-i-i-ver-er? Can't you feel me
> deep in-si-i-i-de?
> Wood-dent you agree, ba-ba-be-e-e;
> You and me! It's a gro-o-o-o-ovi kind of lo-ov-ov-ov-ov-e?"

There was no time for applause! Panic-stricken, the curtain panels flew at each other, desperate to shed themselves of their fabric, guide ropes colliding with a thud at center top. The trailing, flying cloth, caught up, spraying itself voluptuously, as if deranged, the panels leaping aggressively over each another.

"Now, list'en up!" Gloria's patience was waning. "I said List'en!" She punctuated her appeal with a protracted shriek: U-u-u-u-p-p-p! KEEP IT DOWN, I SAID!" She gesticulated: frenetic semaphore gyrations. Allsbury, Baques, and Falange peered cautiously from stage left, reconsidered, and retreated.

"Now! That's jest a whole lot better! Now! We got for you! Now, List-Up!" But the decibel rate was mercurial. Far from being 'better', it accelerated. Her temper did the same. "And I ain't jackin' off, with you guys! Not'ny more!" She spread her legs wide, toes pointed out, rocking on her heels, pulling her skirt still higher on the thighs. Had there been a chair, her posture would have indicated the intention of being seated. "We got for your attention now,...". At this point, for some inexplicable reason, her rage shifted to laughter. She cavorted in near-hysteria, arms flailing the air; "That's right, Oh! Gawd Almighty! I can't even believe this! Un-shit-t-ing be-lee-ee-va-bul! Put them hands together for: The E-e-e-ter-r-r-r-nals!"

But it was not to be as simple as that. Teachers—faculty advisors—Vangi Stillcart, assisted ineptly by Laura Yi and, confusedly by Cyril

Jacobs—Milton—were in desperate straits with the maze of electric cords, cables, wires, and metal flex.

Laura was especially vehement in her criticism. "This is the pits! Shit!" The much-heralded *Eternals*, a quartet in cowgirl attire, watched vacantly, occasionally wiggling the twelve-inch fringe dangling from their white vinyl vests, sequined sombreros at a rakish angle, red sateen, silver-belted leotards gleaming, in front of dead microphones.

Vangi was pointing over their heads, gesturing authoritatively. "That's not working! Dead mike! No, not you! YOU!"

To the rescue, Bud Samuelson, Geography, muscles glistening as if polished, tank-top and skin-tight jeans, leapt on stage. His six-pack torso, enormous smile, and flashing teeth, set off howls of appreciation, mostly, but not exclusively, female. Struggling with Vangi and Milton in a Kafkaesque tug-of-war, he fell against Laura, his mouth cupping her ear. They toppled over each other in helpless glee.

"This is funny!"

"Where's the one you just had? That wire?"

"That's the one you just gave me."

"Not that one! You gave me the wrong end!"

"Is it on?"

"Right!" Bud shouted to the boys clustering around the offstage control panel. "Turn it up, guys. It's on!"

Tugging at each other, overly anxious to comply, the students parried the command, one shouting in desperation, "You on over there? Where this one go?"

"Which one?"

"This here. In my hand? Not hooked up to nothin'."

"You on over there?"

"No, not working. Dead mike."

"Where's the one you had on?"

"It's on."

"On? Turn it up some. Higher! Not that! Your other higher."

Throwing up their hands in capitulation, Vangi and Bud, careening against each other, disentangled themselves and picked their way through the tangle to join the *Eternals*, still waiting, expressionless, at their microphones.

"Sorry for the delay, folks. We're having just lots of problems here. Everything that could go wrong is. You name it! Anybody hear?"

A deafening chorus of "No-o-o-o!" reverberated back as a howl. Bud, with a gymnast's agility, always smiling, the center of attention, was in his element. "You on? Over there? You're just going to hear voices," he called into a mike, his body undulating gracefully, tank-top saturated with moisture. "You people just going to hear voices!" Resentment shifting to enthusiasm, the audience cheered, relishing his efforts, however unsuccessful.

He stumbled over an especially obstreperous entanglement falling against Milton, who observed prophetically: "Awake, arise, or be forever fallen," while Vangi and Laura, convulsed in laughter, clutched one another for support.

Bud threw up his arms in frustration. "This wire's gone ballistic! Ape-shit! Can't f-ing believe this!"

At the control box, the boys, using matches and pencil flashlights, reinserted multiple connectors, maneuvered banks of switches, signaled to Bud who shook his mike vigorously. No result! Making a fist he punched it sharply. An answer from heaven? Miraculously, there was an ear-splitting hiss followed by what could have been an avalanche of rocks. A moment of stunned silence. Then a howling, a psychedelic fog horn, blared from the five gigantic speakers. Bud leapt into the air, "Po-o-o-we-e-e-e-r", a vengeful cry of the dammed: a Tarzan to the rescue. *The Eternals* indifferently tapped their individual microphones, eyelashes fluttering.

Four male teachers took positions at other microphones. Mike Moran in his usual sprayed-on jeans and tank top proclaiming '#1'. He needed a shave and exuberant accolades of audience hysteria acknowledged his display of physique. Pete Simms, Jake Watkins, and Brian McCauley were in jeans and tank tops. Each had an electric guitar. They gyrated in unison with the others; humming, harmonizing, joking and occasionally playfully punching one another to reaffirm mutual maleness.

*The Eternals* whispered conspiratorially, tossing their hair nervously, frequently turning their backs to the audience. Petulantly they absorbed the oogling of the spectators; two of them pretending to be absorbed with the tin buckles on their western-style boots. Yolanda Paniguina swayed, humming to herself, chewing a strand of hair, and, with her tongue, pulling a gold neck chain through her teeth.

Bud, Laura, Vangi and Milton joined the girls at their respective mikes and the "show" resumed.

"You cheated, you li-i-i-ed, you said you wanted
me-e-e-e!

The song they're sang-ng-ng-ing reminds me of you-u-u!
I'll always remember that first night we spent al-o-o-o-ne!
Why, tell me why, must I be a teen-aag-aag-aag-ger in
Lu-u-u-vh?
Pul-e-e-e-se, O pul-e-e-e-e-se try to lo-uvh me,
like I lo-uvh y–u-u!
O, what can I d-o-o-o? A teen-aag-aag-aag-ger in
lo—o-o-vh?

The swirling lights gyrated through unpredictable shades of purple and crimson: turning, reversing, and spiraling. Then it happened. The yellow color, truncating the others, began spinning, increasing its momentum, until it became a whirling mass: bronze, brass, flame. The room was ecstatic.

"One day I feel so ha-a-a-pii, next day I feel so sa-a-a-a.
And if you should say good-bi-i-i, I'll go on loving
yu-u-u.
Each night I ask the Lo-o-o-rd up a-bo-u-u-vh:
Why, O wh-i-i, must I be a teen-aag-aag-aag-ger in
Lu-u-u-u-u-vh?"

The performers skipped off stage right, bumping into Johnny Estarca, who delighted the audience but especially himself, by leaping over a chair, landing in a leg-split, punctuating his feat with a huge grin. In camouflage cargo trousers, hanging perilously insecure just above the thighs, he wore a bandoleer, was shirtless, and carefully manipulated his over-developed torso as if participating in a Mr. Body Beautiful contest. Hysteria waved through the audience. "Hey, take 'em off, hot stud!" "Look like he know whats-for! Would you just to check out that equip-ment! *Sest huge*!"

"I'm a wand-er-er-er-er ... I'm a wan-der-er-ing kind of
gu-u-u-i-i."

Overcome with self-satisfaction, he mouthed the rest of the lyrics. It made no difference. They were undecipherable: his garbled pronunciation and the whine of the sound system. The audience was convulsed in appreciation.

Four female vocalists followed. In a varied assortment of tighter and tightest nylon 'short-shorts', sporting enormous earrings of both psychedelic and Christian symbolism, they were riveted on each other, faces inches apart, ignoring the audience.

"Ea-r-r-r-th ayn-gel, ea-r-r-r-th ayn-gel, will yo-o-u be
mi-i-i-ne?
My dar-r-r-l-ling de-ee-eer, love me all the
ti-i-i-i-i-me."

Bud, teeth gleaming through unshaven grin, joined the singers, their petulant expressions framing his huge smile:

"I hope and I pr-ay-ay-ay-ay that some dah-ah-ah-ayy,
I'll be the vision of yur hap-pin-es-ess-ess-ess-ess.
I'm just a fo-oo-oo-ool, for be-i-i-in in lo-ov-ov-ov
with yo-o-o-uu.
O me! O mi-i-i! Why can't I fall in lo-ove to-o-o-o?"

Cindy Zambrosa was next; stretched black leotards, with a flurry of blue lace at the thighs. In caressing, dulcet tones, seductively, she beguiled her listeners:

"I done found my pot o' go-o-o-o-l;
We found our heaven no-o-o-w!
Whenever you need somebo—o-o-dii, I'll be the-e-e-re.
Fo-or y-u-u-u."

The gleaming earrings, gold circles, six-inches in diameter, bumped her shoulders, as provocatively, she tossed long golden hair. And bounded off stage.

For several minutes, the audience saw only a closed curtain. Then, in response to restless jeers, it opened to a pantomime performance by Lynette Fromer, Monica Sembranao, and Marco Smith. The scenario was indicated by the hand-lettered sign on stage left: 'Crowded Bus'.

Lynette, jostled by Monica, dropped an immense armful of textbooks. Indifferently retrieving several, she looked daggers at Monica, raising her fist threateningly. Balancing the remaining books, she grasped the supposed overhead bar. In the process, the bus, apparently, lurched, and she fell against Marco, beside her and clinging to the same bar. They stood, in silence, pressed closely together. Then, Lynette, showing increasing aversion to Marco, shifted her head from side to side, raising it, lowering it, nostrils palpitating, mouth clenched, eyes squeezed, the personification of disgust. Securing no reaction, she squeezed her nostrils with a theatrical hand movement of thumb and index finger.

Marco, unperturbed, remained indifferent. Exasperated, patience spent, Lynette rummaged in an enormous purse and extracted an aerosol can marked with oversized letters: *Spray Deodorant.* Applying it generously to her underarms, it was an obvious hint that Marco do the same.

Obvious to everyone, except Marco, who added insult to injury by bumping Lynette, as he pushed his way to the 'door'. In retaliation, she kicked him savagely. Struggling, not only with the crowd but with his pain—he was holding his crotch—to reach the exit, Marco then was knocked into Monica, who, unaware of the complexities of the unfolding drama, assumed that the bellicose Lynette had pushed him. Raising her clenched fist, Monica glared at Lynette hatefully, then swung her fists into her opponent's breast and stomach.

They all trundled off stage to be replaced by Mr. Warfles accompanied by a costumed oddity that immediately spiraled the audience into paroxysms of confused glee. The costume was, in reality, Randy Pineda, Indiana Simmental, and Geronimo Florencia, covered by a painted sheet: Randy, bottommost and moving on his knees, Indiana sitting on his shoulders, with Geronimo, perched precariously on Indiana's shoulders. Because of the variance in heights, the entire costume resembled an unattractive deformity: enormous head extending grotesquely from a truncated body. The creature's movements were lurching and uncoordinated, accentuated by the bobbing weight of Indiana and Geronimo.

Warfles introduced the costume as a "former student: come back to 'tell us what it's like out there'." Many in the audience, initially confused, reacted by throwing wadded paper at each other. Nevertheless, grudgingly, they were drawn into the intricacies of the questions put to the 'guest'.

"What's your name?"

"Indiana Jones Pineda."

"Did you like it here at school? Here at Fillmore?"

"Yeah! Except for the school work."

"Did you get good marks in school? In your classes?"

"Makin' it! Except for the ones I failed."

Approval thundered from the audience.

"What advice can you give to these students, tonight?"

"Get as much as you can, as often as you can, have all the fun as you can, and party all the time."

Warfles indicated approval of the responses, nodding vigorously, "Here, have a Tasty Cake, Indiana. You earned it."

Spasmodically, the 'student' leapt at the delight with Geronimo unsteadily struggling to adjust the 'mouth' opening of the costume. Randy's knees were hurting, and the costume, combining terror, dementia and aggression lurched at the treat. Warfles kept lunging at the convulsing creature, which suddenly, fell against him, splattering the cake over its entire 'face'.

The revelation that 'Indiana' was, in reality, three persons, seemed to confuse the audience as the performers emerged from under the sheet and bowed, doubled over with delight. Shouting triumphantly, they ran off stage.

Next was a martial arts display, led by the ubiquitous Bud Samuelson. In Karate suit with black belt, he engaged in sparring movements with Buddy Gomez and Randy Ruiz, who sported green belts. The movements looked choreographed, and ended when Bud appeared to knock the boys to the ground.

Marylyn Mijangos replaced them, bounding onstage and locking herself into fighting position, arms and fists at the ready, legs wide-spread, face contorted in aggressive rage. Bud fell back and the girl, spinning, with amazing agility and ferocity, executed several rapid kicks to his groin, sending the man, doubled over in agony, writhing to the mat. Marylyn stood triumphant, clenched fists raised in salute to the cheering audience, united in hysterical approbation of the defeat. The curtains raced closed.

Bud's defeat was followed by a nameless female trio, giggling, tittering, waving excitedly to special audience friends. The girls sported miniscule stretch pants, red, white and green, held up by red carpenter's suspenders. Mike Moran, Consumer Math, joined them:

"Step by step, we can get the-r-r-re...
We can get to the other si-i-i-e,
It's all ri-i, it's all ri-i-i-i-i,
It's O-O-O-O-K-K."

Lacking practice, the choreography failed. They became three colliding soloists. One performer, visibly upset, held the microphone so that her hand covered her face. The audience heard distinctly, "I feel like crying". Her two partners, heads tilted exaggeratedly to the side, anger immediately replaced by compassion, embraced her, whispering protracted condolences—into the microphone. Gaining confidence, the consolée, unpredictably attempted a solo.

"I done foun my pot o'go-o-o-l. Whenever you
ne-e-e-e some-bo-o-o-di-i-i,
I'll be the-er-er-errr for you-u-u-u."

Her two companions, twisted their lips in commiseration.

Three 'contestants' followed: Jess, Manuel and Chico. They were interviewed by Bobby Fuller, Grade 12.

"Are you married? The audience hooted with ecstasy.

"I was but I was in the Supermarket the other day? And when I turned around? She was gone!"

Bobby repeated his question to Jess who replied, "I want to kill the enemy."

His next question drew additional cheers. "Will you die for your country?"

"If I get paid," Manuel responded, slouching grotesquely.

Bobby turned to Chico. "Young man! Will you die for your country?"

"Shit, man! Gooks not touch me! Grab me! Not to finger me! Look at this body! Who ever touch this?" Chico pulled up his nylon camaflauge T-shirt, revealing a muscular chest with strikingly developed abdominal muscles.

Unable to control itself at Chico's display of physique, the audience responded: a delirious paean. Chico, rising to the occasion, turned sideways, flexing his muscles in a professionally executed pose. The audience roared its approval. Without explanation the young men trotted off stage, Bobby bumping one of the enormous stage speakers, eliciting from it a howl of indignation.

The attention span of the audience, sputtering like a spent firecracker, had little patience with the final performer, a female vocalist who, Judy Garland-like, engaged the portable microphone combatively, tilting it upward: draining an empty glass. Little finger arching one hundred and forty degrees, she pressed the object between thumb and middle finger as if touching something at once, both stimulating and revolting. In the foreground, four male drummers, naked to the waist, white stretch pants outlining their jock straps, beat out a Latin rhythm on sets of blood-red speckled tympani. Their faces were enigmatic; eyes trance-like, mesmerized, so that the soloist's provocative efforts, if directed toward them, were wasted. She tossed platinum hair defiantly, unperturbed by a yell from the seething intertwined throng: "You suck, girl!"

"Tell me, does she want you? Want to haunt you?
Does she elect-tri-fi-fi-fi and shock you and rock you the
way I du-u-u-u?
Don't you th-ay-nk I know there are so many
oth-oth-oth-oth-ers?
Tell me: does she lo-o-o-v you, like the way I lo-v
y-u-u-u?

Arms gesticulating provocatively, the singer's eyes raced around the stage, tongue darting in apprehension, seeking support for the fulfillment of a dare, thereby recording her place in the annals of Fillmore High.

"Nobody want you like the way I d-u-u-u-u.
Nobody need you like the way I d-u-u-u-u.
Nobody screw you like the way I d-u-u-u-u?"

Due to the noise, some, in the audience, already slithering, a convulsed mass, through the doors into the darkness, hissing resentment, enmity and confusion, missed the import of her final line.

No matter! The display of student accomplishment—talent—was over. Until next year.

---

# *ENDNOTES*

1. AP: Advanced Placement Tests: to measure student achievement in college level courses—AP courses—taken in high school for college credit
AP: Assistant Principal

2. Assessment: synonymous with testing. Teacher made tests and state mandated tests.

3. ASVAB: Armed Services Vocational Aptitude Battery. Test for military enlistment and placement. Possible scholarship.

4. Bi-Lingual\Bi-Cultural Education. Program ostensibly designed to bring predominately Spanish\Hispanic speaking students to grade level English fluency: comprehension, writing and speaking. May include separate courses. Intended as a remedial program, some students enrolled permanently.

5. CAHSEE: California High School Exit Exam. State test. Pass or Fail. Required to receive a high school diploma but not to graduate. May be taken—every year if necessary—between grades nine and twelve. Academic content: grades Four through Nine.

6. CELDT: Certificated English Language Development Training test: measure student fluency in English comprehension. If below grade level, student may be placed in Bi-Lingual\Bi-Cultural program.

7. Contract: agreement between local School Board and Teachers' Union stipulating mutual responsibilities.

8. CRT: Criterion Referenced Tests: government mandated tests to measure student mastery of specific subject matter.

9. CST: California Standards Test: to measure student achievement on State Standards curriculum.

10. EXIT: synonymous with CAHSEE

11. GATE: Gifted and Talented Education. Special courses for students tested/designated by the school as intellectually superior. Special teachers for these courses. Additional teacher stipend.

12. Golden State Tests: State of California test of academic achievement by subject: Physics, French, Geometry, etc.

13. The Hill: synonymous with Millard Fillmore High School. School is atop a small promontory.

14. NCLB: No Child Left Behind. Federal law requiring students to achieve stated academic levels. Measured annually by AYP, Average Yearly Progress. Schools with failing students could have administrators and teachers replaced.

15. NRT: Norm Referenced Tests: government mandated tests to measure subject matter achievement based on a national level.

16. OCR: Office of Civil Rights. Federal and state programs to oversee school compliance with minority support programs and adherence to non discrimination: race, ethnicity or female bias.

17. PSAT: Pre Scholastic Aptitude Test: practice for SAT.

18. RSP: Recognized Special Placement. Test to determine student placement in a class/course for learning deficient students, i.e. Special Education.

19. SAT: Scholastic Aptitude Test: required by many colleges to determine admission. Administered by national testing service. May be used to determine scholarship.

20. SDC: Special Day Class. Test to determine student placement in Special Education program.

21. Special Education: academic program for students tested as intellectually/emotionally below normal. Requires teachers with special Education certificate and often, separate classes.

22. STAR: Standardized Testing and Reporting: state test to determine student achievement in course content.

23. Title I: Federal and state programs to prevent discrimination by school against any student on the basis of ethnicity.

24. Title IX: Federal and state programs to prevent discrimination by school against any student: primarily, females, on the basis of sex or sexual orientation.

25. Warriors: Fillmore Warriors: mascot. Used interchangeably with Fillmore Knights.

Manufactured By: RR Donnelley
Breinigsville, PA USA
December, 2010